Dream About Lyssa
Naughty Book Two

Christine Young

Published by Rogue Phoenix Press, LLP
Copyright © 2023

ISBN: 978-1-62420-728-0

Editor: Sherry Derr-Wille
Cover Art: Designs by Ms G

Chapter One

London 1837

"It's the duchess, Ella Montgomerie, to see you, Sir."

The Earl of Blackmore, Black to his friends, set his pen in its holder before leaning back in his chair. In front of him he clasped his hands. His brows drew together while he digested the fact the woman, the duchess, was here to see him. He couldn't think of one reason for her appearance at his country estate, since the location was not amenable to calls. The visit must be important. He owned fifty square miles a considerable distance from London. The land was his home away from Lakota territory in the states. Here he could act as he pleased. He could strip to his breechclout then ride the countryside. His war cry would be heard only by the nearby animals. The scents didn't remind him of the prairie, though they were distinctive in their own way. He felt comfortable in the country, much more so than in the city. Though this land was nothing like the land of his birth.

A long slow breath of air sifted through his lips. The sixth sense he always relied on kicked in as the fine hairs on the back of his neck bristled. Ella was up to something. He'd just have to wait a few minutes to discover her ruse. "Show her in. Bring some refreshments as well. I'm certain she will be in need of something tasty to eat after such a long trip. If not hungry, she'll undoubtedly be thirsty. I want my finest Bordeaux to tempt her pallet."

"She has a young lady with her."

Sitting up straight, his interest grew. His eyes narrowed. His gut clenched. He didn't want anything to do with young ladies, a debutante, no doubt. What the devil was she doing bringing a young woman to his home? *The humble abode of a notorious rake and womanizer?* He certainly was not husband material, never would be. All she could do was hurt this lady's reputation.

"Perhaps lemonade with the snacks would be appropriate. How old is the girl?" Curiosity multiplied.

"You will have to ask the ladies." Abernathy clucked his tongue as if he had asked something ridiculous. "Don't you understand it is not fashionable to ask a woman her age?"

Ah, Abernathy was correct, one didn't ask a lady how old she was. Not if a man wanted to keep his head attached to his shoulders. No, the asking of age would be far too delicate a question for him. His butler was spot on in his assessment of the situation.

"No courage, eh?" Black asked as he straightened the papers and folders littered on his desk. He didn't have the fortitude either. A guess of his own when he saw the girl would have to suffice.

"Courage with the ladies is your department, Sir. I would never do half the things that seem to occupy your free time." A smirk on his thin lips, Abernathy, his thin shoulders squared, left the room backing away and closing the doors as he disappeared. "I will show the ladies in."

Seconds later the door opened. Ella Montgomerie entered with a young woman behind her. The duchess was still a striking woman as she passed into her forties. Not one gray hair on her head. Her eyes flashed with amusement when she looked at him.

Extending his hand in greeting, Black walked around his desk. When the woman stepped to Ella's side, his heart stopped. His breath caught somewhere in the back of his throat. Sluggishly, the startled organ began to beat again. Hot air rasped raggedly into his beleaguered lungs. He placed a kiss on the back of Ella's hand before looking back to the ravishing young woman standing behind and to the side.

Except for the curves of her sumptuous bosom, she was rail thin, her eyes a deep dark blue reminding him of the color of a vibrant blue lake deep in Lakota territory; her hair the darkest brown with hints of red highlighting some strands where the sun caught and held. She possessed a pert nose coupled with high cheekbones. Her neck was long, alabaster in color, needing to be explored by his lips. While he stared at her, the pulse at the base of that long neck throbbed invitingly. He wondered if she thought about a man's touch, a man kissing her in that spot where his gaze rested. He wondered then of the intelligence of Ella for introducing him to the most exquisite creature he ever set eyes upon.

The young lady smiled at him, the gesture reaching clearly to her eyes. This woman was no coquette. The smile was honest while the slow curve of her plump bottom lip stole thoughts from his head. Once again, his breath caught in the back of his throat, which he cleared. Those eyes twinkled merrily as if the joke was on him. Boldly, she tilted her head a bit to the side as if perusing him from the top of his head to the tips of his toes if she could have seen them. Somehow, he understood her intent. Indeed, the way Ella stared at him, the jest might be on him. Startlingly changing his mind about the circumstances, he didn't mind if her visit concerned the girl. He would step up to the job.

"What brings you here?" Black had the decided feeling he wasn't going to like her answer.

Possibly, he might like it too much. His friend tread on dangerous ground. In the darkest recesses of his mind, he understood his life was about to be turned topsy-turvy. If he told her no, she would remind him that he owed her. If he told her no, he might regret the decision for the rest of his life. Also, he wondered how long she would capitalize on the fact he owed her. She used that ploy once before. She was solely responsible for his position here in London. She and the duke saved his life. She used her influence to secure his title after his grandfather died. He was the only son of the previous earl. Sometimes, however, he missed his days on the prairie. Missed the hunting of buffalo along with the freedom, the warmth of the sun on his bare torso.

The immense freedom he didn't have here.

"I've a favor."

He'd come around to stand in front of his desk. Now he leaned against the wooden structure, one leg swinging, his thoughts in a tail spin as he tried to keep his gaze from the young lady who had all the markings of a debutante. This was the season. "That seems to be when you visit. Isn't it? When you have a boon to request?" Black watched her stiffen, her displeasure clearly written in her expressive features. Obviously, she didn't like being reminded. "My apology. Didn't mean anything by that comment. You know I would do anything for you. Except perhaps murder. Just a bit testy this afternoon."

She laughed at his statement. "Actually, that statement is not factual. Though we both understand I would never ask you to kill anyone for me. Murder is so messy. Bodies are always hard to dispose of…cleanly."

Her chin lifted just as one would expect of a duchess. Admirably, she fit the role. She had years to fine-tune the characteristics.

"You do have to admit though…"

He didn't think the moment too prudent to belabor the point. He motioned to the girl at her side. "Do have a seat, both of you. After Abernathy brings the refreshments, we can get on with this favor you're requesting. I would like to learn what is expected of me."

"You needn't act so put out. This will take little effort on your part." Ella straightened her skirts before smoothing the fabric. "You might even enjoy the task."

"Perhaps you've forgotten the introduction. Leaving something so important out is not like you, Duchess. Besides I've the distinct feeling this unannounced visit of yours has something to do with this young lady. Is she another one of your charges? I do pray you do better with this girl than you did with the last one."

Ella looked away for a moment, her cheeks suddenly sporting a delightful shade of pink. So, this was something she was having trouble asking. In that case, the task would certainly not be to his liking. As he guessed, it must have something to do with the young lady sitting not so demurely at her side studying him. The duchess understood that fact too. The girl was part of the favor. He supposed he would have to take her to one of those infuriatingly boring balls the debutantes flaunted in search of a husband. He could handle a ball or a recital for Ella, nothing else.

Before Ella could proceed, he stood, his hand outstretched. He wasn't about to get hoodwinked into escorting a debutante without putting up a bit of a fight. What the devil was the duchess thinking? His reputation alone would end her season, which was now beginning in the worst way. "No, Ella. My answer is an emphatic no. You do understand I would not be in her best interest. She can't possibly be seen with the likes of me. This beautiful young lady would find herself ostracized. No one would accept her."

"This is Lyssa Andrews, my niece, my sister's daughter. As you know my sister lives northwest of Baltimore. They own a ranch. Lyssa is very important to me, you see. I wouldn't ask this favor of anyone I could not trust with my life or hers. You would never do harm to a young lady who is so very significant to me. As you are thinking, she is here for the season."

"No."

"You owe me, Black. It will only be for a few days, a few weeks at the most."

Ella looked away for a second. The tone of voice she gifted him with brooked no argument from him.

His stomach clenched, as he understood all too clearly he would eventually give in to the duchess' request. The young lady grinned an all-knowing smile that reached into his soul, possibly even his heart. No woman ever moved him so swiftly and so urgently, never reaching into his jaded heart. He might be doomed before he began. Ella shifted in her chair. His answer remained the same. "No." He wasn't going to give in easily even though they both understood he would.

"Please."

How could he refuse when she asked him so sweetly? "A few weeks of my life, you say. I won't be saddled watching over a debutante. Good God, woman, you know who I am. Better than most you understand my reputation along with my history. This is the single most ridiculous notion I've ever heard."

"You're right. I understand exactly who you are as does the duke, my husband. Indeed, this was his suggestion. I agreed. Despite your reputation you would protect Lyssa with your life. You would make sure no one would take advantage of her as Collin McInnis did with Nickie. You are the only man for the job. She must have a protector we can trust. With this short notice, you are the only one we could both agree on to do the job."

Well, hell, a protector? Her definition sounded as if she asked him to be something besides a chaperone. "I cannot be a chaperone to a debutante. That in and of itself will tarnish Miss Andrews' reputation. It is a ridiculous notion. I'm never seen at the affairs she will be expected to attend. I don't go to balls or recitals. Don't travel in those circles. Won't receive invitations."

"I will have the invitations forwarded to you as they come in to my home. My secretary is quite good at that."

"It seems you have an answer for everything."

He grimaced as his gaze rested once more on Lyssa Andrews then on her lush curves, her bosom rising and falling delightfully. His astonishment lit on the fact she was enjoying herself. This tête-à-tête amused her.

"Good," Lyssa spoke up, a devilish smirk on her lovely face. She winked. "I'd rather be outside riding than attending balls or recitals. Do you ride, Mr. Black? I promise you the man who wins my heart will have to ride and shoot as good as my daddy. Do you shoot, Mr. Black? Can you hit anything except the broadside of a barn? Can you ride a horse as if you are one with the animal?" she challenged every part of him. "There is no one in London who can accomplish what I've described. There will be no reason for you to put yourself out by taking me to a boring ball. As to recitals, I cannot sing or play any instrument."

Ella smiled, momentarily dropping her lashes. Black was positive she was trying to hold back laughter that by the look of her, the hoot threatened to erupt from behind her teeth. Hells bells, he was half Lakota Sioux. He lived the first fifteen years of his life doing little except ride and hunt. He knew he could outride as well as outshoot her daddy no matter how well the man sat a horse.

"I ride, as well as shoot admirably. Rather doubt though if I can do anything as good as your daddy. Rumors abound about Damian Andrews' abilities of that nature."

Yes, Damian was a smuggler in his younger days. Rumor had it he kidnapped Amorica. Amorica shot him because of his profession. Seems he also heard the injury was only a flesh wound. That was over twenty years ago. Now he was about to be saddled with their daughter. Did they have any idea who he was? Apparently not. Ella knew though.

"You're too modest by far," Ella murmured thoughtfully as she gazed at her niece then back to him. "Suppose she will make you prove your statement. Lyssa doesn't believe an English dandy can do anything of that nature. I'm sure you will manage to surprise her, possibly even impress her with your talent."

Black moved to sit behind his desk. Tapping his fingers on the top, he wondered what the little minx was thinking in tossing out that challenge. Ella must not have told her about his background. No, she would leave all that to unfold naturally. The duchess still didn't refute the fact he was the farthest thing from an English dandy a man could get.

"So, if I agree…"

"Which you have," Ella interrupted. "There was no question in my mind. I've known Lyssa her entire life. There is no better man suited for this job than you." She paused for a few seconds. "Since you owe me."

"What are my duties? When do they begin?"

He was resigned. The little lady seemed to be a thought-provoking bit of frippery. She might prove to be entertainment of the best sort. In any case, he didn't think she would prove boring.

"Now, this moment. Her trunks are even now being unloaded. Abernathy has directed your servants to take them to a suitable room. For propriety she should be ensconced in the wing opposite your chambers. By the way, where is Still Water Runs? I expected him to be here. He is usually a shadow to you."

"Running an errand for me. Why?" he gritted out all the while still wishing he dared say no to the duchess.

He couldn't. Never could. When Ella smiled at him, all his resolve vanished. By looking at Lyssa, her smiles might have the same effect. He would have to harden his determination to stand by his dictates. Debutantes were out of bounds to him just as white women were.

"About time you asked."

She rose, walking to the window that overlooked the back of his estate. He didn't have perfectly manicured gardens or a gazebo. His land was natural, extended several miles to the east and north. A large stream meandered through the middle. There was a small pool at the border where he swam naked. Even in the summer the water was cool to the skin.

"This situation you're in is all because of your friend, Collin

McInnis. You can put this quandary you are now involved in directly on his doorstep. He absconded with my niece, right under my nose. I had no idea. Thought she went back to the McClellan keep. By the time we figured it all out, well, it's been several weeks since she left with the bounder."

He tried to recall if he had heard gossip about his friend in the last few days or even weeks as the duchess implied. Rumor had it he kidnapped a young woman thinking the lady was his mistress. That was all he heard. "Another notorious rake who I'm positive you would not entrust with one of your charges. Am I right? Now tell me, what has he done?"

"You understand exactly why I trust you with Lyssa."

He grimaced thinking about the hardened lesions on his back. Because of his audacity to court a white girl, he was whipped nearly to death. Ella along with Drake saved him. Brought him to England to claim his inheritance as well as his title. "Unfortunately, I do. Now tell me what Collin has to do with my chaperoning this young lady despite my character."

"He absconded with Nickie Gray, another one of my charges. Drake is determined to make him pay, as is her father. They mean to chase him down. I have to go with the men to make sure they don't do something they will regret, as in hang him from the yardarm of his ship."

"Collin left for home over a week ago. No, it's drawing closer to two weeks, maybe more. You say he took your niece with him? He wouldn't do that."

"He did," she shot out angrily, her lips tightening into a thin line. "He took her on his ship. We didn't learn of this until her brother returned from McClellan land to tell us she wasn't there."

"I assume you know this for a fact. Kidnapping is a serious charge."

"You doubt the ability of my husband, the former spy, to ferret out all the facts. He still has numerous contacts in the bureau as well as out. Collin took her."

"She went willingly. You can't blame this situation all on Collin. He would never abscond with an unwilling woman."

8

"Probably. She is willful. We all are," Lyssa spoke up in the middle of their argument.

"Neither will appreciate interference," Black reminded her.

"Nickie didn't want a season. Collin McInnis might just be taking her home," Lyssa spoke up again, gracing him with another smile coupled with a subtle flick of her hair, "Although it's apparent neither of you believe that scenario. I do agree with Mr. Black. Nickie won't want interference from her family. I'm certain she is pleasing herself. Just as I plan on doing the same as soon as I find the man I want for the rest of my life. I won't stick to social rules. I will satisfy myself while enjoying the man of my dreams. Just as a man has that opportunity…to please himself…so should a woman."

The Earl of Blackmore couldn't stifle the groan rumbling from his gut. This could be the longest few weeks of his life.

"Her wishes don't make a difference," Ella said. She leaned against the window frame. Her gaze centered on him. "You do see why we must go. I'm traveling with the men to make sure nothing gets out of hand when they find the two lovers."

"You don't know they are lovers."

"No, but I assume the worst in hopes of discovering a different scenario."

"Guess that's prudent."

"You do still own that hunting lodge in the farthest reaches of Scotland. Do you think he would take her there?"

Black leaned against the back of his chair, his legs crossed in front of him, watching Lyssa. She seemed to be studying him. Brazen chit. She was blatant about what she did. Once more, her gaze roamed the length of him. He might be able to deal well with her for a few days; a few weeks, never. Hell, it would take more than that amount of time to sail to his lodge then back. More than a month would pass before he saw any sign of the duchess.

"Collin understands he will always be welcome there. He knows I've no plans to travel that far north until the fall."

"I don't understand why you are in such a rush to find her. She won't be a virgin when you catch up to her," Lyssa said as her gaze raked over him, centered on his mouth before dipping lower.

Fortunately, once again the desk hid the direction of her gaze from her view.

Shameless piece of baggage. He fought the tightening of his body. Fought the rising of his lust, the swelling of his rod. Bloody eyes, she wasn't for him. She was white. Would never presume to court a woman of her caliber. He learned his lesson. Once was enough for a lifetime. He was now this white girl's chaperone. It would be despicable of him to take advantage of the situation. If this one acted the same as the other one, perhaps Collin was the victim instead of Ella's niece.

Second along with third thoughts assailed him. He scowled at Lyssa when once again her gaze roamed his body. The young lady had the audacity to smirk. She knew exactly what she did. His scowl deepened.

"What do I have to look forward to?" he asked once more as he tried to focus his attention on Ella who seemed oblivious of her niece's blatant perusal of his body.

"You are stuffy now, aren't you?" Lyssa asked interrupting her aunt's reply.

Her stare riveted once more on his mouth. She moistened her lips, leaving an inviting dewy trail of temptation.

"Stodgy," Ella corrected her. "He is known as the stodgy Earl of Blackmore, not stuffy."

Black directed his attention to Ella this time. "Perhaps we should get on with my duties."

"You're committing. I knew you would."

He nodded, his gaze moving back to Lyssa, determined to keep a strong hand where she was concerned. Letting her out of his site for even one second was out of the question, could even be disastrous. This girl, as immature as she was, would not run away with a man under his watch. *Unless that man is me.* He meant to stay close.

"Guess I am. Did I have a choice? So, what is the first debutante affair she will attend? Do hope she has a wardrobe ready."

Black chuckled. He didn't think Lyssa would like him to help pick out her gowns. He would make sure she was covered to her chin if he could manage the task. With her bosom, she needed fabric between her and the prying eyes of the lords seeking a young wife.

"Lyssa has more than enough to suffice for the next few weeks. You will not have to help her with her clothing."

"If you're gone longer?" he queried lifting a dark brow skyward in deep speculation.

Bloody hell, he hoped this trip they were taking would end up being shorter rather than longer. He understood deep down it would be longer.

"Then of course you will have to accompany her to the dress shop. The modiste we most often use has her measurements. There will be little for you to do except make sure what she purchases is appropriate."

His frown lines deepened before he turned his attention to Lyssa with a smirk. "It will, of course, be my pleasure to accompany her. Anything for you, Duchess."

Coquettishly, Lyssa lowered her lashes before she stared at him again. His gut tightened. Her lower lip slipped beneath her teeth. He thought she needed discipline. Perhaps she understood life would not be quite the same with him, as it would have been living at Montgomerie Hall.

"Tomorrow night is her first ball. The invitation is here." Ella fished the gold engraved paper from her reticule before handing it over to Black.

He swallowed a deep breath of air as he studied the invitation. His gut tightened. This was his worst nightmare coming to fruition. "We will stay in my townhouse for the night. First thing in the morning we will travel to London so she can prepare herself."

"I'd rather go riding, or fishing," Lyssa said sweetly before adding a saucy smile for more affect.

What effect she was trying for, he wasn't positive. What he knew was that this spicy girl was trouble of the worst sort. This kind of behavior would have her increasing sooner than later. His breath left him in a slow whistle. She would be a handful.

So are her breasts. Possibly two handfuls.

This wasn't at all what he should be thinking. Ella would have his head if she understood the drift of his thoughts. With his eyes closed, he could almost taste her sweetness. She wasn't sweet. No, she was spicey and hot. His scowl deepened further, if that was at all possible. This lady wasn't for him. She was white, snow white, pure white, impossibly white. New fallen snow would not be whiter.

Bloody eyes, she was a debutante, innocent, a virgin. He meant to remind himself every day that he was her chaperone. She wanted to ride instead of dance. The deal was, he wouldn't mind a good hard ride with her. Either kind. He groaned again. What the devil was Ella thinking leaving her with him? His thoughts were drowning him.

"Would you like to stay for dinner? Black asked as he rose from his chair meaning to summon Abernathy.

"No, Drake and I are leaving first thing in the morning. The ship sails with the tide. Don't believe Drake would be pleased if I detain the sailing. He's in a bloody hurry to get his hands on the McInnis. He'd most likely go without me. I cannot let that scenario play out. Drake sent a guard in case it gets dark before I reach London. So, no worries in that regard."

Ella placed a kiss on Lyssa's cheek. "You behave yourself, sweetheart. If you don't, I'll have to answer to your mother, my sister."

She turned to Black. "Don't let her do something she'll regret. I trust you implicitly. Don't forget she is my sister's daughter and very dear to me."

Lyssa walked out with Ella. He chose to stay in his office until he heard the door close.

A few minutes later, Lyssa stood in the doorway. She was beautiful. "Can we ride?" Pink rose to her cheeks. "Can I pick out a horse? Aunty Ella told me you have about ten horses. She also said there is an Appaloosa you brought over from the states." She whirled to leave the room or to show her ankles as if she was certain he would follow.

When he didn't trail along behind her, she was back in his office. "Don't you think you should dress for dinner?" he asked.

"Thought we were riding. Doesn't take me only a few minutes to change my dress. Dinner won't be for another couple of hours. We have time."

She grabbed his arm, attempting to tug him along with her.

"You actually believe I would let you go now? Before we get a few things straight between us? There are rules for you to know, to learn as well as to obey. Consequences, too, if you misbehave. Don't want anything to happen to you on my watch."

He tried not to smirk at her horrified expression, which turned from an arrogant grin to a scowl. Bemused, he waited for a comment or two. He didn't doubt there would be more than one remark coming from her saucy mouth. If he was putting his life on hold, she would do things his way.

"I don't misbehave unless I'm living with a tyrant," she shot out as she turned to flounce from the room, seemed to think better of her actions as she reappeared. "Not that I think that's what you are. Just stuffy!"

"Stodgy," he corrected with a chuckle then motioned to a chair near his desk. "Have a seat."

"Don't care for lemonade." She poured herself a glass of brandy. Smirked at him as if she wanted him to comment on her *faux pas*. "Cheers." She downed a healthy portion.

"By all means help yourself."

She placed herself on a wing chair in front of his desk. It was where she sat earlier. "Get on with it. Tell me all your stuffy rules."

She sipped watching him with her vibrant blue eyes over the rim of the crystal she held to her lips.

"You will have gentlemen callers. They will meet with my approval before you go anywhere with them. There will be no rakes. I won't tolerate that."

"No notorious rakes for me." She grinned. "Well one, I guess one is meant to be in my future."

She winked at him. Had the mettle to beam shamelessly. She shifted her position in the chair, her bosom making its debut more prominently than before. "You needn't worry overmuch. Already know the notorious rake I want to court me."

"Care to enlighten me? Give me a heads up so I can prepare myself. If need be, I will chase him off."

He lifted an eyebrow mockingly. This would be easier to keep her away from an unsuitable man if he knew who that man was. Any rake notorious or otherwise was unsuitable.

"You'll have to discover that for yourself," she taunted flashing a devastating grin. "I've made up my mind though. Nothing you can do or say will discourage me."

"Good God, Lyssa, you've been in the city for a week. This is going to be your first ball. How could you have met someone so soon?"

"Just met the man today."

Her smile widened. Behind her lips her straight teeth were pearly white her cheeks flushed a light shade of pink. The fingers holding her brandy glass were slim and long. They were also nicely manicured.

He ran that over in his head until the thought had nowhere to travel. Ah, he would discover who this mystery man was she favored soon he supposed. Perhaps the ball tomorrow night would tell him what he needed to learn. He could wait for the opportunity. He was a patient man. Whoever this man turned out to be, he would never get the opportunity to be alone with Lyssa Andrews. No, he would make sure this debutante remained a virgin until she wed.

"How can you know he's the one?"

This sensation she was feeling couldn't possibly be grounded in fact. There was no logic or rational thought. It had to be infatuation or perhaps lust driving her. "You can't have known him for more than a minute.

"Love at first sight is how I see the situation." She lifted delicate shoulders, her grin giving away all that lustful fascination she must feel. "He checks off all the characteristics I want in a man."

He found himself to be too curious about these features she was going to describe. Was feeling as if he wanted to know what she thought. The devil...he had to ask, a half smile on his face, "What are those characteristics?"

"You want to know?"

She sipped the brandy while her gaze roamed the length of him one too many times, finally resting on his eyes. Moving forward on the chair she sat, she appeared eager to answer. Good God, at least she didn't stare at his mouth this time.

"I asked. Didn't I?"

She had the boldness to toss him a cheeky grin. "Well…to begin with…tall, he is very tall. I always wanted a man with black hair as well as sky blue eyes although those characteristics aren't as important as broad shoulders and stomach muscles that are hard as rocks. Don't like men who harbor paunches. Means they overindulge. Don't appreciate debauchery of any sort."

Shifting uncomfortably, he walked to the window. If he turned now, she would see the growing bulge beneath his trousers. "That's quite the list. You say you met this man today? What about his personality? That's important too." He rocked back on his heels, beginning to get his body under control. "He might be a woman beater."

"Oh, there is more. Would you like me to go on?" She sounded far too enthusiastic for his comfort.

Quickly, he strode to his massive desk to sit down behind it. Hide might be the more appropriate term. The size of the man seemed to swallow her whole. "I believe it's rather obvious what you want in a man. What you are thinking will not last a lifetime. There is more to a man than a hard stomach along with broad shoulders."

"I haven't even begun to elaborate." She shifted in her chair, one finger touching her chin as if in thought.

"Perhaps you should go dress for dinner."

The need for distance from this little piece of baggage prompted the statement. He was uncomfortable with this description, which sounded far too close to him to feel comfortable.

Finding someone suitable to court her would be his mission the next few weeks. He would have to find a way to take her mind from the unidentified man. The sooner she was spoken for the better for him. The sooner she was out of his home he could breathe.

"You always dress for dinner? At my home we don't, simply because we're usually coming in from chores. We wash up. Mother won't let anyone into the house unless they've washed. Father always complains. His complaints are to tease mother"

"Suit yourself," he muttered wishing she would leave for a few minutes. "Dress or don't dress, I don't care."

"Well..." She set the empty brandy glass on his desk. "It might be fun to try out some of the new wardrobe Aunt Ella spent a fortune on for me. If I dress for you, can we see the horses after dinner?"

He grunted.

~ * ~

She took that as a good sign.

Lyssa was pleased. The moment she saw the man, she fell head-over-heels, hopelessly in love with him. More than anything else she wanted to see him smile. She supposed being an earl he had a lot of duties that would keep him serious. Uncle Drake had a lot to do. He always found time to smile. Of course, his smiles were most always directed toward Aunt Ella as well as his children. She wanted Black to smile at her the way Uncle Drake grinned wickedly at Aunt Ella. Wished his gaze would lovingly follow her around the room just as her father watched her mother. The two of them were still madly in love with each other. She wanted a man who would be irrevocably in love with her in twenty or thirty years; longer, if possible, if life looked on them favorably.

Lyssa stepped back from the mirror in her room. She turned sideways to examine herself, shoved her face close to the mirror to pinch her cheeks. She applied a small amount of makeup to highlight her eyes as well as her lips. The color was not overdone, still she wondered what he would think. Jess complained about makeup on the women he saw.

Now, she stood back. She wanted him to see more of her. Needed to find a means to tempt him. Jess, her brother, told her inadvertently all the ways to drive a man crazy with lust. Lyssa was certain doing so would take all that and more to entice the stuffy earl. She sensed he was a man of inordinate control. Known as a rake around town meant he would know women as well as how to give a woman pleasure.

Damn and blast his power. She didn't understand this pleasure thing.

For now, she understood that he liked her breasts. He stared at them often enough. This gown was too modest by far. All she need do would be to remove the modesty piece. Quickly, she did just that.

She smiled. Her corset thrust her breasts upward. The valley between them was quite visible. Flaunting herself might not get the desired result. No, she meant to play coy as if she didn't understand what the sight would do to all his male sensibilities. He wouldn't know that aunty Ella made certain at the dressmakers all her gowns were suitable for a young debutante. This gown with the lacy piece removed was anything but appropriate. Unable to help her wayward thoughts, she grinned at herself in the mirror then thought of the French court, the decadent fashions that came from the country.

Lyssa didn't care. Not when the man she meant to be her husband was the only male seeing more of her than was deemed proper. She shivered suddenly understanding implicitly there was a fine line that would separate her from a naïve debutante solely relying on her elders' opinions and the trollop he might believe her to be. No matter the cost though, she meant to be his. She could play the innocent with him. Never in her wildest thoughts would she do something so obvious when there would be other men seeing her. From the moment she set her eyes on him, she knew they were meant to be together. He was the man of all her dreams. She hoped someday she would be the woman of his dreams.

With trepidation in her heart and mind, she walked down the long winding stairs to the drawing room. Her heart thundered beneath her chest, pounding painfully. What little oxygen she could draw into her lungs did little to help her nerves. Negligently, he leaned against the mantle by the fireplace drinking what she assumed to be brandy. Instinctively, she absorbed a deep breath of air that didn't seem to go past her throat.

Her wish came true.

As she prayed, his gaze rested on her breasts, specifically on the exposed valley between them.

The ever-present scowl that seemed to be always a part of his features deepened. It appeared he wrestled his gaze from her breasts to her face. Her smile was hesitant. She tilted her head demurely, innocently, while she fluttered her lashes.

"You look lovely tonight, Miss Andrews," he murmured as he

stepped forward offering her his arm before proceeding to the dining room as if she wasn't showing him exactly what she shouldn't. When she looked down, she almost saw her nipples. He would see what she offered to him.

His comment was not what she expected. Damn and blast, she anticipated a comment of disapproval, anger possibly. His glower certainly spoke that way. Perhaps he was biding his time, working to control his irritation.

He always glowers. He's stuffy. No, he's stodgy. Well, damnation, what difference did the word make?

What did she foresee? After the first sighting of her blatantly revealed charms, it appeared he ignored her. Found no interest in what she deliberately exhibited. He pulled out a chair for her to sit before walking to his own chair. All the while, his gaze remained fixed on her face, her eyes, not her lips which she moistened. She ran her tongue along her bottom lip then repeated the performance. Jess told her men couldn't resist a woman who did so. Blatantly, she stared at his mouth.

"What are we having for dinner?" She set the tip of one finger on the moistened bottom lip imploring his gaze to rest there also.

It seemed to her he looked as if he wanted to devour her as his gaze slipped from her mouth to her breasts then back to her mouth. His silver blue eyes darkened to deep pewter rimmed in blue.

"Haven't the vaguest notion, nor do I care."

His bland voice told her he was indeed seeing her in a different light. He wasn't immune to her charms. He was interested.

"Oh. Aren't you hungry?"

She positively hoped he was now hungry for her. Lyssa imagined the way his mouth would feel when his lips covered hers as well as when his tongue touched upon hers.

The dinner proceeded in stilted silence. As he ignored her, Lyssa's appetite dissolved. She picked at her food. Whatever thoughts he formed about her were going to remain in his head. She fidgeted with her silverware. Looked at him beneath lowered lashes for heart stopping seconds.

When he sat back seemingly finished, his hands folded and resting

18

on his hard belly, he observed her. Finally, he spoke, "Would you like to pick out a horse? I'll have your mount brought into town for the duration of our visit. The duchess told me two days after the ball there is to be a recital. You will sing. You are supposedly very talented. Ella also pointed out you have the voice of an angel." He met her gaze with his own. "Do you? Do you have the voice of an angel? Perhaps your aunt is prejudice. Maybe she misspoke."

"I wouldn't know."

She wanted to toss the glass of wine in his face. Needed to spark some emotion rather than the bland indifference he courted her with. Instead of his interest flaming, she received bored unresponsive looks for her efforts. Perhaps she needed to try something different, another ploy Jess spoke of.

Well, tomorrow would be another day. She would think on the measures she could employ tonight. There would be time for further thought during the carriage ride to the city. They headed to the stable. Outside, the night was warm. Before she left the house, she wrapped a shawl around her shoulders.

Inside the earl's stable, the sight of magnificent horseflesh greeted her. She ran her hand down the nose of every horse, sweet-talking her way down one side then the other.

"The Appaloosa, I want that one to ride while I'm here. The mare is gorgeous."

She wanted that horse forever. The only way she would accomplish that was if she won the earl's heart. The stuffy man was proving more difficult than she thought. Quickly, she reminded herself she'd known him for less than eight hours.

What had she believed? That one look at her cleavage would leave him drooling for her. That he would bend his knee to the ground then propose she spend a lifetime with him. The man must see cleavage whenever he wished.

Hah!

She now understood a bit of cleavage would not bend a notorious rake to her will. He probably saw cleavage most every day of his life. The only reason Ella picked him for the chaperone duties were because she knew he wouldn't cave to her wiles. Of course, Ella didn't know she fell in love with the man the moment she saw him. Her aunt also didn't know she would do absolutely anything to win his heart. If she had to, she would climb into his bed.

"I'll have the mare brought to the city tomorrow morning. Unless you would like to ride her there."

"You would allow that?"

Lyssa didn't comprehend the underlying note of sarcasm in her question. What she did note was the lifting of his raven-black eyebrow.

"I'm not the ogre you seem to believe me to be or a tyrant as you implied earlier. If you wish to ride part of the way to the city, I've no objections. For myself, I do prefer a good horse beneath me instead of a closed in carriage where there is little to no air to breathe. That environment makes a man claustrophobic."

His comment about the ogre-tyrant stung. "It's just the rules you laid out for me. I don't like to think I have to ask every time I want to do something or go somewhere. That's not something that has been a part of my life. I rarely have to ask permission."

"The rules are for your protection, not to make you irritable. Since I've taken over this chore, I mean to do the chaperoning right. I'm assuming where you live you've trusted ranch hands that oversee your quest around the range"

"Me? My protection. I don't need to be safe guarded." She placed a hand on her chest exactly where she wanted his gaze to travel. "Irritable? I'm not the least bit..." she broke off then realizing that was exactly what she was, although her burgeoning annoyance was his fault.

He let his head fall back as he roared with laughter. "Yes, you. Irritable as well as conniving. I know Ella well enough to know she wouldn't allow you to wear a dress that revealed so much of you. Where is the modesty piece? If you show up in something so skimpy tomorrow, I'll march you upstairs then dress you myself."

That was the best idea she'd ever heard. Lyssa beamed at his suggestion then thinking better of her smirk, dropped her hand, noting with satisfaction the direction of his gaze. She set her hands on her hips while she thrust out her large chest for his scrutiny. Perhaps she did interest him.

He turned away.

She smirked.

"You should retire for the night."

His voice was gruff, didn't sound at all like him.

She recalled his father's voice when he wanted her mother in the bedroom. They were much the same. "We should ride. The moon is bright. It will make the jaunt enjoyable."

"Do you need help with your saddle?" he asked while he leaned against the stall, his pose giving none of his emotions away.

She was thrilled he wanted to ride tonight. Had not expected agreement to her proposal. "No, just point me to the saddle you'd like me to use. I've always saddled my horses. If it is not too heavy, I'm fine."

"Even in that gown? Never mind, I suppose you ride astride too."

The tone could not be ignored. Censure seemed to coat every word as if he disapproved. His annoyance over this small issue surprised her.

Damn and blast, the earl was going to have to get used to her if they were to do well together. "Bottom line, if forced to ride sidesaddle, I'd fall off. I cannot ride in such a ridiculous manner. Have never done…tried that horrific position? Have you?" Her sarcasm as well as her meaning was obvious even to a deaf ear.

One eyebrow rose. This was his turn to smirk. There was no other word for the expression. Well, she wanted to see a full-blown grin, not a smirk at her position. He went on to say, "A woman, a debutante, should understand the complexities of riding both ways. The nobility here in London look down their long-pointed noses at a woman who chooses to be too unique. I would warn you, though, to be aware of that fact. As for me, don't see how a woman stays on a horse when she doesn't open her legs for the ride."

She comprehended his words held a double entendre. She just didn't understand the second meaning. Mayhap she should ask. No, another time might work better. "Do you?" Lyssa was creeping closer to losing her formidable temper at the man.

"Do I what?" he asked sounding totally unknowing as to the question at hand.

"Look down your long-pointed nose at women who...? Who doesn't open their legs to ride?"

She couldn't repeat the words. If he answered yes to the question, she had a great deal of work cut out for her.

She was annoyed and irritated by his bark of laughter. He didn't answer her question.

Faced with the saddling, she grunted. Heaved. Grunted again while she tried to saddle the horse. Her arms shook with the weight. Despite her best effort the damn saddle was too heavy for her. At home she had a saddle she could easily take on and off her horse. She let out a puffy breath of air thoroughly frustrated with her inability to prove herself competent to this man she wanted to adore even while at this moment she was having the greatest urge to cosh him over the head. In this she wanted to prove to the earl she was capable. He'd already told her she couldn't pick out a stallion because her arms were too scrawny to keep the animal under wraps. Now this. Giving up, she finally admitted defeat. "It's too heavy."

His grin widened. He told her so, by his expression. If she couldn't presume to lift a saddle of his choosing, she wouldn't have the muscle if the stallion decided he didn't like the direction she pointed him to keep the horse in line. She had strong legs, knew how to use her knees to guide a horse.

He didn't say anything. In a blink her Appaloosa was saddled. She could not complain over much. The mare was gorgeous. Her front was a blanket of dark brown. Her white flanks sported irregular shaped brown spots. After Lyssa mounted, she set off at a brisk canter, not caring if he wasn't ready.

Suddenly, he rode beside her. He rode bare back, his hair rakishly long having lost the ribbon that held the length in place flew in the breeze they created. The man was as majestic as the nearly pure gray stallion he rode. Black was one with his horse.

Magnificent.

Splendid.

At the sight of man and beast working so well together, her heart beat double time. Lyssa knew all along the man would ride brilliantly.

Every muscle in his body exuded primal masculinity. Before she could move her horse away, he grabbed the reins.

The earlier smirk vanished to become another deep scowl. "Never take off without me again," his words a low growl. "Not only is the night dark, you have no notion where you are going."

Taken aback momentarily, she rambled, "The moon..." she looked upward to the black velvet of the night laced with twinkling stars then back to him, "is bright."

It wasn't. However, she thought the suggestion might help him overlook her foolishness. At home she was never foolish or impulsive.

"Manages to conceal in shadows what one should be able to see. As I said, do not ever ride alone. I will be with you or you won't ride. I can just as easily have the mounts taken back to Blackmore estate if you choose to disregard my ruling."

Even though she knew he was right, indignation rose, fluttered in her chest before her furry erupted. She wasn't accustomed to be chastised so blatantly. "You cannot dictate to me! I'm not a little girl!"

At that moment she experienced a decided change of heart where the man was concerned. Damn and blast, he hadn't bothered to saddle his stallion.

"Stop acting like a spoiled brat."

"How dare you?"

She wanted to spur her horse forward, escape this humiliation.

After that, he had the boldness to remain silent. The man wasn't going to gift her with a retort. Well, he'd find out soon enough she was a liberated woman. She would come and go as she pleased with or without his consent. Telling him her every move would preclude her future with the man. She had to set him straight before doing so was too late. Training as well as taming this man to her way would not be an easy task. Nonetheless, they were tasks that needed to be done.

First things first. Before she could have a future, she needed him to see her as someone other than the helpless debutante he was supposed to chaperone. He needed to see her as a woman; powerful, independent.

"Are you intelligent enough to understand?" He tossed the reins back at her. "Do I have to elaborate further?" He cocked an insipidly condescending eyebrow.

The tilted supercilious eyebrow was a gesture she positively wasn't enamored of. If she never saw him raise another eyebrow at her, the moment would be too soon. "I know what I think as well as what I want. No one has ever tried to be my watchdog. At home I was allowed to come and go as I pleased. That won't change here no matter your commands."

By his expression she comprehended her words would never sway him to allow the freedom she craved. There were other ways to get what she wanted as she understood she could turn the situation around to her favor.

"Very well. Where are we going?"

"Your easy compliance doesn't ring true, Lys. It would behoove you to take my words seriously. If you don't, you won't enjoy the consequences of your disobedience."

Consequences of my disobedience?

He was just too damn calm, too domineering. It seemed he thought he had the entire world under his thumb. She didn't intend to find herself under his thumb despite her mushrooming love for him. She paused in thought. Perhaps it would be nice to find herself under his big muscular body. Her imagination kept falling short of those feelings though she wished to discover more.

Prudently, Lyssa decided not to pursue the topic of consequences coupled with disobedience. "Where did you get this horse?"

That question seemed to be a good diversion for her.

"Changing the subject, are we? Maybe that is a splendid idea. I did, however, expect you to ask about the punishments. I would expect you to be curious. Your overactive imagination must be doing tailspins."

She tossed her head back. Pins holding her hair in place flew. Strands of her long hair fell down her back. The feeling of her hair unbound always delighted her. It was also a means, as Jess told her, to catch a man's attention. A man liked to run his hands through a woman's hair he told her one day when he found her cursing the tangles.

"There won't be any consequences to my behavior."

She literally loved the slant of his mouth, as he seemed to mull over her words.

"Why is that?"

She detected a note of laughter in his question. He was pursuing the topic. She liked that while she did want to learn what he would do if she disobeyed one of his rules, she wasn't going to push his hand tonight. She would be a model prisoner to the tyrant's ruling power; the very picture of decorum until she wasn't.

She flashed him a saucy grin. "Your rules won't be broken by me. Hence, there will be no punishment or consequences. Nonetheless, I don't believe you've the right to dictate as you seem wont to do."

She meant to be constantly at his side asking permission for this or that. He wasn't going to find a single moment of peace for himself. By the time she finished with him, he would cave to her every wish.

"You are welcome to your belief. Come, let's return to the stable. The carriage will depart in the morning at six."

If he expected to get a reaction from the early hour, he wouldn't. Working on the ranch all her life, she woke up early. The hour of departure was nothing new to her. She wasn't enamored of lying around in bed. Although, she paused in thought, while she stared at his profile, lying in bed all morning with that man might indeed be something she would enjoy.

"So late," she asked while she lowered her lashes for a moment. "We could leave earlier. Didn't you tell me I could ride the Appaloosa?"

"You can, you might not…well, it's a long ride. You might want to take the carriage the latter part of the trip."

She bristled, her back rigid with the implication he slashed out to her. Truly, he had no idea what type of woman he dealt with. This man didn't know who she was. "I can sit a horse for hours on end. My father's ranch is a working ranch, you understand. Can you?" she challenged. Couldn't help the grin when she looked at his sour disposition.

"We shall see."

She pulled a sharp breath of air into her lungs before she sent it out in a rush of understanding. "You don't like me."

Her blurted words got her another frown from him. If he didn't like her, she would have to change that before she could win him over.

Maybe she shouldn't be so sarcastic. She did want him to like her before he loved her. She thought of her parents' love story. Her mother liked her father then she despised him for what he was. After that she turned an about-face when she fell in love.

"It isn't that," he began by hedging. "Your presence here has come as a shock. This is a bachelor abode as is my home in London. Never expected Ella to call in a favor such as this one. Don't know what to do with a young debutante."

"It's true. Ella did."

"Ella did," he repeated. "I'm sorely inept at chaperoning a young lady, a debutante."

"Can you please stop referring to me as a beginner. I'm not." The gallant earl did not miss her huffy tone.

"You are not a beginner? Then what pray tell are you?" Once more an eyebrow lifted. "You have vast knowledge as well as experience in the art of love? In what men and women do together when they are in bed?"

"Didn't say that," she muttered dispirited by the turn in conversation. It seemed every word she spoke made matters between them worse.

"You are a beginner."

"Told you I wasn't," she shot back, determined to make him understand.

"Are you purposely trying to confound me?"

"Well, no, of course not. I don't know anything about love, save what Jess tells me."

Lyssa had not meant to blurt that. He would query her. She didn't want him to know things about her until she was ready.

"Who is Jess?"

"My brother."

Damn, she should have told him something else, anything else. Should have told him Jess was her lover.

"Your brother talks to you about love?"

His voice faltered for a moment. He seemed to come a bit unhinged.

Lyssa would love to know what he was thinking. "As I said before, he doesn't know he's telling me. He's either talking to his friends or he allows little things to slip. I've seen mother and father in bed. She's always hiding beneath the sheets. He's always laughing. They both tell me to leave. Since I've grown up, haven't ventured into their domain again."

"Thank God!"

In her defense she felt as if an explanation was needed. "We were little. Sometimes I'd go in there because of a nightmare. Sometimes I just needed to cuddle."

"You never saw them...?"

She laughed at his look of horror. "Never saw much. They were always underneath the covers. Heard some things though." She grinned at his look of displeasure. "Have a few thoughts. You could tell me or explain more thoroughly."

"This conversation needs an end."

Boldly, she continued, understood this was not the direction he wanted to take. "I was going to ask you what some of what I overheard meant. Most the time it was just masculine groans along with puffy little feminine sighs. I did hear father growl mother's name once."

"Lyssa." He waved his hand in the air. "This is something your new beau will want to speak of with you or teach you. It is not suitable for me to commence explaining to you what any of this means. I'm your chaperone not your lover."

His voice turned husky. She had an idea what that might mean. She'd heard that sound before from her father as well as the duke when he thought he was alone with Ella.

It was appropriate, she wanted to yell at him. *You're my new beau.* "Didn't think about that," she told him feeling subdued for the time being.

It was far too soon to tell him he was the man she fell in love with at first sight. There were no thoughts in her head as to how to proceed with that information. To fight another day would be her mantra. Tomorrow would be soon enough. The ball would serve her purpose. Jealousy might be a good ploy to utilize. After tonight, she didn't think he would be jealous if he watched her dance with someone else. He told her in vivid terms that he wouldn't allow her to be in the presence of a known rake.

None except him. She beamed. She was living with a notorious rake. He was the rake she fell in love with. Could her life be any better?

The thoughts did give her good reasons to smile, at least for a few seconds.

They were at the stable. The night ride seeming to be over before the jaunt began.

"Do any of your lady friends ever scream your name?" she asked while she watched him hang her saddle on a rail.

Lyssa kept her face averted. She heard Jess speaking about just that very thing. "Jess told his friend that the woman of the night before screamed his name. He was very pleased with his prowess."

"Lyssa…" he growled. "Enough questions."

"Does it puff up your chest when that happens? Jess says it makes him feel really good because it means he gave his lover pleasure. Do you give your lovers pleasure? I know you have them, lovers, mistresses. Do you have a mistress? So, don't deny anything."

"Wouldn't dream of denial," he said, his voice lacking emotion.

"Is that what it means?" she persisted while she understood she ventured into dangerous territory. "I'd like to feel pleasure, whatever that is, in my lover's arms."

"Lyssa!" he growled out her name again.

She looked at him. Well, her gaze riveted on him. Followed the line of his body to his crotch. He looked different. Immediately, as if he had something he wanted to hide, he moved to the other side of his stallion to give him food. She wondered at that.

"You can't blame me for my curiosity. While I told you I'm not a beginner, there are questions in my head I've no answer for. Do your ladies scream your name?" Courageously, or maybe foolishly, she asked again.

She understood he wasn't at all pleased with the question.

Keeping her queries in her head was not something she was used to doing. "A girl should know. I do believe if you gave me pleasure, I'd scream out Blacky."

The tick in his jaw increased in speed. "It's time you went to bed, little girl. I'll finish up here."

"I can take a hint."

The little girl part was a slap in the face.

"Can you? I haven't noticed."

"You should look more closely. I didn't mean to make you angry. You're so easy to tease. If I wait for you, will you walk me to my bed? Will you tell me more about pleasure? Perhaps tuck me in for the night?"

"Lyssa!"

~ * ~

"Not at all certain paring Lyssa with the earl was a good idea." Drake Montgomerie leaned on the rail of the ship as they pulled up anchor.

In a few minutes, they would leave London behind. Their search for Nickie would take them east then north onto the North Sea. Their first stop would be McClellan Castle. If Nickie wasn't there, they would continue to Dornoch, Collin's ancestral home. If not there, they would try the Earl of Blackmore's hunting lodge in the far reaches of northern Scotland.

"It's all wrong to allow Black to chaperone Lyssa Andrews. I do, however, believe with all my heart she is the breath of fresh air the man needs. I'm hoping a bit of matchmaking on my part will help our friend find love. Do you realize the girl was so bold to tell Black she would make him smile? He's been a good friend. I want to see him happy. Truly believe Lyssa can do that for him," Ella said while she leaned against her husband, his strong arms surrounding her.

Drake always, well, almost always made her happy. Once she got by that first rocky decision she made, she understood he was the only man for her. It wasn't easy though, putting her reputation on the line for his insecurities.

"What if she runs off with him?" Drake asked squeezing her closer to him. "We'll have two charges to search for. I don't like the thought that history might repeat itself. Good God, he could take her to

Lakota territory! We would never find her."

"He will resist her until he can't do so any longer. If that happens, I believe he will marry her in the way of his people, the Sioux. That will suffice until she can wed him in the way of the English. I did see the way they looked at each other."

Behind her Ella felt his hard arousal. The steel rod against her backside pleased her.

"He will compromise her. You know that. Is that what you want?" Drake said as he placed tiny kisses along the back of his wife's neck.

His hand now cupping her breast beneath the shawl she wore. He flicked his thumb across the tight bud.

She turned in his arms. His kiss stopped the words she planned to say from bubbling from her lips. When he finished the kiss, "Black will resist her until she has him firmly wrapped around her little finger. As I said, he will wed her in the way of Sioux. If you recall, you compromised me. All turned out well in the end."

"Think so?"

One of his ducal eyebrows shot upward in a perfect arch.

"Know so," Ella told him feeling smug about her plan to find a wife for Black as well as a husband for Lyssa.

The pair were made for each other. "I don't care if he makes love to her before the wedding. We both know someone who did just that. All turned out for the best in their case, now, didn't it? I'm not a hypocrite where love is concerned. Will never judge anyone, especially my nieces."

"You're making a damn bad chaperone for your charges. What did the first duchess say to you?"

Quickly she shot back, "Time will tell."

"For now, I'm going to accept what you've told me. Lyssa is your sister's daughter. She's been brought up in the west. I'm sure there will be no end to surprises for Black. She seems to have a way of saying what's on her mind without thinking."

"Like I said, a breath of fresh air for the stodgy man."

"Impulsiveness is not always the best."

"True, all that you say. I'm not implying their journey will be easy. It won't. I know Lyssa is in love with him."

30

"If she is anything like you, he will not be able to resist her persistent nature," Drake said as he ran his hands along Ella's arms.

She shivered with the passion he so easily created. "He will find himself blindsided by her innocence. She will be blatantly surprising. While she is nothing like the white women he is used to, he will fall victim to her honesty. He will want to touch her, make love to her. Eventually, he will give in to his needs."

"You believe he will keep his hands to himself."

"No, however the question is how long it will take him to give in to his passion for her. I saw that desire blossom the first time he looked at Lyssa. The passion shimmered in her eyes too."

"Just be advised this scheme of yours could all backfire."

Ella pulled in a large breath of air, thinking on all Drake said. "I will take that under advisement. Right now, however, our biggest concern is Nickie. I'm sure she also follows her heart. She might be increasing by the time we reach her. She will have a big decision to make."

"The McInnis pup has a great deal to account for. A man can't run off with a well-born lady. He's not above the law."

"I won't have you threatening them. Not when I'm sure the pair are in love and will eventually do the right thing. Just as we eventually did."

Drake turned her in his arms. His kiss was devastatingly sweet. Ella knew Drake would do as he damn well pleased in this matter. Damn the consequences. If Nickie loved the rake, she would fight for him.

"You know I will. I plan to put the fear of God in the young'un. He has to understand the family he is dealing with. When he does, their future together will go much easier for him. Shall we retire down stairs to discover further pleasures?"

"Thought you would never ask."

Chapter Two

Black, his given name Kane, watched Lyssa while she floated around the ballroom in her new gown. Her feet barely touched the floor. She moved with sublime grace. The picture Kane watched stunned him. Brought forth all his protective instincts. Before they left the townhouse, Kane made sure she was covered appropriately. The little minx did indeed remove the modesty piece last night before she came down to dinner. The act was either in defiance of his suggestion she dress for dinner or a not-so-subtle attempt at seduction. The answer was hers to tell. He would never ask. Tonight, her parents would be proud of her. They raised a beautiful daughter. He was certain they knew that for a fact. Lyssa's beauty wasn't just on the surface. Her beauty glowed from the inside out.

Ah, seduction...the reason she might want to seduce him clearly eluded him. He was not a catch any young debutante would consider. He was half Sioux warrior. He had women who fell over their heels to get him into his bed because of that fact. They all wanted to know if someone so primitive might stir their passion more than a titled gent born and bred in England.

Those were all widows or women unhappy in their married life. Virgins, he didn't take to his bed. Once though, a long time ago, he allowed himself to dream, thought he was in love. Discovered he was more in love with the idea than actual love. The woman he desired was beautiful as well as white. She didn't know he was part Sioux until he'd already made love to her, took the virginity she willingly gifted him with. When she discovered his heritage, her father had him whipped. He was tied to a post, nearly died there.

Drake and Ella rescued him. Ironically, they were in the west, the Dakotas, searching for him. He was the man who would become the next Earl of Blackmore. Together they nursed him back to health. His mother was Lakota Sioux. He had more the look of an Englishman than a Sioux, which was why the woman thought him white. Believed the color of his skin was due to the sun not his heritage. Part of that was true.

He owed the duke and duchess his life. Would always owe the pair. Without their care, he would never have survived the whipping. While he implied to Ella she was taking advantage of his good nature, he would do anything for her. What she asked of him this time was not too much. The problem, which he attempted to deny, was that he was attracted to Lyssa. She was amazingly beautiful, a stunning beauty. She was white, pure as the driven snow.

Beauty wasn't the issue. Indeed, there were women who were more stunning than Lyssa. Her temperament was sassy and sweet. He could listen to her bluster all day never growing bored. He already knew he loved to tease her. She possessed a sensual innocence that stirred every male part of him. Ah, but the questions...did she or didn't she understand the blatant sexual innuendos she tossed his way? She queried about anything that popped into her beautiful head.

The conclusion was apparent when she gaped at him, her mouth opening, the subtle shift of her shoulders giving all away. Obviously, her nimble mind rattled his answers around coming to no conclusion she understood. This was a game he thoroughly would enjoy playing more often with her.

In the arms of a portly young man, she danced past him. For his benefit, Lyssa made a sour face of distaste. He chuckled while he recalled the list of attributes she wanted in the man she would wed. This dandy didn't fit into any part of her list. For making sure the least threatening men were on that dance card, he should have a bit of remorse. He didn't.

Lyssa's dance card was full. He'd made certain there would be no time for her to pursue a dance with him. The devil take him if he held her in his arms. Much to her chagrin he left no spaces. He also made sure he approved of all the men who held a spot on the card. Understandably, the men he chose would not be to her liking. She wouldn't lose her virginity any time soon.

As the dance ended, Lyssa's partner stopped in front of Black. He bowed then thanked her for the dance. She cringed. Black grinned.

After her latest dance partner left, Lyssa turned on him, her eyes blazing. "Damn and blast, Blacky, what the devil do you think you're doing? These men are horrible. None of the men you allowed to dance with me have one redeeming quality." She was seething, her anger palpable. "I couldn't breathe he smelled so bad."

He smirked. Asking nonchalantly, "What do you mean? These men all have titles. They are perfect for a young debutante."

"These men...they..." It seemed she couldn't get the words out that would describe her dance partners."

"They?"

He watched her lips smush into a thin line. Lips he would like to taste, savor for a very long time.

"You're doing this on purpose. I won't court these men you've picked out for me. There is nothing attractive about any one of them. I've told each and every man I've danced with not to bother calling on me tomorrow afternoon. Hope you're satisfied." Her tiny hands were fisted at her sides. "If we weren't in the middle of all these people, I'd start throwing things at you. I'd toss a glass of that horrible punch in your handsome face."

She was delightful. He chortled, sincerely reminding her, "You filled out the card. Has it been so long that you forgot?"

"I didn't know who any of the men were. You did." She poked him in the chest to better make her point. "You planned this. I hate you…"

"They all meet my approval. That was my condition. Come, the musicians are taking a break. We can get something to drink. If you don't mind being seen with me, that is."

His hand lightly on her elbow, he steered her toward the glasses of wine. Taking one for each of them, they moved to a spot on the balcony. He knew she seethed. Her temper flared easily. He did enjoy a woman who showed honest emotions. Lyssa didn't hide behind false words. If he could have found a man who fit all her chosen characteristics and was also acceptable to him, he would have added the name to the dance card. As it turned out, there were none in attendance. No one here could ride as well as her daddy…except him.

He turned to her. "Not trying to make this difficult for you. I do

34

want you to find someone."

"No? Not difficult? What would you call your atrocious behavior?"

"No, what I'm attempting is to keep you out of trouble until Ella returns."

The fact of the matter was that he didn't think any of the young lords at this ball would suit her, even the ones who were not simpering fops or mama's boys. She was such a free spirit. A man who was not adaptable would crush that wonderous spirit of hers.

"Would you dance with me?"

She smiled widely, her eyes alight with mischief.

He wanted to kiss that little dimple that seemed to wink at him with her changing expressions. "We both know it would not be proper for the chaperone to dance with his charge. The scandal would follow you the duration of the season."

"Damn propriety, what do I care about scandal? Nothing," she murmured as she turned away from him. She pointed, "I want to dance with either one of those two men, both if possible. You don't happen to know them, do you?"

Black couldn't hold back the groan rumbling from his chest as Drew and Jeremy stopped in front of them. "What are you two doing here? You never attend these affairs."

"Hells bells, thought I'd ask you the same. These balls are not ever in your element," Jeremy said as his attention moved to Lyssa to linger on her mouth then her magnificent bosom. His ardent gaze roamed the length of her then back to settle on her exquisite features. His grin stretched across his face. "This one is quite fetching."

"Can I dance with him?" Lyssa asked her voice turning sweet while she looked into his eyes. "He fits some of the characteristics on my list. No blue-grey eyes however," she spoke softly.

"No."

"Why?" both Jeremy and Lyssa seemed to ask at the same time.

"My friend here," Black paused to look sternly on the man, "Jeremy, is a rake as is Drew. I won't have you dancing with a man who is likely to toss your skirts if given a chance. If given the opportunity, he would waltz you onto the balcony and have his way with you."

Lyssa snorted, something else that gave Black a reason to smile. It was so Lyssa as well as so unladylike. The girl truly didn't care what others thought. "I won't allow Jeremy to do that since I've picked out the man I want to toss my skirts. Unfortunately, he's yet to show a smidgeon of interest in me."

Black let out a deep breath of air as he looked from his friends to his charge. Both Jeremy and Drew were laughing, howling would be a better description. They laughed as if they knew who this man was.

"Oh, it's that way then," Jeremy said a chuckle on his lips. "She wants the chaperone."

The music was beginning. While there was a name on her card for this dance, the man wasn't here. Black gave up. "Go ahead." To Jeremy, "Don't take her on the balcony, mind you."

She flashed her dimple at him again. Jeremy grinned as if to say I'll do as I please then pulled her into his arms. He held her too close. His hand at her waist the tiniest bit too low. Black wanted to know what they spoke of when he bent to whisper something close to her ear. They disappeared for a moment only to reappear in the farthest away corner of the room.

Jeremy had no shame. If he wasn't mistaken, the man was waltzing her onto a secluded balcony meant for kissing. In his earlier days, he made use of the trysting places located at far ends of the room. He wasn't about to trust his friend. He knew him too well.

When he spotted them, she was leaning on a pillar, her breasts rising and falling as if she'd been running. Jeremy's hand was braced on the same pillar by her head. He was grinning at her. Had the look of moving in for a kiss.

Black didn't understand the jealousy raging through him. Nor did he understand the sensual thoughts rushing through his head concerning Lyssa. What he did comprehend was that he wanted to be the first man to set his lips on hers. He reached the couple before Jeremy could take advantage of the opportunity he single-mindedly created.

"Not so fast!" Black said as he pulled Jeremy away by the back of the collar on his frock coat.

Jeremy winked at her. He saw the dimple. Wondered if he'd just been set up. No, Jeremy intended to kiss her. Would not think for one second, he would feel that green-eyed bug of jealousy biting him in the butt when it came to a female. He'd never cared before.

He wasn't jealous. He was her chaperone. What the bloody hell was he thinking?

The first man to kiss her?

As brazen as she was, she most likely had been kissed numerous times. He wasn't about to give in to the wishes of his unruly body. Ella charged him with a job to do. He would make bloody sure he stayed within the parameters of chaperone.

He might die trying.

"What's up with you? It's just a kiss. Not like I'm taking her outside to do a bit more than kiss." Jeremy sounded indignant. "You would have done the same."

If that wasn't enough for one night, Drew tapped him on the shoulder. "Don't suppose I could have this dance? Promise I won't take her to the balcony." The man grinned shamelessly while he asked. "Maybe outside though for a bit more than a kiss. We could walk among the roses."

Lyssa returned the grin. "I'd like that. No kissing though. Blacky might not approve. He's hovering over me. The man's like an old woman."

Old woman? Blacky? No one calls me that that and gets away with it. She's already done so numerous times.

Both Jeremy and Drew hooted at her comment.

That was taking it too far. When she waltzed away this time in the arms of his other friend, he knew he wanted her in his arms before the night finished. One dance. That was all he needed to have her out of his system. He pulled out his pocket watch. The night had only just begun. He would wait until people were leaving. The chaperone dancing with his charge would not be quite so noticeable or scandalous.

If he could find a way, he would dance with her then make sure they were on their way home. Watching her dance with other men when he needed her in his arms was sheer torture. What the bloody hell was he thinking? He'd gone stark raving mad.

One dance. One time in his arms then he could focus on finding her a suitable husband as well as running off all the unsuitable ones. The rest of the night passed in a blur. Jeremy and Drew showed up at the ball only because they wanted to peruse the new flock of debutantes. They left after both secured a dance with Lyssa. Black was certain they would end up at their favorite pub with their favorite ladies of the night.

Presenting yourself in front of debutantes along with their doting mothers or chaperones was always dangerous. Once in a blue moon though they would give in to temptation. After that bout of ridiculousness, they would leave swearing off balls and young women whose only interest was in securing a titled husband.

Lyssa didn't seem to care about titles or finding a husband. After all, she told him she knew who the perfect man for her was. She stared him in the eyes when she said the words. He groaned. His member grew hard.

The last dance of the night found Lyssa with no partner despite the fact he painstakingly filled her card. When she looked at him, her blue eyes wistful, he gave into his urge to hold her. Wrapping her in his arms, he pulled her close. Let the sway of her body ignite his. It wasn't so much that he allowed it to happen, he didn't seem to have a choice where his body was concerned. She inflamed him. He settled his hand where it shouldn't be. Thought better of it, forcing himself to place his fingers on her waist. As she leaned into him, her generous breasts pushed against his chest. The softly rounded globes felt divine. He held her to close. She knew it. He knew it. Everyone watching would think the same.

She tilted her chin to look up at him. "Thank you for dancing with me. All night I hoped you would find an empty spot on my card. It was rather fortuitous that the man who was supposed to have this dance left early. Don't you think?"

There was nothing fortuitous about the man leaving. Black paid him to do so with a threat along with a few groats.

"Indeed." Was all Black was willing to say.

Certainly, he wasn't about to enlighten the little minx what he did so he could hold her in his arms. If Lyssa understood how much he wanted her, he would never be able to withstand her charms, in the interim keep her chaste.

Lyssa set her hand on his chest instead of his shoulder. "My mother always does this when she dances with daddy. I feel your heartbeat. It seems to beat the same pace as mine. We seem to be in tune with each other. Do you think so?"

He gulped in air. Her words always had this way to unnerve him. This innocent statement wasn't even an outrageous statement of fact. Still, the words had the same effect on him. If he could, he would find a way to make love to her. As soon as they reached the townhouse, he would do just that.

That was the crux of the matter, making love to this woman was not possible. He wouldn't take her virginity; a gift she would give the man she was meant to marry. Although there wasn't one doubt in his mind, he was the man she described in her imagination. He could never wed her. While he understood he needed a marriage to gain an heir, no one in England would do. Risking courting a white woman again sent terror racing through his veins sweat coating his palms. Courting a white woman was the only thing he was afraid of.

Ella explained to him time and again there were many women who wouldn't care about his heritage. Didn't know if that was true or not. He wasn't in such a desperate need for a woman he would risk another encounter with a female whose color was like fresh-fallen snow. Hell, he was only twenty-nine. He had more than enough time to sort as well as sift through London to find the right woman. One who could love him for who he was not who she thought him to be.

Before Lyssa fell in love with him, he would have to tell her more about himself. He needed to make certain she understood they would never suit. Finding a woman in London seemed prudent. They would not have heard the stories surrounding the Lakota nation. Might not consider him a savage. Lyssa was from the states. She would hold many of the same prejudices. The native people who lived there for centuries were savages to most white people who didn't understand their way of life.

Yes, Lyssa would know. Her parents settled on the outskirts of tribal land. Bought land that once was owned by native people. If she knew his background coupled with some of the things he did in his younger years, she would be terrified. Finding the right time to tell her was the problem. He didn't want to burst the small ray of hope surrounding him when he looked at her lovely features.

The woman enticed and intrigued like no other. Thoughts of resuming his life when she no longer needed him left him with feelings of despair. He didn't want to be honest with himself. If he were to do that, he would admit he was enamored of the little minx the moment he spotted her standing behind Ella while framed in the doorway to his office.

Everything that transpired after that served to deepen his feelings. Even when she rode off without him caused him to feel more for her.

She touched his chin. He jerked. His expression tightened. He sifted in more needed air just to deal with what was to come.

"What are you thinking? You seem so far away." Her voice softly purred as her breath whispered against his skin.

He closed his eyes to ward off the powerful sensation that tiny fluttering of air caused.

He had been far away, adrift in his thoughts. "Thinking I'd like to go back to Blackmore Hall tonight instead of in the morning. Not possible though." There was more to his thoughts. He wasn't about to share. He wanted her in his big bed, beneath him while he taught her about love, what a man and a woman could share. Wished he could answer all her questions by showing her how love between them could be. She had so many delightful questions. Ah, if he could...

That was the major obstacle, love between them couldn't be. He was the chaperone. She was the debutante. No, he was a man well and truly damned. Resisting her beautiful charms for very long would be impossible.

"I'd like that too. The recital is in two days. I don't need to go to the damn event. Don't believe singing a few songs will find me a man. Or...we can travel between the two places. Your estate is so much nicer than the city."

"Why is that?"

He grinned now as his fingers tightened on her waist. Pulling her even closer than he should, he wondered if she felt his steel hard arousal against the softness of her belly, wondered too if she knew what it meant. If she asked the question, it wouldn't surprise him. Lyssa said whatever popped into her fertile and curious little mind.

"There are so many reasons. Where should I begin?" she began, tilting her chin as if she wanted to see him more clearly.

She ran her tongue across her bottom lip, leaving a dewy, tempting trail of wetness behind.

"Tell me."

He whirled her in a tight circle holding her closer to keep her from stumbling. The way her body pressed against him brought him to rock hard arousal. Tonight, he would find no satisfaction in the soft velvet of her body.

"The country reminds me a bit of home. One can hear the birds sing along with the sifting of the wind through the trees. The stars are brighter, the scents pure and natural. Don't enjoy the smell of the city. There are other things too."

"You like to listen to birds?" He swept her into the same alcove Jeremy did earlier. "What about the other animals? Do like to hear those too?"

"Y-yes."

She sounded breathless, winded from the dancing or in anticipation of a possible kiss? He didn't know nor did he care. Her mouth parted slightly almost as if she invited him inside. The dimple he adored showed itself. Too bad she had no idea what she was about.

"Why else do you like the country life?"

His question whispered across her ear he was so near to her. He touched the lobe with the tip of his tongue before he pulled away, understanding a kiss would lead to more of the same. Dancing was so much different than kissing.

Dancing would have to do.

They weren't dancing now.

"You along with your servants are the only people I see. We can ride anytime I want. There is so much space. Believe I could ride forever."

She set her fingertip on his chin. Her dimple played with his senses. He wanted to see what the tiny indentation tasted like, perhaps dark sweet honey. "If you say I can, that is. I mean to follow every autocratic rule you set down. You know that don't you? I'm going to be a model prisoner." She gifted him with a huge grin.

"If you say so," he chuckled at the expression on her delicately delicious features as he allowed his thumb to travel across her bottom lip. "Don't want you to think of yourself as a prisoner though. You don't need to ask to leave the house as long as you stay close. Rides in the country are a different matter."

Flirtatiously, she lowered her lashes for a moment, as she seemed to wonder how far she could push him. When her gaze returned to his, she smiled. It was almost as if he could see the naughty thoughts dancing in her mind.

"Would you kiss me?"

Her question jolted him back to his senses. The devil, he was about to do that very thing. She was pliant in his arms, all womanly curves. She was soft in all the best places, ripe for seduction or a bit of coaxing. Her lips would part for his tongue. Stunned by his carnal thoughts, he pulled away.

"No, Lyssa. I must apologize for allowing this to go too far. I forgot myself."

He let go of her. She stumbled backward. He reached out to steady her. "It's getting late. We should leave. Do you still wish to return to the estate? No, you will have gentlemen callers in the afternoon. Wouldn't want to disappoint any one of them. We will stay in town until the morning after the recital. Tonight's ball, along with the recital, are the only invitations Ella gave me. I'm certain more will come your way."

"Hope not," she muttered while she stole a deep breath of air. Her once dreamy eyes were now defiant. "I didn't enjoy this ball except for the last five minutes with you. You should have kissed me. I will keep trying for that kiss," petulantly, she went on to tell him as she poked his chest with her finger, "I'm not going to accept an invitation to do anything tomorrow. The men I danced with were horrid. If you would think about it, could you see me in bed with any of them?"

Again, she shoved him from his thoughts. *In bed with one of those men?* When she put it that way, his only recourse would be to agree with her. The thought of Lyssa in bed with any man except him turned his gut sour. "That's an image I don't have nor do I want to think of you in bed with a man while he..."

Well now he was almost down right crude. He almost said a few curt words that would have been inappropriate in most settings, especially this one.

"Except for Jeremy, Drew also. Those two are quite handsome if you want my opinion. I might, as you so put it, let either one of them toss my skirts. Nonetheless, I doubt if they ride as well as my daddy."

"You're not allowing any man to toss your skirt, especially not Jeremy or Drew. You're right. They don't ride as well as your daddy."

He growled the words. If they came to court her, he would shoo them off.

He scowled before taking her hand in his. They said their goodbyes to the hosts.

Once in his carriage, he felt relief wash over him. The last hours strained his nerves, stretched them thin. However, he meant to enlighten her about a few things. If necessary to drive home his point, he would tell her more than once. "If Jeremy or Drew come to call on the morrow, you won't accompany either one of them anywhere."

She sat forward. Her eyes deepening in color, she cleared her throat. "I understand they are notorious rakes here in London just like the man who absconded with my cousin. I believe I'd like to know either one of them better. If Jeremy or Drew does come to court me, you could go with us on a ride. You've nothing to worry about if they don't ride as good as my daddy. I do so want to learn more about love as well as what happens to a woman when she is in bed with a man."

His jaw clenched with her words. That was not going to happen. "No! That won't be possible. My friends aren't ready to choose a wife. Not old enough either. Won't be for years. Not letting you waste your energy, not to speak of the time wasted on men who can't reciprocate the feelings you require in a man who will be your husband. A male who would break your heart."

"Not if I'm in love with someone else. I am, you know, in love. What could seeing Jeremy or Drew along with having a bit of fun hurt until the man I want comes around to my way of thinking? Perhaps one or both could teach me the proper way to kiss a man."

"The man you want will never come around."

He crossed his arms over his chest while he tried to ignore the restlessness of his body, the stirring beneath his trousers. She provoked and prodded emotions best left dormant.

"You don't know that."

"I do."

"No, the man I want almost kissed me tonight. If he did, I would say I'm one step closer to my dreams." Her smirk was blatant. Infuriatingly so. "Perhaps he could still be persuaded."

"Jeremy? He's not..."

"Quit denying the facts looming in front of your face. You know exactly who I'm speaking of. The man is not Jeremy or Drew. Although if either man kissed me, I would have something to compare since I've never been kissed. However, you must kiss me too. Oh, dear, if you didn't know it's you I want. You must understand now. Should we see if the man I want more than anything will kiss me now?" Lyssa moved so she sat next to him. "You could take me onto your lap. I'd like to sit there, cradled on your thighs. You could take other liberties. I would allow anything."

With all the willpower he possessed coming into play, he set her to the opposite side. This wasn't happening to him. Lyssa wasn't attempting to seduce him? "You're too brazen."

"If courage gets me what I want, then I applaud myself. Are you afraid of me, Blacky?"

"Call me Black or Kane."

"I think not. Blacky suits you."

He gritted his teeth trying desperately to ignore her blatant invitation while he understood this conversation was going nowhere. He was tempted to give her a taste of what she asked for. The little girl would turn tail, run, hide so terrified she'd wet her pants. Perhaps, if he frightened her, she would back off. If he took a few of those liberties she blatantly told him she would give. No, she would probably pursue this further.

She was incorrigible.

"We're almost home. I trust you to find your room by yourself.

"You could tuck me in."

She batted her lashes while she grinned sweetly.

~ * ~

From her bedroom window, Lyssa watched Kane ride out of sight. She'd done that to him. Exactly what that was she wasn't at all positive. Jess always told her he didn't like women who reserved favors until they had a man riding hard and fast. Tonight, she did the opposite. If she'd known what he was about, she would have followed him. Blatantly, without reservation, she threw herself at the stuffy earl. She wanted that kiss more than anything. She wanted more too. The trouble was she didn't understand what exactly it was she wanted. She meant to discover the truth of the matter though. The kissing thing in the carriage wasn't well done of her. She provoked him. Knew enough about the male body to realize, he was aroused.

That was before the near kiss on the balcony.

She shouldn't have asked. Chalking that revelation up for future use, she gathered asking him was what kept their lips from touching. Damn and blast, she wanted that kiss, his lips joined to hers. Now, she didn't know when she would get another chance. That moment in his arms, dancing, had been the perfect opportunity. When they stopped on the balcony, she felt as if she was in heaven. Everything was ripe for that kiss.

She wasted the golden opportunity by words that brought him back to the reality of his position as her chaperone. He'd been just as caught up in the moment as she had been. The moment was a misstep that was all. She would correct her mistake. In time, he would kiss her. He must want her.

Once during the night when she said something outrageous, she caught his smile. She did that to him, helped him smile. Her intention was to do that more often. She thought him the handsomest man alive when he scowled. Oh, when he smiled there was no one who would compare.

She truly hoped he would kiss her soon. Thought for a few seconds he would do so. A kiss wasn't to be. He possessed too much will power. Somehow, she would have to find a means to break him of that indomitable strength of his. If she couldn't, she might not ever get that sought after kiss.

A thought of something Jess told her before she left for England gave her a little giggle. He'd said a man could never resist a naked lady. Why he told her that went beyond anything she could imagine. Still, perhaps if she met him naked in his bedroom when he returned, he'd lose the power of control.

Heat flooded her face. She could never be so shameless. Thinking about taking all her clothes off in front of the man was bad enough. Doing it was something altogether different. Doing went beyond the pale. If she did so, he might send her home. That just wouldn't do.

Tomorrow would prove to be a long boring day unless for some reason his friends came to call. She didn't want either of them. They seemed fun however. They reminded her of her brother only a bit older. When she danced with Jeremy, he laughed at her. Told her because of her brash nature she was not of the fairer sex. The stodgy earl should have words with her. He didn't like to be called Blacky. Many tried. All failed.

It seemed she did try to needle him. Kane took all her provoking in stride, merely mentioning a different name could be used in place. Ah, she wasn't one bit tired. As a matter of fact, she was wide-awake. If she knew where Kane was, she'd ride out to meet him. She would take a blistering of words if she did so. What punishment or discipline would he dole out? Finding out would almost be worth the effort to discover the punishment. The more she came to know Kane, the more she thought he was all bluster when the time came to his words about disciplining her. The question looming in her mind was if she wanted to discover if she was correct in her assumption.

That decision could wait until later.

Lyssa brushed her hair until the locks glistened in the soft firelight. She paced the room at least one hundred times. Plumped the pillows on her bed each time she passed by. The view out her window remained unchanged. He would return soon. She made a decision. It might not be the smartest. Might not be the worst. Only time would tell the truth of her actions.

Quickly, she slipped a robe over her nightdress. Barefoot, she walked to the drawing room and poured herself a hefty glass of brandy before curling up in a wing chair by the fire with her feet tucked beneath her robe.

Flames danced while embers glowed in the darkness. Glowing orange firelight flickered against the wall giving an eerie feeling to the room. One oil lamp remained alight at the door to the room where she waited. She closed her eyes thinking about their almost kiss. Vividly, she recalled the feel of his arms around her, the mint scent of his breath when he bent so very near. In his elegant eveningwear, he was dashing. When he pressed her against him, he was hard everywhere. His body was the perfect fit for hers. If she was of a different temperament, she might be disappointed in the fact he didn't show interest in her. Might even give up on him. Not yet. She needed to make him smile all the time. She wanted his gaze to follow her around the room.

When his fingers touched hers to remove the dangling glass, she jerked up, startled. She pushed hair from her eyes before blinking a few times to confirm the fact that Kane stood in front of her. She'd decided to call him Kane since everyone she knew including the duchess called him Black. His dark hair appeared wind disheveled. The strands were damp. A rakish lock fell over one eye. His deep blue eyes flashed with pleasure at seeing her, at least she hoped desire was what she saw.

"I must have fallen asleep," she murmured sleepily wondering when that could have happened. "Didn't mean to do so."

A bemused look on his face, Kane appeared for a moment at a loss for words. "Always thought a person should sleep in his or her bed. What are you doing in the drawing room?"

Lyssa wasn't at all sure how he would take the truth. She wouldn't lie. Perhaps part of the truth was prudent. "I saw you ride off. Was waiting for you. Thought about following you." She lifted her shoulders. "Didn't know where you were going."

"You did? You were?" His eyebrow lifted in speculation. "Pray tell does that have something to do with you sleeping in the wing chair?

Couldn't be comfortable."

Expecting a scowl coupled with derogatory words not the pleasantness she was now hearing, she was delighted with the outcome. With nothing left to say, she chose to repeat herself. "Would have followed you. Wanted to do so. Didn't know where you went in such a hurry or why."

She looked down to her hands that were now folded innocently in her lap. When she met his gaze again, she lifted her shoulders in what she hoped was a womanly shrug, one that might present her bosom in an enticing manner. "Didn't have your permission either."

A short bark of laughter followed her outrageous comment. "Were those the only reasons that kept you in the house?"

He filled her glass then another for him. He sat down opposite, his legs stretched out in front of him. Negligent could be used to describe him, curious too.

Liking Kane that way, she flashed him a cheeky smile deciding she wasn't going to use feminine wiles to get her way. Was no good at them in any case. "Didn't know where you rode off to," she repeated the first reason.

"If you knew, would you have followed?"

The tenor of his speech alerted her to the fact all was not serene in his mind.

Her gaze shot to his face. Needed to read the expression, the underlying look to his eyes, the way the lines across his forehead deepened. She wanted to trace those creases with the tip of her finger "Can I be punished for words and thoughts as well as deeds? Something I didn't do?"

"No, only deeds. You can think whatever you will. If you have the control to stop yourself from doing something stupid, I won't punish. However, I'm beginning to think you lack control. You, my dear, need a firm hand."

He was almost smiling. His eyes shimmered merrily. She liked that about him. One smile along with one almost was most likely all she would get for the night. She was satisfied.

"It did cross my mind to follow you." She held up a hand to stop his comment from leaving his lips then perhaps turning ugly. "Conversely, as I told you, I'm not going to willingly or even unknowingly break the rules you set out. Now, you must promise me that you won't make another rule up after the fact so you can punish me. That would not be fair at all."

He appeared taken aback by her comment. After that moment, he started shaking his head. "Truly, this isn't as if I would take delight in giving out discipline. Is that what you think?"

"You could have fooled me. First thing you spoke to me about after Aunt Ella left the room was rules that couldn't be broken."

She turned her head so he wouldn't be able to see her grin.

"Listen, I'm not a tyrant!" With those words his voice was harsh. He calmed himself. "You know that. So, from now on, I'd appreciate it if you did not create situations that make me appear that way."

Lyssa pointedly felt the stab to her heart his statement was meant to create. Though she had no intention of apologizing. Everything she told him was the truth. In her mind, it was time to move on to some other topic. Figuring out what that would be was difficult.

"Where did you go? If the place is close, can we ride there tomorrow?"

She slanted a timid smile his way. She didn't feel timid. However, there were certain things he needed to understand about her. One was that she didn't back down. Something else her brother taught her inadvertently. Men appreciated women who stood for their beliefs. Of course, Kane might be that one man who would rather hold a woman under his thumb. She didn't think so. However, it was disconcerting to her to not truly know this man.

"For a cold swim," he answered rather quickly.

"I did that to you?"

This time her smile was plastered to her face. Jess would go for cold swims at night if he didn't get sex from the woman he was with. That didn't happen often, only when it was a new lady for him. He told her cold swims were the only thing that would cool his ardor.

Kane scowled. "You've no idea what you're talking about. Either that or your brother has told you far more than is appropriate for a young lady to understand."

He downed his brandy in a gulp. Poured himself a second glass. "As I said before, he doesn't exactly tell me..."

"You hear him talking with his friends. That's not much better. He needs to be more aware of his surroundings. I'm sure you make a habit of blending in so no one notices you."

Her smirk brought on a deeper frown. "A brother rarely notices his little sister unless she is annoying him in some manner. When she is simply doing her chores as expected without saying a word, he doesn't know she is there. It isn't my fault you know, if I can manage to hide in plain view."

His snort of derision didn't surprise or bother her. There was no other way to explain the sound he made. Well, she didn't expect him to believe her.

Long strides sent him to the fireplace. Now, when he stared at her, he had a cocky look to his face. "Tell me exactly what you did to me to tease me to the point I needed a cold swim. I'd like to confirm or deny this ability you think you have over my body."

She blanched, felt all the blood drain from her face. It was one thing to imply knowledge, quite a different happenstance to speak of the details. Even if she knew the particulars, she'd be too mortified to tell him in specific terms what she thought. She had an idea though. Facts she wasn't entirely positive about. Lyssa knew the only way to get through this was to brazen the moment out until he grew tired of the topic. He might forget his question. She stiffened to rigid, her chin tilting upward. "A woman doesn't speak of such things, intimate things to a man she barely knows."

Kane grinned. It wasn't the kind of smile she wanted to put on his face. He was about to draw blood, hers. He was probably thinking she didn't act like most women.

"Tell me, Lyssa. Tell me what it is you think you did to my man's body. Didn't take you for a coward. After all, you started this conversation. Possibly we need to finish the tête-à-tête."

"Well."

She hesitated while she wondered what to say to him. As it was, she truly didn't know the exactness of what her brother and friends spoke of, just that they needed a cold swim in the pond so they could sleep. She lowered her lashes. Swallowed the lump growing bigger in her throat. Brazening this out was a good idea, but how?

"Perhaps I should tell you. Even though I would rather hear you speak the words."

His voice gruff and whisky smooth began a firestorm in her belly to eventually seep lower to this spot between her thighs she'd never been aware of before Kane almost kissed her.

Her gaze shot to his face, her eyes wide. While the smile didn't reach his mouth, his eyes seemed to twinkle with laughter. Damn and blast, he appeared to enjoy this discomfort of hers. She could only blame herself having carried the dialogue too far. Time for her to excuse herself then go to bed.

"No, believe I'm tired now. Should go upstairs. Tomorrow will come far too soon."

She started to rise. His large hand settled on her shoulder, pushing her down. His flesh felt warm as the tender caress enflamed her senses more.

"Why don't you stay and have another brandy. You said you weren't intending to see any callers on the morrow. We can explore what it is you did to my man's body to make me search out a cold lake."

"I'd rather not."

However, she did want to stay with him for a few more minutes or hours if he wanted to talk. She would like to know if she was the cause of his ride to the lake or pond. Prudently, she decided dancing around the topic or finding a new one would do more to suit her purpose.

"I think you will."

He handed her a freshly poured glass of brandy. It was her second in so little time. Her mind felt a bit muzzled by the effects of the alcohol. If the strong spirits went to her head, she didn't know what she'd divulge. While she blurted out things no other lady would, she always, until now, tempered those impulses to some degree. Until now, she was always in command of her words.

"Very well." This time she sipped, watched him over the rim of the expensive crystal. "You first."

He sat down next to her. His long legs stretched out in front of him, the thick muscles, contained enticingly in the buckskin pants he wore. To go for the ride, he had changed from his eveningwear. The shirt he wore now was partially buttoned, still damp in places from his swim. His broad chest was smooth beneath the opening. He didn't have black hair on his chest as her brother did. He didn't have any hair at all. She wanted to test the texture of his sun-darkened skin. The urge to feel him rose fast and furious.

"I'm waiting," he spoke softly, determination to his tone that didn't go unnoticed by her.

She widened her eyes, feigning unawareness. "For what?"

Ignorance could sometimes be used as a ploy to divert from one topic to another. She used the ploy quite often with her brother. The scheme usually worked.

"For an answer. What do you think you did to my man's body? It's something you need to know so you won't do it to some other poor soul you catch unaware. It's a quite painful state for a man to find himself in with no possibility of relief in his future."

"Painful? How?" she queried, swiftly sitting forward, her eyes wider now that she wasn't pretending. Yes, Jess did say something along those lines. "I did something to you that hurt? Certainly didn't mean to."

Her bravado was slipping fast. She knew nothing, absolutely nothing about pain. Thought the sensations between a man and a woman were all pleasure. Now she was lost, totally lost, floundering in neck deep mud barely keeping her head high enough to breathe the air.

"Your words not mine."

Damn and blast, what the devil was he speaking of. He did say painful first. He did use the word first. In any case she owed him a heart-felt apology. "I'm terribly sorry. I..."

The breath he let out seemed to go on forever. "Go to sleep, Lyssa. Finish your brandy first. Truly, you shouldn't be so barefaced as to toss out the implications that you did. You are an innocent, flaunting knowledge you don't have. These last few moments were intriguing though. I've learned a great deal about you." He leaned forward, his huge forearms resting on his thighs. "I've no intention of enlightening you. In this case what you don't know can't hurt you."

She downed the brandy regaining some of the lost courage. For a reason she didn't fathom, she needed to learn more. "How is it painful? I know from my brother that women can do that to a man. He said as much one night when he ended up at home a bit tipsy from too much to drink." She held up her hands as his scowl deepened. She understood from his expression he meant to interrupt. "I'm not implying it was me that did that to you. However, don't you think if I'm going to see men, I should understand what I shouldn't do to make them hurt. Don't you think?"

"Where are you going with this?"

Amusement now tinged his voice. He was grinning which surprised her.

She shrugged slightly wishing she had an answer for his question. For the moment, she didn't understand how he went from pain to amusement. "I don't know."

"Before you start something you can't finish, you should keep your foot out of your mouth." He seemed to have an additional thought. "Perhaps you should keep it in so no words you'll regret will pop out unbidden."

His new sarcasm irritated her. She didn't know what to make of the rapid change of emotions.

Her anger rose to the surface. Going down in defeat was not part of her style. "I do know more than I said, just reluctant to say the words in front of you. Know it's because a man wants sex with a lady and doesn't get it. My brother..."

He held up his hands, the scowl on his face growing. "Don't mention your brother again in my company. While I'm sure he has had a hand in your limited and very inappropriate education concerning sex, we will proceed without his advice or the parts you overheard. Most likely you heard bits and pieces of a conversation not meant for you to be part of. Nothing that would put the whole of the situation into context, am I right?"

Again, wisely she knew she'd gone too far. However, she wasn't feeling the least bit wise at this point or prudent. She had something to prove. When she got that bee in her bonnet there was no way to get rid of it accept to charge forward. "Your rod was stiff. You needed to make it relax to its normal shape. Did the cold-water work?"

She tried for a serene, flirtatious smile. The pretense might work to her advantage.

Brandy spewed from his mouth, splattering down his shirt as well as the soft buckskin of his pants. His mouth gaped open. Quickly, he stood brushing the droplets off his shirt and pants.

"Whether the swim worked or not, I won't be discussing my rod with you. I'm your chaperone, not the man who is to see to your education where relations between a man and a woman are concerned." He was livid now, the muscles on his jaw ticking his face red.

"By the look of your crotch it didn't work at all. The bulge there seems to be growing."

Fascinated with the obvious change in his anatomy, she stared at the spot between his thighs unable to shake her gaze.

"Bloody, bloody hell! Go to bed, Lyssa before, I do something we will both regret!" He downed that glass of brandy.

"Did I say something wrong?" She knew her innocent act didn't fool him. Found she'd be disappointed if it did.

"Something?" he choked. "More than one something."

"Are you going to tuck me into bed?"

She watched the rigid shoulders of his retreating back. His powerful long strides seemed to eat up the floor then the stairs to his bedchamber. Closing her eyes, she tried to recall what was said. Understood all too well once again she overstepped what a lady should or should not say in the presence of a man. Unfortunately, around Kane she couldn't seem to curb her unruly tongue. Watching the ever-changing emotions on his handsome face was just too much fun. He delighted her in so many ways. She hoped for a lifetime.

Slowly, she walked to her room. Sleep would not be forthcoming in the next hours despite the fact the night had been exhausting. Still, she settled onto the bed, one of her pillows tucked between her arms.

Tomorrow, she hoped Jeremy and Drew would call on her. They were the only men at the ball she encouraged to do so. Kane would scare any suitors who attempted to stop by, not his friends though. His scowl alone would send any man or woman running in the opposite direction. His friends understood the man was harmless.

Why didn't she run?

Because she understood below that ruff exterior he was soft and warm. He would be tender with her. When he almost kissed her tonight, his touch was gentle. She knew he would never hurt her.

Her body longed for him. Places she never knew existed ached. Was that the same type of pain he felt?

Maybe or maybe not, in time she might know the truth. If so, she didn't understand how a swim in cold water would help. In his case tonight, the ride and swim didn't work out the way he hoped.

She woke to the pounding on her door. "You've a caller downstairs. Says he'll wait for you to get up."

"Kane?" Lyssa ran to the door. Tossed it open. "What time is it?"

Her earl stood outside the door. "Cover yourself." He turned from her continuing to speak. "I've ordered a bath. Food will be up in a few minutes. It's past two o'clock."

She looked down. Her body was perfectly clear to anyone looking beneath the sheer lawn of her nightdress. Heat raced to her face. She picked up the robe she'd worn last night then slipped her arms through the sleeves before pulling the fabric closed in front of her.

"Who is here?"

Curiosity coupled with anticipation that either Drew or Jeremy would come to see her gave her reason to smile. They wouldn't though. Both men knew precisely she wanted Kane. Too bad Kane didn't know the truth. Well, he knew now. He just wouldn't accept that certainty.

"Your third dance partner, Lord Ritter. Apparently, he didn't believe you when you told him you wouldn't entertain callers today. He says he'll wait since last night was late. A woman, after all, needs her beauty sleep."

A man doesn't?

"He said that?" She was incredulous at the horrible man. "Send him away. Still don't want to entertain callers. Won't allow a court dandy into my life."

"I won't do that. If you don't want to see the man, you will have to tell him yourself."

"I've already done so!"

~ * ~

Lord Sinclair Ritter sat in the elegant wing chair Lyssa sat in the night before. He watched the play of the sunlight as it filtered through the window. Lyssa Andrews was a beautiful *lass*. Though she needed taming. From what he heard circulating last night, the man who wed her would gain the family title as no man in her immediate family wanted anything to do with moving back to England.

He was just the man to do so, tame her as well as gain the title. She was shameless, a born and bred hussy. He didn't like that in a woman though he knew there were ways to take the spontaneity out of her.

One thing he meant to discover was why the Earl of Blackmore was her chaperone. That didn't bode well. No, the earl might be known as stodgy. He was also a womanizer. Black was a poor choice for a girl's chaperone. Nonetheless, that was what he was. Sinclair would offer for the girl despite her willfulness, despite that horrid sense of humor she possessed. Nothing she said to him last night could be considered funny.

He grinned, hoping she was a virgin. There was only one way to discover that truth. Considering the title, her innocence didn't truly make much difference to him. He would have to sire a son. After that he would do as he pleased. Even while he was bedding his soon to be wife, he would continue with his entertainments.

"Brandy?" Black asked when he stepped into the room. "Lyssa will be down shortly. I had to wake her up. While you must agree, last night's ball was exhausting. She did need her beauty sleep. She is quite lovely don't you think?"

Sinclair couldn't help himself, he snorted. She shouldn't still be abed unless Black kept her up doing things a chaperone shouldn't be doing. He would discover the truth soon enough. He had doctored the wine they would drink later with a potent relaxant. She wouldn't be able to tell him no. He would compromise her. She would have to marry him.

The plan was flawless.

"Thank you." Thoughtfully, he eyed the earl over the rim of his glass before swirling the amber liquid.

The earl sat. "What are your intentions today?"

Not that it was any of his business. "Brought the carriage. Heard there are some nice places down the road for a picnic. Thought we could take a spin through Hyde Park on our way out of town."

"Wine and sandwiches? Enough for three I do hope." The earl grinned sending a slight shiver of apprehension down his spine. "I'll be coming with you. In this instance three isn't a crowd. It is a necessity. I won't allow her to be alone with a man I don't know and trust."

"No."

"In that case, I'll have to inform my cook to add a few things to your basket. Perhaps a second bottle of wine would be in order also."

Black's presence would positively put a damper on his actives. "Didn't plan on having a third party on this outing. Need to get to know the girl better."

If Black wouldn't desist from this, he wouldn't be able to compromise her. He knew he needed to do just that if he was to get her to agree to marriage. The Andrew holdings near Dover were perfect for his objectives.

Kane directed his attention to his butler. "Inform cook to send a basket of food with me and Lyssa. Lord Ritter didn't bring enough for three."

Sinclair's face heated. He tried to tell Black he wasn't invited. Ended up sputtering just as Lyssa entered the room. "Bloody eyes, what are you wearing? You need to change yourself."

"My riding clothes," she told them smoothly in a fleeting attempt to ignore Ritter's contempt and Kane's grin. "Trousers are the only way to ride astride." She smiled sweetly before tossing her long braid over her shoulder. "Ever attempted riding in a dress?" She lifted perfectly shaped eyebrows. "It's rather difficult if you ask me."

He didn't ask her.

Kane let his head fall back then roared with laughter. When the first round of laughter ended, he hooted. "Sinclair here was planning a carriage ride."

"Not for me." Lyssa sauntered to the brandy bottle. Without looking at him, she poured a stiff drink, downed the contents. Her eyes wide, a smirk on her lips, "Nothing like a good drink to start out the morning. Oh, it's no longer morning now, is it? So, this is perfectly acceptable, not that it makes a bit of difference to me. I do as I please."

She set the glass down, turning to Black, "Do you have a spirited stallion for Lord Ritter to ride. If I'm going to let the man court me, he needs to ride as well as my daddy, shoot as well too. Otherwise, I won't have anything to do with the man."

"I never...we..."

He cleared his throat thinking what he was about to say would not serve his purpose here today. This woman was going to be his wife. He understood there were some things he would need to put up with if he was going to make that happen. Once she found herself wed to him, she would learn to obey. Thoughts of obtaining more land in Baltimore through her father sifted through his head. He wanted land in the states as well as on the Dover coast. Both places would increase his standing in the ton.

"You don't ride?" she sounded incredulous. "You're not the man for me. Besides, your paunch is not becoming. Means you're a wastrel."

He blustered. She was a daring piece of muslin. "Of course, I ride. It's just that I'm dressed for more casual courting."

He tried. Truly he did try to keep his anger and rage tamped down to the barest minimum. This situation wasn't to be. It would not do well to allow this female to take charge of the afternoon. However, if he didn't stamp his foot on her audacity, she was doing exactly that.

"You afraid your britches will split?" she asked her voice so soft Sinclair had to lean forward to hear.

His face heated. He wanted to slap the smirk off her face. When she was his he'd thrash her for her impertinence. She was an outrageous piece of fluff. One who needed a firm hand. "We will ride. Don't know where we'll carry the lunch."

"I'll stuff it in my saddlebag. Squished bread is just as good as the plump pieces." She looked to Black. "You can pack the wine in yours. Wouldn't want wine to stain my saddle if anything brakes."

Sinclair tugged in a deep breath of air. He should rethink this notion. It might be prudent to find her alone sometime. He could take advantage of her if she was minus a protector. Obvious to him now, that for the time being, Black wasn't about to let the brazen chit out of his sight. While he rode from time to time, most of the horseflesh he saw was from behind in the carriage he drove or at the races. He followed them to the stable.

When he saw the prime piece of horseflesh Black offered for him to ride, his gut churned. At first glance the stallion appeared skittish. The feeling this was going to turn out very wrong passed through his head. He had serious doubts about riding the stallion.

The saddle Black placed on Lyssa's mare was not a sidesaddle. Bloody hell, she did ride astride. No lady rode astride, doing so was nothing short of indecent. Perhaps he didn't want that land and title after all. No, he did. He would have to discover a different means to court her. Absconding with her, keeping her with him until he could manage to curtail his distaste of her and compromise her was the obvious solution.

He was positive crying off this afternoon was the best solution to this dilemma. With a quick thought, he pulled out his pocket watch.

"I'm sorry," he turned to Lyssa. "I've forgotten I've another obligation waiting for me in London. This can wait for another time. Mayhap I'll call on you tomorrow."

"Don't bother."

Chapter Three

Kane was shocked it took Lord Ritter that long to decide Lyssa wasn't the biddable young woman he met at the ball. Although according to Lyssa, she'd not been the least bit biddable except toward his friends. She did tell everyone she danced with she would not see them the next day.

"Why didn't you tell him you didn't want to see him?" Black asked the most obvious question.

He wasn't positive he understood anything concerning his charge. She befuddled him at every turn.

"Thought it would be easier to show him how much we don't suit. I racked my brain to think of something outlandish to say. Decided that showing up in trousers, boots and a shirt would put him off better than words. Daddy always told me if you wanted to convince a man as to what you're thinking, show don't tell."

"Sage advice." Kane grinned at her appreciating her antics more with each turn of events. Life surrounded by her would be anything except boring. "Should we ride to the lake on Montgomerie land? We can share the lunch and wine. Lord Ritter's lunch. It will taste even better knowing he left it behind."

"Don't mind if we do. Believe the sandwiches will taste heavenly when shared with you." She laughed, the sound more a giggle than anything. "We've two bottles of wine, one for you and one for me." She mounted. This time she waited for Kane to ride up next to her. "Can we swim too?" she asked when he and his horse were next to her.

"So, you do want to ride to the lake? It's about two miles east of here. It's on Montgomerie land." He repeated before he watched her ride away.

She was one with her horse. He admired her ability. The last time he didn't notice. He was too furious with the fact she left him still saddling his horse. He supposed he made his point that day.

"Is that where you took your cold swim?"

She tossed him a spicy smile while sweet innocence simmered in her eyes.

Thinking about last night and the condition he was left in after nearly kissing her was not strategic to his comfort. He needed to figure out a way to keep his hands to himself during this outing. Wished he could also figure out a way to keep his body from responding to her womanly charms.

"Well?" she prompted tilting her head sideways when he declined to answer.

"Yes, we could swim today if you wish. As it turned out the water wasn't all that cold."

It was cold enough. His trouble centered on the fact he couldn't stop thinking about the way her body molded so perfectly to his when he held her close. Nor could he get the image of her breasts pushing so delightfully from her corsage or the soft scent of woman mixed with jasmine from his head when he pulled in a deep breath of air. More than anything at this moment he wanted her beneath him. He wanted to bury himself deep inside her sultry warmth. Heaven and hell that was what this woman presented to him.

"Would like to do just that, swim. Don't have a swimsuit though. Do you? No, you wouldn't. Men swim in the buff."

He realized he put his foot in his mouth with the suggestion of a swim. Though he thought a dip in the cool water would be a welcome diversion from his inflamed emotions as well as his swelling manhood. "Do you swim in the buff, Lyssa? Would positively like to see that."

The challenge he issued would most likely result in one of her own choosing. The color staining her face was charming. He enjoyed the fact he could do that to her, embarrass her so completely. She would come back, give him as good as she got.

She pushed her horse to a canter, her back stiff, chin held high. Despite the fact she was brought up on a working ranch, her ladylike bearing was regal. He followed, keeping abreast of her waiting for an answer. It seemed she meant to temper her words. Maybe she was only thinking about her response. He couldn't wait to hear what outlandish thing she would come up with. He hoped whatever she had to say would shock him.

She didn't look at him, kept her gaze straight ahead. "Sometimes when there is no one around I do. As to the other part your question pertains to, yes, Jess and I used to swim naked all the time. That is until we were older. Mother explained we couldn't. Now, I pretty much swim in my camisole and drawers."

"So," he paused as he tried to think of a way to form his question, "you've seen all there is to see of a man?"

She no longer looked straight ahead. Myriad expressions played across her lovely face while her eyes seemed to cross.

She pulled the Appaloosa to a stop. Turned to stare at him directly. Her voice held a hint of indignation. "What's that supposed to mean?" She frowned, her brows almost meeting. He wanted to trace those frown lines; smooth them out so they were non-existent.

"You always answer a question with a question?" His dark brow shot up. "Do you?"

He enjoyed watching the breath of air puff out from her lips.

"Jess was ten, I was seven when mother told us in no uncertain terms, we weren't to do that anymore. He was hardly a man. If you're asking if I saw him naked, then the answer is yes, however not since that last time. Don't you have brothers or sisters?"

Kane didn't like the thought of her seeing a male naked, even a ten-year-old naked brother. What was this green-eyed bug of jealousy that kept biting him in the butt? Where Lyssa was concerned, he needed to get over that strangling emotion. She wasn't for him.

"True, a ten-year-old is not a man with a man's body."

What else could he say? He wasn't ready to tell her about the life he lived with the Sioux. The devil, if she only wore her camisole and drawers to swim, he was darn sure he would see everything he saw this morning. When she opened the door and was greeted with the sight of her, the barely hindered view of all of her, he almost pulled her into his arms for that kiss he didn't take last night. It was a damn close call.

That was the problem. He'd be taking. Even though he was certain she would be in the giving mood from the way she acted, he didn't want to take anything away from her. She was supposed to come to her husband a virgin. One kiss from him would lead to another then more until he'd be unable to stop unless she told him no. He was positive she wouldn't stop him. If he started, he would finish what he began.

"Is that what we're going to do? Go swimming? It is hot enough." She loosened a few buttons on her shirt. Waved her hand in front to cool herself. She was trussed up tight beneath her shirt with some material that seemed to keep her generous breasts from moving. It wasn't his place to figure out this tiny mystery. In time she might tell him.

His body tightened. Her breasts from what he witnessed first-hand this morning were bountiful, perfectly shaped jewels tipped with tender pink buds. Finding out how sweet she tasted was on his mind. Dark warm honey, he mused. He needed to get a hold of his thoughts, send them in a different direction. He was afraid talk of swimming just wasn't going to do the trick. From the notion of swimming in her underwear his mind spun in more delightful ways.

"It's hot enough," he agreed while tempering his growing smile. While she rode ahead of him, he adjusted his buckskins to a more comfortable position. The only way he'd be more comfortable was to rid himself of them.

If he did that...all bets were off.

Though he brought up swimming, he wasn't sure he should pursue the topic when they reached the lake. They were now out of the city heading toward the Montgomerie estate. He liked his country home so far from the city. Though there were definite times where the closeness would be appreciated.

"When we get there, you can show me if you ride as well as my daddy. I'm betting you do. Don't understand why I might think that, you an English lord of all things. You wouldn't have learned."

"If I understand your parentage correctly, Damian Andrews is also an English lord. Been told by the duchess that your brother has inherited the title your father doesn't covet. Does Jess want a title?"

"You're right about my father. He had to learn to ride dangerously as well as with breakneck speed, though for reasons I can't divulge. You, on the other hand, have had no reason to become an expert horseman."

"You've no idea, Little Bit. I've had more than my share of pursuits along with chases." All of her was itty bitty except her breasts. The thoughts swimming through his head brought back many pleasant memories. The hunt for buffalo, the excitement of the chase, the freedom of the prairie along with the mountains. He missed the people of his tribe. Missed his mother.

"Tell me."

"We can talk after our swim. Talk while we enjoy Sinclair's contribution to our afternoon pleasures. I'll tell you something of my life before the earl, for the first time, brought me to England kicking and screaming. I wasn't always as I seem now."

"With your permission," Lyssa pointed to a tree a quarter mile down the road. "Race you..." Her horse jumped forward. She rode hard. He wanted to laugh at her underhandedness. He loved the spontaneity she brought to his life. Even though she asked, she didn't wait for his permission.

Obvious, she didn't wait for his go ahead, his consent. If she had, she wouldn't stand one chance of winning. Lyssa was two lengths ahead of him before his stallion began the chase. It was debatable if he could catch her. The distance was short. A bit longer there would be no contest. She would have known that when she pushed her horse to run. For twenty-five yards they ran neck and neck. He couldn't let her win. With a softly spoken word to his stallion, Kane burst ahead of her.

Stopping at the tree where they raced, he was mesmerized by her flushed features, the way her silky hair fanned in sweet disarray around her face to pool at her slim waist. The plaited braid vanished during the wild ride. There was nothing left of the hairdo.

She was laughing, grinning from ear to ear. Her laugher contagious, he joined in.

"You won."

"Was there any doubt?" He chuckled watching as pink stained her face. "You do realize you cheated."

She was flushed, so very beautiful, her body tugging in breaths of flower-scented air. For a moment her lashes fluttered delicately against her cheeks. To Kane, she was the image of what as well as who a woman should personify. She would never allow him to make all the rules. He supposed they should sit down together in order to hash out the further restrictions he meant to place on her. The day before they barely touched on the most important let alone the dangerous places that loomed in the city.

"If the distance had been shorter, I would have won." She wrapped her hair in spirals before looping the long dark strands around itself until it was a knot on top of her head. How the devil did she do that?

"I would have worked harder sooner. As it was, I let you have the allusion that you might win."

It appeared she wanted to toss something at him. She didn't have anything she could throw.

She cocked her head a bit sideways, a flirtatious look on her delicate features. You should know, "I allowed you to win. Didn't want to hurt a fragile male ego such as your own. Masculine egos you understand are very delicate."

He hooted foregoing his usual scowl. "My ego, fragile? Delicate? You've got to be kidding."

"You must have missed the sarcasm. I've lost count of the number of times you laughed and smiled today. Perhaps you aren't so stuffy after all. Maybe that's the allusion you want people to believe. Keeps people from seeing who you are. Are you hiding, Kane? If so, what are you hiding from?"

Stodgy. Kane wasn't about to remind her any more. Hiding? He'd never hidden from anything in his entire life. She was a woman who would challenge as well as test until one way or another she got her way. He gave up that battle. Not that it mattered. When a person got to know him, he wasn't stuffy or stodgy. Just as she guessed, it was all a persona he put on to keep people he didn't like away from him. He'd been using that ploy since he ended up in England, the new Earl of Blackmore.

He liked Lyssa. Enjoyed everything about her too. "So, are we going to swim?"

They faced the lake. Ripples shimmered sliver on the surface of the water. More than anything he wanted to swim with her. The situation would have to be handled delicately. Neither could swim in their clothing. This would be a test of his ability to keep her at a distance.

Lyssa looked so longingly at the water he felt the urge to laugh. He had a pretty good idea what thoughts traveled through that saucy head of hers. In order to swim, she would have to disrobe partially. While she could be a brazen piece of baggage, she most likely never did anything like this with a man other than her brother when they were both quite a bit younger.

Ten-year-old brothers didn't count as experience in a situation such as this one.

When she finally turned her attention to him, she spoke softly. "Truly, I want to swim. While I don't care a fig about proper and not proper, you're still a man. I want you to kiss me but..."

Yes, there would undoubtedly be a 'but' in this. He expected that. "I'll turn my back until you're in the water. Will that work? I won't see any part of you except your face." Being a gentleman in this situation seemed too hard. The job was necessary though. No one would know.

Her smile was a beaming testament to his saying the right words. Too bad she didn't understand in the crystal-clear water he would be able to see all of her unless he kept his distance. He would have to try to do just that.

Quickly, she slipped from the horse handing him the reins. He watched as she strode to a place behind a large boulder. She waved her hand in a tiny circular motion. "Turn around."

He grinned.

A moment later he was dismounted, his back to her. "I'll wait until you're in the water. Holler when I can look."

His imagination kicked into a hard fast gallop creating a firestorm inside. Every male sinew in his body tightened to explosive levels. This might be conceived as hell. He could tell himself a thousand times he wasn't interested in Lyssa Andrews. He was though. With each passing second, his interest grew.

"You can look now."

When he turned, she was about twenty feet from the shore. Her hair was plastered around her face and shoulders. She must have dipped underwater. He could see her shoulders along with the straps of her frilly-white chemise. While he still watched, she dove underwater to resurface later about ten feet from her first position.

"Are you coming in? The water is pleasant, not too cold. Actually, just right."

"I'll join you in a minute."

He had to chuckle as he unbuttoned his shirt. Her tiny face was riveted on his chest. How long would she continue to watch without turning away? The little minx most likely wouldn't take her gaze from him unless he requested her to do so. Well, he wasn't about to do that. She might get more than she bargained for if she kept staring at him. Instead of ten-year-old boy, she would see a grown man.

His shirt hit the ground while he shucked off his boots. A few seconds later, his hands were on the laces of his buckskins. Still, his little bit stared at him. He grinned as he shed the trousers. When he looked up again, she was underwater. Unless she told him, he would never know what she did or did not see. Didn't think she would tell him either. This might well be a lesson in dealing with grown men.

Kane had been naked around more women than he cared to count. Except for her brother, he might well be her first naked man. He wondered what questions or comments she would come up with when presented with the fact she stared at him. Supposed a girl could be inquisitive. He smirked. She might be curious about him. He certainly responded eagerly to her questing gaze.

Long strides took him hip deep into the water before he dove. He headed for the last spot he saw her. When he surfaced, she was no more than ten feet from him. She was treading water. A water scuffle might be in order.

Playfully, she splashed him then turned to swim away. In two strong strokes, he caught her foot, pulling her back toward him. She slipped through the water then into his waiting arms.

So much for keeping my distance.

"Kane!" she cried out, kicking her legs to get away. She turned sideways to splash him.

Drawing her back, he caught her around the waist. "Take a breath," he urged.

His hand on the top of her head, he pushed her underwater. She came up sputtering. He didn't expect retaliation as she tried to do the same to him. When she pushed on his head, he didn't move. She wasn't strong enough. Much to his chagrin, her barely concealed breasts pushed against his chest. She rose above him to get enough leverage to push him under. The hard tips were so close to his lips, he had a swift urgent need to taste. His mind traveled to more delicious pursuits than a water fight.

He groaned, as he pushed her away. "You play with fire, Little Bit. You don't understand what you are starting." His voice was soft but the intensity seemed to surprise her.

She scowled at him. "You started this."

He guessed he did.

Before he could look away from her breasts that seemed to float in the water bobbing with each gentle wave created between them, she said, "Race you to the rock."

Once again, she took off before he realized what she asked. For a couple of seconds, he watched mesmerized by the sheer power of her strokes. She was a good swimmer, better than most women…or men. Everything he took for granted about the female sex she proved to be wrong. Her life before London must have been very different.

He shook the daze from his mind. Letting her win this was out of the question. After all he had his masculine pride to deal with…his fragile male ego. Forcing a hard, powerful kick he propelled himself forward. He caught up with her before she reached the rock. His fingertips touched first. Laughing she launched herself into his arms. "I almost won."

"You cheated again. Is that the only way you think you can win?" He laughed with her.

She placed one finger on his chin. "Against you, yes."

Well, hell, she was in his arms. Her dimple called to him. This was exactly what he'd been trying to avoid while at the same time attempting to figure out how he could get her there. He held her face in his hands. His mouth formed gently on hers. He nibbled the corners, touched the small indentation with his tongue. When her legs rose to

68

circle his hips, a low husky groan rumbled from deep within his chest. He ran his tongue along her bottom lip. Tugged a moment with his teeth. Hoped she would open for him. In her innocence, she didn't understand what he asked.

"Open for me, Little Bit," he whispered softly, knowing he was a man truly damned.

This was the kiss she wanted a day ago at the ball. Last night he possessed more restraint. He didn't mean to do anything except kiss as he prayed he had the self-control to do so.

Eventually, Lyssa did open for him. Hesitantly, her tongue touched upon his then withdrew. Low in the back of his throat, he growled his pleasure, her taste honey-sweet. Her luscious breasts pushed against his chest. He felt the heat between her legs against his swollen member. Prayed he didn't frighten her. For a few seconds, their tongues danced and played with each other. He ended the kiss, understanding he just jumped into forbidden ground as he sucked in a shaky breath.

"Kane?" she asked her voice soft yet questioning too. "You don't need to stop."

For a few breath-stealing moments, he was terrified she might want a second kiss. Stopping this now was the only way. "It's time for lunch. I'll wait until you're dressed. Go on." He didn't want to dwell on that kiss as well as what it made him feel. Didn't want to look into her eyes to see the disappointment she didn't seem to be able to hide.

He should not have kissed her. Well, the devil, this situation placed him in a devilish spot. He never kissed virgins. Damn, he was her chaperone not the ravisher of innocents.

Reluctantly he understood that at least for him there were no regrets even though he knew better. There was no going back either.

None at all.

Leisurely, he swam, parting the water with long sure strokes. It took a few minutes to reach the end of the pond; a few more to swim back. He found he was winded, not from the swim. Instead, his nearly breathless state came from the kiss. Beneath the sheer fabric of her underwear, he felt all of her pressed against him. During that time, his arousal pushed against the softness of her belly, just as it did the previous evening. This time when he strode from the water, he hoped she wouldn't look at him. It wasn't his embarrassment that bothered him. It was hers. Since he was fully aroused. His naked body would appear far different from what she could remember of her ten-year-old brother or what she might have seen as he stepped into the lake.

Once she was dressed, she sat on the blanket she spread out for them. The basket of food sat in front of her, the bottles of wine standing within the confines of the fabric. He saw the glass she poured for herself. She drank deeply.

Lyssa did like her spirits. Once on land, he dried himself with his shirt. He draped it over the nearby boulder where her chemise and drawers were also arranged. Her clothing was so small. To him, she didn't appear tiny simply because she possessed such a huge personality. Lyssa was most assuredly a little bit of a woman, except for her breasts.

He waved off the wine she offered, preferring to wait until she was the tiniest bit tipsy. The way she drank the wine, it would not be long. "Are you nervous? I'm not going to do anything."

"It's just..." She stared at his lips as if she remembered the kiss then back to her glass of wine.

"What type of sandwiches did Lord Ritter pack for today's outing?"

Changing the subject might be in order. If she were nervous, she probably wouldn't say so. He leaned against the rock, his legs stretched in front of him, content to watch.

"Looks like ham. Do you like ham?" She handed the wrapped parcel to him before opening her own.

Again, she drank deeply of the wine. They ate in silence.

"You were going to tell me about your past. Now would be a good time. You haven't told me anything about yourself while you know so much about me."

She sipped some of the wine. He topped her glass then poured one for himself.

"You might not like what I'm about to tell you. It's been a long time since I've divulged my heritage to anyone. Many whites don't like me for my parentage. They especially don't want me around their daughters. Your father might have the same thoughts."

He set his wine on top the boulder while he waited for some reaction on her part.

Her fingers trembling as she brought the glass to her mouth, she drank more as she still seemed overly nervous to him. "Believe I'd like to hear anything you want to tell me. You're not thinking I might be disappointed in your life, are you? I'm not bigoted. None of my family are." She leaned forward. "There is nothing you can tell me that would disenchant me."

It was all he could do to think while he watched her breasts sway beneath the soft material of her shirt. Whatever she wore earlier to keep them in place was gone now. She didn't fasten the shirt to her neck, as she should have. He caught glimpses of her rounded softness. Just as in the water saw the rosy tips of her hardened nipples through the sheer fabric of the shirt she wore. This was more than any man should have to endure.

"Yes, most women are disgusted when I tell them where I spent the first fifteen years of my life."

He didn't know if that was true. He did understand first hand he almost died because of one young lady's aversion to his upbringing along with his heritage. He still bore the scars on his back.

"Disgusted? That's harsh. Where did you spend those years?"

She smiled at him. Her grin appeared more delicious to him than either the wine or the food. Her dimple winked at him. If she agreed, he would have one more taste of her today. Poured herself more wine. The first bottle was nearly gone.

Kane stared at her pallid face suddenly concerned. "Lyssa…" He rested his hand on hers. Her eyes were dazed when she met his gaze. "Maybe you shouldn't drink more wine this soon. We do have to ride home. You look as if you're going to be sick."

She smiled, waved a hand in the air her eyes wide pools within her pale face. "Just a bit dizzy, that's all. Nothing more. It's just one bottle. You've part of it in your glass. It's delicious, so sweet." Her words slurred slightly then she giggled. "I'm sleepy. Must be the swimming, all the exercise. Since I left home haven't done much in the way of exercise."

This was not like Lyssa. He reached out to take the glass from her. Hesitated. After tasting the contents, he swore softly beneath his breath. This was the wine Lord Ritter brought for the picnic. The liquid was drugged. He didn't know what the drug of choice was. He needed to get her home then call for the doctor.

"What's wrong with me?" Lyssa's head lolled slightly forward. Her body began to topple. The drug seemed to take affect all at once. She slumped forward. The glass she held toppled to the green grass. Red liquid pooled around it.

Kane caught her. His arms around her, he held her up. Her head was upon his chest. Bloody, bloody hell, the man had a lot to answer for. As soon as he got Lyssa home then tucked into bed, he meant to call on Sinclair Ritter. He didn't believe this was poison. No, Ritter wanted something from her. The man wouldn't get what he sought if he killed her. This was probably something that would help him deflower her, something to relax her so she would put up no protest or struggle beneath his hands. She wouldn't remember, so she couldn't claim rape. The man was a despicable man. No, he was less than a man.

Well hell, the man's intent was obviously clear to anyone willing to look. He meant to get her so relaxed she wouldn't tell him no when he fell upon her. She was in no condition to think let alone respond to anything sexual, too sleepy to say no. He was pretty sure this would wear off in the next few hours. Again, more determined than ever, he meant to pay the man a visit.

All he needed now was to get her home. Supposed this afternoon he would tuck her into bed. She wouldn't even know.

~ * ~

A long drink of air swept into her lungs. She felt so relaxed. The world seemed to spin and dance around her. Colors of the lake along with the pond blurred into beautiful blues and greens tipped with silver from the sunshine. With the tip of her finger, she touched her lips. He kissed her. Kane kissed her on the lips, mouth against mouth. Lyssa didn't think she would ever forget those amazing feelings that gentle caress generated inside her. Enchantment still pulsed inside eagerly anticipating the next kiss. She wanted to savor the sensations for as long as possible.

When he walked into the water, she watched the tiniest bit too long. At the memory, heat flooded her. She saw all of him, all his wonderful male parts before she gasped then turned away. By the set of his shoulders, she understood he challenged her to look, to soak in all his male beauty. She did exactly that. Given the opportunity, she would do the same again.

She giggled. "More wine?" she asked reaching toward her glass. Her body wavered again. One more time she fell into him. Giggled again. Her hand pressed against the smooth bare flesh of his chest. She moved her fingers, passing across his nipple. His sharp gasp of air startled her.

"You've had enough. I'm going to get you home, Lyssa. Either that or you'll have to sleep the remnants of the drug off right here. If I can't get you on my horse, you will have to remain here despite my efforts."

"Sleep what off?" she asked, pushing hair from her face then slightly away from his chest. Wishing she could taste him; she ran her tongue across the bottom swell of her lip.

"Look at me." His hands were bracketed around her face. Her eyes shimmered with dark sparks of blue. Now they seemed rimmed with violet.

Lyssa clung to his wrists, her nails biting into his skin. Kane was going to kiss her again. She sighed softly, once more moistening her lips as she waited for the tender and oh, so sweet touch. "Kiss me," she giggled.

Now he scowled. What happened to his laughter? The lines on his brow deepened. He was back to stuffy...no stodgy. "You were drugged. We're going home now. No more nonsense about kissing."

Kissing wasn't nonsense. She wanted to scream at him. Suddenly, she found herself cradled in his arms. He strode to the horses. Lyssa didn't know how he managed the feat or when for that matter. Now she rode in front of him, on his stallion. She recalled he was going to tell her where he lived the first fifteen years of his life.

Did he? She didn't remember. Her eyes closed. She didn't sleep though she felt as if she existed in a blurry haze. Sounds intensified around her. Her skin seemed overly sensitive. She felt hot. No, it was just that she was touching Kane.

Now, one of his arms circled her waist. Through blurry eyes, she saw his right hand held the reins to his horse, her little mare as well. If not, she hoped her mare would follow. Didn't suppose Kane would leave any of that to chance though.

Dreams of him kissing her, shuffled woodenly through her brain. She hoped the kiss she recalled wasn't a dream. Against her, his back was strong and hard. She liked the way his forearm felt beneath her fingers. He pulled her closer. She fell forward. His arm came up to rest just beneath her breasts as he tugged her against him.

Once more, he swore foully beneath his breath. For a few moments today, she coaxed him to laugh as well as smile. Something happened to change that. She wasn't sure exactly what occurred for his mood to about face so drastically. Suddenly, she thought she would be sick. Bile rose in her throat.

"Kane!" A frantic plea whispered from her lips. She grappled with his arm trying to get him to let loose of his hold around her waist as she twisted and turned.

He must have understood. Gently, she was set on the ground. Her knees touched the earth then her hands. Unbound hair fell around her. He held her hair back. Bent over; she lost the contents of her stomach. His big hands soothed her, running along her back repeatedly. Kept her hair swept away from her face. She whimpered softly, wishing the nausea away. Her stomach ached and cramped until she vomited again and again.

He murmured something she didn't understand. Was certain the words came from a different language. This man must have some feelings for her.

Again, she heaved. It was wretched, horrible. He gave her wine from the other bottle to sip.

"This is to take away the bad taste in your mouth. The wine will help."

She nodded her thanks, since she couldn't speak. Wished this were over. Didn't like the nausea curling within, threatening to erupt. Her stomach churned and rolled. She sucked in air, filled her lungs. Still, the sickness continued.

So preposterous, she was never sick.

What seemed like hours passed. He held her in his arms, patiently rocking her, chanting words she didn't understand. She closed her eyes, wishing she were in her bed at home.

"Sip some more."

"No." She pushed the bottle away. "Don't want more wine. Sick. My stomach. Hurts."

He chuckled, "Very well. You ready to try the horse again. We should, you know. If possible, would like to be home before dark. I've an errand to run that can't wait for the morning."

A quick peek to the horizon told her the sun would descend behind the hills soon. She agreed. Didn't want to ride in the dark.

"Just want to be in bed," she groaned while her stomach cramped again.

"Are you better?"

He seemed to wait for an answer.

She nodded, "Let's try the horse."

~* ~

Kane spent the evening searching the various establishments where Sinclair Ritter was known to frequent. Luck didn't seem to be on his side this evening. Finding Jeremy and Drew at their favorite pub, he easily enlisted their help telling them part of what transpired this afternoon.

Perhaps his luck changed.

Splitting up they agreed to meet back at the Dark Horse Pub in an hour whether they found the man or not. Individually, they scoured the gaming halls as well as the established brothels that catered to the more affluent. At one place he missed the man by a scant five minutes.

His patience wearing thin as the hour passed, Kane stepped into the Dark Horse. Sinclair sat between Jeremy and Drew. His breath caught in the back of his throat while his heart lurched. The man would pay at his attempt to hurt Lyssa.

They found him.

Whether to hit him first then speak to him later was his present thought. He supposed a few minutes of speech would help the pompous weasel understand why he'd have a broken nose along with two black eyes by the time he left him tonight.

"I say..." Sinclair rose his rounded stomach bouncing as Jeremy set his hand on his shoulder to push him back to the chair. "What do the three of you think to be doing? I came in here for a friendly drink at their invitation."

"What?"

Kane lifted his eyebrow. Disdain for this poor excuse of a man filled him. His anger simmered deep inside. The image of Lyssa losing the contents of her stomach and suffering by Sinclair's hands were etched in his brain. Thoughts of the man's intentions simmered in his head. He'd like to do more than just break his nose. Castration might do the trick.

"You've no rights here, Black. These men tell me you want to speak to me. Get on with it. I'm a busy man."

He waved his hand in the air. The gesture would do no good to sway him.

For a few seconds Black grinned at his friends. After that he turned his attention back to Sinclair. "What should we do with him? Take him somewhere he can defend himself like a man? Should we give him some of his wine first?"

Kane stepped back his expression bland, unwilling to give Sinclair any idea of what he truly felt or the fury simmering deep within.

"Put him in the boxing ring," Jeremy said while they watched him sputter. "He can defend himself there. It will be all right, tight and legal."

"You're all joking. Got to be a misunderstanding that can be cleared up with ease. I haven't done anything to any of you."

Across the table, Kane wrapped the front of Sinclair's shirt in his fist. "Drugging a young woman so he can rape her, you call nothing?"

Anger spurring him forward coupled with disgust, Kane pushed him so hard he hit the wall behind him with a huge thud, rocking the glasses of ale on the table in front of him.

"What makes you think that?" Sinclair began. His face turned white. "I haven't been with a woman today. You saw to that, Black. You would not allow a simple outing with your ward." His thin wavering voice held no conviction.

It seemed the self-important lordling realized what must have happened this afternoon. Kane burned for a fight. His fist clenched then unclenched curling into tight balls. He wanted to pummel that man until he understood pain. A fight wasn't something this simpering dandy could give him.

"Thought I made it clear this afternoon you were to leave Lyssa Andrews alone." Kane turned to his friends. "Bring him outside. He's a bit more convincing ahead of him to do if he wants to come out unscathed."

Black wondered if he could keep himself from killing the man. His fists tightened at his sides once more. He heaved in several deep breaths. He would have to give the man ample opportunity to hit him first.

"You can't do this. It's against the law," Sinclair blubbered, his body shaking with the fear that seemed to envelop him. "I'll call the constables. Have you sent to Newgate if you—"

"Believe what you intended is also against the law, Sinclair."

Good, he wanted the man to fear the next few minutes. Terror would help him remember why he needed to stay far away from Lyssa. In the darkest part of the alley, the men let him go. His head turned one way then another as if searching for an escape route. He was cornered. There was nowhere for him to run or hide.

"Drugging a lady with the intent to rape is also against the law. Where I was brought up a man would die for that act."

Kane knew he'd never been this angry. His fury seethed deep inside rolling then churning.

"I didn't rape her."

Saliva rolled down his chin to end up on his protruding stomach. He tried to wipe the spit away with the back of his hand. Sweat ran down the sides of his face. "Please...please don't hurt me."

He cried now, huge sobs raced in strangled gasps from him as his belly bounced. Tears combined with his slobber landed on his coat.

"You plead so prettily. Would you have listened to her pleads for you to stop? Would you? I rather doubt that fact." Kane held nothing but loathing for this man. Bloody eyes, he wasn't a man. He was a sniveling coward.

"I wasn't going to rape her. Just wanted her to be a bit more willing when...that's all."

"You wanted her so relaxed she couldn't say no. If she were able to get the words out, they would be so weak you could claim that you thought she was telling you yes. You delude yourself if you believe that isn't rape."

"No, no that's not the way at all. I..."

He licked his lips his hands rising as if he could ward off the blow coming his way.

"You will keep your distance. If I ever hear that you were anywhere near her, you'll regret ever making my acquaintance. If you happen to be at the same social function Lyssa is attending, you will turn around and leave. Do you understand?"

Sinclair nodded, shaking his head madly as if that would give him the respite he wanted.

"I want to hear the words. Say you understand."

Seconds turned into a minute. Kane saw the muscles in Sinclair's neck straining, his jaw working. Liquid ran down his leg soaking the crotch of his pants.

"Say it."

Again the man was nodding, finally, very slowly, "I...understand."

"You can take the first shot. Hit me, you pompous weasel."

"No." Tears ran down his face. "No..."

"If that's the way you want this."

Kane swung. His fist landed on the bridge of the man's nose. Sinclair crumpled to the ground, blood spewing from his nostrils.

All Kane wanted now was to get to Lyssa. She should wake up soon. He needed to be there for her when her eyes opened.

~ * ~

The next time Lyssa woke, she was on her bed. She still wore her pants and shirt. Her head wasn't so dizzy. Nonetheless, it ached terribly. Her hands at her temples, she hoped the pounding would cease. The pressure she applied changed nothing. When she ventured to open her eyes again, the walls of her room didn't spin in a constant blur. She wanted to understand what happened as she searched her mind in a blind attempt to remember. When she looked at the ormolu clock on the shelf in her bedroom, the hands said ten minutes after midnight.

Damnation, what happened to the evening? She had no recollection of how she ended up in her bed. She sat up, inhaling gulps of air. With the walls whirling, she slumped back to the bed. All she remembered was that Kane had been angry, very angry.

Lyssa was wide-awake as well as famished. She didn't remember eating. What she did remember was downing most of the bottle of wine. No wonder her head ached. She'd never been able to drink very much. She recalled her sickness along with Kane's cursing, needed to understand what had happened. Needed to find Kane.

Moving slowly, holding on to furniture to keep herself upright, she changed her clothes, putting on a simple lavender, muslin day dress before she slowly tottered down the steps, clinging to the banister as her unsteady feet threatened to topple her. She went in search of food. She could discover Kane's whereabouts later. He was the only one who could tell her why she didn't remember anything from the afternoon. Her first stop was the kitchen. A loaf of bread sat on the counter. She sliced two pieces then did the same with the cheese. Before she left, she broke off a piece of each, chewing now as she continued her search. She wondered what happened to the ham sandwiches.

Feeling stronger by the second, her next mission was to discover the location of Kane. She hoped he wasn't in bed. If he had gone to bed, he would just have to get up and dress himself. She needed to talk. When she stepped into his office, she found him sitting behind a mahogany desk, sipping what appeared to be brandy. His feet propped on the top, he looked perfectly at ease. As if nothing untoward happened this afternoon.

"You're awake. How are you feeling?" He appeared concerned

yet totally relaxed. "I expected you a bit sooner."

She sat down, her hands holding the bread and cheese she pilfered from the kitchen settled on her lap. She broke off more food. Set a tiny piece inside her mouth then chewed slowly. "As if I've been run over by stampeding horses."

He chuckled softly, "I was thinking more along the line of buffalo."

Lyssa wished she could find something humorous about his words. "Why? Why buffalo?" She was suddenly reminded of the conversation they did not have this afternoon. This was not the time for that, she guessed by the new scowl lines forming on his forehead he wasn't amenable to telling her his life story. She so liked the chuckle better. What did she say to make him frown?

He sat up. His heavy booted feet landed with a thud on the floor. Now his forearms rested on the desk. She remembered the way they felt when they were around her waist. Together they rode his horse. She couldn't remember why she didn't ride her little mare.

"Just a thought rambling in my head. Buffalo seemed more intense than horses." He paused for a moment." You were drugged, Lys. Thought you should know I've taken care of the matter."

"When?" She was more curious than ever. "It wasn't just the wine giving me a headache and making me tipsy. I did drink too much." She lowered her gaze to stare at the bread in her lap. "That's never happened to me before. Truly, I've never overindulged. Always know when to stop."

"When? Thought you should know I visited your friend, Lord Ritter. No, you might have been a bit tipsy too. However, Sinclair wanted you drugged so you wouldn't be able to tell him no when he tried to rape you. He counted on being alone with you. Having his way so that he could force marriage."

She sifted a stiff breath of air. Her hands trembled so hard, the bread and cheese dropped to the floor. "Are you positive?"

He nodded his answer.

"I'll kill him. Scalp him with a paring knife if necessary or a butter knife might take more time. I'm certain it would be more painful."

Kane sat up straight. She watched him as he grimaced at her violent words. For a moment, she wondered where his mind went. He looked as if he were in a far distant space. The expression on his face unreadable, "That's a bit vindictive. If you wish it however, I'm sure Still Water Runs will be able to accomplish that feat and keep him alive until the very end. After all, one can't live without his scalp."

"Is that possible?" This conversation was clearly beyond her knowledge.

Kane waved his hand in the air. "Yes, though I've taken care of the matter for now. Don't believe he'll have designs on you again. I visited him while you slept. Let's just say I left him with a broken nose along with two black eyes. He will think twice before threatening you another time. Nonetheless, I do believe the hazard of scalping would have an immense impact on the little lordling if I had thought to mention the deed could be done with little effort."

The wealth of sarcasm Kane projected for Sinclair Ritter was overly obvious. She smiled then grimaced. Her head hurt. She shouldn't have poured the brandy. She truly shouldn't drink the potent liquor.

As if he understood her thoughts, Kane took the glass away. "Don't believe this will help your condition. Why are you down here? Thought you would be sleeping. Well, knew you would seek me out as soon as you woke. Although I'm glad to see you, it is a bit late in the night."

She made a face at him. "Couldn't sleep. Wanted to talk to you."

Did she? Yes, the need to know about him seemed too important to gloss over. He let out so many subtleties that pointed to a life other than one groomed to rule his little earldom.

"About?" He leaned back in his chair resuming his nonchalant position, his feet back on top of his desk.

Understanding this question might stop all the others, Lyssa still needed to ask. "Why did you kiss me? You positively didn't want to last night. Every time I've suggested the contact, you backed away, horrified by the mere thought then reminding me you are my chaperone. Although I liked what you did, wanted the kiss, I didn't expect you to do something so out of character."

His scowl deepened as he seemed to regard her question with no enthusiasm. Why did he do anything? Probably, because he wanted to do so. "You're a lovely girl, Lyssa. In case you haven't noticed you could tempt a saint. In case you haven't noticed, I'm no saint. Every time I look at you, you tempt me."

Her lips twitched while her heart leapt. He thought she was lovely. She tempted him. "Here I thought you didn't think me attractive. Believed you disliked me."

"Fishing for compliments?"

One of his black eyebrows arched upward. He could do that, move only one. She tried. Failed completely.

"Yes." Her voice was whisper soft. "I believe I am. Since you know I'm attracted to you, enticed by everything about you, it's nice for me to know you have at least noticed me."

"More than I should." He tossed back the remaining brandy in his glass. "What else would you like to know about me? Ask me anything. If I don't want to answer, well, then I won't."

She was intrigued by the fact that now he might be an open book. Of course, she understood, open only as far as he intended his life to become. "Why do you think you ride as well as my father?" Hers was a loaded question. She understood the answer might give her a great deal of insight into the man she intended to marry despite his reticence. She felt certain eventually he could be persuaded to her way of thinking.

Before answering he tapped his finger on his desktop. "You should know the truth as you seem to have made up your mind about wanting me. That doesn't change anything since I'm not planning a relationship with anyone, especially not a white woman."

A white woman? "Truth is always valuable. Don't think there is anything you can tell me that will change my mind. Go ahead, do your worst."

"I ride well because I've always ridden. Before I could walk my uncle set me upon my first horse. My mother bit back her anger. It wouldn't do for a woman to voice her opinion in a man's world. My mother could never gainsay a man. My uncle did as he pleased."

Her hand cut through the air as she clearly didn't believe that statement. Standing with both hands flat on his desk. "Balderdash. A man's world? A woman always has the right to at least voice her opinion. Men, good men, usually pay attention to a mother's opinion when it comes to her baby."

He chuckled softly, his eyes taking on a faraway look. "Not where I lived. Not in this man's world."

This vagueness was going to have to change. She tried to calm her escalating emotions, succeeding a bit. "Where was that?"

He would have a hard time with this explanation. To her knowledge there were few cultures left that would claim such backward social values. Maybe not.

"Lakota territory. In the heart of it." Kane filled his glass while he watched her eyes narrow. "Deep in Lakota territory where it wasn't safe for a white man to travel. Fortunately, for me my father took the risk. He fell in love with the country along with a woman, native born."

Believing that bit of nonsense was hard to pallet, the fierceness of his gaze seemed to dare her to challenge the truth of his statement. "Lakota territory...you were raised in the Sioux nation?"

Kane nodded his agreement.

She couldn't tell if he was scowling or amused. The two expressions seemed to meld together into one. "Would you like me to continue? Or, have you heard enough for this evening."

Of course, she wanted him to tell her as much as he was willing. With this bit of information, she understood more thoroughly why he intrigued every sinew and bone in her body. Kane was more than a lord of the realm, more than a title or a notorious rake. He was real flesh and blood man. She'd always wanted a man as strong and determined as Damian Andrews, her father. She wasn't convinced any but her brother and male cousins would be good enough. With the telling of his story, she would be positive.

"I want to know everything."

Lyssa found herself mesmerized by the words. She clasped her hands tightly on her lap, holding her breath as she waited. He barely touched on anything about himself.

"Do you now?" He poured another full snifter of brandy.

"You sound as if you've changed your mind? I can always talk to Aunt Ella if you refuse to enlighten me. She will tell me everything about you. Why would you do anything for my aunt, even something so detestable as chaperone a debutante?"

While she waited for him to continue the story, she slowly let out the air she'd been holding inside her lungs.

"In case you've forgotten the duchess is not here."

"Aunt Ella will return."

His gaze met hers, daring as well as challenging. "My mother is Sioux. My father was supposed to become the next earl of Blackmore, much to his chagrin. The man needed adventure more than the breath he inhaled. Didn't care a fig about his title or wealth. When he was seventeen, he left England telling his father, my grandfather, he didn't want to become an earl. In the way of the Sioux, he married my mother. Stayed with her for two years. I don't remember him. Vividly, though I recall my uncle. He was the one who set me on my first horse. Taught he how to shoot and ride like the wind."

"Did you count coup?"

"Yes."

"Hunt buffalo?

Kane nodded watching her carefully.

Her heart filled with anticipation of the rest of his story. "You've walked in the Rocky Mountains?"

"Many times."

"Jess wants to live there. Two summers ago, he rode west with one of our cousins. They hunted and fished, made friends with some of the tribes. It seems he is always looking to the west."

"He would claim land that belongs to the Sioux or the Cheyenne?" The censure in his voice was obvious. "He has no right to that land. No white man does. Still, they claim land that is not there's. They build houses, raise cattle. Start wars. The cavalry murders innocent women and children."

"The Sioux don't build there. Instead, the tribes roam. How do they call it their land?" Curiosity spurred her. She wanted to understand.

"The tribes look for game. They follow the trails. No, they don't build homes to live in. Nonetheless, they bring their homes with them. The land is their land, theirs by right. Gifted to them by their Gods. White men have no business living on that land."

"Perhaps we should move on. Although, all the information intrigues me, I do want to learn more about you. This is just the tip, isn't it? Why did you come to England?"

He chuckled seeming to let go of his anger. "Tell me something about yourself," he encouraged.

"I can imagine you're tired of speaking of the past you loved. Did you have a choice in coming here?"

He lifted his broad shoulders. She recalled what they looked like beneath her fingers covered with moisture from the lake, droplets slipping on along his neck. Her belly seemed to be filled with butterflies.

"No, not much choice."

"But you came."

She heard the puff of air, which was barely a sigh. "It was either stay there or come here. I chose the lesser of the two evils. It seems half-breeds can't live anywhere as an equal."

That answer left her with more questions. "You're more than equal in England. You're an earl, part of the aristocracy." If she sounded indignant, she was. "You've no reason to feel sorry for yourself."

Again, an eyebrow arched upward. "Is that what I'm doing?"

"You're trying to tell me you're not?"

"Not attempting to tell you anything. People draw their own conclusions. I wouldn't be able to sway your mind nor would I want to do so. Know this, the duchess and her husband saved my life. If they had not done so, I would not have followed them to England. Needless to say, Grandfather was pleased with their endeavors. He got me here once despite my avid protests but I returned to Indian territory only to find that life there wasn't what I hoped."

"I bet he was content. Now he has an heir."

"Most likely after I'm gone there will not be a legitimate heir. His work was for naught."

At this point the conversation lagged. She didn't think she should ask him anything more. He seemed satisfied with his thoughts. If she had her way, she would be more than willing to help the Blackmore line continue, gifting him with a legitimate heir.

"Believe I should go to bed."

"Yes, the recital is tomorrow afternoon. Do you think you can sleep now?"

"I don't want to go to that damn recital!"

She didn't want to sing for the fops who would attend. "Don't want to be paraded in front of drooling lords who are looking for a wife. Who will drug unwilling women in order to force a marriage."

They're not for me. She wasn't going to see men the next day who would try to drug her so they would get the title neither Damian or Jess wanted.

"You don't want a husband?"

She laughed at his question. "Suppose all women are expected to crave a man's protection. However, I do want a man who will return my love, someone who will protect me if necessary. As I'm thinking of Sinclair Ritter, I shudder. He's a man who takes. Thank you for coming to my defense."

"Truly, it was nothing."

"Not to me. You know who my father and mother are. I've told you a great deal about my brother. What else would you like to hear?"

"If you're so set against the English lords, why did you come for a season?"

That was a fair question. She lifted her shoulders. "Guess you could say, I gambled and lost."

"A bet with whom? Your father or your mother?"

"Mother. She wanted me to at least meet someone besides the men in our area since no one caught my eye so to speak. Even when we spent last summer in Baltimore, I didn't like anyone I saw enough to want them to kiss me." She couldn't help staring at his mouth, smiling when he appeared a bit discomfited. "As you know, I wished for you to kiss me."

His glass landed hard on the table, his eyes narrowing. She wished she had the nerve to ask him what he was thinking. She was positive she wouldn't like the answer.

She continued though. "You should understand I was brought up in a world few men understand. Most of what my brother was taught about ranching, I was also taught. On ranches, when necessary, the women folk must do their part. They go out in the winter blizzards to round up the livestock. I've spent a night in a line shack holed up because the drifts were too high for the horses to walk through."

"Your father was worried?"

"Terrified. That only happened once."

She recalled that day all too well. She wasn't worried until the second day. When the third day came and went with no sign of the weather clearing, she thought she would die.

"You should not have been allowed that far from the house in a blizzard. That's men's work."

"Rest assured, Daddy did apprise me of that later. He wasn't at all pleased I went out in the blizzard. The following years, he was more attuned to where I was if a winter storm did hit." She laughed softly. "I see you don't approve."

"I don't. If I had a daughter as beautiful as you...hell...if I had a daughter, I would watch her more closely. I certainly wouldn't leave her in the hands of a jaded earl, who is part Lakota Sioux, who would more than likely take her innocence without batting an eye."

She wanted to touch his cheek, sooth his aspersions about himself. He was sitting too far away from her. He called himself jaded. Said he would take her virtue. What truly happened to him to feel so intensely that he wasn't worthy? "You haven't though. I wish you would."

"You don't want anything of the sort nor should you want anything to do with the likes of me if you understood the entire truth." He growled the words while his scowl deepened further.

"You check everything I want in a man. All I've ever wanted in a man. Aunt Ella obviously doesn't agree. If she did, she would never have left me in your protection."

"I'm a half-breed. You've yet to see if I ride and shoot as well as your daddy."

His sarcasm wasn't missed. He stood. The anger in his voice didn't deter her.

"You're a man first. Quit feeling sorry for yourself. When you do, you can get on with your life." She rose from the chair ready to end this argument so they could move on to something more pleasant. "I will wait for you for as much time that it takes. I guarantee you won't be sorry. First, however, did my aunt and uncle rescue you from a vindictive white woman? Is that why you're jaded? Why you scowl and grump around. Why you're trying to tell me you will never marry never have an heir."

At the rapid change of expression on Kane's face she knew she hit on part of the truth if not all. In an instant, his countenance went from startled too stuffy or was that stodgy? For some reason she could never remember. What did it matter?

Before he could answer, she straightened ready to shock him again, "Was this white woman one you were courting? She found out after the fact, after you took her virginity, you were indeed a half-breed? Know that I will never belittle you in any way. I want you to be my first as well as my last. Don't want any other man. You are mine, Kane."

She understood that might be too bold, too brazen. Lyssa didn't care.

Chapter Four

Even before Lyssa told him for the thousandths time that she didn't want to attend the recital, he saw the stress lines in her face. This was something he promised the duchess he would do. Reneging was not possible. He would make sure she attended every event she received an invitation for. After all, he took on the position of chaperone. It was his duty to present her to London society, to give her every opportunity of meeting a respectable man. Even though she made it clear to him she wanted him, only him. He wasn't a respectable man.

Lyssa would find a handsome man who would possess all the characteristics in her long list of must haves in a man. It wouldn't be easy. However, given enough opportunities, she would find the man of her wildest imaginations. She would be happy. Would forget about him. It was the best for both of them.

Though, he would never forget her, never forget that virgin kiss, the way she tasted. The devil, she twisted him every which way with her constant questions. Seconds ticked by while he paused in thought. The chance to teach her the answers to all her inquiries could prove to be fun. The man she found would have to possess a wealth of patience, in addition ride as well as her daddy. The notion brought a thoughtful chuckle from his lips. There weren't many men in England who could perform on a horse to her satisfaction. He was among the few.

The broadmindedness part of his thoughts left him out of the running. He had little to no patience where women were concerned. Tolerance wasn't part of her list. Bedding a woman then leaving her was all he ever intended for a relationship. He never slept the entire night with his women. Even though he understood he would have to have a legitimate heir someday, that for him was far in the future. Lyssa would not be part of that future. She would remain in London for the duration.

If she didn't find a suitable husband, she would return to the States.

She told him she could sing as well as play passably. Their family would gather around the piano on special occasions to sing. Her mother and father sang together, their voices melding beautifully. The duchess told him Lyssa's voice was as sweet as an angel's. Lyssa told him her voice was passable.

There was a contradiction here. Even though he didn't expect her to tout her praises, she might have described her ability as something more than adequate. He felt sure the duchess's assessment of her talents was closer to the truth if not the absolute truth. Avoidance caused her to lie. She must have thought he would give in to her whim.

Kane found he was more than eager to hear her for himself. For his purpose, the recital couldn't come soon enough. He promised her they would leave for the country first thing in the morning as he longed for the smell of clean country air. The fact was, if he thought she would have gentlemen callers that afternoon they would wait until evening to leave. He needed to give her ample opportunity to meet suitable men.

Now, he wasn't at all certain how he could break that news to her. So far, he hadn't seen her too angry. While she seemed to wear her emotions on her sleeve, anger didn't seem prevalent. She certainly could have been angrier last night when she discovered Sinclair's ruse. Simply put, she took the possible drugging along with the planned force in stride as if the man had not intended to take her against his will.

Well, she did tell him she wanted the portentous lord scalped. Too bad he couldn't do as she suggested. Kane wondered if Sinclair would show up at the recital. He certainly hoped he would think about attending the event more than a second or two. He probably wouldn't appear, he guessed he'd put the man out of commission for at least a week if not longer.

Kane chuckled softly. He would enjoy seeing the man again just to see if the damage to his face was as extensive as he thought it would be.

If Sinclair tried to press charges, the issue would be his word against three others. Kane wasn't worried about that possibility. Sinclair Ritter didn't have the nerve to stand up against a man.

He'd been sipping brandy waiting for Lyssa to make an entrance. Kane felt relaxed for the first time since learning about his duty to the girl. She had this way about her that put him at ease. It wouldn't surprise him at all if she chose to come down in her riding attire. She did promise him though that she would be on her best behavior.

Nevertheless...

Lyssa was a woman true to her word. She would not default on her promise to show up in correct clothing for a recital even one where she was loathe to make an appearance. After that, he couldn't be sure as to what would transpire. He grinned thinking on that, knowing Lyssa that could be just about anything. Suddenly, he felt excited about what would occur in the ensuing hours. He was eager to see what would follow.

When Lyssa walked into the drawing room, he wasn't surprised. She stood in front of him. What he did feel was deep amusement, as she seemed to appear meek. Lyssa would never personify a humble woman. This was as close as she would probably ever come. She had some ulterior motive, something planned that might get her out of the recital. At this late hour, he could think of nothing.

A perfect personification of a biddable woman, she smiled softly at him. "Do I please you? This doesn't break any of your rules, does it? Am I modest enough?" She twirled in a small circle, her gown flowing delightfully around her slim ankles, her smile hesitant as if seeking his approval.

The answer forming on his lips might shock her. No, he didn't think anything would astonish this young lady. Her brother didn't pull punches when it came to his little sister's education. She spent too much time in the company of her older brother along with his friends to be totally innocent of the way of men.

"What do you have up your sleeve, Little Bit?" He tried to scowl. Instead, he smirked, one brow arching upward. "I can see mischief in your eyes. Tell me so I can brace myself for the repercussions."

"Told you I would do my best at this. Don't want to be an embarrassment to the duchess or me. Sometimes I forget..." She hesitated a moment too long, wetting her lips, "At this endeavor as much as I dislike the fact you are making me attend, I plan to behave. However, you might not be pleased with the outcome. I get nervous, always have. Every time I've done something such as this, I've forgotten the words to the song, or turned them all topsy turvy. After that I blurt out whatever pops into my head. There are always repercussions."

"Your voice isn't passable? Is it?"

He didn't believe for a moment Ella lied to him. She wasn't like that.

"Aunt Ella says it isn't, says I've the voice of an angel. Who am I to disagree?"

She lifted slim shoulders, her flesh as white as moonbeams.

Yes, she was clearly planning something. Well, he was positive whatever she was thinking of doing would shock the poor people in attendance. Typically, these events bored him to tears. He had the distinct feeling today would be anything except boring.

There was a clear possibility she spoke the truth. What if she did always forget the music or the words? She would be humiliated. He wasn't at all optimistic how to deal with an embarrassed or humiliated woman. That was out of his scope of expertise.

"When was the last time the duchess heard you sing or play?"

He wasn't too sure why he pursued this. Probably because he'd like to be forewarned before all hell broke loose this afternoon. By the slight smirk on her dainty features, he once again felt certain his guesses were not wrong.

She meant to make certain he wouldn't badger her to go to another recital. If things turned out the way they should, he wouldn't be chaperoning her much longer. Although, he was also positive if Collin was trying to elude the men searching for him, it might be longer than the few weeks the duchess intimated before they found the runaway couple. If he knew his friend, they could be gone for months.

Once more, her slim white shoulders lifted slightly. "Don't recall. Could have been a century ago for all I know. I don't tend to keep track of events that I despise attending."

Well, Lyssa might despise recitals nonetheless she would sing at this one. "Come along."

He offered her an arm while he studied her expression. She looked like a cat that licked all the cream from the bowl. All he could think was that she meant to screech while she missed the notes on the piano. He supposed that would keep him from forcing further attendance to these events.

That wouldn't do. It was too easy. There was something else she intended. Maybe she told the truth. She got nervous then did the unexpected. "Not going to ask you what you plan on doing besides singing and playing simply because I know you won't tell me. Besides, I do believe I'd rather be surprised. Promise you won't bore me."

"That's just the point, Kane, recitals are tedious events. No one enjoys them except the proud mamas of the sweet little debutantes who caterwaul their songs to the masses in attendance. The first time I made a fool of myself, mother promised me there would be no more of them. Now, look what is happening." She spread her arms wide to make her statement more dramatic. "You're too afraid of Aunt Ella to disappoint her by letting me have my way. I assure you Aunty would never insist I attend if she knew what happened to me every time I tried to sing at a recital."

"You said you've only been to one."

"I did, didn't I? Perhaps I exaggerated. I need to make my point before it is too late to do so and I embarrass everyone including myself."

"Maybe you did. No matter what happens I won't be embarrassed."

The ride to the Mayberry townhouse took too long. An eternity could not describe the length of time better. Her chatter, which was not normal, began to amuse him. Clearly his little bit appeared nervous about something. Maybe she did tell the truth. Her fingers wound in then out of the fabric of her gown creasing the fabric so much that he was certain the material could not be smoothed out. From time to time, she looked at the ceiling as if she tried to remember something. This might be the torture for her she told him it was.

That wasn't all that unusual by itself. Her complacency was the abnormal detail in this situation. Lyssa Andrews was not a woman who would go down in defeat. Falling in defeat was exactly what she was doing now by accepting the fact she had no choice. The truth would be nice to know.

They reached the Mayberry place. He stepped out of the carriage allowing the driver to place the steps before taking her hand to help her down. Her hand in his was ice cold, sweaty as well. He squeezed hoping that would give her the courage that seemed now to be lacking.

For a moment she pulled back, her deep blue eyes wide with trepidation. Very seriously she proceeded to tell him what would be the last time, "I don't want to do this."

Kane felt as if this was her last plea to stop the shenanigans she planned for the afternoon entertainment. Truly, he wasn't at all positive why he thought she was up to something, after listening to her as well as watching her attentively his mind was in a muddle, changing its tune constantly.

He did still believe she planned some secret entertainment for the attendees. Then…perhaps not.

Nothing she could do would discomfit him. At least he didn't believe so. Kane was certain he'd seen as well as done just about everything in this world. Although what his little debutante might do, could surprise him. She was a wealth of surprises.

Inside, some of the most elite members of the ton mingled. There were chairs set behind the piano for easy listening. She clung to his arm, her fingers clenching then unclenching as they strode through the room. Her gaze roamed. She held back when they stepped closer the groups of people conversing. If this was an act of sheer terror, she was bloody good.

"Miss Andrews." A young man took her hand in his. "It's so nice to see you again."

She pulled back. He kissed the top. She made a face over the young man's head while shooting daggers at him.

When Lyssa turned to him, a beaming smile on her face, his heart took a sudden lurch. She'd turned away from the young man who addressed her. In a whisper for his ears only, "I'm going to make you regret insisting I attend. I know it for a fact just as surely as I'm breathing. Don't know what yet, nonetheless you will regret what happens. As will I. You could have made apologies to the hostess. We could have left. Singing in front of strangers is not something I do well."

"How? Apologies? Regrets?" He bent close. Knew his breath whispered across her cheek. "How could you possibly make me regret bringing you here?"

He wasn't certain that he might already regret this stagnant scene. Tedious didn't begin to describe how he felt. Bored to tears came closer. He'd much rather be out riding as he knew so would she.

Lyssa ran her hands up then down her arms a look of distress crossing her lovely face for an instant before she smiled at him again. "If I told you, it would ruin the surprise. Don't you think?"

She winked at him. With that single gesture he no longer felt sorry for her.

Bloody hell, she unnerved him. One second, he felt sorry for her, the next she blustered on that she was going to make everyone regret her attendance here. "I'll never regret keeping a promise to a dear friend. If you think to embarrass me, you will fail miserably. Haven't been embarrassed in years. Not since mother caught me kissing Little Pearl in the stream behind our lodge. It was also the fact I had my hand on her breast that caused the embarrassment not just the kiss. Learned then I had nothing to feel shame about. Little Pearl liked my attention."

Lyssa giggled. "I'm surprised that embarrassed you."

"I was just twelve. Feeling my sexual prowess. Now, should we fetch ourselves something to eat or would you rather sit while you wait your turn on the piano. I for one can hardly stand the expectation as to what you have planned for this nonthreatening audience. I'll bargain though that whatever you have up your tiny sleeve, it will humiliate you more than me."

"Twelve? So old? I would have thought... I've nothing planned!"

"That was when I got caught," Kane smirked at her.

"Oh..." She turned to smile at him her face flushed a beautiful shade of pink. "You have vast experience in that area. I believe I like that. You will give me pleasure when you make love to me."

"That's not going to happen, Lyssa. If you look, I'm positive you can find that one man who will make you happy. That man isn't me."

His voice was a low growl. Kane didn't know whom he tried to convince, Lyssa or himself. The convincing wasn't working. With each passing second, he fell more completely in the spell she wove around him. He wanted her more than he needed to breathe.

"Only if he's you. There isn't anyone else in this town who can ride and shoot like my daddy. For that matter you still have to prove yourself. You've only intimated that you could. Though you did beat me soundly in our little race the other day."

"Unlike you, I don't have to do anything or demonstrate a point. If I wanted to prove myself, would have done the deed yesterday afternoon when we had the picnic. I'm not in line for your attention. Keep that in mind. You'll be happier."

"Someday you will show me your riding skills then I will show you mine."

The challenge was clear to him. Her riding skills, he had a powerful feeling he wouldn't be pleased. His gut was always right.

At the mention of riding skills, his thoughts traveled to a place they shouldn't be. She had no idea how what she just said could be misconstrued. It seemed that happened once before, maybe more than once. Lyssa Andrews was more innocent than she portrayed at first glance.

For several seconds, he studied the quarter sliced cucumber sandwiches. The crusts had even been cut off the bread. He liked the crusts. Tiny lavender teacakes sat on a piece of China. Silver spoons lay in a row waiting for use. Nothing here appealed to him. This was going to be the longest afternoon of his life. Perhaps she was right. He shouldn't have insisted. They could be outside riding in the fresh air, sunshine beating down on his face.

Once again, he bent close to speak, "You could volunteer your talents. Go first. We could get out of here after that. Go get a bite of real food."

"You want me to go first or not at all?"

Her smile brightened. He was certain at the thought of not at all. "If it's not at all, I won't get to embarrass you. However, you are right about the food. What they are serving couldn't fill the belly of any one in this room." She was shaking her head, "Cucumber sandwiches. Not my taste at all."

It seemed her attention centered on a portly young man. Kane chuckled. No, that man would not be to her taste.

"The punch I'm positive is no better."

"I'll volunteer to be first. Would just as soon get this over with. After that we can have fun. Where will we go?"

He could only think of one place. The Dark Horse Pub wasn't exactly appropriate for a debutante. Well, they could sit in the back in a shadowed corner. The food was good as was the ale. After they ate their fill, they could leave. No one would be wiser.

When a young woman began to play and sing, he realized Lyssa must have missed her chance to go first. Approaching the matronly Mrs. Mayberry, he inquired about the order for the young singers and discovered there was a list by the door. Also found out she would have to wait until the end since they didn't see it when they first came through the opening. To keep his mind healthy, he thought he should bribe one of the young debutantes to perform later. Discovered the mother would have to be the one he bribed. He would have to smile all the while pretending interest in the young lady. At the very idea his gut cramped.

After speaking with the first ten ladies on the list he secured a place for her close to the beginning. She would be fifth in line. He sat down with Lyssa beside him and tried to enjoy his cucumber sandwich. It curdled in his stomach. The teacake tasted a bit better. At least the confection didn't make him gag. The punch was not as bad as he expected.

While waiting for her turn, Lyssa acted as she did in the carriage. Her fingers wound in and out of the fabric of her gown. She looked to the door as if all she wanted was to escape. Deep sighs emanated from her every few seconds. If he didn't miss his guess, she was truly terrified.

She leaned close to him whispering softly, a slight tremor in her speech. "What if I don't remember the words? What then?" There was a fine line of sweat beaded across her forehead. "I can't breathe. Do believe I might faint. Will you catch me?"

"You're next and you're not going to faint. I'm sure you will do fine up there. If you forget the words improvise with something you know, as if you remember the crease lines on the palm of your hand.

Nothing is going to go wrong. I'm sure of it."

By the paleness of her face, he wasn't at all convinced what he said was true. He would have liked to promise her. Understood he couldn't. What happened up there was her responsibility. It wasn't in his domain to change anything.

She nodded. Gulped air. When she walked to the front of the room, she appeared to be going to her execution. For a moment he felt sorry for her. After that he wondered if he'd been wrong. Before she sat on the bench, she tossed him a hesitant smile. She warmed up her voice with a few melodic notes breathing deeply between phrases.

He leaned back crossing his arms over his chest. She would do fine. He didn't want to ride in the same carriage with her if she didn't. Knowing what to say to her if she embarrassed herself was far from his expertise.

Lyssa began to hum softly as she gained confidence. The sound of her voice seemed to float on the air. Ella was right about her talent. She did have the voice of an angel. He grinned as he sat back to enjoy her short time in the limelight.

Her fingers roamed over the keys for a few more seconds before she began to sing the words. Amazing Grace was the song she chose. The lyrics flowed sweetly. Her voice filled the room with softness. She seemed to gain more confidence with each crystal-clear note. Indeed, he was listening to the voice of an angel.

Her words stilled. Her eyes widened. She grimaced, frowning.

She looked to him for direction, her eyes appearing to cross. Her face pinkened. The earlier smile vanished. In its place was a look of terror. He nodded hoping he could help her remember his advice. If you forget the words, change songs. Sing something you can remember. Something you know by heart.

No one will care. For that matter, who here truly cared whether a potential wife could sing? What mattered was how the woman responded in bed. There were no recitals for that.

She smiled at him. He watched her suck air, her large bosom heaving with the effort the rounded globes nearly spilling from her gown with the concerted effort. Looking away was impossible.

She began softly at first then growing louder as she seemed to forget her nerves. Her confidence showed.

By the light of a candle I happened to spy
A pretty young couple together did lie
Said Nelly to John if you'll pull up my smock
You'll find a young hen as good as your cock
Then Johnny kissed her and pleased her awhile
When he pulled up her smock it made him to smile
Instead of a hen it appeared like a cat
For there was her beard and her rough hairy back
Then Nelly she opened her lily-white thighs...

Bloody, bloody eyes! Kane shot to his feet. This was not what he expected. Not what anyone expected. What the devil did the girl think she was doing? She would be ostracized. Thrown out of good graces. The duchess wasn't in residence to help right this horrible *faux pas*. He certainly didn't have the power to do such a thing. He was known throughout the city as a cad and a reprobate. He'd never done anything to change any opinions.

"Oh my..."

"Well, I never..."

"Who does she think she is? An American barbarian!"

"She's a savage."

"A little twit of an upstart."

"A little ninny with no social graces!"

More exclamations littered the air. Mothers covered the ears of their girls. Whispered titters and laughter followed joined by the deep guffaws of the men in attendance.

Lyssa had done it now. She completely made the situation impossible for her to receive more invitations. Young lords seeking a wife would want her for their mistress instead. A woman who would sing such a song would not be a suitable life mate among the aristocracy. To calm his fury, he drew in a deep breath of stale, perfume scented air.

"Excuse us."

Kane strode quickly stepping around chairs to a spot beside her.

His hand on her arm, he helped her to stand. Bending low, "Are you crazy?" he whispered hoping no one else heard the words. "Did you intend..."

No, she would not go that far. He would guess she had no idea what she sang so sweetly that had every patron gasping in air. "We'll talk about this later."

"What do you want to talk about?" When she stared up at him, she blinked a few times. Though her smile didn't reach her eyes. She appeared totally unknowing.

"That sounded too innocent to be believable," he muttered as he ushered her to the coats, nevertheless wishing he'd not given her the advice to sing a different song if she forgot the words to the first. Amazing Grace was safe. She shouldn't have gone wrong. "You might have just gotten your way about one thing. You won't have to go to another recital or ball this season. You won't find yourself asked to anything important. You're Aunty Ella will be mortified when she hears about this travesty. I hope that's what you wanted."

His voice turned gruff, he tried to temper his seething emotions. He found that impossible. When he stopped to think, he chuckled, tried to keep his chortle of laughter behind his lips.

She looked at him bewildered before she tossed him a cheeky grin. Good God, what had she done besides ruin herself for any possibility for further invitations, for a husband. She'd be labeled a pariah. He had to concede though; she was getting exactly what she wanted.

"No more balls? I could sink my teeth into that notion. Was it the song?" she asked sounding far from innocent.

"You don't know?"

He knew she was innocent. "So...so," she stammered softly, her eyes wondering.

He couldn't understand. Didn't understand Lyssa Andrews at all. "You know the problem was with the lyrics, not your voice."

The devil, he'd been so immersed in her lovely and haunting rendition of Amazing Grace the words to the new song didn't hit home until she finished a couple of versus. If he caught the change before she finished the first verse, the damage would not be so devastating to her reputation. He cringed to think what type of men might show up tomorrow to court her. They wouldn't have wooing in mind. The intentions they would have would be the same horrible objective Sinclair Ritter had. Only they would expect to spread her legs without drugging her.

"In case you haven't guessed, we're leaving now before Mrs. Mayberry tosses you out on your delectable little fanny," he whispered to Lyssa. "I hope you understand what you unleashed with this travesty. No, I don't guess you do. You should comprehend this wasn't good. The song was a poor choice, a very bad choice. The worst choice you could have made."

He was so frustrated as well as annoyed with her he was repeating himself. While he wanted to be angry now that he had time to digest the situation, he couldn't for the life of him bring forth that emotion. As more time passed, the sight of all the horror-stricken mothers was amusing. He didn't dare laugh.

When he looked at her, her eyes were huge pools of shimmering blue. Moisture clouded them. She was so lovely. For a sudden moment, he thought she might cry. She stiffened her shoulders then lifted her chin. Indignation rose in her tone as she spoke, "Jess sings that tune all the time. Why him and not me? The men always laugh." She hesitated for several seconds. "Though I'm not sure what all the lyrics mean." A long pause followed. "I don't know what any of them mean. They are just words that go with a catchy tune."

He sucked air, revelation-sinking in. "Let me get this straight. You sang a song with bawdy lyrics. The worst part is that you didn't know what they meant. Are you stupid?"

He thought he must have asked her that same question earlier. He couldn't remember. Kane helped her into the carriage. He sat down across from her. She stared at him, her eyes questioning.

She mushed her lips together, her gaze roaming out the window then coming back to rest on his eyes. "Didn't think the words could be all that bad. Once I heard Jess sing them in front of mother. Thought if they were bad, she would have washed his mouth out with lye soap or boxed his ears."

"Guess that's what I should do with you. What do you think?"

It seemed he considered the possibility of that ridiculous notion even though the notion held no appeal for him.

"You wouldn't?" Her eyes flashed with indignation. Her little fists clenched. "You wouldn't dare! Truly, Kane, I didn't know."

She was so damn adorable. He couldn't think straight. What was wrong with him? He wanted her. Was having the devil's own time resisting the charms she appeared too willing to give. "Your brother seems to get you into trouble without you knowing the situation, doesn't he?"

The circumstance was almost amusing. He wasn't about to explain the lyrics to her. Perhaps her future husband could do so.

"Tell me what they mean, the words to that song? Don't you think I should know? I did sing the lyrics."

"More importantly, remember that you shouldn't sing tunes you've heard your brother tossing about with his male friends. I'm certain your mother was out of hearing distance. She would not have approved. Either that or she didn't know you were nearby or perhaps she didn't understand. You should tell me how you could remember the lyrics to that song and not Amazing Grace? You sing that one at church, right?"

He was no longer positive about anything. Maybe she didn't go to church. How the hell would he know? He certainly never found the need to sit in a church and listen to a lecture he didn't agree with. His church, his solace and peace he found outdoors listening to nature, God's animals.

"Where are we going to eat?"

She changed the subject. Her face turned straight ahead.

He appreciated the tactic. Thought he should do the same. "I should send you to bed without dinner," he mumbled, as he had no idea how to continue with her. Damn his promise to the duchess. Giving up on the pretense, he informed her, "The pub we spoke of earlier. My driver has the directions. At least we will have a round of good food to ease the disaster that was today."

He sat back, legs stretched negligently in front of him, watching her closely. Most likely there would be no gentleman callers tomorrow, at least not of the suitable kind. He hoped there wouldn't be any of the unsuitable kind either as he wasn't in the mood to chase them off or offer explanations.

"You wouldn't do that. Would you?" She sat up straight, hands folded primly in her lap a saucy smirk on her face. "Mother used to do that when we were terrible. However, she would always sneak something for us to eat when father wasn't looking."

He let lose a long slow breath of air. "No, I wouldn't. Want you strong and healthy before I punish you."

"You're not going to do that either," she told him her smile reaching gigantic proportions. "I'm not sorry if you're looking for an apology. I'm pleased with the results you predicted. Doubt if I'll ever see these people again. So, what does it matter that I embarrassed them? I'm sure they are all too caught up in themselves to have fun."

"It will be the reason that will send you home."

She hissed in a breath of air.

~ * ~

Hell and damnation, Kane had believed she planned the song. She didn't. What could she expect after the way she teased him, tossed out grins as well as words implying she planned to do something to sabotage the outcome of her recital. The truth of it all was that she had no idea what the words to the ribald song meant. Not only did her brother sing the bawdy tune but the ranch hands did too. She'd heard the catchy tune countless times. Even going as far as singing silently when no one thought she was nearby.

Lyssa wanted him to take her seriously. If she kept making mistakes like the last one, he would never trust her or think of her as a mature woman. He tossed out sending her home. She wouldn't allow him to do that. As it was, he still thought of her as a debutante, possibly even a child. He would never touch her. She wanted him to kiss her again. He tasted so sweet, his scent provocative, his muscles rippling beneath her fingers. Wished he saw her as more than the debutante he had to chaperone. Wanted more than a kiss, whatever that entailed.

She intended to gift him with her maidenhead. She wasn't about to give her innocence to any other man. She didn't know how to go about doing that or even exactly what it meant.

"What am I supposed to do now?" he asked, his voice soft. His eyes shimmered with an emotion she couldn't read. "Since you've closed a lot of avenues to a successful coming out, do you want to go home? Perhaps you could return next season. People might have forgotten about you in a year. I could arrange a ship on the morrow if you'd like."

She tried to stifle the gasp of horror that rippled from her lips. He suggested she leave a second time. He couldn't possibly be serious. Leave before he fell in love with her? She couldn't do that. Her stubborn pride would keep her from that along with her need for Kane to change his opinion of her. If she had to attend balls to stay here, attend she would.

Lyssa waved a hand in the air, choking on her words. "Going home is out of the question, Kane."

She didn't mean to return to the states until she was wed to the blasted man. That might take a great deal of time since he was so stuffy, no stodgy. What was his nickname? Well, he was too tense all the time, that was for certain. He was too stubborn to see what was right in front of his eyes; a woman who fell in love with him the moment she set eyes on him. A woman he could fall in love with, one who wouldn't hurt him even though she was white. Her father would never have him whipped for any reason. He should be more appreciative. She closed her eyes recalling the time when she heard her mother speaking to her father about a man her aunt and uncle rescued. A man who'd been beaten almost to death. They rescued that man. Lyssa didn't doubt for a moment that man was Kane. All that he told her coupled with everything he didn't say pointed directly his way.

He lifted broad shoulders, ones she touched when they swam, ones that undulated beneath her fingertips. She remembered the way he felt, the rippling of his cool flesh when she ran her hands across his broad chest. He'd been naked beneath the water. She should have looked her fill.

Clearing his throat, the gesture seemed to her he proceeded with reasons for her to leave. "Don't see why you should stay here. There is nothing for you to do."

"I like swimming with you as well as riding. Want to get to know you better."

She was fishing here. She wasn't positive what she was searching for. What she liked was his kisses. One kiss from him right now would be more than pleasant.

Even one more kiss was not enough.

"You have no need to get to know me better."

He leaned forward, picking her hands up so his surrounded them. Warm, he felt warm, the slight caress sensual. He would protect her, not that she needed to be protected. He would come to cherish her. With time, she knew he would fall in love with her. She would have to figure out a way to get that necessary time.

He laughed at her impulsive questions. Grinned when she told him something outlandish. She did see the almost smirk when he wrested her away from that horrible recital. He enjoyed shocking the stoic, stiff members of the ton.

Perhaps he didn't think her questions and statements as amusing just eccentric. Her brother told her it wasn't proper to ask the male species some of the things she asked him. Jess did relent by telling her she might ask a husband to show her or talk to her. Kane was going to be her husband so who better?

She grinned thinking of the lyrics to the song Kane called bawdy. He could tell her what the lyrics all meant. She understood he would never do such an outlandish thing. Poppycock, what did she care about proper? Proper was for debutantes not for her.

"What is wrong with getting to know each other better?" she asked even though she felt positive she knew what his answer would entail.

She would argue with him. Make him believe she was good for him. Hadn't she made him smile? More than once.

He didn't scowl as often.

Almost as if he didn't know what he was doing, his thumbs traced lazy circles on the inside of her wrist. The sweetly gentle caress sent sensations straight to parts of her she didn't know existed until he kissed her the other day. She wanted more of the same. Did he know what he

Dream About Lyssa

was doing to her? She wasn't sure she understood. Nevertheless, she liked the wicked and ever so naughty sensations that heated then sent flames soaring through her to newly discovered secret parts.

"We won't ever have the relationship you seem to want, Lys. I'm not going to marry you. So, I don't intend to ruin you in any way for someone else," he told her his voice so very throaty, husky.

It seemed he straightened, forcing himself to be stern. His voice was ragged as he spoke. "You have to get that notion out of your pretty little head."

She witnessed his eyes warming, smoldering with what appeared to be the same heat he created within her. Inadvertently, she ran her tongue along the outline of her lips. She wished she knew what else she could do to make him want her.

"As I mentioned before, you check all my requirements. I'm not going to stop trying," she protested his ludicrous statement with the only reasons she could think of at the instant. Well, now, he must not understand what he did to her with his thumbs, coupled with his warm hands, hands she wanted other places. She just wasn't too certain where those other places should be.

If he meant to convince her he wasn't interested in her, he needed to stop touching her. Needed to stop sending those heated bolts of red-hot desire through her. Good God, in a few seconds she would be panting for air as well as fanning herself to chase away the raging inferno.

Suddenly, as if he just realized it himself what he was doing, he dropped her hands. After that he cleared his throat. His voice strangely husky, "It doesn't matter that I..." He jabbed his hands into his hair several times, swearing beneath his breath. "I'm not going to marry you."

For a moment his statement sounded to her as if he tried to convince himself. "It does matter. You're the man I want. I won't give up. Although you don't realize the truth yet, I'm what you want. Not going to settle for less than the best possible choice for me." She paused avidly watching him. "You kissed me." The line sounded like as accusation.

He sucked air, his gaze moving to look outside almost as if he sought an argument for that. A long time passed before he finally said,

"I've kissed a great deal of women. Those women mean nothing to me. In my life I intend to kiss more but not you. Just because I kiss a woman, doesn't mean I'm going to marry them."

"That's because you mean nothing to those women. The situation is different with us. We care about each other."

She hoped he wouldn't deny that statement as she was dreadfully hurt he told her he wasn't going to kiss her again. She would find a way around his ludicrous statement. Find a means to tempt him.

Again, in the moment it seemed to Lyssa he struggled for words. "Yes, I care for you as a cherished sister. I'm like your brother to you. You only think you want to marry me because I'm the first man who has kissed you. That's the only reason. A brother doesn't kiss his sister."

The carriage rolled to a stop. "We're here."

Yes, she was disappointed as well as disillusioned. Mayhap in the pub they would have the chance to continue along this same vein. She sensed she made headway. Since he protested so vehemently, she felt positive his heatedly spoken words were meant to convince himself. She saw the way he looked at her, seemed to study her when he didn't think she was looking.

Inside the pub, women walked by swinging their hips, flashing bright smiles while they showed off bosoms barely covered by fabric. Men talked as well as laughed in loud voices. The air smelled of smoke along with whiskey. A blue haze filled the air in the room. She thought she caught the scent of fresh baked bread. Her stomach rumbled. She was hungry.

The door to the kitchen swung open. A woman backed from the door with a tray full of drinks as well as platters of food. She didn't see any women except those in low cut gowns with hems that reached above the knees serving the customers. This place was indeed something new to her. Jess would like this pub too. It was far from a place an earl took a debutante. This was perfect to ruin even more a battered reputation such as hers. She should thank him. He might not like that.

She grinned, the realization hitting home. Kane took her somewhere that was not proper. The stodgy earl brought her to a pub where only men and lose women went. A lady waltzed by, her skirts swishing showing more leg than was appropriate although that wasn't the only part of her she showed too much of. The lady sat down on Kane's lap while she wrapped her arms around his neck. Her lips were too close to his. Lyssa wanted to slap her silly. Jealousy rose then twisted in her gut.

How dare she? Kane is mine just as I am his.

"Not now, sweetheart," he murmured, his hands on her waist, a feeble attempt to push her away. "There's a lady present." He nodded his head toward her.

"A lady? Is that wat she's callin' herself? Doesn't look like no lady to me. If she's a lady, wat's she doin' here? Kiss me, Black. You know how I like it deep and hot, the harder the better. Don't stop until I can't breathe no more." She brushed her lips across his.

Lyssa bristled. He groaned. "Not now, sweetheart." He set his hands on her waist, pushing her from his thighs while she clung to his neck. Her rump stuck upward, into the air. Her garters showed. Despite her jealousy, the scene purely fascinated Lyssa. She wondered what he would do if she dressed for him like the woman. If she pressed her lips against his without asking.

The woman purred softly while she moved her heavy bosom in front of his face, "Later. I'll be upstairs waiting for you, Black."

She continued her enticement bending over so he could see the swell of her breasts. Her large pink nipples showed beneath her corsage. Again, Lyssa wondered what he would do if she acted the same. Most likely that discipline he spoke of.

"Not tonight." His voice turned harsh. It was a tone she'd never heard from his lips before. "Go on now, you've work to finish. I'm positive there will be another customer who will love to see your charms." He swatted her on the bottom.

Lyssa grinned. Now she could clearly see the woman's nipples. So, this was the type of white woman Kane sought, one with no scruples, one who flaunted her feminine jewels in front of him. Perhaps her very own nipples against his lips would lure him. Trying to break down the wall he built around himself might be fun. She watched as the woman sashayed her large rounded bottom to the bar. If that's what it took, she was certain she could sashay too. She recalled the way he stared at her breasts when they were surrounded by water. If she'd any idea what to do then she would have tried something. She decided to file this notion in her brain for another time.

A glass of ale for each of them was set on the table followed by a basket of bread. She grinned at him while she picked up a slice. Waving the bread in the air, she said, "So that's who you come see when the hankerin' gets to you? Do you like this type of woman? She's not good enough for you, Kane."

She didn't need to know the answer to her question. When he said no to the lady's request to meet her upstairs, the woman appeared more than disappointed.

His scowl deepened. He drank long and deep from his glass. The glass landed on the table with a bang, ale drops toppling from the rim. "Who I see doesn't concern you. I'm your chaperone. Best you remember that fact, not a suitor."

Of course, it concerned her, "You do comprehend, she could give you the pox."

Once again, it seemed she blurted her first thought. She should bite her tongue. Maybe he would do that. She'd heard Jess saying something along that line when he was speaking with one of his friends. Tongues dancing while playing together, a tiny nip here and the woman would moan with her pleasure. Big brothers sometimes were useful.

Kane sputtered. It appeared he wanted to reply but held back. Instead, he looked away for a moment. She wanted to know what he was thinking, wished she could see inside his head. Seemed he might oblige her. When he looked back, she knew he was going to tell her what she wanted to understand. Well, at least one of the things she needed to comprehend before he finally made love to her.

"I use a condom." He was stoic, his handsome face void of emotions. "Not that you need to know."

She would give him kudos for keeping the scowl on his face. "Jess does too. He's told me...what's a condom?"

Kane rested a slightly calloused fingertip on her lips. She touched his flesh with the tip of her tongue. He didn't jerk back as she suspected he would. Instead, he slowly ran the callused pad of his finger across her bottom lip which seemed to swell with his attention. The sensation delighted while tempting her to do more daring exploits. If she only had any ideas what those adventures would be.

His deep blue eyes darkened to the same color she remembered the day he kissed her. "You're going to be the death of me, Lys. I can't help myself..." He bent close as if he meant to kiss her.

Her name said in that manner sent shock waves of pleasure heating her insides. She swept her tongue across her lip following the same path that his finger took. In silent anticipation, Lyssa held her breath until it scorched her lungs. His thumb replaced his finger, tracing, stroking the caress so soft and tender. She closed her eyes. A sigh filled with desire fluttered from her lips. Her stomach coiled and ached anticipating what was to come. Butterflies danced and played where she'd never experienced sensations until Kane came into her life.

"Well, hells bells, Black, what have we got here? You taking advantage of the girl you're supposed to be chaperoning? Must say it's not a'tall like you," Jeremy asked grinning as he sat down sliding across the bench so he was close to her. Lyssa felt his leg touch hers. She scooted closer to Kane then shot him a furious glare daring him to give her space.

"You going to kiss your charge? Didn't think you had the balls in you to keep your hands off this one. The duchess won't be too pleased if she comes back and discovers what the two of you have been up to in her absence." This time it was Drew who spoke. He sat down opposite Kane.

Lyssa heard Kane's groan of despair or frustration. Now she wasn't certain. She hoped the low rumble meant what she thought the throaty sound might. He wanted her. Slowly, he was losing his control. It seemed to her the loss of control might only be a matter of time before he gave into his vows of abstinence where she was concerned and kissed her one more time.

"What you saw is not what you think," Kane mumbled his voice hoarse. His words seemed to rumble from him with a husky tone from the back of his throat. "We are having a pleasant dinner then we're headed for the townhouse. Maybe the two of you can find somewhere else to sit down. We've things to talk about."

Yes, it did seem he wanted to be alone with her. If his earlier declaration was true, Kane should welcome the added company. Now, Lyssa didn't believe that truth.

"Looks as if you're planning on doing more than talk. Heard about today's debutante recital," Jeremy tossed out while he grabbed a piece of bread from the basket. "Wasn't pretty...not pretty a'tall. It's all over the city. Everyone who is anyone is talking about what happened."

Her breath hissed into her lungs while her stomach churned. *No.* It was one thing to make light of what happened with Kane, quite another when his friends were involved. By the deepening lines on his forehead, she knew he wasn't pleased about hearing this. If anything, she felt horrible that her behavior gave him reason to feel uncomfortable with his friends.

"Is it as bad as I've heard?"

Worse, infinitely worse, for herself she didn't care. Everything she told Kane was true where her feelings were concerned. She didn't care if one member of the ton or all of them shunned her. All that mattered to her was what Kane thought of her as well as what his peers thought of him.

Kane's voice was infinitely calm when he responded. "Lyssa made a mistake, one that in the eyes of her peers won't be corrected soon. What did the two of you hear? The knowledge might help me correct the mistake."

"She sang a bawdy song about lifting smocks and seeing cats' hair," Jeremy laughed out loud. "Wish I'd been there."

His voice seemed to carry around the room. She wanted to cover her ears. Shame filled her. "Told the perpetrator of the lie that the gossip he was expounding wasn't true. Lyssa wouldn't do something so bold and brazen. But then..." he paused staring at her. "The way you're blushing I see the rumors are true."

Lyssa sipped the tiniest hint of air, her face now draining of color, her emotions swirling. Thanking them for their defense would be logical. First, she would have to tell them the truth. "You're right. I sang a song I shouldn't have," she murmured her gaze focused on Kane. "Thank you for defending me."

The jaws on both his friend's faces dropped. What was an astonished expression turned to what seemed like approval. Drew tipped his hat. Jeremy nodded. They both grinned.

"Hells bells," Jeremy said laughing, his eyes lighting with humor. "You're just what all those simpering ladies and doting mamas need to liven up the events. How did you dare?"

"I didn't dare. I didn't know what the words meant, still don't."

"Don't believe there will be more events for you or dashing young suitors to court you," Drew pointed out. "Do you mind too much?"

Drew's words generated a beaming smile from her. "I don't mind at all. What does bother me is Aunt Ella. She doesn't deserve the censure she will receive. Neither does Kane."

That was the truth of the matter. She would never lie.

"You mean, Black? He'll be thrilled to know he doesn't have to escort you to more balls," Jeremy tossed out, looking from the one to the other as if he was seeing his friend for the first time. "He hates balls as well as recitals. Never attends."

"We've things to discuss, Lyssa and I," Kane reminded the pair. "Go find someone else to plague."

"I say, despite your reputation, you're usually friendlier than this," Drew said with a blatant smirk.

"How about you, sweet cakes? Want to have some fun upstairs later tonight?"

It was the same woman who sat on Kane's lap earlier. No sooner than she set the tray of food Kane ordered on the table, the lady perched on Drew's thighs, her heaving bosom pushed against his chin, her lips pouting as if asking for a kiss.

"No, not tonight, Janey. We've got business to discuss with Black. Maybe another time."

"The loss is yours," Janey huffed away clearly displeased with the rejection the second and third of the night.

"Well, I say. She didn't ask me," Jeremy complained while watching the lady.

"You tell her no every time she asks," Kane reminded him. "Did you expect her to seek another rejection?"

"So do the two of you," he grumped. "A man enjoys the asking. Wants to know he's appreciated."

Kane stared at them hard before he spoke. "We'd like some privacy to eat. The two of you are not invited."

A waitress set glasses of ale in front of the two men. "See, everyone here expects us to stay," Jeremy drank before ordering. "Delicious. Fish and chips for both of us."

The deep scowl on Kane's face must have finally registered with Jeremy and Drew.

"Guess you don't want our company. We'll sit over there." Jeremy quickly nodded toward a table far enough away they would never hear what was going to be said between the two of them.

"Wise choice," Kane told them his eyes dark, his scowl blacker than midnight without a moon. He looked as if he wanted to stake them out on the desert sand.

While she watched them walk toward the empty table, she held her breath. The mood Kane created before the two of them showed their faces vanished. Silence permeated the surrounding atmosphere. Lyssa picked at her food while she searched her brain for something to change the atmosphere back to what it had been. Could think of nothing to change Kane's scowl to a smile or even see the desire flashing in his eyes again. If he would only look at her with such tenderness in his eyes as he did earlier, she might be able to breathe again.

She was afraid nothing she could do or say would accomplish that. Frightened she would have to begin again another time. Charming him was certainly not easy for her. Enchanting him wouldn't be tonight.

"Not hungry?" he asked his voice soft with concern. "I'm sorry they showed up, sorry they hurt you. I understand what happened there was an accident. I'm not going to pretend otherwise even though earlier I thought you planned the scenario."

His heartfelt words sent a bolt of relief into her. She tossed him a cheeky grin waving her fork in the air. "They didn't hurt me. Just told the truth. Still, I'd appreciate you much more if you told me just what the words of that blasted song referred to. I believe the meaning of the lyrics would be nice to know. So I don't give a repeat performance."

An eyebrow slashed upward. "No, you don't want to know."

"Of course, I do. Wouldn't you? If you sang something that would make you a laughing stock you would want to know why. Please..."

"I wouldn't sing."

"And," she paused mulling over the words in an attempt to remain rational instead of impulsive, "Isn't that just like you? How many times did I tell you I didn't want to go to the damn recital? Damn and blast, you don't listen well. You caused this." At the pain in his eyes, she felt a sudden bout of remorse. "Since you won't tell me, I'm going to ask Drew and Jeremy what the lyrics mean. At least I think they will tell me the truth." She rose. He reached out and stopped her.

"Thought you were just nervous. Nerves will vanish in the wind if you confront them. Anyone ever tell you if you fall off a horse the only way to chase the fear away is to mount the horse again?"

"Hells bells, that's why I messed up. My bloody nerves got in the way. Always have messed up at recitals. Would have thought Ella comprehended that fact. Too bad they won't vanish in the wind because I'm never going to sing or play at a recital ever again. If anyone forces me, I'll remain mute. Not going to open my mouth to sing ever again!"

"You shouldn't swear so much," he grinned, his eyes once more deepening in color. He seemed to look at her heaving bosom before searching her eyes again. "Cursing is not lady like."

It was her turn to scowl at him. If she didn't want him to stare at her bosom, she would put her hands there to hide herself. With his fingers he picked up a chip. When he bit into the morsel, she stared at his lips remembering the taste of him. Slowly, she let her gaze drop.

After he finished chewing, he looked at her again. It seemed to her he didn't acknowledge where her gaze dropped. "Just curious. Why do you wrap cloth around your upper half when you ride? When you do that..." He choked then quickly drowned his mistake with a gulp of ale. "Never mind, don't suppose that question was appropriate."

Absolutely true, the question wasn't at all proper. It didn't bother her, not one bit. He could ask her anything he wished. Didn't mean she would answer. Feeling impulsive, she tilted her head slightly, a lone fingertip on her lips. He ventured into a land where a gentleman wouldn't go. She meant to give him an honest answer.

Her eyes widened as devilish thoughts entered her mind. She could hardly wait. "The answer seems obvious to me."

"Don't bounce? Your breasts? Why?" he asked with a strangled sound. "Like it when they bounce…" he cut himself off.

At this point, Lyssa wasn't at all sure he was asking a question. If he was, she had no idea how to answer. This line of questioning was inappropriate to her. *In for a penny in for a pound.* "When I ride fast, I'm not comfortable. When I do tricks…" She flashed him a saucy smile. "I'll have to show you my tricks someday, tomorrow? Maybe I can teach you then you'll ride as well as my father. Anyway, I'm much more comfortable if they don't move all the time and get in my way." She leaned forward impulsively challenging him, "You might have the same problem with your manly parts. Do they bounce when you ride? Maybe they are not big enough to bounce. One day I asked Jess but he didn't answer. He scowled at me just as you are doing."

Ale sputtered through the air. He coughed as if trying to clear his passageway. Suddenly, Kane was looking away from her, wiping the ale from his shirt as well as his trousers. Now, he wasn't scowling. She wasn't sure if that was good or bad. He also wasn't answering. She decided why not go for broke?

"Well, do they bounce?" She watched as a hint of a smile touched his mouth before the smirk vanished.

"No. Should we proceed to a different line of questions that are more suitable for a debutante? Seems that once again you've managed to shock me out of a gulp of ale. What do you plan next, Little Bit?"

"Can we ride tonight?" She attempted a diversion. She wanted to yell at him that she wasn't a debutante. Instead, she kept the words to herself.

"No." He ate before he responded more fully. Chewed as if he meant to prolong the following conversation. "Perhaps in light of the words in your song as well as your intentional questions meant to embarrass me, we should move on to something other than riding together."

When he answered, her cheeks heated, the firestorm she created for herself swept down her neck. Trying to shake the strange sensations off she leaned toward him, her eyes flashing. "Does that have a double meaning? I'd like to try riding with you if it does."

~ * ~

"The duchess' charge did what?" Jonathon White sat back in his chair, his glass of brandy to his lips. He could help himself he hooted.

Now he smirked, his mind reeling with all the possibilities. If the rumors were found to be true, her conquest would be easy. She was a ripe little piece of muslin just waiting to succumb to his manly and very irresistible charms. He wasn't certain how to approach the pending courtship since he didn't meet her at a ball or the recital. Steps to hurdle would be in front of him.

"Tell me again?"

His hands formed a steeple beneath his chin. He wanted the chit from the first time he realized she was the heir to Damian Andrew's title. If he wed her, he would be the proud possessor of an English title as well as wealthier than he could imagine. Though in his line of work, he made money easily, he would never complain if more dropped into his lap. As far as he was concerned, the wealthier the better was his motto. A title would be icing on the cake.

What he didn't have was the word "lord" in front of his name. A heading to his name was something he coveted. Now, he had the chance. She was simply an awkward woman coming from the states, a backward place spawning homely women easy to influence. This minor task should be accomplished in record time. Jonathon heard about Sinclair Ritter's attempt to seduce the girl, how the attempt failed as well as how Kane reacted. The Earl of Blackmore would not be an easy man to deal with. He could find a way. The man must want to get rid of the unwanted piece of baggage. He would take her off his hands.

He might be worried about the Earl of Blackmore flaunting his attentions on the girl. Hell, the rumor stood that the earl was a half-breed. He had nothing to worry over. She wouldn't want anything to do with the man. While he understood Black would put impediments up to stop his courting of the chit, in the end he would win. Where women were concerned, he could seduce any female to go to bed with him. He positively didn't lack charisma.

Jonathan also comprehended that after the uniquely bawdy performance today, she would be bombarded with unsuitable men. She would be vulnerable. On the morrow, he would have to be the first to arrive at Blackmore's townhouse. Would have to prove what a refined gentleman he was.

Harry sipped his brandy eyeing him thoughtfully over the rim. "She sang a bawdy song. Shocked everyone in the room to the tips of their pointed little slippers. Black hauled her out of there as fast as he could go. The feat didn't happen soon enough. They left all the mamas along with their daughters in astonishment mouths gaping open."

The earl must be simmering mad that she embarrassed him," David laughed. "Should we all court her? That would be fun. We could draw straws to see who gets her first."

Jonathon was clearly irritated. He tapped his fingers on the arm of the chair where he sat. "No, she's mine. Don't want competition. Not going to draw straws for the girl now. Eventually I will share this one."

He had plans for her. A little smooth talking after a soft kiss here or there in strategic palaces, if he had his way, she would melt in his arms. The idea held a great deal of merit.

"Maybe I don't care about that," Harry said eyeing him over the rim of his glass. "You don't have carte blanch where all the females are concerned in this town. The title that would come with a marriage would be an added benefit, if you get my drift. Believe I'll call on her tomorrow. See who she likes best, you or me."

"She probably won't appreciate either of you," David gave his opinion with a leering grin.

Jonathon didn't dare show his fury. It would give his friends more reason to torment him along with his plans. He pulled in a long deep breath of tobacco-scented air. The calm he didn't feel persevered with his next words. "You can try. Don't be surprised though when she picks me."

His mind travelled through all the possibilities of a first outing. After hearing about the song, the little chit couldn't be a virgin. No, she couldn't be. Any young lady who would sing something like that would be well versed in the ways of men and women.

"What about the earl, her chaperone? Heard when Ritter approached, he insisted on being part of the excursion." David tossed out, his even white teeth showing. "After the performance he might not wish to let her out of his sight, especially if he's coming to realize she isn't as innocent as she might seem at first glance. He might want her for himself. I've heard she's very attractive."

"What about him? He doesn't ever attend the functions during the season. Rarely attends any gatherings. The man won't be interested in her. His likes have never travelled to the debutantes who flock to London during the season."

"Didn't mean that. He was appointed her chaperone by the duchess. Undoubtedly, he will take his duties seriously. You truly believe you can waltz into his townhouse then expect that man to let you take her out riding? If you do something that riles the duke and duchess, there will be hell to pay. You can count on that for a fact. Heard tell Montgomerie is ruthless when it comes to his enemies."

"I won't rile the duke. Intend to convince the little piece of baggage she's in love with me. After that, I'll get her with child, my child. Lyssa Andrews will have to marry me when that happens."

"Wouldn't count on her wedding you for that reason," Harry mumbled. "You recalled what Kane did to Sinclair when he tried the same thing. The half-breed busted Ritter's nose. If you succeeded, he might kill you." After a lengthy pause Harry continued. "Most likely scalp you too. You do like your hair on top of your head, don't you?"

With the word scalp leaving Harry's mouth, Jonathon couldn't suppress the shudder. Yes, he liked his hair right where it was, "That won't happen."

Bloody eyes, he didn't appreciate the idea of losing his scalp.

"You're mighty arrogant for a man who hasn't even shown up to court her. What makes you think she'll take a second look at you? After Ritter, she might be leery of any man. The fat idiot did try to drug her so he could have his way with her."

Jonathon understood he was a good-looking man. Didn't all the women he meet fall head over heels for him? He never had difficulties obtaining women. Debutantes were no different from his other conquests, other than the complication of a chaperone he would have to deal with.

"Ritter was a bumbling fool. His appearance probably turned her against him the moment he set his feet in the drawing room. He's not a man worth taking a second look at if you get what I mean. I did hear even though she's unique in her actions, as you said, she's also quite beautiful." Jonathon stood then assumed several different postures meant to show off a few of his best qualities. "She won't be able to refuse this man's body especially when she sees me naked. He flexed his buttocks. What do you all think?" His query was smug. He knew the answer before anyone blinked. Undoubtedly, he was a fine masculine specimen.

"You don't live up to the likes of Black. He could lay you flat with one solid punch to the chin. The man is a living, breathing mass of muscle," David said blandly. "Think you to challenge him in any competition, you would lose. Rumor has it he's not just a half-breed but a damn Sioux warrior. If I were you, I wouldn't take him lightly. That is, if you value your life."

"Ritter told everyone Black threatened his life. What do you think? You going to stay on his good side so you see your next birthday?"

"If Lyssa Andrews likes me, he will too."

"What if she doesn't?"

Bloody hell, the question irritated him. "You just playing devil's advocate? Don't show up tomorrow either of you."

"Or what?" Harry challenged. "Where the girl is concerned, you don't have rights that none of us have. Until she agrees to your suit, we plan on taking our turn with courting. Wouldn't mind acquiring a title along the way. Wouldn't mind a kiss or more if she's willing."

"You won't if you know what's good for you," Jonathon spoke softly hoping to talk his friends from courting the Andrews girl. It seemed they were determined to do just that.

"Think I'll see you there tomorrow," David said laughing. "What about you, Harry?"

"I'll be there," Harry replied.

Chapter Five

The day was sunny and warm. The carriage to take them back to the country estate was waiting for them outside the front porch. Lyssa rose early so she could pack, singing in her angelic voice. Kane cursed himself every time he thought about the kiss they almost shared yesterday at the pub. If Jeremy and Drew didn't interrupt them, he would have set his lips upon hers. Touching her intimately was exactly what he swore not to do. He wasn't suitable to be her chaperone or her lover. He was too old. She was a white woman, innocent in the extreme. Long ago he wrapped his heart in a steal band to keep something such as this from happening.

The truth of the matter was that he couldn't keep his hands off her. She was all he thought about during his waking hours, all he dreamed about when he was asleep. Purging her from his mind was the only way for him to once again feel in control of his life. He didn't know how to vanquish thoughts of her out of his head. Every time he turned around, she was there, smiling, laughing, flaunting her beautiful charms in front of him.

What the devil was he to do about Lyssa Andrews? If she were any other woman, he would take her to bed. When he did that, she was bound to be instantly out of his system. He would be able to breathe again when he looked at her. As it was now, when she was in his presence, he couldn't think straight, his heart thundered, the sound of his heated blood pounding in his ears.

Kane told her they would wait until after the noon hour to leave just in case any suitors came to call. In a huff, waving her hand in the air, she told him not to bother. After yesterday's fiasco, she didn't want to see anyone. He understood she didn't want to encounter men who would have heard about the recital. Comprehended the fact she wanted him. Allowing that to happen would be idiotic, stupid. He was neither. Giving her a chance in the debutante whirl was important to him.

The first knock sounded on his door at half past noon. Still Water Runs strode outside to escort the young man inside. Abernathy hovered in the hallway, a bland expression on his face. They'd all been told how to handle the possible situation. Now, Still Water Runs stood beside his carriage. Kane stared out the window for a few seconds. When his gaze locked with the man, he recognized him. He realized immediately why he was here.

The bloody song would haunt her for longer than one day. He knew that for a fact a few seconds after he rushed her from the Mayberry home. Now, he watched holding the air inside his lungs until Still Water Runs delivered the man into the drawing room. Politeness along with the need to test the man's mettle caused him to offer his hand in greeting.

"Jonathon White," he introduced himself as Kane accepted the offered hand.

"I know who you are, young pup. What I don't know is why you are here. You can't possibly be interested in Miss Andrews."

She wasn't his type. Kane wondered if the man would be honest. Of course, he wouldn't.

Taking full measure, he felt positive the man wanted what he could gain from a union between the two of them. He wasn't looking for love. From his prior knowledge of Mr. White, the man had wealth. So, what he sought to gain here was a titled heading to come before his last name. He wanted to become an aristocrat. White was also a womanizer if everything he heard about the man were true. Beneath his breath, he chuckled softly. A womanizer was far different from a rake. The man would be just as bad as Sinclair Ritter was; out for whatever he could gain by the liaison.

Taking absolute care Lyssa was never alone with this man was uppermost on his mind. He doubted if she would want to see him. She told him early this morning she wasn't about to entertain suitors today. Or ever, she followed with a last parting shot.

Jonathon stepped back before clearing his throat. He looked beyond Kane to the stairway. "If you haven't guessed as much, I'm here to court Lyssa. You've no reason to deny me the opportunity."

"Miss Andrews to you if you know what's good for you," Kane growled low in his throat, his scowl deepening. What he needed to do was intimidate this man into leaving as well as never returning. He didn't think that would happen. White appeared determined.

"Miss Andrews," Jonathon hastily corrected himself. "I'd like to take her for a carriage ride in Hyde Park if that is allowed."

"If she wants to go, absolutely. Be advised though she goes nowhere with you unless I accompany her." He hoped his words along with the tenor of his voice scared the devil out of the man. He doubted the man was bright enough to be frightened. Though the heated words might make him back down. Kane never met him before, only heard rumors. What he saw now did little to impress. He prided himself on first impressions. This man did not fare well.

"Is she still asleep? I gather yesterday's events must have exhausted her."

He spoke at Kane while watching the stairs as if he'd see her floating down the stairway, hand extended in greeting. More likely she'd scamper down the steps ready to ride the Appaloosa, in the process shock him.

"Yesterday?" One eyebrow arched upward speculating as to Whites intentions once more. Growling, he asked, "What do you know about yesterday? You were not in attendance at the recital."

White shuffled his feet, looking back to the stairs to avoid his gaze. Then with a practiced lift to his shoulders, "Everyone knows what happened."

"Is that why you're here? To offer best wishes to Miss Andrews or to take advantage of a situation she didn't understand?"

The odious man had the nerve to bristle. Kane hoped he could push him to misplace his temper. If that happened, he could easily terminate this man for the day. Perhaps the dismissal would last through eternity. He could only hope. Well, damn hope, he would have to make sure his wishes came true.

"No, I'd like to get to know her better. Will you send someone to tell her I'm here?"

Kane turned to Still Water Runs. "Tell Miss Andrews she has a visitor, a man. If she wants to see this man she can come downstairs. If she doesn't, please relay the message."

Still Water Runs nodded, turned on a moccasined foot then strode silently up the steps. Kane didn't offer a chair or a drink, as he was positive Mr. White would not be staying to take Lyssa anywhere. He understood this would happen. At this point, he cursed himself for not leaving the townhouse this morning when they were both ready. This encounter was distasteful, so much so the meeting with other men didn't bear repeating.

This man might pester them later at the country estate. Kane didn't have any intention of returning to London until the furor over the horrendous recital ran its course. The duchess, if she were here, would feel the same.

Deep Water Runs returned, no expression on his face. From the Lakota plains, the Sioux warrior had followed him to London. He called this man friend. More than once he saved his life.

"She says, 'no' to this man." He stepped back, his hands at his sides. "He is like dust in the wind to Miss Andrews. She doesn't want to see him this afternoon or ever."

"Dust in the wind?" White asked looking as if he had no idea what happened or what the words meant. "Did she say why?"

Still Water Runs didn't answer the question. Kane thought he would enlighten the man. "Miss Andrews, after yesterday, wishes to retire to my country estate. I believe she wants to find some solitary time to herself as well as a bit of peace for her shattered emotions. She is not used to the expectations of the season. Nor has she grown up in London. In her life she was free to come and go as she pleases. For the duchess, her aunt, she felt obligated to attend the recital even while she didn't want to be present."

"A woman shouldn't be allowed such freedom," White's voice was nearly a snarl. He was clearly displeased by the fact a woman didn't want to see him. "You should not allow her to dictate the terms of her courtship."

"Who better to dictate than her guardian?" Kane smiled. If she didn't tell him no, he certainly would have. He would always allow her a say in her life. However…there might be cases he would have to override. "I will tell her you were disappointed. That you regret the fact you couldn't meet her."

Kane didn't have any intention to say anything of the sort. He disliked this man with intensity. He was a pompous ass as far as he was concerned. Lyssa would not fall victim to a man such as this, not if he had the means at his disposal to keep her safe.

Still Water Runs walked with White to the door. When he returned, "I would have liked to kick him down the porch steps."

"Would rather have taken his scalp," Abernathy said fiercely, "If I knew how."

Kane chuckled at his friend's and servant's ardent declaration. Lyssa had become special to both men. "You and me both. Please tell Lyssa we are ready to leave unless she wishes to stay in the city."

"I'm ready." Lyssa flew down the steps her skirts swishing, tiny ankles flitting beguiling with each step as her dress swayed with her mad rush. By the time she skidded to a halt in front of him, she was panting for air, her breasts heaving delightfully with the tiny exertion.

He saw the mischievous twinkle in her eyes as she dashed toward him. The little minx had listened to the conversation. Her cheeks were bright with color. Her dark hair, unbound now tumbled down her back. He could see himself naked with her, the ink black locks wrapped around him. She appeared ravishing. His thoughts traveled to the long ride in the carriage with her sitting close to him. No, she would want to ride the distance on the Appaloosa. She wasn't dressed to ride, at least not in her usual britches and shirt. He noticed her breasts weren't bound tight.

The chuckle he held back was difficult. She appeared bright eyed, eager to leave. As usual her candid charm unraveled him. "You don't want to ride?"

"Do you? I could change." She seemed hesitant. "I would have to…" She looked down, not at her feet but at her bosom.

Kane felt positive he knew what she was thinking. Before he could look away from her breasts, her gaze shot to his crotch. He felt a sudden urge to cover himself. Still Water Runs laughed as if he knew what both were thinking. Abernathy looked away for a moment, red staining his long neck. The men didn't, couldn't. His thoughts were impossible for him to know.

"Lyssa." He tried to avoid those eyes. "If you want to ride, change your clothes now. If you want to sit in the carriage, we can be on our way."

She tossed him the cheeky smile he was coming to adore. The way she looked at him set his blood boiling. She played a dangerous game. "The carriage is my first choice if that is where you will be."

"If not?" he asked, positive he knew what was on her mind.

Another kiss also dominated his thoughts. He had no business thinking about intimacy with Lyssa. She was too young for him as well as to white for this Lakota warrior.

"Then I'll change now. Give me five minutes, maybe ten. I'll have to have one of my trunks unloaded."

At the thought of the wasted time, Kane decided the carriage was his first choice. "We will take the carriage." He wondered what outlandish question or comments she would utter during the following hours. Wondered too, if he could stop himself from pulling her onto his lap for shared intimacies. He couldn't think of a better way to pass the time from here to there.

Lyssa rushed out the door, her skirt flying around her ankles again. He wondered if she ever did anything slowly.

Before he could help her into the vehicle, White was beside her, his hand on her elbow. She jerked away. For a fleeting moment, the man's eyes shimmered with hate. The look vanished leaving Kane with the decided impression this man might indeed mean her harm. White appeared to be a man who did not handle rejection well. A shiver of apprehension for Lyssa swept inside. None of her suitors were acceptable. This man was worse than Sinclair. He was dangerous, arrogant in a malicious sort of way. Sinclair was just a bumbling idiot.

"You were told the lady didn't want to see you, White. What makes you think she would change her mind after a few minutes?"

Kane stepped forward seething inwardly, anger momentarily clouding his judgement. For a moment, he was reminded of the blundering Ritter. Except this man was calculating as well as cold. If he continued in this vein, the man might cause problems.

"I needed to hear the rejection from the lady," he ground out.

When White stepped toward Lyssa, Kane blocked his path. "No, you don't."

It was all he could do to stop from beating the man senseless. His temper escalated when White tried to step around him. "Get in the carriage, Lyssa. I'll be with you in a moment."

She did as he said. With a nod from him to Still Water Runs, he set the carriage in motion. His friend understood he would catch up to them when this matter was taken care of to his satisfaction. White would be more difficult than he thought previously. Kane's stallion grazed nearby waiting for him.

"You can't..."

"Go home, White. Don't come back. Miss Andrews won't change her mind about seeing you. Find another debutante with a title you can court. You won't get close to Miss Andrews."

The man muttered, cursing him as if he couldn't hear. The names he called him were far from flattering. Names he'd heard numerous times before this. Jonathon White could mean trouble. He would have to watch his back. Would have to make certain Lyssa was never left alone.

A few seconds later, Kane watched as White climbed inside his carriage. As the ostentatious vehicle trundled down the street, he said a silent prayer that the man would never return. He understood all too well the prayer was useless. White's transport turned the corner. Kane let out a slow even breath of air.

A few minutes later, he sat inside his carriage on a seat opposite Lyssa. She smiled at him. The soft way her lips parted coupled with the shine of pleasure in her eyes sent his body into a tailspin. Tender feelings for her erupted throughout his hard body. Slowly, this tiny young woman with her delicate features and large heart wormed her way into his heart. He didn't believe for a moment he could let her go. He was two kinds a fool.

She was his or would be soon. When the time came, he didn't quite know how he would explain his feelings to Ella. This attraction for her wasn't something he could fight. The emotions weren't something he'd ever felt before. Lyssa Andrews was made for him. They would fit together perfectly as one. Their hearts would share a beat.

At that moment, he wondered how well her father did ride. Well, if his talents were as good as his, he was a damn fine horseman. One day soon, he intended to give her proof of his abilities.

"Did the recital cause this man to come calling? I've never seen him before," she asked, her voice breathless, soft, and whispery. Her arms wrapped around her, it seemed she was protecting herself. "I don't like him. He makes my skin crawl along with the hair on the back of my neck to prickle. In many ways he's worse than Mr. Ritter. Don't understand why someone like that would come to court me. I haven't even met the man."

He imagined that very same whispery voice beneath him when he made love to her. Couldn't help the way he reacted to the sound. His masculine body was thoroughly aroused by the tenor of her words. He wished he could chase away her fears. Only time would do that.

"Suppose the performance did give him a reason. More men might come to call for the same motive. You did create quite the scandal."

He hated to tell her the man wanted something from her other than her love. The thought demeaned her, would make her feel less than she should. As she appeared now, she seemed remarkable to him. Strong. Vibrant. Intelligent. All woman.

"I know that type. Even in the states there are men who looked at me the way he did. They want only one thing." She held up her hands to stop him from talking. "They either want to tumble me in the hayloft or they want a piece of the Andrews Empire. What they don't seem to realize is all of it goes to Jess." Slowly, she let a breath of air sift silently from her lungs. The soft sound whispered in the thin tightly stressed atmosphere. "Jess didn't want either the title here or the land father built. He wants to find his own place then create his empire. He never wished to be given anything."

"I'm sorry, Lyssa. It can't be easy to know someone wants something from you besides your love."

He did feel sorry for women who so often were used as pawns by the men in their lives. Lyssa would not be hurt that way. He was the man to make certain love was what she found. Where Lys was concerned, his about-face didn't surprise him. She was unlike any woman he'd ever met. For now, he needed to come to terms with his new-found insight.

"Don't feel sorry for me, Kane. All I want is a man to love me for me. I will find that man."

She stared at him hard her gaze searching him as if she could find answers.

"I believe you will."

He meant his words as he was beginning to hope that man would be him.

"What did Mr. White want? Did he tell you? Damn and blast, I've never met Jonathon White. Never set eyes on him before this afternoon. He wasn't at the ball. Was he? The recital?"

"From what I know of the bloke, what he wants is the title that comes with your hand in marriage."

Leaning over, his forearms on his thighs, he took her hands in his. She was warm and soft, so delicately built she stole his breath. The slight trembling was something he wished he could stop. "I'm sorry, Little Bit. You're right about men though it doesn't please me to say the words."

"My imagination soars to find a man who will dream about me, a man who will put me first as I will put him first. It's what mother and father have though they didn't come by the emotions easily. Believe my father loved her from the moment he saw her then never stopped loving her. She loved him too until she discovered he was a smuggler."

She laughed softly, warming him from the inside out, wishing he could create more laughter to share with her.

"Remember, you shouldn't bandy those words anywhere else. From what Ella has told me your, parents still visit England from time to time. He could still be accused of the crime, perhaps even convicted."

"My aunt and uncle always protect them when they visit. You understand Uncle Drake has important and powerful connections. I'm not worried. You're right though. I've no business tempting fate. Though I trust you."

She brought his hands to her lips, kissed his knuckles one at a time. When she turned her gaze toward him, the blue of her eyes darkened. He wanted to remove all her sorrows, fix all her problems. He should have listened to her, never insisted she perform at the recital. The past was a mistake he would never make again. He would never make her do something that wouldn't please her.

He cleared his throat as he drew in a fresh breath of jasmine scented air. "Despite all this time, there are still wanted posters with his likeness sketched on them," Kane reminded her as his body hardened further under her gentle kisses.

She smiled at him. His heart lurched. He felt like an untried youth with his first girl.

"Father knows. Uncle Drake has tried to get rid of those hated posters. Hasn't succeeded. Though the likeness could be just about anyone with dark hair."

"I've seen one poster," Kane admitted wondering about her father.

Wondering too how she was brought up so free and independent. It was the way of the Sioux to nurture their children in this manner. During his childhood, he roamed free. Did what he liked without consequence. Women though were treated differently. They never had as much freedom as their male counterparts. The time didn't come for him that he had to bow down to rules until he became the earl. At that time his life held boundaries he couldn't easily circumnavigate.

"So, what did you think? Is my father devilishly handsome? Mother thinks so. I've heard her say that fact too many times to count. I do believe you are more handsome than father."

She laughed softly.

Unable to resist, Kane pulled her onto his lap.

"What are you doing?"

There was no sound of fright in her voice, not that he expected to hear fear. This is what she'd been after for days. "Don't care. Men are men, what's inside their heart is most important, not the pretty face. Sometimes a man with a pretty face is more dangerous than a man with a scar to detract from his looks."

Gently, he ran a fingertip along her jaw. When she looked at him, the look held an infinite amount of tenderness. The emotion was written there for him to see. Ah, he knew she wanted him. Understood she needed his love. If that were true, she would have everything she wanted. He would give her the moon and the stars if he could. It seemed to Kane, in that moment, he did succumb to all he'd ever felt for her. For him there was no longer any hesitation. He wanted her, needed for her to become his wife.

"Have you ever loved a woman, truly loved her with all your heart? I understand you thought you did."

His gut tightened at her innocent question. "What I felt was lust. At the time, I did believe the feeling was love. Suffice it to say I was wrong. I was too young to know." He didn't understand his blatant honesty with her. He wouldn't lie to her. "Young lust for that matter. I'd never been with a woman for any length of time before her. You might say she was my first actual relationship. She did things to me that changed my life forever."

"I've never been with a man. Shared a few kisses behind the stable, one by the pond near our home. Those kisses didn't move me as yours did. I wanted you to kiss me the day at the pond as well as the time before that. Though you knew that."

Lightly, he touched the tip of her nose. Trailed that fingertip along her neck then across her collarbone memorizing every delicate part of her. He wanted to follow the path his finger traced with his lips and tongue.

Wanted so much more.

"Do you wish for me to kiss you now?" His voice grew husky with the building desire only his Lys could inspire.

He prayed her answer would be in the affirmative. The carriage ride would pass with blinding speed if he did so, if she gave her permission, he chuckled softly.

"Yes," the one word was a breathy whisper in the jasmine scented air.

She closed her eyes as if waiting.

Kane held the amusement he felt behind his teeth. "Open your eyes, Little Bit. Need to see them sparkle with passion when I kiss you. Want to see them darken so I know you truly want me."

She did so.

He touched the corner of her mouth with his lips then the sweet dimple. The caress was barely a murmur in time. He felt the soft breath of her air move across him. The sensation touched him deeply. His trembling hands held the sides of her face as he continued with tiny kisses, coaxing kisses, seducing kisses. Her sigh rippled in long ribbons of desire tearing at his senses. The kiss was short and sweet. He wanted the opposite, long as well as deep, heated.

Kane felt as if he was a man well and truly damned. The more of her he tasted the more he wanted. While he shouldn't be sweet-talking Lyssa, coaxing her to want him, he couldn't help himself. She was so bloody sweet and adorable, honeyed, and spicy, saucy at times. Her taste of innocence coupled with a woman slaked with passion along with desire was his undoing, had been from the beginning from the moment he saw her standing behind Ella. He needed to thoroughly love her, as she deserved to be loved, with tender loving care. For the first time in too many years, he could see a future with a woman, this woman. No one else would do for him. She was the woman he'd been waiting for.

He ran a hand along her back, gently pressing her closer. Her rounded breasts pushed against his chest. She didn't wear a corset. Her nipples hardened where they touched the hard wall of his chest. His teeth tenderly closed over the tiny lobe of her ear. She sighed softly fitting herself against his body.

It seemed she melted against his chest turning to liquid warmth. Her hands circled his neck before her fingers swept through his hair. He undid the pins holding her raven locks in place. As each strand fell loose, he ran the silk through his fingers. Everything about her touched a place in his heart.

Once more his lips touched upon hers. Nibbling and coaxing he wanted her to open for him. She didn't seem to know what he wanted. He tugged on her lower lip. She ran her tongue across his. His groan rumbled up from deep in his belly. She had no idea what she did to him with that simple caress.

"Open for me, Little Bit. Let me delve inside. Allow me to taste your sweet nectar." Once more he tugged. Her lips moved apart. His tongue slipped slowly inside the heated warmth she so willingly offered.

She whimpered then purred as he explored the warm inner sanctum she presented to him. The tempest inside escalated. He covered her lips with his mouth. Repeatedly he tasted and caressed with his teeth and tongue. Tentatively she reciprocated pushing her sweet little tongue between his teeth, exploring him, investigating with open curiosity. She tasted of mint, smelled of jasmine and her own special womanly scent. Her fingers clutched his shoulders as if she hung on for dear life.

He slid his hands along her sides. His fingers touched upon the ladder of her ribs stopping below her breasts. The tender undersides connected with the back of his hand. He swallowed hard, understanding he couldn't toss her skirts in the carriage. Making love to her inside the vehicle was out of the question. He wanted her first time to be special.

Suddenly, guilt assailed him for even thinking about making love to this inquisitive lively young woman. He was a jaded bastard for assuming she would be his. After all he learned the lesson a long time ago. Somehow, he could not seem to stop the wild yearning she generated in him. Understanding he was taking advantage of her inexperience was not going to stop him. If she was willing to give herself to him, thoughts of marriage collided with the hate he understood grew from white women.

Lyssa wasn't like any white woman he'd ever known.

As if sensing his momentary hesitation, "Kane? What's wrong?"

"Nothing Lys, nothing a few more kisses won't help alleviate."

Where she was concerned coupled with the way his traitorous body felt as his sex rapidly turned to steel, more kisses would increase his problem not diminish the ache escalating between his thighs.

Once more his lips covered her mouth. She responded, her body pressing against his with fervor he never felt before in a woman.

"I want you, Kane," she whispered when the passion slowly ebbed with the cessation of the kiss. "But...I don't know what exactly I want."

"Do you understand what you are implying?"

"No," the word was thin, a soft whisper in the heated air.

With gentle hands he moved strands of hair that had come undone from her face. Tenderly, he touched her mouth with his lips. When he looked into her eyes, she smiled beautifully at him. "You are so bloody sweet."

"No." She touched his chin, the tip of her finger moving slowly across his flesh. "No, Kane I don't understand. Nonetheless I want you to teach me, show me what love between a man and a woman is supposed to be."

His big body shuddered at the tenderness he felt from her. Slowly, she was becoming everything to him. Lyssa would never betray him. The first time with her he wanted her on his furs in his lodge. He wanted to see her in the wedding dress his mother lovingly crafted for his bride so many years ago even though there was no woman fitting that role at the time.

~ * ~

Lyssa was afraid he would stop. Afraid he wouldn't stop. All her thoughts centered on him, the incredible sensations he generated with the gentle touch of his lips against hers.

His finger tucked gently under her chin, he slowly lifted until she looked into his eyes. His were a dark shimmering shade of blue, rimmed in dark blue-velvet. He lowered his mouth once more to caress her lips with his. He tasted so warm.

"You taste so bloody good, Little Bit. Open for me one more time. Let me savor you. I've wanted to do this since I first saw you standing behind the duchess and framed deliciously in my doorway. I need to taste you, to keep tasting you. His hands rested on the small of her back. God knows I've tried to resist your sweetness."

It seemed he meant to continue this until they reached home. She had no objections, not one.

She didn't say anything but she opened her mouth for him. Damn and blast his taste was heady as he explored inside her mouth. He touched his tongue to hers. Teeth, tongue, lips; everything to savor left her breathless with longing. Hanging on to this moment paramount in her head, she met his tongue with hers, danced then played with him until she whimpered. The small broken sound flowed from deep in the back of her throat into him. She clung to him, hoping then praying he wouldn't stop.

Moving closer to his large body, her hands resting on his shoulder, she ran her fingers through his hair, reveling in the soft, silken texture. The strands were so dark, midnight black it seemed to be. The leather thong he bound his hair with fell to the floor so she could sift her fingers through the long silken length.

Suddenly, she became the aggressor, the leader in this new game of love he was teaching her how to play. If she didn't want him to stop, she would have to show him how much she needed him. Her fingers gripping his shoulders, she pulled him closer. She tasted him. Her tongue ran across his teeth then into the sultry depth of his mouth exploring the dark recesses. He growled softly as he responded to her hesitant steps to keep him close.

"Not here in the carriage, Lyssa. Won't make love to you here, at least not the first time. I'm not going to teach you more than kissing until I've soft furs to set you upon."

His hands roamed over her, soothing, caressing then enticing more and more. The buttons down the front of her dress were flicked open by his nimble fingers. It seemed he stared at her for the longest time, seeming to drink in her body. She reached with her hands to cover herself, flushed as well as embarrassed by his ardent perusal. She didn't understand her sudden embarrassment. This was what she wanted. Wasn't it? Butterflies danced deep in her belly, a strange, heated ache between her thighs escalated.

"No, don't cover yourself," he murmured as he held her hands away. "I need to look at you."

"S-so, what are you doing? Undressing me, is that part of what we are supposed to do?"

Of course, it is, ninny. You know your brother doesn't make love wearing his clothes. Her hands found purchase behind his head while he kissed her. His lips trailed just above the fabric of her chemise. It seemed an inferno blazed within seething through her, pounding until she could barely think.

"Th-that's not kissing. Is it?"

The way her words squeaked out she didn't recognize her voice. She wanted to be a woman in his arms. Now, she sounded like a child, a little girl.

He chuckled softly while his teeth pulled on the ribbons holding her undergarment closed. When he looked up, his deep blue eyes were tender. They also burned and shimmered in the muted light of the carriage. The fabric fell apart. Her bountiful breasts were bared to his gaze as well as his lips. He touched one crest with his thumb lightly rubbing across the tip. She swallowed hard, needing more than he gave. Tempest, flames…swept through her.

"Other places on a woman's body respond to kisses. Do you want to learn about all those places? I think you must. Tell me where you want me to kiss you."

It seemed he didn't wait for an answer. His teeth grazed across the fullness of her breasts, moving from one to the other, giving equal and devoted attention to both. His large callused hands roamed, searching for what she wasn't all that sure. What she did understand was that she never wanted him to stop.

She mulled his question over in her mind unsure of letting him see her nearly naked. "Kane you can see me..."

"Yes..." he whispered while he slipped his mouth beneath fabric of her chemise until his tongue curled around a hardened peak. He suckled then nipped, grazed the tip with his teeth until she cried out in a burst of air from her lungs.

Her gasp surprised her, as did the burning ache between her legs. He made her twist and coil deep inside. She arched against him, silently begging for more. With his lips and teeth, he teased one hardened crest then with his fingers he tormented the other. It seemed she pulled him closer, her sharp nails biting into his shoulder through the fabric of his white lawn shirt. When his mouth returned to hers, he continued to caress and tease other parts of her. His large hand rested on her belly before traveling lower. She felt the touch of his calloused hands on her leg as a breath of air whispered against the naked length.

She found her legs slowly parting for him. He trailed his fingers along the inside of her legs to the top of her thigh before heading back to caress the back of her knee.

"You're opening your legs for me. Did you know that?"

He continued the assault, playing havoc with her senses. She ran her hand along his back, basking in the width and breadth that so fascinated her. He was so big and strong. He dwarfed her completely. Amber sunshine sifted across his strong, chiseled features. Light shimmered within his deep blue eyes. He looked upon her with admiration glittering in his eyes.

"I..." she stammered unknowing what to do next. "Is that what you want?" She sucked air that didn't pretend to go inside her lungs.

"Only if it's what you want."

He switched his attention to her other leg, roaming, sightseeing, until she jumped, startled by the result of his quest. His fingers touched her, stroked her more intimately before backing away. "You are so wet, so ready for me. Did you know that?"

"Ready?" she queried, her voice trembling with the passion he generated as she found her legs were opening wider.

She found she wanted his hands, his fingers to continue their exploration. Lyssa didn't understand any of this. All she knew was that she wanted more of Kane. Needed everything he could give. She felt as if she waited a lifetime for this moment.

"You are so bloody adorable. I'm damned if I do and damned if I don't." Kane continued his assault for a few more minutes. He explored until he touched her most intimately again.

Unexpectedly, he stopped. Beneath his breath he swore softly while he pulled her skirt to thoroughly cover her legs.

"Kane?" She touched her lips with the tip of her tongue then her fingertip. They were swollen, slightly sore. "Don't stop? I want you to..."

She didn't know how to tell him what it was she wanted. Her brother and his friends spoke of this in lewd terms. What he was expertly doing to her body didn't feel lewd. The ways in which he touched her felt so right the thought stole her breath.

"We must cease. We are almost home. I need to put your clothing to rights before anyone sees you."

With slowness that felt reluctant on his part, Kane's hands left her. Slowly, he held the ribbons to her chemise between his long fingers. "This is not the way," he pulled in a deep breath of air, "not the way I wanted to leave you. You understand that don't you? I would have liked to give you more pleasure."

"P-pleasure, you...I don't want you to stop," her whisper was halted by a broken sound as he gave one last nip to the tender bud he wrestled with earlier. He stared at the tip for the longest time.

"Don't want to stop either. Stopping is a necessity though."

With finesse she understood was born from experience, he laced her chemise, pulling the fabric together before he buttoned her dress.

Lyssa didn't know what to think or for that matter how to feel. Unexpectedly, he seemed detached as if he hadn't shared the most intimate moments of her life with her. For reasons she didn't understand, she was certain he wouldn't take up where he left off once they were inside the house. She could tell by the grim slant of his mouth as well as the deep creases in his forehead he easily, too easily, put this behind him. It seemed to her, he regretted his actions. She didn't want him to regret what they did together. She certainly didn't.

No, when they left the carriage, there would be other things to do. She would need to unpack. Dinner would be served. A bath would be in order. Still Water Runs would do his duties throughout the house. Abernathy would arrive later then hover in different places overseeing the other servants. Privacy would be nonexistent unless he carried her to his room. He wouldn't do that. Moisture hovered in the back of her throat. He wanted her on his furs...

She noticed the bulge at his crotch before looking into his eyes. She couldn't believe how bold she was about to be. Seconds ticked by while she thought, "May I touch?"

He seemed to understand what she asked. The dark blue shimmer of his eyes grew hotter. His smile flashed, his even white teeth showing against the bronze of his flesh. He caressed her cheek with his knuckles then lower. The look he gifted her with seemed to appreciate her. "Not tonight, Lys. I would explode if you touched me." His voice was strained, almost brittle.

"When?"

Her question seemed to startle him. "I don't know. Though now is not a good time."

He glanced out the window. She wished she could find a means to climb into his mind so she could be privy to his thoughts. The carriage rolled to a stop then swayed as the big man Kane called friend jumped from the driver's seat.

Lyssa didn't like the fact that he refused to answer her question. An answer was what she deserved. It didn't seem he meant to give her one. She wanted him to tell her he would see her in her room tonight. He wasn't going to do that. She sensed the knowledge as if the information simmered deep in her gut. He didn't have to say the words.

"I don't regret anything you did, anything I did," she blurted the words, wishing she could erase the intense heat stealing across her face. Every caress of his lips she remembered vividly. Every place his teeth grazed and his tongue followed was scalded in her memory.

Kane touched her, ran his knuckles along her cheek one more time before following the column of her neck. "I'm glad to hear that. I wouldn't want you to feel any other way."

"Do...do you regret what we shared? The kisses? The other?"

She knew she shouldn't ask. This was too much for her though. She smoothed her skirts. Pushed at her hair. His stony silence both unnerved and terrified her. She wanted to kick him so he would snap out of this strange distance he generated between them.

"You look as if you've been thoroughly ravished, as if you've just come from my bed."

A shaky breath entered her lungs. Desperate, she clung to his arms. "If that is so, I don't want anyone except you to see me."

She did feel ravished. Only his eyes should see her this way. She didn't want his friend to make assumptions. Even if those assumptions were true.

"Still Water Runs, go on. Leave us to follow. Seems the lady..."

He stopped speaking as if he didn't want to finish the sentence.

Her face heated even more, as did the rest of her. When she tried to stand, her legs wouldn't hold her weight. "Kane?"

With her hand placed on her chest, she felt confused, disoriented. Dazed, she thought for a moment she might tumble to the ground.

"You're all right. I feel the same. In time we will finish what was begun here. I've a powerful lot of thinking to do before that happens."

Warmly, he touched the tip of her nose, after that roamed across her lip. "Know you hold great importance in my heart. There is much that lies between us. I will have to come to terms with those things that have shaped me for a decade. I cannot do that in an instant."

Lyssa knew he lied about feeling the same as she did when he scooped her into his arms. His long, booted strides carried her up the porch then into the house. He set her on one of the wing chairs facing the fireplace. A few minutes later, he handed her a brandy.

"Drink, the liquid will warm you. Would like to say the alcohol will clear your head. I can't do that."

"You carried me...why?"

Lyssa followed his command, sipping the drink letting the liquid warm a path down her throat to her stomach.

He chuckled; his grin broad. "It seems I had no choice. You couldn't walk worth a damn. Didn't want you to have to crawl. That would not have been gentlemanly of me."

Her eyes widened as she stared at him. The brandy she drank continued to burn all the way to her stomach. "You said you felt the same."

"I did. Still do for that matter."

"You could walk," she accused him feeling out of sorts with the notion. "I couldn't."

Kane sat down next to her. His long well-muscled legs stretched out in front of him. He closed his eyes while he sipped, his thoughts private. "True."

"Then...?"

His glass sat on the table between the two chairs. His dark gaze fastened on her. "I've had more practice at this sort of thing. You've none. After love making of that intensity, it takes powerful concentration to walk. You've no experience whatsoever."

Love making of that intensity?

Insecurities assailed her. In his assessment, he was correct. She had no experience. Didn't know why that would matter. She thought, well she thought men wanted chaste women. Kane was so different in so many ways. Maybe he didn't want a woman with no experience. "Was I that obvious?"

She felt so inadequate she didn't know what to do.

"Your lack of experience is adorable, Lys. I wouldn't have you any other way." His heated gaze turned to the red-gold flames in front of them. He stared at the fire, twirling the amber liquid in his glass. "You melted in my arms. You know that I felt wonderful at your response to me."

Despite what he said, his lack of interest in her now hurt. "Are you going to finish what we started?"

She caught her trembling lower lip beneath her teeth. Lyssa didn't know why she asked such a stupid question. He'd withdrawn from her just before they left the carriage. She saw the indifference in the way he looked at her.

"As I said earlier not tonight. We'll have dinner. Perhaps we can talk at that time. Maybe not," he said after a moment. "I want you to understand that what happened in the carriage cannot continue until..." he paused in thought. "Well hell."

Her understanding of the previous events traveled as far as she could toss him. Moisture filled her eyes. Attempting to blink back the tears, she looked away. She didn't want him to see how his words affected her or how they hurt her. When she turned back, the scowl she knew so well deepened. "Did I do something wrong?"

The question seemed to jerk Kane from his distant thoughts. The grin he turned on her widened. "No, Lys, you were perfect in every way. The fault is with me. Don't worry about things. What is happening between us will all work out for the best."

It didn't seem he wanted to continue the conversation even though she felt lost and vulnerable.

For the best? In whose opinion?

She wasn't about to allow him to stop with those hasty pitched out words. Though she understood if he chose to remain silent, she wouldn't have much to say about what they would and would not do. Still, she was going to ask, demand a better answer if possible. She wasn't perfect at anything. "Why then? Tell me."

"Before I make love to you Lys, I've some serious thinking ahead of me."

If he had to think seriously then she should do the same. She almost gave herself to him while he sweet-talked her innocence away. He must understand how easy she was. He wouldn't want easy. She wasn't like the bar maid, flaunting herself. She had though. Humiliation at her easy compliance swamped her.

He cleared his throat before he continued. "Taking your gift of innocence from you without promises of a future together is not something I can acknowledge. You're precious to so many people. Whether you care or not the fact remains the same, I'm a breed. People will look down upon you. They might hurt you just to get at me. Need to make sure your parents won't come at me with a branding iron or a whip if I marry you. If I take the step, it's permanent, forever."

With that said he turned inward, his thoughts shuttered from her. Most likely he said as much as he intended to say.

Lyssa didn't want to appear too eager about the way he worded his thoughts. He did mention marriage. Perhaps, in time he would make love to her. She was a lot of things, however patience was not one of her stronger suits.

His words were something she'd wanted to hear from him. He said more though. Implied things she guessed at. He had no idea just who her parents were or how they thought. They weren't prejudiced. "Mother and father won't care about your heritage if I love you. You're a good man, not like some of the men who came calling on me the last couple of days or even before I left for the season. Those are the men they wouldn't like even though they seem to have everything in order even though they are not breeds as you so describe yourself. Those men, their heart is not where it should be."

For a moment, he pinched the bridge of his nose. His eyes narrowed as he stared at her a lazy grin hinting at taking the crease lines from his forehead. "I would give you whatever you asked. Want to hear the song in your heart. Want to know how to make you happy. Want to hear you sing the bawdy songs your brother inadvertently taught you, perhaps the next verse to the one you sang at the recital. As I told you earlier, I've much to think about. The future must be taken seriously.

Your innocence is precious."

"Being with you makes me happy. You've already created a song in my heart, one that sings for you, only you."

She wondered if he rode as well as her father. If not, she no longer cared.

He shot her a look she didn't understand. The expression seemed to be a cross between a smile and a scowl. "If I made love to you now, tonight, I would be as bad as the gossips make me out to be. I'm a rake, a cad of the worst sort. I'm not going to take advantage of you now or ever."

"No, no you aren't a cad. You are wonderful. If I'm willing, that's not taking advantage."

Kane groaned low as the sound rumbled from deep in the back of his throat. "You don't know me. You don't understand that I've always taken what I wanted including women. They are always eager, too eager sometimes. You were willing because I played on your innocence. I've ignored..." He blew out a long stream of air, "I've ignored what is in my heart, until I met you."

"Do you want me?" she interrupted a bright smile forming as she waited hesitantly for his answer. Perhaps he was being noble and possibly he did want to continue. "If you do, you can have me. From your words, from what you are telling me, it sounds as if you do."

Lyssa felt crushed when he didn't answer. Instead of giving her a response, he stood. Wiped his hands along his pants. He slanted her a cursory look before his long strides took him from one side of the room to the other to repeat the process several times. When he finally left the room, she was terrified he wouldn't come back inside. She recalled when he rode from the townhouse to the lake on Montgomerie land for a cold swim. Now, to get away from her he simply walked out the front door.

Her heart dropped.

A few minutes later, the rhythmic chopping of wood coming from outside startled her curiosity. Slowly, she walked to a window where she could look toward the sound. Kane stood near the stable, his shirt tossed haphazardly on the ground. His bronze flesh glistened in the light left by the lantern. His broad, muscular chest was naked to her gaze.

He chopped wood. A simple act yet so strange after the intense conversation they just had.

Jess chopped wood whenever he was frustrated about something or with someone. Fascinated, she watched the rhythmic play of his muscles while he worked. The easy way he swung the axe. His arms were powerful, more so than either Jess' or her father's.

She started for the back door intent on continuing their conversation even though it seemed Kane wanted nothing to do with the discussion they'd begun a few minutes past. She needed to understand.

"I wouldn't do that." Still Water Runs spoke from behind her, his presence imposing.

She felt his disdain without looking into his eyes. "He needs time and space. Believe he told you as much as he is now willing. He is not used to this type of dilemma, a problem he cannot solve easily."

Whirling, her hand at her throat from the shock of his voice so close to her. "Why ever not. I'm a dilemma now? We've unfinished business to talk about. He's running from me. I need to understand why."

"I've known my friend all my life. This journey with you that he is taking is not easy for him. The way he feels about you confuses him, going against all the basic rules of his life. His emotions are at odds with everything he's believed for the last years, since he was horse whipped nearly to death for courting the wrong girl. Since the duchess saved his life. Since he rode free on the plains, only the wind in his hair and the sunshine overhead to warm him. There are so many things you cannot begin to comprehend."

It seemed she heard only two words. Her gut churned as her mind imagined him tied to a stake, a whip lashing his back until he almost died. Would have perished that day if the duchess didn't step in and save him. She'd made guesses about this. Now the vivid truth was put in front of her.

"He was what?"

Her heart caught in the back of her throat at the thought of someone lashing him of blood and scars. No wonder he scowled. There had been little in his life to smile about.

"Black Thunder asked me to make sure you remained comfortable as well as inside the house. My friend needs to be alone with his reflections. If you walk out there, to watch or to talk, he will not be able to put his beliefs into a coherent line that will make sense to him. There will be nothing gained. Your presence will not help him achieve this task he is set on. He needs to come full circle so he can walk a path to you. The trail to you is the path I think he wants to find."

"Oh..."

Walk a path to me? Come full circle. At this moment her emotions were a jumbled mess. She didn't have wood to chop so she could ease her frustrations. If he owned a smaller axe, she could chop her own wood. No, tomorrow, if he were still distant, she would ride. She could do that. Only she wasn't allowed to go very far just to the edge of his property, to the tree line. Restrictive walls began to close around her. Suffocation gripped her throat. Never had she been confined. He was not her jailor. Why did he act that way?

"You will come eat?" he asked as he showed her the way to the dining room. "There is plenty of food. Black Thunder might not eat tonight so there is no reason to wait for him. I will keep something warm waiting so there is food for him before he goes to bed."

The dining room was large, the table almost as large. Loneliness assailed her. One place setting was laid out on the table. She didn't want to eat by herself. The place felt empty. Moisture hovered in the back of her throat threatening.

"Will you eat dinner with me?" she queried, watching as he seemed to back into the kitchen.

"It would not be proper to do so. I'm a servant."

"Damn and blast proper. You're also his friend. I hope mine also. If you won't sit with me, I'll take the food to my room." The window in her chamber looked toward the stable, toward the chopping block where he worked. She could watch him. "I'll have a bottle of wine too." In her entire life, she never felt this alone or vulnerable.

He kissed me. He touched me in places...

She placed a finger on her mouth. Her lips were slightly sore, could tell they were inflamed. She'd melted into his embrace. Opened for him, surrendered. Would have given everything of herself to him.

He rejected her.

She didn't understand anything Still Water Runs told her. *Walk a circle back to me?*

"I will put the food on a tray, the wine also. Go to your room. I'll bring your dinner to you. I'll also send hot water for a bath. Ring for me if there is anything else you might need."

This was not what she anticipated when he was kissing her in the carriage. Didn't expect him to run from her. He had to think about making love to her. Lyssa supposed she must have done something right even though she didn't comprehend why he had to think about his feelings.

He certainly knew how to kiss. She touched her still puffed-up lips with a fingertip thinking about how she felt when his lips molded so gently over hers, when she tasted him. Caught the scent of him. Her brazenness astonished her. When she closed her eyes, her imagination brought back all the sensations.

In front of Still Water Runs, she turned to him. "You called Kane Black Thunder? Is that another one of his names? He has so many." Yes, Kane Michael Murphy, his English name. Black, by his friends and now Black Thunder was the name Still Water Runs called him.

"Black Thunder is his Sioux name given to him by his father. Black of course is because he is the Earl of Blackmore. His father seemed to know he would return home someday. Go on, Miss Andrews, retire to your room. I'll be there with your food in a few minutes. Where he is concerned use patience. If you do so, you will reap the rewards."

Rewards? She wondered what exactly those were.

Her footsteps led her to the room assigned to her. She was to sleep in the wing as far away from his bedroom as he could get her. The smile forming on her mouth, caught in her heart. If she could, she would find a way to share his bed.

~ * ~

Kane looked to the window, Lyssa's room. Her gaze on him warmed his heart. He liked nothing better than to watch her. He understood by leaving her tonight, he hurt her. That wasn't something that made him proud. Loving her went against all his intentions. For him, white women were taboo. Kissing her that first time was a colossal mistake. The soft and so very tender caress caused him to need more from her to want more. After that one small intimacy, he saw her in his future. The one thought terrified him. Wrapped up in that single kiss was everything he'd been missing in his life. She was nothing like the other women he'd known. Nothing like the first woman he thought to fall in love with, the woman he thought at one time he might find a long-term relationship with. That was so very many years in his past. He was older and wiser now.

Miss Andrews touched a place in his world-weary soul. Slowly, this tiny slip of a woman mended that part of his heart he thought would never heal. He would not hurry to become intimate with her even though he wanted desperately to possess her, to bury himself deep inside the heat of her body. To know her completely as a man would know his woman.

The instant she walked into her bedroom and the light flickered there, he understood she would watch him. It didn't seem she could help herself. He didn't know how he felt about that prospect. Her eyes upon him, watching and wondering what he thought. How could he keep his distance from her when all his being cried out that she was his woman? All he needed to do was to go to her. She would surrender herself to him.

He wanted to marry her. She had no idea how drastically her life would change when she married a breed. The word was horrible. The sentiments attached to it worse. Even so far away, the dear English people seemed to feel the same as they did in the States. To some his being a breed, he was less than human. If he did come to terms, he would wed her in both worlds. He intended to marry her in the Sioux fashion then when the duke and duchess returned, he would wed her in the church. Hell, he'd take her to Baltimore and her family for a third wedding if that was something she would like.

It was a fine notion.

So terribly unpractical.

The first time he made love to Lyssa, he wanted her beneath him on the furs in his lodge. Perhaps if he took her to his teepee, she would begin to understand him better. He would show her the way of his people. That would be a fine thing. If she accepted him wholly, that would be even finer.

Bloody eyes, he didn't understand himself at this moment. She was willing. He was outside chopping logs. He could have her tonight if he came to terms with the outrageous escalation of his emotions. In his wildest dreams, he never thought to meet a woman like his Lys.

She was all he wanted. So, why the devil was he waiting? Why was he tormenting both of them?

When he looked up from his musing, Still Water Runs stood close by. "She is taken care of though she is not pleased with her abandonment by you. I'm sure she will talk your ear off when given the chance. You should not ignore the young lady for too long. She cares deeply for you."

"There was no choice." He didn't like himself now. When they parted, she was aroused to the point where he could have slipped inside her with great ease. He could have satisfied her without penetrating. She was passionate and enticing. He wasn't proud of what he did in the carriage, yet he didn't regret one moment.

"You did too much sweet-talking on your way here. Your actions as well as your words are like sugar to her. They taste sweet but they vanish after a moment. Possibly it would have been best if the two of you rode your horses instead." Still Water Runs chuckled seeming to find amusement in his distress. "You would not have spent the hours kissing if you'd done so. Both of you would not be in a state right now. You have an outlet, the chopping of the wood. How do you think Miss Andrews is going to ease the arousal you generated in her?"

"It was that obvious?" He did tell her she appeared as if she'd been ravished, that she looked as if she'd just risen from her lover's bed.

"You didn't fasten her gown correctly." Still Water Runs chortled at his words.

Kane felt heat rise to his forehead even while he saw the devilish smirk grow on his friend's countenance. "I didn't?" He must have been more distracted than he thought at the time.

"Her lips were swollen and slightly red, her hair disheveled while her bodice was fastened haphazardly as if done in haste. As I said before, she looked as if she just came from her lover's bed."

Sighting in on his friend's smirk, "She came from her lover's arms not his bed." It was only a matter of time before she found herself in his bed. "Don't see anything amusing here."

"If I were you, neither would I. Shall we leave it at that?"

"What else did she have to say?" He looked to the window. She wasn't standing there now staring down at him.

"She is quiet, hurt, introspective. Your woman doesn't understand why you abandoned her. Hers is a fair question. Don't you think? Possibly a few answers would be appropriate. She is an innocent, unwise to the ways of the male species."

Guilt swallowed him whole. True enough, he was a bastard of the worst sort to leave her the way he did. It was not well done of him. Again, the thought he should never have kissed her blindsided him. It was the kisses that brought him to this point. Every intention he possessed warned him from growing too close to her. He ignored his inner advice simply because for some reason he saw a future with her.

Somehow, he understood his Gods brought her to him, to heal his soul along with his heart. Lys said as much. She told him she meant to create smiles for him to see the world with. He was supposed to laugh not scowl.

What did he do in return? He brought pain to her life while she taught him to laugh and to love. He never thought to fall in love or marry. Now that was all he could think about.

Lys was his.

"Hers is a question I want to answer. I didn't speak false when I told her I had to think."

He didn't know where the path he was about to walk led. All he understood was that he meant to walk that trail of life with her. They would find a way to live in this world together. She would help him figure how to do it.

When he closed his eyes, he saw the prairie running endlessly in his sight. Saw the mountains rising high on the horizon topped with snow. He also saw England, his townhouse in the city along with his country estate. He had one foot in each world. When he agreed to leave the prairie with his grandfather, he put the plains and the mountains behind him. His deepest fears fought with his deepest wishes. He would have to choose.

All were part of the trail he might decide to walk with Lys. He made promises to his grandfather. If he left England permanently to live in Lakota territory, the lies he spoke would settle hard around him. He was a man of his word. Lys would never be happy living on the prairie. His people ran from white soldiers. Her life would be at stake. He couldn't do that to her.

Shouldn't she have a say?

By the beliefs of his people, she would not. His woman would follow him wherever he chose. Somehow, he didn't think Lys would prove quite as obedient as all that. He looked to the window a smile on his lips. She was not brought up in the Sioux fashion. No, she lived her life believing she had a voice…that her opinion counted.

Once again, she stood behind the panes watching him. Her small fingers were fisted in the curtain. By the way her body moved, he was certain she sobbed. His heart split into two pieces. Still, he didn't dare go to her.

When he did make love to her, claim her as his wife, he needed to be sure of his path. At this moment he was not.

Chapter Six

Two weeks passed. It seemed to Kane he made no progress with his decisions except in the chopping of the wood. He had enough piles chopped to last two maybe three winters. Now he alternated between his lodge and the house. Frustration ate at him. With each passing second, he wanted and needed her more. What was holding him back? Fear…terror he was making a foolish decision kept him from going to her.

Dinners were accomplished in silence. After a tension filled meal, Lyssa would excuse herself to go to her chamber. She no longer seemed to appreciate his company. Her entire demeanor changed perceptibly over the weeks he avoided her. What could he expect?

To follow her into her room would be heaven. He didn't dare take the next step until he was certain of himself as well as his feelings. His mind wavered between his promise to himself and what was in his heart.

His people believed duty and loyalty to be fine, strong qualities. His duties lie here in England. He didn't know if she would agree to travel with him to the plains. Didn't know what was in her heart. Why would she want to spend winters freezing in a lodge made from animal skins? He sensed though, she yearned for adventures. She was entirely happy in England. His was a conundrum he couldn't figure out. The worst part was that he was afraid to ask. Where Lys was concerned, he was a coward. Never did he recall such naked terror.

Still Water Runs would remind him she wasn't happy, because he gave her a cold shoulder. While he spent his time chopping wood and doing whatever backbreaking work he could find, Still Water Runs informed him she rode.

Every day after he left for the lodge she would go to the stable. According to his friend she didn't ride with a saddle. Instead, she draped a blanket over the Appaloosa secured with a surcingle. He chuckled to himself. The one time she tried to put the saddle on her horse, she couldn't lift the weight. The surprise was that she could ride bareback.

That was an oddity for an English woman. She wasn't English. He supposed he should spend more time at dinner asking her about her family, her life in the States. Before he could make any decisions, he needed to learn about her basic needs as well as what would make her happy.

These last weeks, he'd been too damn caught up in his wishes coupled with indecisions to consider Lyssa's. Bloody hell, it was long past time to speak with her. Tell her what he decided, at least what he hoped she would agree with. He spent the last two days putting all his hopes and dreams in order. He tossed the blanket over his stallion then secured the material.

When he looked up, Still Water sat on his horse in front of him, his expression grim. His heart slid to his throat while the breath he held whooshed out. His friend nodded toward the house.

"Lyssa?" His pulse beat hard and fast. "Is it one of her suitors?" Neither White or Ritter had enough guts to return at least not in broad daylight. What brought Still Water Runs to him?

Still Water Runs nodded, his eyes so dark they seemed black. The message, the look simmering intensely in his eyes sent fear sweeping into Kane. "You will not like what you see. Your woman takes liberties with her life she should not. You have been absent far too long. My friend, the time has come to make your decision about the lady. If you don't want her, let her go. She deserves your honesty."

"She isn't hurt?" Kane leapt on his horse.

Takes liberties with her life she should not? What the hell was Still Water Runs talking about? The stallion pranced around in one spot seemingly as eager to ride as his master.

"Not yet. At least she wasn't hurt when I left. You need to hurry if you expect her to be in one piece when you reach her."

"Bloody, bloody hell!" When did his speech become so English? He even cursed like a damn Englishman. He whirled his stallion in a tight circle, eager to race against time.

"You will have to see for yourself," Still Water Runs muttered, his voice hard.

With that said, Kane spurred the big gray horse toward home. "Ashes, go like the wind." Still Water Runs turned to follow him.

He raced the wind, terror for Lyssa rushing through him flooding him with worry, sweat beading on his body, his heart pounding with distress. What did Still Water Runs mean she hadn't hurt herself yet? The ride from his lodge to his home lasted an eternity, yet only a few minutes passed. By the time Kane reached the edge of his estate, bowling from the trees his nerves were laced thin, stretched to their limits. His fear for his woman unraveled his heart.

When he saw her riding, he pulled his horse to an abrupt stop. Cursed. The stallion's hooves pawed the air. For a moment he couldn't breathe nor could he think. This was too damn impetuous. He would have never guessed she would test the limits of her strength in such a death-defying manner. She could die with one slip of a foot or a hand. Could find herself trampled beneath the hooves of the sweet mare she rode. Dread gripped him so hard and fast for an instant he couldn't move.

"No!"

Still Water Runs stopped beside him. His gaze riveted on the young woman who didn't seem to care if she lived or died. "What do you intend? She must not pretend to be a man. This will bring dishonor to you."

Who the hell would know? His English cronies certainly wouldn't care if she rode this way. Only his brothers, his people would have that reaction. His breath caught in his throat while Kane continued to stare at Lyssa, amazed and horrified at the same time. She never failed to shock as well as captivate him. In his wildest dreams, he never expected to see something such as this, a woman playing a warrior's role. He would have never thought she could attempt such a feat let alone live to talk about her artistry.

How dare she risk herself in this manner? Didn't she understand she was his? It was one thing for a warrior to ride with breakneck speeds risking life and limb, however for her to do this in play, made a laughingstock of all he understood as a constant truth.

He tried to calm himself as well as his initial reaction to the sight in front of him. Dragging in a deep breath, he proceeded, "Lyssa doesn't know of our laws regarding women. She isn't even mine yet. I've no right by our people's laws or hers to discipline or chastise her for actions she doesn't understand. A lecture by me would not be appreciated."

He did though. As her chaperone, he possessed that right. He would make damn certain she understood his thoughts.

"The woman puts herself in danger for no apparent reason. She is simply amusing those you employ," Still Water Runs' growl resonated from deep in his throat. "You cannot allow her to continue in this reprehensible manner. If she gets trampled, how will you feel when you sit by and watch her in pain? If that happened, she could die."

Kane tried to disregard his friend's words. Instead, he admired her abilities. When he first arrived to watch, she rode standing on the Appaloosa's back. Her slender form was tall and straight. As she always appeared when riding, now she performed as one with her horse. In a matter of seconds, she dropped to ride astride, hooking her foot through surcingle, she slipped beneath the belly of the little mare. He gasped air when her tiny backside bumped the ground below. She pulled herself up. Didn't seem to have the strength to remain above the ground. He counted five times her adorable butt hit the dirt. She would be bruised. His fists tightened. He couldn't do anything until she finished the crazy entertainment she provided for his staff. Frightening her might cause her to lose hold. His thoughts centered however on thrashing that charming backside until she couldn't sit. If she kept this up though, all the times her butt hit dirt as he watched she wouldn't be able to sit, even without his intervention.

Still Water Runs was correct in all he said. He needed to do something about this activity of hers. He wondered if this is what she did every morning when he was gone, making plans for their future together. Cautiously, he rode his horse toward the spectacle. Lyssa was no longer beneath the horse. Now, she rode sideways, her body stretched parallel to the earth. She picked a hat off a pile of hay. Pulled herself to sit astride once more then donned the hat while she sported a cheeky grin.

She whirled the horse in tight circles one way then the other. The wind carried her laughter. Her smile wedged into his heart. She was happy. When he curtailed her activities, she would no longer laugh or smile. If she wanted to be with him, as she said, she would have to learn his ways. She could never put her adorable person at risk ever again.

The minute she saw him, he knew. Her horse stopped. She held perfectly still as she watched him approach. Her grin did little to ease the fear still surging through him at her terrifying ride.

Her death could have been eminent if she slipped.

He would not have been able to do anything to stop it. All he would have been able to do would be watch. When he closed his eyes, his imagination saw her trampled beneath her mount's hooves. At the image he saw, his body shuddered with fear. His stomach catapulted. He found he was shaking, anger along with fear surging through him. He would have to put a stop to this.

As if nothing was untoward about what she'd done, she waved then urged her horse forward appearing eager to meet him. They met just outside the corral. When she saw the way he looked at her, her smile changed to a frown. She looked to the house then back to him. He watched the hand holding her reigns tremble. For a brief instant, he thought she might run from him. Fearlessly or perhaps foolishly, she held her ground.

"Follow me." He turned his horse to begin the short ride to his lodge expecting to hear the beat of her horse's hooves behind him. Privacy for this discipline was needed. He would not allow Still Water Runs to witness her shame. Yet to decide on what form the punishment might take, he didn't realize she wasn't meekly behind him following as he commanded.

When he turned to look toward her, she rode in the opposite direction. Well hell, was it something he said? No, he gave her a direct order. He expected to be obeyed. She didn't understand the gravity of her actions. He supposed he would have to be patient while he taught her what would be expected of her as his wife.

"Lyssa! Come here! Now!" His voice thundered across the open meadow. He hadn't meant to show his anger quite so clearly or so soon. Since she ran from him when he issued a mild order, she certainly would never heed this threatening command.

As if she didn't hear him, she continued to ride toward the stable.

At her evasion, more anger escalated, seethed within his veins. He urged his stallion forward until the mount thundered toward her. Ignoring him would do her no good. She was simply forestalling the inevitable.

The beat of thunder on the ground must have alerted her all was not as she expected. With a panicked expression when she looked back, she thought to race from him. In seconds they rode side by side. He scooped her from her mare then across his thighs. For several seconds they rode until his hold felt secure.

"Swing your leg around, Lys. Don't want to drop you." He whispered close to her ear. His voice was as harsh and unyielding as his thoughts. When he noticed the pulse at the base of her neck, he saw the wild racing of her heart.

"Kane!"

She cried out his name, but this time she did as told. She swung her leg over so she sat astraddle the horse as well as his thighs.

His arm circled her waist. Her fingers dug into the flesh there as he raced toward his lodge, eager to find privacy. This little incident touched on every protective instinct he possessed. He wanted to shake her until her teeth rattled. After that he wanted to touch and caress every sensitive place on her tiny body. He couldn't believe what he just observed. She risked her life for no reason. Even though he didn't want to do so, he had to admit the horsemanship was remarkable.

When he witnessed her riding beneath the horse's belly, he understood she would never survive with his people. They would never accept her ways. She was too willful, stubborn as well. Her wildness and shocking questions attracted him to her. It was all those characteristics that would not serve her well with the Sioux. Women were supposed to act meek as well as biddable. They obeyed their husband's tiniest command even if they disagreed. If she disagreed, she would never obey without a heated argument. Instead, she would vent her spleen and after that do exactly as she pleased.

In the stilted London society, she was outrageous, charming at times. She forged her way as she liked. Her family's name however would see her through the worst of her outlandishness.

Her bawdy song at the recital gave him reason to smirk. He would have liked to hear her finish the tune.

Now, though, he needed to instruct her. "You need to learn what a woman can and cannot do. Lys, your actions today were unacceptable."

Once more, he whispered close to her ear as they rode, while her rounded breasts pushed against the top of his arms giving him ideas that did not coincide with discipline. Today, she had not bound the rosy tipped mounds. He wondered at that. Perhaps, she had not intended to push the limits of what she should and should not do. Possibly, she had not thought to ride so recklessly. Why did she?

In his arms she stiffened. "Kane?" Her voice held warning; a fire seemed to rise from the depths of her lungs. "Put me down this instant. I don't like what you're doing or what you're saying. I don't want to be here with you. Now I don't even like you!"

"Not on your life."

He didn't like the fact this close contact aroused him when she was telling him she disliked him. Talking to her about this misbehavior would not be easy when he wanted something else from her. She would fight him. He was sure of that. Her anger seemed to vibrate throughout her slender form. Now, he didn't care what she liked or asked. After he explained everything to her, he would make his actions up to her.

"You can't just manhandle me because you're stronger. There are laws!" she yelled at him as she turned on him, her tiny fists pummeled his chest. Her eyes blazed her defiance.

She was furious, fighting mad furious. Nothing she did affected any part of him except his heart. "I can hear you just fine, Lys. I can handle you anyway I please."

Yes, there were laws. English laws that gave a man permission to discipline those he was charged to look after. She would have to learn that in his care, she could not do just as she pleased. By this evening she would be his wife. She would be his. Finally, he made up his mind. All it took was this extreme act of courage or perhaps defiance to make everything he felt startling clear. Over the last two weeks, he'd put the wheels in motion. Now it was up to Still Water Runs to see to the small details.

"Doesn't seem like you can hear a word I say. Don't my wishes count for something?" She sat back against him, seemingly resigned to accept her position such as it was. With her meager strength she couldn't move.

"Don't fight me, Little Bit. It won't do you a moment of good."

Her body pressed so close to his after such a long abstinence sent ideas flooding his brain that had nothing to do with a discussion over compliance.

The rest of the distance they rode in silence. It wasn't far. He struggled to hold his baser instincts in check. Without conscious thought, his thumb rubbed the underside of her breast. She sat stiffly. Didn't attempt to move away from him though. Her quiet resignation disturbed him. He figured she'd probably come at him hissing and clawing when he finally set her on the earth. He understood she would fight simply because he intended to take something precious from her. This time it wasn't her virginity. What he meant to take was some more of her precious freedom that independence she seemed to crave.

This would hurt him as much as it did her. She wouldn't believe that nonsense for one second. The fact was true though. Keeping her alive was more important than her tender sensibilities, her wishes, too, or even her independence.

Kane tried to concentrate on the wind and the sun as nature filled the earth with beauty. Light shimmered with silver and gold on the leaves of the trees they passed under. Wind brought the scent of wildflowers along with freshness of the country to his senses. Animal sounds reverberated throughout. With all his heart, he missed the plains. He could never go back. He would never watch the buffalo roam the prairie nor would he hunt them. He needed to resign himself to his new home. Until Lyssa appeared to him, his hopes remained. Now he understood his destiny, one she was meant to be part of.

This was his home. He understood that now more than ever. Perhaps it took a feisty little American to make him see where he belonged. He understood the plight of the Sioux nation wasn't good. Settlers continued to migrate west. Americans consumed the land as if they had every right to do so. They murdered buffalo for no reason except for the sport of hunting large animals. They left dead carcass scattered across the land. The Sioux needed to go farther and farther into the mountains to hunt to provide food and clothing for the people. There would be war between the white man and the Sioux. He couldn't take her where her life would be in jeopardy.

He allowed a huge breath of air to fill his lungs until he thought they might burst. The promise to his grandfather was not the sole reason he would stay. If he were to have a future with the little lady sitting so close to him, he would have to remain in England. Until he met Lyssa, he rarely thought about returning to the plains. He'd accepted his life as an English lord. She had this way of putting new thoughts into his head of complicating his life. She was the free and independent spirit he wished he could be.

The animal skin lodge he erected in this far corner of his property waited for them. Tonight was the night for him to claim her as his. After the lecture he planned, she might not be receptive to him. He would find a way to convince her this was right.

Over the weeks that he stayed away from her, he bought horses, fine horses her father would appreciate. He bought from some of the best horse breeders in Ireland and England. Potentially a fortune of horseflesh waited to board a ship to Baltimore then on to the Andrews' ranch farther inland. Lyssa would not understand the meaning or the honor of such a bride price. He hoped her father would. In this there were no guarantees. Lyssa's father might feel insulted. Her father should not.

The horses were meant as the bride price to honor her as well as what would be their life together. If her father understood anything of the way of the Sioux, he would accept the gift as it was intended. Lyssa might believe he bought her. For now, though, if he chose to wed her tonight, the ceremony would be final in his heart. Still Water Runs would say words over them. He would wrap her in his blanket then claim her. There would be no procession of women, no gifts, nothing else. The deed would be done. As soon as he made love to her, there would be no going back.

After he allowed her to slip to the ground, he nodded to a place by the fire. "Sit." The rebelliousness he saw in the depth of her simmering blue eyes challenged his soft command.

"I prefer to stand if I'm to meet my executioner." Her back was rigid, her words stiff. "Actually, I prefer to leave."

Her executioner? Prefer to leave?

Behind those words he saw new words. She was waiting for the discipline, or was she? Lyssa appeared baffled by his anger, his abruptness. The way he chased after her when she rode in the opposite direction should have imparted a wealth of information into that head of hers. Was it possible she had no idea how angry he was at her riding this afternoon? Did she not know how dangerous her actions were to herself? Explanations before discipline might be in order here.

With Lyssa anything was possible. He chuckled. Her father must have been overindulgent with her. From the few things she told him about her life in America, she was allowed to run free on their land. He couldn't fault Damian. If he could, he would indulge his children every way possible. Not this way however, not when her deeds put her life in danger.

"Sit down, Lys. I will explain everything to you. If you have questions after my clarification, I will answer whatever I can."

He watched the play of different expressions dance across her beautiful features. She was so sweet, so adorable, saucy at times. He would have a difficult time with discipline. He resigned himself. This must be done. She must understand.

The first words coming from her startled him, "You're an ass."

She sat by the fire. Her chin stuck into the air. Her fingers wound tightly into each other. The stubborn nature amplified the longer she waited for him to speak.

Fascinated, he decided to give her time. The wait would do her good. "Yes, I am at times. This situation, as I see it, is meant only to protect you from yourself. You weren't thinking clearly."

The wild look in her eyes changed to a modicum of recognition. Perhaps she understood that when she attempted to ride like a man, she could hurt herself.

"The situation as you see it?" she asked him sounding totally baffled. "What situation is that? I was riding the horse you gave me. Is that such a great sin? I've no idea why you are acting this way. I rode in the designated area even though I would have liked to explore the countryside."

Struck by the realization his worst fears were true, he attempted a different attitude. He would come at this from a different angle. "Riding is no sin. Taking risks with your life is." He was surprised when she still didn't get the gist of his words, having never thought he would have to point out each indiscretion.

"I've ridden like that since I was a child. A Cherokee taught me. Father allowed me to do so. He always told me to be careful. I am!"

Her tiny fists were clutched tightly, her body vibrating with her fury and indignation.

"I'm your chaperone. I won't allow you to risk yourself!" Suddenly, he found himself in a shouting match with her. He lowered his voice. "You cannot do that again. You cannot ride like a man, a warrior."

"That's it, isn't' it? You don't want me to be better than you at riding. Should have guessed as much. I don't care any longer." She turned her back to him which infuriated him even more than he thought possible. She turned back. "I don't want anything to do with you. Not now! Not ever!" She waved her hand in the air, "To me, you are like dust in the wind. Nothing. I don't have to chop wood to find a path to you or come full circle. There is no path that leads me to you."

Still, he ignored her statement as well as the hurt bursting inside. He needed to stand by his resolution. "You're not to risk yourself by the tricks I saw today. That's an order."

Her chin rose higher. "You're not my father. You've no privileges with me."

She still ignored the inevitable. It seemed she would argue with him despite the fact he was dead-on about this.

"True, the way I feel about you, a father would not. You will listen to me as well as heed what I say." Time needed to separate him from his anger, hers as well. He took care of his horse, watching from the corner of his eye. "When I'm finished here, we will talk."

"Don't bet on it."

Ah, he would do more than bet. Gambling on something as important as Lyssa, he would never do.

From his lodge he brought out a bottle of wine along with a pouch of nuts and dried fruit. More food would come from the house shortly. Still Water Runs would bring the delicacies he asked his cook to make earlier in the afternoon before he arrived at his lodge to prepare for their joining. A joining he wasn't certain of until he watched her nearly kill herself. He poured wine into two mugs then gave her one. The planning began last week continuing to this morning. He just never expected this explosion of wills.

She drank the wine. Held out her mug for more. "I don't want to talk. Think I'll just have more wine. I'll drink so much I won't hear a word you have to say." She set the mug next to her.

"No?" He arched a brow in conjecture. "Fine with me if you want to get foxed. Either way we will speak of your riding. You can answer, give me the reasons you were risking your life. If you don't, the horse will be forbidden to you."

He understood she would not like his words. Waited for the repercussions of the threat of discipline.

"You can't do that!" She jumped to her feet, once again her hands clenched desperately to her sides. "I won't stay here."

His gaze riveted on her unbound breasts as they softly moved. Mesmerized, he couldn't take his gaze away. The hardened tips of her nipples pushed against the thin fabric. He swallowed hard. His body hardened to steel. This task of discipline would not be easy.

He needed to figure out what should be said before he lost all semblance of rational thought then gave into her as he was certain her father had done. This wouldn't do at all.

"As it stands now, the horse is on loan. If you break my rules..." He shrugged. "It's a simple result of your actions. You won't be allowed access to the mare." He let out a rush of exasperated air. "Lys, sit, relax, finish that mug of wine if you'd like, pour another one if it suits your fancy. What I mean to focus on is not taking away the little Appaloosa you seemed to have grown fond of."

"Focus? Focus on what? What has you so angry it appears you're spitting nails at me. I've no earthly idea why you swept me off my horse. Why you were yelling at me back at the house. I've done nothing wrong. You have barely spoken to me in weeks." She crossed her arms beneath her luscious breasts thrusting them forward.

He swallowed hard.

Truly, she didn't know. He pinched the bridge of his nose, as if the gesture would stop his growing headache. "The way you were riding, Lys. No more tricks, no more risking your life to show off. I won't have you endangering yourself."

"You won't have it!" Each word distinct coupled with a short pause after uttering the word. "Kane Michael Murphy, you cannot tell me what I can or cannot do. Those tricks are easy for me. I'm not at risk. Nothing will happen."

"If you fell, the horse would trample you, grind you into the dust beneath the great beast's hooves."

Frustration eating at him, he gestured with his hands. "It makes no difference what you say. If I see you or if Still Water Runs tells me that he saw you riding in that manner, you will not be allowed to mount your horse. That is all I will say on the matter."

Her hostile glare tore at his insides. Now, he didn't have one doubt that she despised him. He hoped that wasn't true. Knew at this moment it was. Hell, he'd hate himself in this situation. Nonetheless he needed to make her understand.

She turned from him, her back stiff. He understood what she was thinking. Lyssa would tell him that she wouldn't fall, would never fall. Accidents happen. There are no assurances in this life.

"Is that your final word? Suppose I don't have a choice except to follow your male inspired dictates as misguided as they are." Her words held a wealth of sarcasm coupled with bitter distaste.

"Final." He agreed suddenly relieved that she might be willing to end this here and now. "Now, we will talk of other things."

"You want to talk now? I don't. Will you take me back to the house? I don't want to be here with you? At the moment, you are the last person I want to be with. If you can't tell, you thick headed man, I'm angry, furious. Annoyed. Irritated. Ready to spit nails." She stood, wiping her hands on her pants, looking toward the house.

"You aren't going anywhere." She wouldn't walk all the way though she might try.

"Don't want to be with you," she muttered saying the words once more.

"Why?"

Kane didn't appreciate what she was telling him. His plans would be dust in the wind if she left. Didn't like the notion she wouldn't fight for what she thought her rights should be. Damn, wasn't that what he wanted, a submissive woman? No, he wanted Lyssa in all her radiant and confusing glory. The thing was, she needed to learn when she could fight him, when there was a chance, she would win the battle. This was not one of those times.

She tossed a stick into the fire then another, her gaze riveted on the red-yellow glow of the flames. He wanted her to look at him, face him with her anger. "Because you've gone all autocratic on me. You haven't wanted to talk to me in over two weeks. You seduced me in the carriage then didn't want anything to do with me. You have any idea how I felt? You are a horrible man."

Her anger began to simmer. He could hear the fury rise in her voice. She was letting off the steam that had been brewing over the last weeks.

Well hell, it appeared he just learned the true reason she was fuming. Her irritation wasn't about the lecture. Her coloring turned bright as the anger developed. Perhaps it was the memory of the carriage ride that caused the rise of color on her face. "Well, I do have a pretty good idea since I felt the same. Have felt the same for over two weeks. Why do you think I was chopping wood?"

"Why don't you tell me? Since I'm so inexperienced I wouldn't have a clue as to why you've split enough wood to last forever plus another day if you're conservative. Looks as if you've done the same here."

It seemed to him this was the first moment she noticed the lodge. Her eyes widened before she turned her attention back to the fire and her mug of wine. He wished she would tell him what she was thinking.

"You should eat." To put more emphasis on his words, he picked up a chunk of cheese. "Hmm...good. Food will help you forget your annoyance with me. It will satisfy one's needs."

If his plans went as he intended, another need would be satisfied tonight as well.

She turned. Clearly, he could see her face, the drawn lines of stress. "Still Water Runs told me you had to think about things. Did you? He said you had to walk in a circle to discover your truths," she asked while she did what he suggested this time.

Food in her mouth she waited for an answer. "What does that mean, walk in a circle?"

He would have to give her some of what she wanted. She tossed out the question even though she used the words earlier to insult him. "I did. Would you be happy living in England with me?"

"What? You want to stay my chaperone forever? If you still want me to find some lord who will give me a title, I flat out refuse to do so. You've known from the beginning the only man I've ever wanted is you, until tonight that is. Tonight, as far as I'm concerned, you're a bloody bastard...and an ass. I wouldn't have you if you prostrated your big body at my feet."

He winced. Decided he should continue with the plan despite the road blocks. Speaking plainly, "Found the lord who will give you a title. Won't let you refuse him."

She stood then faced him hands on her hips. "Damn and blast Kane, this...this is the nineteenth century. You can't make me marry some old doddering lord just because you think he would suit. You're not going to pawn me off on some womanizing rake I can't stand. I won't say, yes! If you persist in this scheme, I'll jilt him at the altar." With that said she sat down, crossing her arms again in the process pushing up and displaying her beautiful breasts.

He smiled while he watched her vehemently refuse his proposal. Of course, she didn't know the truth. Tonight, she might refuse him. Feeling a tiny bit hesitant, he went on to say. "I'm the lord who will give you the title. Marry me tonight in the way of the people."

~ * ~

The chunk of bread she chewed caught in her throat. The slice of cheese she held between two delicate fingers fell to the ground. She coughed several times before she gave up and tried to wash the offending food down to her stomach with the little bit of wine left in her mug. Finally, it seemed she found her voice. "You want me to do what?"

"Marry me tonight. All you have to do is say you are my wife. It will be done."

His words sounded emphatic. "In the ways of the people? How is that? I want to be wed in the church. Vows need to be said, a commitment made. Papers signed. Doesn't that take time? I want a dress and cake. Need my family to witness." Her breaths didn't make their way into her lungs. He wanted her to marry him without benefit of clergy.

"Which is why I don't want to wait. I made up my mind, Lys. I know this is what you want too."

He couldn't possibly think she would consider herself his wife by simply speaking the words. How she wed him didn't matter to her. She wanted Kane for her husband more than anything. This was ludicrous though. *The way of the People?* Her parents would never condone a marriage such as what he planned. If this was done his way, he could set her aside with little provocation whenever the mood hit him.

"You ignored me for days, endless days, nights as well. Now, you expect me to agree to this preposterous proposal. I know you think you can have anything you want. Know now, this instant, you cannot."

Lyssa was angry and hurt. He didn't understand how horrible she felt when he abandoned her their first night back. She still nursed the wounds created by that horrible recital.

"If I told you I was sorry, would that help?" He sounded hesitant for the first time in their too short relationship unsure of himself. "I would do most anything to set this right. I want you tonight, Lys. The only way we can have what we both want is to wed my way. I won't make love to you unless you are married to me."

"I'm not going to marry you tonight, might not ever after this insane suggestion."

She finished her wine. Compared to the conversation at hand the liquid was delicious. Not waiting for Kane to pour her more, Lyssa upended the bottle refilling her mug until the wine reached the top. She meant to drink the contents. If he wouldn't take her back to the estate, she'd steal his horse. He wouldn't like that. She didn't care a fig if he appreciated her attempt at freedom or not.

"You will." The two words were a command.

She didn't intend to obey. "No!" She knew he was frustrated with her stubborn stance on this marriage request. Knew he wanted her. She wanted him too. The entreaty had come as such a shock, as she hadn't expected him to ask. He wanted to marry her so he could have sex with her. After that he would dump her. Damn and blast, she wanted him to continue what he started in the carriage even though she was terrified. She trusted this man with her life. He wouldn't hurt her. The feelings he elicited were intoxicating, more so than the wine.

"If you wish there is more wine."

He stretched out on his side, a lazy half smile stretching his lips as if he tasted victory. His head was propped up with one sturdy hand while one knee was bent. He plucked a blade of grass, played with the length. Seemed to study her.

She knew what he was doing. Didn't give a fig if she got drunk. She wouldn't change her mind, at least not tonight. She wouldn't do this in any way except the one she'd expected since she was a little girl. A minister needed to perform the ceremony. "Would marry you tonight if there was a man of God here who would say the words of the church," she blurted the statement immediately regretting them when she saw the half smile on his handsome arrogant face grow to a wicked size.

He nodded his head not toward her but to her eternal dismay to Still Water Runs who stood nearby. He hadn't left after he delivered the food. She didn't realize he was still waiting for further direction. Oh god, oh god...no she didn't want this to be so easy for him. She needed for Kane to grovel, to feel at least a small measure of the pain he inflicted on her. Needed for him to understand her frustration. With her hasty words she'd given her feelings for him away as well as free reign to have what he proposed.

"You sent him for a minister, didn't you?" Irritated and more than annoyed, her voice wavered with the realization tonight she would be married to this man. She loved him. In too many ways to count, she was afraid of what they didn't finish that day. She needed more time. She just didn't want to feel ignored.

"That is what you asked for. Was it not?" He smiled at her. "Just as you promised me you would do, you make me smile every moment I think about you. I won't ever hurt you, Lys. I promise this to you."

"You know I won't marry a man who can't ride like my father, or better."

She sent that message loud and clear. His lack of riding ability was her only hope of escaping his wicked plans tonight. There was no way he could sit a horse better. He grew up Sioux. Dear lord, he most likely was more competent at this feat than most any man including her daddy. The challenge was sent. She couldn't take the words back. Once again, her stupidity was clear. The last chance vanished on the wind.

"A demonstration is in order. If I do better than your father, you will marry me tonight," he challenged, his smile growing even broader. He knew he would win the contest.

The blasted man knew he could outride as well as outshoot everyone in England and probably on the North American continent.

That was another order. His words were not phrased as a question. While she melted for him, she wasn't sure she wanted to finish the melting so totally unsure of what came after all the kisses. Kane was on his feet walking toward the tepee. A few seconds later, he emerged in a breechclout striding toward his big stallion. Before he reached the horse, he grabbed his bow and arrow.

Dear Lord, she'd never seen a man nearly naked. He was magnificent, muscles rolling, seething, and rippling as he moved. Oh, she'd seen both Jess as well as her father without a shirt. Kane wore only a small piece of cloth covering his maleness. His legs were long and corded with thick, hard muscles. His body was bronze. She knew the strength of his forearms. His biceps bulged, his thighs also. Power emanated from every pore of this man's body. The broad chest he showed her now narrowed to a lean waist and trim hips. His stomach rippled in corded sinew. He slanted her a look of wry amusement. His grin told of a man so sure of himself he couldn't lose. The blasted man knew she stared at him.

A target sat nearby. Did he intend to shoot at that target while he rode? Surely, he would miss. No man could do such a thing. Was that how the Sioux did battle? She groaned. It wasn't that she didn't want to marry him. It was that he had everything his way. Over the past weeks she'd felt so insecure, so much pain, so much confusion. He ignored her all this time, increasing her insecurities. Now he wanted her to instantly forgive him. She couldn't. Wouldn't.

With easy grace he mounted. She should have realized what he was capable of before she gave herself no possible way out of this wedding he planned for tonight. In his eyes, she was most likely wed to him at this very moment simply because he said the words. He didn't have to do this, didn't have to prove himself. Well, in her eyes there would have to be a minister present along with vows said before she considered herself married. He sent for the minister. The man would be here soon. She was sure of that. He must have had this planned before he brought her to the lodge.

"Ay-ee, ay-ee," the war cries echoed through the still air, ripped through her. Alarmed as well as excited, she watched while she held her breath. The cries were terrifying, chilling. Again, and again the words filled the silence "Ay-ee, ay-ee." This was the man she was about to wed. This man she witnessed now was a part of him she didn't know, part savage and ruthless, part lord of the realm and gentle. Riding his horse, he personified poetry in motion.

Shivers flooded through her body. Wrapping her arms around her waist, she held her breath while she watched in fascinated wonder. His skill was remarkable, breathtaking. With his knees, he guided the horse in a wide circle. First, he mimicked her by standing, the horse moving at breakneck speed. Still, he stood majestically atop the animal. While he rode past the target, he shot two arrows. Both landed dead center, the tips touching each other. Quickly, he dropped to the side of the horse. More war cries emanated from him. Again, he passed swiftly by the target letting fly two more arrows. One hit dead center, the other a finger's width from the other three.

Before she could concede the win, he dropped below the horse riding close to the powerful stallion's belly, his buttocks never touching upon the ground as hers did when she attempted that position. Once more arrows flew, all landing so close only a hair would separate them. She found she was still holding her breath, deeply immersed in the vision in front of her.

Lyssa wanted to change the subject of marriage to the burning question in her head. If he could ride his horse like that, why couldn't she? He would never allow that conversation to proceed to a coherent end. His mind was made up the moment he observed her. Slowly, she was beginning to have some semblance of understanding for the man she loved. His word was law. She would obey that law. If she didn't, she would pay some type of consequence. He would discipline her in some way.

Like hell she would. She would fight every step of the way if she disagreed. See if she wouldn't.

He slowed the horse, still guiding the animal with his knees. He rode the stallion proudly as he stopped in front of her. "I can do the same with a rifle, a pistol as well as a knife. Do you need more proof?"

She could do nothing more than shake her head, her mind reeling with the images she just witnessed.

"You will become my wife now."

Well, if he put the offer that way, she didn't have much of a choice. Damn and blast did she want a choice? Her breath caught in her throat. Lying to him wasn't an option. She never lied. What about the crying of the banns? For some reason, she wanted to postpone this marriage. She didn't understand why. She never cared if she had a wedding dress linked with all the craziness of a marriage. There was no crying of the banns in Maryland. Planning events was not something she enjoyed. Although she understood Aunt Ella would love to sit down with her to help orchestrate the ceremony.

"The minister isn't here. The banns need to be read." She looked down at herself, all the way to her toes. Not that it mattered, "I'm not wearing a dress." She never thought to get married in her britches. A tear slipped from her eyes. Hastily, she brushed the moisture away.

"I see that you're not. Don't understand though what it is you're attempting to tell me. Do you want to wear a dress? That can be arranged in an instant." He slanted her a slow lazy smile.

She slid her sweaty hands along the sides of her trousers. Another small thing that might slow this process, might give her one more day before she became his wife. "Yes. Yes, a dress would be nice. Much nicer than these pants I wear to ride."

"When it is only the two of us, I appreciate the tightly fitted britches."

He looked to the lodge. That lazy grin turned to what seemed a smirk to her. He knew...he knew she was attempting to put this off.

"If you walk inside my lodge, you will find a white doeskin dress fit for a wedding to a Sioux warrior."

"You think of everything."

She couldn't believe what he said. He was that prepared. A dress waited for her just inside that flap of animal skin.

His all-knowing smirk seemed to be his answer.

"That wasn't exactly the type of dress I was thinking of."

Finding a way out of this tonight seemed to be a losing experience. The kind of dress she was thinking of would take a few weeks to sew. She deserved a wedding dress.

He lifted his broad, naked shoulders still grinning as if the world was his. "The gown is the only one I have for you. Take a look. Tell me if you don't find it beautiful. If you don't want to wear the gown, you can wear what you have on. I will be quick to remove whatever you wear when the time is right."

"We don't even have a wedding cake or flowers."

What did she care about cake? She didn't know. The list she was making for him was just something to postpone something that was beginning to feel inevitable.

I can say no.

Don't want to say no.

At this point, Lyssa didn't know what she did want except for this wedding to occur a different day. She needed time to get used to the idea, this all happened way too fast. An engagement, a nice long engagement first would have been nice, a month perhaps two.

"In that you're wrong. My cook sent a wedding cake with Still Water Runs when he brought us the small picnic. Inside the lodge we have enough good food and wine to sustain us through the night, possibly into the next week. "Go on, Lyssa. Look at the dress. I'll give you five minutes."

A lump clogged her throat. "To dress?"

"No, to look at the dress so you can tell me if the gown will suit." He dismounted. His long strides took him to a point in front of her. With the tip of his finger, he lifted her chin. "You are acting strange, Little Bit. Are you afraid of the wedding night? I promise I won't hurt you."

"You can't promise something like that." Her voice wavered, shook so hard, he would know the truth.

"Ah, the problem is apparent. You're right. Since you are a virgin, you will experience minimal pain. I'll replace that small hurt with a great deal of pleasure. You will remember the pleasure not the tiny ache that has to be inflicted before you can become my woman."

That was easy for him to say. However, he sounded so sincere. She wanted to believe his words. Studying the tips of her toes seemed easier than looking at him. She was acting like a ninny. He was about to give her what she wanted. She denied him. When she finally looked at him, questions rose to the forefront of her mind.

"Are you going to wear that?" While he was incredibly virile with every muscle on his rugged male body clearly delineated, she wanted something more. "Perhaps you could put on clothing. Maybe you could wear your buckskins."

"You don't want me to wear a shirt?" He chuckled, clearly amused with her questions.

"Don't laugh at me! This is all, all, well, it's all so very disconcerting. Of course, I would like you to wear a shirt, trousers as well. Even though no one will see us get married except the minister and Still Water Runs." To no avail, she tried to swallow the growing lump in her throat. "The memory would be nicer if you were fully clothed."

"Memories are always nice. Whatever you would like, Lys, I will do. Go, tell me what you think of the dress that was made for the woman who would become my wife." He braced his feet apart, as he seemed to study her.

Slowly, she walked into the lodge, sensing he watched her. Going to her execution could not be so terror filled as this silent walk. On the pile of furs, she saw a pure white doeskin dress just as he told her. It wasn't a dress as she thought of one. It was a blouse and skirt. Beads were sewn on the blouse as well as the skirt. White fringe fell from the hem of the skirt and blouse. It was beautiful.

Lovingly, she ran her fingers along the soft fabric. How did he get this here? Tears shimmered in her eyes. Moisture clung to the back of her throat. This was nothing what she expected. She didn't have words to express herself properly. To do something like this, he must love her. Thinking of marrying Kane would be easier to do tonight if he did love her.

The words never passed his lips. Two weeks passed while they spoke over dinner, the conversation almost nonexistent between them. He could have told her what he was feeling. There was so much left unsaid. Her mouth was too dry now.

"Lyssa?"

"Oh! You startled me." When she turned, he stood a few feet away from her. He was so tall, so very tall as his body seemed to fill the entire space. He dwarfed her.

"Didn't mean to do so. Were you woolgathering?"

Her hand held tightly against her chest as if the small gesture could ease her pounding heart, "Yes, I guess I was. I was wondering." She swept her tongue across her lips. "Was...it doesn't matter."

"What you were thinking makes a difference in my mind. Care to tell me where your thoughts led you?" His voice held a wealth of amusement.

Nothing funny about this came to her mind. "It was nothing."

He nodded seeming to accept the answer. "Do you like the dress? My mother made it years ago. She gave it to me when I left the People. Mother asked me to save this gown for the woman I intended to marry. Now that I've finally come to my senses, that woman is you."

She had the horrible thought this dress was meant for the white girl who had him whipped. If that were true, she wouldn't wear the blasted thing. No, she would burn the horrible pieces of clothing. He had no right to even think...to expect her to wear something so loathsome.

When she turned her gaze to him, all expression drained from her face along with the blood. She swayed slightly. He reached out to steady her.

It seemed he guessed the direction of her mind. Must have felt a need to explain, "The dress was not intended for the other woman. We never got close to discussing marriage. This is meant for you, Lys, only you. I would have no other woman wear the soft doeskin that was so lovingly crafted." His voice gentled and whispered to her so low, she nearly swooned.

"We..." She licked dry lips, "We haven't discussed marriage either. You just told me I'm your wife." She wondered how he could presume so much. Gesturing with her arms, "No discussion, just orders. I don't like the way you command and expect me to do what you've...what you've commanded."

He mimicked her, his hand in the air before gently caressing her cheek. "It is done. In my eyes, you are my wife. In a few more minutes, we will wed according to your customs, English customs. Marriage doesn't need to be discussed in our case. We both understand it is what we want. What our souls cry out for. Tell me you don't want to be my wife."

She couldn't. At this moment though she wanted to lie to him.

Reaching around her, Kane picked up what appeared to be his wedding finery. His buckskins and shirt were also white. The silver medallion he wore stood out against the bronze of his naked chest. Unable to help herself, she stared at him, tried to absorb the image of him into her soul, tried to imagine touching him, caressing him.

"I'll dress outside. When you are ready, come out. I heard the hooves of our approaching witnesses, the minister and Still Water Runs. I believe Abernathy has come with them. He is truly quite fond of you. It is time. You won't regret marrying me. I promise."

Before he left, he let his gaze wander the length of her. She burned from the intimate caress bestowed by him.

Her heart pounded against her ribs. The meager breath she held in her lungs whispered through parched lips. The lodge was empty. Her fate waited for her outside. Sounds of men talking greeted her ears. The minister and Still Water Runs returned in record time. This must have been something else the two of them planned. Either that or, either that or...Black Thunder might have threatened the minister, had him kidnapped. She wouldn't put the deed past him. In many ways he still reacted as a Sioux warrior. He grew up believing he was. Could a few years in London change the man?

Truly, she didn't believe that he would do something like that, kidnap a minister. There weren't many men of the cloth who would wed two people without reading the banns or a special license from the church. Lyssa could do little more than shake her head at all he seemed to bypass to wed her. If she didn't change, Kane would be back to help her into her wedding finery. She didn't know who she would get, Kane or Black Thunder; the English lord, or the Sioux warrior.

Who would make love to her tonight? Anticipation along with fear flooded her.

Quickly, she shirked from most of her clothes leaving her chemise along with her pantalets beneath the soft doeskin. The clothing felt as if it had been made for her, which was impossible. How would his mother know the size of her future daughter-in-law so many years in the future?

As she stepped from the lodge, she saw the four men. Kane strode toward her with his hand outstretched. He stopped, a gentle smile on his lips. "I want your hair down," he murmured while he proceeded to unfasten every pin holding her braid in place. When he finished, he ran his hands lovingly through the strands until her hair fell loosely around her shoulders. "It's beautiful as are you."

It seemed to her he devoured her with his eyes. She shivered once more, her body heating with the intensity of his gaze.

Kane held out his hand for her again. With a deep breath, she let him take hold of it. He wound his fingers through hers. While they walked toward the large fire, he rubbed lazy circles on her wrist. He chuckled at the small shiver of passion that seemed to flow from her into him.

This was the hour she would become his wife. He would be intimate with her. She swallowed hard, pushing the apprehension searing through her head to the back. They stopped in front of the minister.

"Make this quick," Kane murmured. While he gazed at his soon to be wife, he spoke, "We've things to do."

Heat rose to her face while he squeezed her fingers seeming to understand her embarrassment. All the words were said. She didn't hear much of anything. Didn't know what to say until the words were repeated more than once. He had to nudge her when it was time to respond.

"Do you have a ring?" the man performing the ceremony asked.

To her surprise, Kane turned to Still Water Runs holding out his hand. "This was my paternal grandmother's. It was given to me with the intention that my wife must wear this to carry on the tradition."

Deftly, he slipped the ring onto her finger. This, she was certain was not in the way of the People.

To Lyssa's amazement the ring fit her seamlessly as if the jewelry was made for her, just as the skirt and blouse fit her to perfection. The minister must have given Kane permission to kiss her because he was. His finger beneath her chin, he lifted her face so their lips would meet. Briefly, she felt his tongue against her lips. The kiss ended before it even began. Even so, her knees nearly buckled. She wavered, leaning into his huge body allowing him to support her.

The ceremony was over. The minister pronounced them husband and wife. This was the time. Now, what would happen? Lyssa reminded herself this marriage to Kane was what she wanted, what she dreamed about. He was the man she wanted more than anything. She'd known the fact the first time she saw him sitting behind his big desk, scowling about something.

So be it. The deed was done. For her there was no turning back. If she meant to refuse his suit, she should have done so when there was still time.

With one arm around her, securing her close to his chest, they watched Still Water Runs along with Abernathy and the minister leave. They were alone. He would do what he wished. The heat from his body poured into her, flooding her with warmth. His heart thundered where her head rested against his chest. She wondered if he was nervous.

They were married.

He was hers now as she was his. What the devil did all that mean?

"Are you hungry?" His lips brushed lightly across her forehead.

"My stomach is turning over and over, somersaulting. So, no, I don't think I could eat one thing."

For some reason she couldn't fathom before when they kissed, she never thought about the fact he would come inside her. Now that she did, she was terrified. She needed to see him entirely naked. While she remembered seeing her brother when he was ten with nothing on, she knew Kane's body would not be the same. She remembered how he looked at the pond before she turned away.

"Perhaps we should consummate the marriage so you won't fear the act. I will be gentle. When we are done, you will be able to eat and relax. I don't want you to be less than enthusiastic," he laughed while he hugged her close.

"You said the joining would hurt." She sounded like a frightened little girl afraid of a scrape on a knee.

"I did, just a tiny prick, nothing more, nothing to be afraid of. You need not fear me." Lazily, he ran his hands through the length of her unbound hair. "So soft...so very soft...all of you...soft and white. I will make sure you find your pleasure before the tiny hurt. You won't even notice the prick."

That was easy for him to say. He wasn't the one who would feel this tiny prick as he called it. "Some wine would be nice."

"You cannot put this off forever. Don't you think we..."

"No, just a bit more wine then I'll be fine."

~ * ~

Sinclair Ritter sipped brandy with Jonathan White. Jonathan didn't like the portly insipid man. He was everything a man shouldn't be. Good God, he even drooled when he ate. He couldn't imagine Lyssa Andrews beneath this man while he sweated and pumped above her. The thought was incomprehensible even though his intentions toward the girl weren't noble. At least he wasn't a slob.

"We will share?" Ritter asked eagerly as he searched the room. "I can tell you though, that man put fear into my heart. He threatened my life if I ever looked at that girl again. I would bet he might take my scalp if I went against his orders."

"Ah," Jonathan gently tapped his glass on the table while he thought on something he could say that might ease some of Ritter's fears. "It's all bluster. He doesn't mean anything he's said to you. He's a lord of the realm. Murder is not something for an aristocrat. Going against the law would not be wise for him." If he could get the man to approach Lyssa, he would have half the work done for him. Ritter would bring her to him at no risk to himself. The marriage would be easy to accomplish. As soon as he had her secured in his carriage, they would go to Scotland for a quick informal marriage.

"I don't know about that. Seemed pretty threatening to me. Thought he was going to kill me right there in the alley. The other one's just as scary."

"The man is all talk. All he wanted was to frighten you into doing things his way. I see his ploy worked. Here you are blubbering about the man when you could be planning the abduction of the Andrews girl. Would you like that more than running scared?"

Jonathan clenched his fists until nail marks were left on his palms. He hated working with bumbling idiots. This man was more than likely to cause him problems he hadn't foreseen than to help solve any. "What can I say to convince you to work with me?"

When Ritter brought his glass to his lips his hand trembled. "Nothing you can say. I'm looking for someone else. If he didn't frighten me, the girl does. She is wild and rebellious, uncouth too. You heard about the recital. She rides astride. Wears pants just like a man. Don't want a woman like that. Don't want to be forever shocked by what my wife does on an impulse."

Lyssa Andrews was exactly the type of woman he wanted. She would entertain him with all her strange quirks. More than anything on this earth, he wanted that title she came with. He supposed if kidnapping her and taking her to Scotland were to come about, he would have to enlist the help of his friends. Sinclair Ritter would be useless. Even the thought of sharing her was not incentive for the man to help.

"He's a breed. That's the rumor. He might take your scalp if you cross the man. Heard half his life he spent living with the Sioux. The earl of Blackmore is no one's fool," Ritter blurted, spittle spewing from his fat lips.

"That's all probably true, expect the part of knowing how to scalp a man." He leaned forward. "I'm no man's fool either."

David and Harry joined him. Sat down with drinks in hand. It was time for him to do some serious thinking. For the last few weeks, Black kept Lyssa isolated at his country estate. The place was a fortress. He would need to figure some way to bring them back to town.

"You've been plotting how to get the Andrew's girl into your clutches?" Harry asked grinning. Before he sat down, he poured himself a drink. "Could help if you give a tiny bit of incentive."

"Not getting anywhere though. I want that title she holds, don't care if we pass her around after I'm sure it's my heir growing in her womb. Don't want there to be any confusion or doubt about that." Thinking, he drummed his fingers on the glass, watching his friends, wondering how they felt about the Andrews girl.

"What if her brother wants to claim that title? You will have gone to a lot to obtain something that won't ever be yours. Understand the rumors say he doesn't. Just tossing out a what if. You don't want to be stuck with her if that happens. Maybe you should reconsider," Harry put the question out there for him to deliberate.

It was a damn good question as far as he was concerned. No, without the title she was too crazy to put up with. He didn't have to see her though, at least not after he got his heir. She was the only woman who had a title worth wedding for in the entire lot of debutantes. Damn, sometimes he wondered if he had all his oars in the water.

"Heard she married the earl," David said smoothly his gaze fully on him. "What do you plan if that's true?"

Jonathan felt the floor drop from beneath his feet. He hadn't heard that yet. The gossip couldn't be true. Hell, anything was possible. More than two weeks passed since he saw her at the Blackmore estate. "Figure out how to get the blasted thing annulled. If it's true that is." He tapped his finger on his chin for a moment. "A man like Black won't want a used woman. If we take her, well, then she'll be used thoroughly by all three of us. Even if they are wed, he won't want her. Most likely a divorce will be in order. After that she is ours."

"What the bloody hell!" Harry jumped to his feet. Before he left, he said, "I value my life more than that. No woman's worth losing a scalp over. You've got to be crazed to suggest something that crazy."

Chapter Seven

Kane didn't have one clue as to what to make of Lys's reticence when it came to saying the marriage vows. He'd not expected her to resist. In truth, he anticipated the exact opposite feelings. Thought she would be eager to tie the knot. Now, second along with third thoughts assailed him. He didn't know how to proceed, except perhaps with great caution. Thoughts of the stolen kisses, the passion coupled with all the desire he felt in her small form swamped him. All he knew was that he wanted her, desperately.

For the moment, he studied her from the corner of his eye. She sat with her long white legs tucked beneath her in front of the fire, sipping her wine. Her lovely blue-eyed gaze appeared to be focused on the flames. Christ, all that went into her stomach since he brought her here was wine. She needed food. He didn't want her to pass out when he made love to her if she allowed him the privilege.

When she finally looked at him, her eyes held a distinctive shimmer, moonlight reflecting off the deep blue color. He didn't want her to cry. His wants didn't matter much. She was going to cry. There wasn't a damn thing he could do about that horrific fact.

Her fear radiated from her. She'd never been afraid of him before. Why was she now? His gut twisted and coiled as he watched the nerves seem to take control of her slender body. He had to do something about this soon. Letting her sit and wallow in her thoughts might not be a good way to go about this night when all he wanted was to hold her, to make love to her to feel the rising passion of her slim form.

As best he could, he gentled his voice, hoping she would open up to him, tell him what troubled her. "Want to talk about it?"

Finding out what 'it' was seemed to be the only way he could approach this problem head on.

To his eternal dismay, she shook her head while she whirled the contents of her mug. The movement of the liquid appeared to fascinate her. With her free hand, she smoothed the fabric of the doeskin dress. The cloth hugged her curves, her nipples pressing outward from the large rounded globes he so longed to explore. The sight aroused him, hardened him to steel. He would have to figure out a way for her to respond to him. As she was now, she seemed to him to be a broken shell of herself. Somehow, he single-handedly did this to her.

"You need to talk about what is bothering you. I'm not going to let this go. Talk to me, please," he persisted on that vein. How the hell was he going to learn anything if she continued with this damnable silence?

For too many seconds she stared at him. Her expression masked behind large blue eyes and a soft mouth that was pressed together in what he could only term disillusionment or perhaps disapproval. When he told her she couldn't ride in such a manner as he discovered today, he understood she would be angry with him. That was her nature. In all his wildest imaginations, he'd not fantasized this total withdrawal.

"Would you listen if I did?"

When she set her gaze on him, she appeared deeply wounded.

Her question felt like a slap on the face. He prided himself in his ability to listen along with his patience. Did she actually believe he didn't listen to her? Perhaps he didn't, not when he was terrified for her life. In those instances, her wishes held little value to him, listening to faulty reasoning unimportant.

"Come here." He patted a place in front of his spread legs. "I wish to hold you in my arms while we speak to each other. I promise I'll listen to whatever you want to say. However, I can't promise that I will give in to your request or agree with what you say. Is that fair?"

There were things he anticipated. Now he expected her to tell him why she hated this marriage. It was, after all, a marriage she proclaimed she wanted the first day she became his charge.

So, what terrible fact made her change her mind? One guess was all it would take.

Her eyes clearly asked the question. *Do I have to?* He patted the spot again thinking he needed to give her a few more choices. That wasn't going to happen anytime soon.

"I would like you to do so. Is that enough?" he said softly while her body shuddered.

The question in her eyes had not been answered yet. Quickly, so as not to burn the bridges he was trying to build, "Only if you would like," he finished thinking this time he would give in to her wishes. If she found a way to come to him on her own, he would be happier. "I was under the impression you wanted me."

An ember popped from the fire. He pushed the burning coal back with the toe of his moccasin. Her shoulders were suddenly not quite so stiff. Kane sensed a softening of the expression on her face. His breath stopped in his lungs while he waited. Maybe all she needed was to feel she had a choice.

She moved slowly, making her way to the spot between his legs. When she sat down, he let the air he'd been holding slip away. A silent feeling of relief swamped him.

Her body fit his to perfection, soft curves molding against hard muscles. In his embrace she was all warmth and tender woman.

She leaned against him. Her pulse at the base of her neck beat rapidly as he placed a finger where the blood beating from her heart throbbed. He wanted to return to his original question. Needed to discover what she kept inside, hiding from him.

"Can you tell me what is bothering you?"

He did stay the course. Would continue to persevere until he knew the answer.

Her chest rose as she tugged in what seemed like a huge breath of air. "I'm not used to having someone order me around. This day has been one order after another. You didn't even give me a real choice about marrying you. You assume you know me. You don't, at least not that well. Neither do I know you. Yet...now we are wed."

Kane always persevered until he got what he wanted. He needed Lyssa more than he needed to breathe. Until now, he believed she felt the same way about him.

"You put your life in danger. If I remember correctly, this is the first issue that has come between us as well as our happiness. I can't allow something like that to continue. You risking your life is not something I will ever allow."

The truth now would help. Her anger over the riding was obvious. There was more though.

"It's not your place to dictate to me," she shot back, brushing tears from her cheeks as if she didn't want him to see she cried. "I hate it when you are so underhanded."

His hand on her shoulder, he squeezed slightly. "Everything you do is now my business. I'm your husband. I will dictate to you only when I feel the issue is necessary. Otherwise, all the choices are yours to make."

She turned to face him, her hands on his chest as if she meant to push him away. Instead, she gripped his shirt in her tiny fists. "Is that why you wanted to marry me so you could order me around, Kane. So you could dictate to me the rest of my life?"

"No. I never intended to marry anyone. Until you…"

He ran his knuckles along her jawline, watching as her tiny pink tongue moved slowly across her bottom lip jolting his body to instant life. The movement left a dewy trail of moistness on her pink flesh. Desperately he wanted to taste her sweetness, the sauciness of her he adored.

"No? Then why?" she asked a perplexed look appearing on her face. "You've given me no reason to even believe you are interested in me. Suddenly, you want to marry me."

Because I love you.

The thought jolted him. Holding her chin in his hand, he let his thumb roam tenderly across her bottom lip. "Is that all that's bothering you? The orders, the command that you don't put your life at risk or possibly the reason is because I didn't get down on one knee to propose marriage to you, or perhaps the motive behind your anger is because I wanted to wed you in the way of the Sioux?"

"Why can you ride that way and I cannot?"

Her anger radiated from her. The grip she held on his shirt tightened perceptibly straining the fabric.

Before he could take her to his furs, he needed to tamp down that rage. The most logical answer was that he was a man and she wasn't. The distinct feeling that if he said as much, her fury would escalate to such gigantic proportions he would never be able to consummate this marriage, at least not tonight. As things between them stood now, his prospects of doing just that diminished more with each passing second. Nipping this tiny bit of rebellion in the bud sooner than later seemed necessary.

He still held her chin, his hold light. "Lys, before tonight have you ever seen me take risks such as I did to prove to you that I'm an accomplished horseman? I took the risk, placed my life in jeopardy so we could put one of your marriage concerns to bed. I've always understood how important certain things were to you. Thought you would be pleased to discover the truth about me. Whether you want to admit to the fact or not, we are suited. Given a choice, I would never risk my life in such a callous manner. I never use my skills to show off."

Silence between them lasted an eternity. Kane wasn't sure she would answer. Whatever response she gave would mute the very point she tried to make with her question. There was only one way she could reply.

"Well?" he prompted while he tried to hide the smile growing behind his teeth.

She would admit to the truth. Confessing would take a bit of time. He was patient. He understood she wanted him. What he didn't comprehend was why she backed off now.

She shook her head, cascades of silken hair fluttering across his fingers. "No," she murmured softly.

"No?"

"I've not seen anything such as that," she finished lamely her delicate and very fragile shoulders lifting a tiny bit. It didn't appear she wanted to concede the truth. Kane knew in the end she would never lie.

"Rumor has it this last two weeks you've been practicing these tricks. How many days is that? Fourteen? I only wish I'd been told earlier of your antics. I would have put a stop to them before they got out of hand. A Sioux warrior practices so he will not die in battle. You, Little Bit, will never be in battle. So, to risk your life in such a way is outrageous." He splayed his hands around her ribcage. "Is there anything else you would like to warm my ears about? Anything else you've been doing that will cause concern. I don't like surprises."

"How did you accomplish this wedding without banns being read? It's not possible, is it? Three weeks, right? Do you even go to church?"

"Ah, a good question from you. It wasn't easy. I had to work hard to get the proper papers in order. If I had decided to marry you two weeks ago, there would not have been a problem. As it was, two days ago when I made up my mind this was the only course for the two of us, I approached the bishop with my needs. He gave me a special license called a marriage bond, which enabled me to forego having the banns read. After that, all I needed was a minister to conduct the marriage ceremony along with your consent. Finding a minister was not too difficult."

His thumbs moved gently along the underside of her breasts. He wanted to entice her, to coax and wheedle until her tiny sounds of pleasure rippled from the softness of her lips, until she no longer feared what would come between them in the marriage bed. From the carriage ride he remembered how she sounded when he sweetly coaxed her. She moved as if to get closer or to avoid. He wasn't positive. What he was certain of was that he enjoyed watching the subtle sway of the beautiful globes beneath the doeskin blouse she wore. Soon he would see them, taste them, caress her sweet jewels. Pull them deep into his mouth, play then arouse, suck each one deeply into the warmth of his mouth. How he wanted her.

"You went to the bishop?"

She gulped air when the back of his hand brushed across the hardened tip of her breast. "Thought you intended for this marriage to be of the People's ways."

"It was. Both ways. What the marriage lacked is the usual bridal gifts and fanfare. It was still a true marriage. Even though I didn't care, I understood you would want a marriage in the English tradition. Besides, I didn't want anyone questioning the status of an heir when you do conceive. We needed God's blessing as well."

That was the truth of his decision. Except for the title passing on to a legitimate heir he would not have cared. In this instant no questions or gossip could surround their joining or the conception of the next earl.

After moving her hair aside, he trailed kisses along her neck, nibbling here and there; enjoying the soft feminine sounds she made relishing the movement of her hips, movement that beckoned him to give her more sensations. His thumbs rose higher tempting and teasing reactions from her. A tiny broken sound emanated from her lips while she pushed back against him. She couldn't stay angry with him for long. Soon, he would carry her inside and set her on his furs. If all went well, tomorrow night they would make love in his bed at the estate. The marriage just as the wedding would be consummated in two different ways, two different cultures. On second thought maybe they should stay here for a week or so. Still Water Runs along with Abernathy would make sure they had everything they needed.

"I would not have considered this a true marriage without the minister. You knew that. Didn't you?"

Despite her initial lack of enthusiasm, her body responded to him. The tips of her breasts hardened. She moved against him as he coaxed responses from her.

Everything about her enticed him.

Tempted.

Seduced and cajoled.

Carefully, he allowed his thumbs to brush across the hardened tips of her breasts that pushed so delicately against the doeskin. Disrupting his subtle coaxing, he reached for a berry, traced the fruit along her lower lip tantalizing and luring her in a different way.

"Take a bite, Little Bit. You need to eat. We will bring the tray of food and wine inside once we are finished here. I want to make love to you all night, perhaps into the morning. We can stay here as long as you want."

As if in a trance she bit down. She closed her eyes. He turned her, their lips touching he accepted the other half into his mouth. Before he left her, he touched her lip with his tongue. Placing his teeth on her lip he tugged. In response, she purred softly.

"Is there anything else you want to talk about?"

He did the same with a second berry. His hands cupped her breasts now. Her fingers rested on his thighs squeezing then relaxing.

She tried to turn in his arms.

He stopped her, needing to take this slow. Before he came inside her sultry warmth, he wanted her so ready for his entry she would beg. He wanted her desperately hungry for him. The pain from their joining would be minimal. This first time with her scared him. He didn't want to hurt her. Understood there was no choice in the matter.

"Did you know I wouldn't protest the marriage?" she asked softly as she ran her fingers along the length of his thigh then back.

He shuddered at the soft hesitant touch, knew she would feel the bulge of his arousal where she sat against him. His hand splayed on her belly drawing her closer, so very tempted to pull her skirt to her waist so he could feel the feminine mound between her legs.

"Do you?" He tossed the question back at her.

That was another truth he needed an answer to. If she protested, he might have to change his plans where this evening was concerned. He'd never taken an unwilling woman. As it stood, unless she wanted this marriage, he would have to consider her unenthusiastic.

"Do I what?"

She looked confused, her eyes so wide moonbeams seemed to glisten within.

"Protest the marriage."

His mouth closed over hers, giving her no chance to reply. Her hands rose to his neck then into his hair as she drew him closer. His hands roamed, exploring and discovering, finally to settle on her tiny waist. He tightened his hands. She was so damn small. God, he didn't want to hurt her.

When he pulled away from her to gaze once more into her eyes, he expected an answer. He kissed the tip of her nose before he tasted the corners of her mouth, "So sweet, so much sass."

"No. It's what I wanted. You know that. What I protest is how you went about this," she whispered softly. "The marriage was sudden. Too abrupt. I didn't have time to adjust to all the changes."

"I wasn't romantic?"

He'd never thought to be saying those words to her. Nothing about his life spoke of romance. Never thought to bend a knee to the earth when he wished to wed. His life until he traveled to England was harsh. Survival was the incentive for everything.

The soft breath of air leaving her lips told him a wealth of information. Perhaps she was wishing for him to act more in conformity to the white man's ways. It wasn't in him to do so. Somehow, he would have to try harder. If she could accept him the way he was, he could give a few concessions. He would try to meet her half way.

"Every girl wants a bit of romance. Didn't believe I required a great deal," she spoke softly. "Thought I was above that. Guess I was wrong."

"By the morning you will have no reason to protest anything. What can I do now to make this evening...romantic for you? Tell me."

When he scooped her into his arms, she was light as a feather. His long strides took them into the lodge. He closed the flap that was letting in the light. Still Water Runs would stand guard tonight along with a few other men. He still had misgivings about White and Ritter.

They would be fools to try anything. With a woman in his arms, he could be caught off guard. Kane didn't doubt for a minute they would try to get to Lyssa even though the marriage should have put them off their game. He wrote an announcement in the London Times to be published tomorrow. Everyone would know they were married in the morning.

The beautiful sight of his wife lying on his furs was a striking apparition. In luxuriant waves, her dark hair was spread across the furs. He needed to make this first time right for her. Watching her, his breath caught in the back of his throat. He didn't understand the turmoil he went through to come to this decision to marry her. She was his now. For the first time since he left the People, he felt happy. Perhaps content was the better description. Felt as if the rest of his life would be filled with love. This was right in every way. They would work out whatever differences lay between them.

Kane stretched out beside her, his fingers running the length of her arm and back. His gaze traced the path wondering how to proceed, he'd never made love to a virgin or a wife. He remembered the time in the carriage. She responded passionately to him. She would do so again. Taking his time, he bent forward to kiss her. Touched her mouth with his, traced the seam with the tip of his tongue. She closed her eyes, her lips forming into a tiny sign of satisfaction.

"Don't be afraid of me," he whispered close to her ear, grazing the lobe with his teeth, nipping gently, licking, pressing his tongue into the center.

Her hands clung to his shoulders. "Only a little," she murmured softly. "I do want you."

Tenderness assailed him. For her to remember this night with wonder was his intent. He moved to take his shirt off. When he settled next to her again, his chest was naked. She touched him, running her fingers along the broad expanse of his torso, exploring the width, grazing his hard nipples as she did so. With the virginal caresses becoming more potent as each second passed, he sipped in a scorched breath of air. His body shuddered while she trailed one nail down the center of his chest to the top of his buckskins. This was a dream come true.

"Sit up, Little Bit."

She blinked at him as if he just brought her from a trance. Her eyes seemed slightly glazed, the dark color of hers deepening with each passing second. "Why?" Her question floated on the sultry air in the tent.

"Why do you think?" He kissed his way along her jaw while he helped her to sit. His fingers slipped beneath the hem of the blouse she wore. As he lifted the fabric, she held to his arms.

"Y-you want me naked?" The question was shaky, hesitant at best. "I-is t-that the way it is s-s-supposed to be done?"

He grinned at her, "Have you forgotten the carriage ride so soon? Do you want me without a stitch of clothing? Both can be accomplished with little fanfare."

"Do you...?"

"Yes, to both questions. Making love isn't too much fun wearing clothing. Clothes makes everything damn near impossible."

"It's embarrassing."

"In the carriage you let me see your breasts. My job is to change that emotion. You should never feel embarrassed when your husband admires you. Lift your arms." In one swift motion, he divested her of the blouse. She wore her chemise. He laughed, seeing she tried to put what she might consider armor between them. "I had not expected you to wear clothing beneath the blouse. What do you have on beneath the skirt? Hmm...should I see?"

"I..." It seemed she lost the ability to speak. She blinked a few times before she turned her head away.

"I...?" he parroted as he pulled her skirt down her hips. She wore her pantalets. "You are making a great deal of work for your poor husband. Work I did not expect. Did you think you could prolong the lovemaking with more clothing? Really, Lys, you couldn't possibly have believed something so shocking."

Bloody eyes, he could tell by the soft shimmering of her eyes that was exactly what she assumed.

Several minutes passed while he studied her. Lys' cheeks as well as what he could see of her breasts turned a deep shade of crimson. The light from the fire flitted across her features enhancing every bewitching curve she possessed. Shadows danced along the length of her. He rose to pour more wine for them. Brought slices of fresh fruit to the bed.

More than anything he wanted her to enjoy the evening. He hadn't quite figured out the best course to take for that to happen. He would though. For the moment, he would give her time to adjust. He didn't understand how exactly. Urgently, near desperate for a man who prided himself with his patience. He wanted her now.

She sipped her wine, a thoughtful expression painted on her lovely face. "I'm afraid because I don't know what will happen. Don't want to ask you to just get this task over with because I doubt if that will please you. However..." She had a faraway dreamy expression on her face. "That is what I want."

To his amazement he understood. While he craved to prolong everything, she needed to discover what was so wonderful about making love with one's husband. "Would you like to forget the food as well as the wine to explore each other more thoroughly? If you like, you can take off my buckskins for me. I won't protest. I would enjoy the experience. Will relish feeling your fingers against my belly as well as my other manly parts. You may touch as well as kiss me anywhere you would like." He bent over to remove his moccasins.

"You would let me undress you?"

The soft sound of amazement seared into him would have brought him to his knees if he'd been standing. Her soft smile sent lust surging straight to his groin.

He nodded. "It would please me to no end if you did so. Is it something you would like to do? Touch as well as kiss all of me?"

"I don't know. Maybe. Yes."

He chuckled, watching as her eyes seemed to cross. With one eyebrow lifted, grinning besotted at her, "That tells me so very much."

"I can leave..." She looked down at her chemise and pantalets before returning her gaze back to him, "...my small clothes on. I would be more comfortable."

"If that is your wish," he grinned thinking about the torture his body would endure when her small hands began their virginal exploration. How well he understood the fire that would surge through him. He would have to grit his teeth. Would have to make sure his hands didn't take on a will of their choosing.

"I can do anything I want?" She sounded hesitant yet at the same time willing to try. Excitement colored her voice.

"Anything."

He choked as her fingers played with the front laces of his trousers. He felt her knuckles graze his belly. The muscles constricted. He swallowed hard, tamping down his lust.

She tugged at them. He groaned. His imagination played havoc with his body, swamping him. The small pressure of her hands against his throbbing arousal nearly unmanned him. He clenched his teeth together so hard his jaw ached with the pressure. This was insane. He might explode.

Her wide startled eyes bored into him. "Are you alright?"

"Never been better," he ground out as he tried to block the path her nimble fingers took from his mind.

Giving her this erotic experience would be his part of his wedding gift to her. He did have others. They were at the estate.

The laces were undone. She sat back on her legs a worried expression on her face. "I don't think I can pull your trousers down unless you help."

"What would you like me to do?"

He tried to keep the grin from bursting from behind his lips. She looked so adorable dressed all in white except for the pale blue ribbons holding her chemise together. He itched to see her completely naked. In time, he would do so. He had the rest of the night, longer if necessary.

"Lift your hips, maybe."

Her fingers at the top of his pants grazed his skin. Beneath his breath he swore softly. He arched his back as she slowly, excruciatingly brought his buckskins to his ankles. The tips of her fingers tickled his feet when she slipped them over his toes. The soft caress seemed feather light, intoxicating as well as exciting, shudders reverberated through his entire body.

Completely naked and open for her very intimate perusal, Kane propped his head with his hands while he watched her. Studied the way her eyes glowed with what he hoped was pleasure. He knew the moment she saw his arousal, hard and thrusting from his body. Before this second, he didn't think her eyes could grow wider. They did.

Unsteadily, she reached her hand in the direction of his rod. He gulped air as he thought about the gentle caress of her hands, even her mouth on the length of him. She didn't touch him there. Instead, she set her splayed hand on his belly. Moved her fingers enough to make him groan again. Seemed to experiment with shy caresses.

"You're so big. Are all men this large?"

Her breath swept across his chest, across his belly then lower to caress that part of him that needed her dreadfully. He wanted nothing more than to feel her warmth surround him, feel her throb with the ecstasy he meant to introduce her to.

He laughed then, "I wouldn't have the foggiest notion. I suppose so. Never seen a fully aroused man before."

Lys stretched out beside him. He felt her breasts through the fabric of her chemise push against the side of his chest. Wished she was as naked as he was. For the moment, her explorations were limited to her hot little fingertips. If she started to use her mouth, he was sure to detonate from the blazing inferno she created. Gritting his teeth, he fought for control.

Didn't want to be embarrassed before the wedding night was barely begun. He wasn't a randy boy with no experience. She would never believe he was experienced if he exploded before he came inside her.

She rose over him. Beneath the chemise her large breasts swayed mouthwateringly. Her mouth closed over a nipple. He jerked to attention. She twirled her tongue around the small nub while her fingers played with the other nipple. His body responded with intensity. She bit down lightly. He gasped his hips bucking into the air his arousal becoming steel-hard even more so than before. Bloody eyes, he told her she could do this. It was all to make the transition to becoming lovers easier.

Easier for who?

Kane decided at this point he might just be up for sainthood. All her actions were hesitant, untried. So stimulating he thought he would surely jump out of his skin. If she was knowledgeable, she couldn't have aroused him more thoroughly. It was the very fact that she was innocent that made each caress so very intoxicating. He was drunk on sinful pleasure.

Wide-eyed she stared at him, her tiny pink tongue on the edge of her lip. "Did I hurt you? I remembered when you did the same to me. The bite didn't hurt. The act generated deep hot feelings in parts of me that are different from you. Does it do the same to your dissimilar parts?" She paused in thought, an impish smile decorated her sweetly kissable lips. "Can I kiss you anywhere?" Lys didn't wait for an answer. She was kissing her way downward closer and closer to that hard swelled part of him that wanted her more than anything, needed to feel her sultry heat surround him.

"Not tonight," he groaned scarcely able to put a coherent thought into his man's brain. "Maybe another time."

Just to keep himself in check he'd closed his eyes straining for the reserve he needed. His fists were clenched at his sides while she stimulated every sense he possessed.

"Oh? Why not tonight?"

Her voice purred over him, soft and so very sultry. The scent of her ingrained in his mind

~ * ~

More than anything she wanted to give Kane pleasure, the same ecstasy he promised for her. She didn't know how. Desperately wanted to learn. Didn't understand why there were some things she could do later but not now. All she did understand at this moment was that everything she was doing to him was affecting her too. Her heart galloped beneath her ribs. Each breath seemed to be a tiny pant. She sipped the much-needed air. Fire enflamed her body when the heat from his hands roamed down her back. She was so hot she wanted to dive into the cool, refreshing waters behind the lodge.

Playing with the ribbons on her chemise, they seemed to fall apart beneath his fingers. She understood he wanted to see her naked. Lyssa also knew she wanted to please him. Quickly, she slipped her chemise over her head watching for his reactions. Her breasts swayed with the slight movement. Cold air swept across her, hardening the tips.

There was no reaction or sign that he saw her naked. She felt disappointed, saddened that he no longer cared.

Her gaze rested on his face. His eyes closed, his jaw set tight, he looked as if he was in pain. At the sight of him, she didn't know what to think. His eyes were still closed. When she pressed her body against his, his lashes flew open. She looked into vivid silver-blue eyes simmering deeply, fervently.

"Lys!"

He jerked, startled by her. His hands that once carelessly held her waist tightened, moved upward across her ribs, stopping beneath her breasts.

Hesitant, hoping to gain some idea about his thoughts, she smiled at him while she ran her busy hands across his chest, sweeping her fingers across his tight, hard nipples. By the look in his eyes, he wasn't displeased. Yes, he appeared very content. Firelight danced in the depth of his eyes as his smile grew large. After she sat back on her knees, she slowly worked her pantalets from her legs then tossed them to join her other clothing. Now, she was exactly how she thought he wanted her. She pushed her hair over her shoulders. Her breasts thrust forward. He stared hard. He swept a calloused fingertip across one hardening crest.

"I never thought," he murmured as he framed his hand to cup her breast. "You are so beautiful, every part of you."

His thumb glided lazily across the hardened pinnacle back and forth until she thought she might scream from the frustration eating her senses. He inflamed her, enchanted, enticed with each sweep of pleasure he generated. She stole a gasp of singed air, held the oxygen deep in her lungs until it burst forth in a rush.

"I didn't know what else to do. It seems I've wanted this forever. I've only known you a few weeks though. Is that all it takes to know the depth of one's feelings?"

Her head fell back, her dark hair spilling around her shoulders down to her bottom as she absorbed all the sensations he generated. His touch was so very erotic, dreamlike, bewitching. Every part of her seemed to swell with softness and heat. She never wanted him to stop.

"You are perfect. You are so soft," he murmured, his voice rough the texture invitingly throaty as he seemed to watch her waiting for whatever part of him she decided to torture next.

Lyssa didn't know what to do now. "I've never seen..."

She swept her tongue across her bottom lip. Well, she'd never seen a totally naked man before. This man, her husband, was her first. She didn't think any man could be as beautiful. "Never seen..."

He was grinning obnoxiously as if he knew exactly what she tried to say, arrogant man. His was a dangerous smirk. Of course, she'd never seen a naked man. Of course, Kane would know that or at least assume as much. If she had, would he still want her?

"I know. Do I measure up to your imagination?" he queried softly his hands still working magic.

Now they danced and played with her breasts. He bent to touch one peak with his lips, grazed with his teeth.

She wanted him to take them into his mouth, suck them deeply into his moist heat. He tempted and excited. His every caress heated and melted. She was certain if something more didn't happen, she would shatter into a million tiny pieces. Her nerves were stretched to the breaking point.

"Yes," her voice was quivering while she tried to put forth more words. "You are beautiful. I never thought," she swallowed hard, "a man's body could be so stunning. You are hard everywhere, even here. Her fingers rested on his belly. "I want you but I don't understand what to do. What you would want me to do. You said I could kiss you anywhere. Is that true?"

"True. Just not this moment." Kane looked as if he liked her answer. "Are you through sightseeing your husband's body?" he asked softly. "I'd know before we take this farther. If you are done playing with this man, I would make to love to you now. Would you like that?"

Her nod sent tendrils of hair cascading around her, running like heated silk across his belly. The tender very sensitive pink tips of her breasts peeked out from between the long midnight-dark strands. Through her hair he flattened his hands against the hardened tips. She'd never seen the tips of her breasts so hard. Then he kissed her there. Suckled the rounded globe deep inside his mouth. She cried out. The sound of her voice was harsh and needy. He bit softly on one tight crown. Her body coiled and arched while her hips seemed to rise against him. Parts of her tensed and squeezed as if needing something only he could give. She throbbed in her most private and intimate places.

This was heaven.

Quickly, he flipped her onto her back. He stretched his hard body over hers, one leg coming between her legs to spread them apart. For a moment she panicked. Reared up. Didn't understand her fear. The terror was real though. In that second, she understood there would be no turning back.

"Easy, Lys," he murmured close to her ear. "I'm not going to hurt you, at least not, well hell, just a little. Your first time, a little bit of pain can't be helped. Spread your legs wider. I want to see all of you, all the swollen pink folds of your woman's body."

"Are you going to come inside me now?"

She felt the hair on his legs against her thighs. Felt him push hers farther and farther apart. Knew he looked at her. She wanted to cover herself. He held her hands by the side of her head while he gazed into her eyes.

"Not yet, soon though. I'll let you know when it's time. Is that satisfactory with you? Can you wait a bit longer for your woman's pleasure? I've so many places to taste and touch. Doing so will take more minutes."

How could she question or protest when he bent over backward to ease her feminine fears. She understood her body would protest if she told him no. Didn't want to do so. More than anything she wanted him to well and truly make love to her.

For a moment she lowered her lashes wishing she could give him a different answer. "Yes. I can wait."

She didn't want to. She could though. She was primed and ready for something indefinable to her.

"Yes? Yes, it's acceptable?" he asked seeming concerned, solicitous even.

His knuckles brushed gently across her cheek then down her neck. She shivered in response.

By his tone of voice there was no doubt for her about his apprehension. She felt a ninny to question him in any way at all. He would make this right for her, better than right.

As if he didn't want to talk any longer, he rose over her. His lips crushed softly against hers then harder. He kissed her and kissed her pushing her lips apart. He sent his tongue between her lips to dance and frolic with hers before allowing her to change the tune he played. Her hips rose touching the hard planes of his body, feeling his smooth hot sex against her belly. She felt as if she begged him for his favors.

She did then. "Please..." Her nails bit into his shoulders, before trailing down his back. Beneath his big body, she twisted and curled seeking, requesting seeming to implore the heat his body promised along with the fulfillment she knew nothing about, just understood the ecstasy existed. Knew too, if she allowed him free reign, he could give that fulfillment to her.

His lips traveled along her neck then lower to make their way across her collarbone. He bit then laved where he left a tiny mark. He kissed the spot again, sucking there. She wasn't at all sure why except the erotic exploration sent more penetrating and powerful sensations coursing through her, swamping her, flooding her with a deepness she didn't recognize. The next phase of his exploration sent him to her breasts. He pulled one deep into his mouth, teased and danced with the tip just as he'd done with her tongue.

She was beyond herself with need.

He moved lower. His hand splayed across her belly. He kissed her there let his mouth explore lower then lower still. Until her body soared tensing with the exquisite pleasure he doled out to her. Suddenly, his head rested between her legs. He teased her inner thighs, slipping lower until he found tender erotic spots behind her knee, lower still until he reached her toes. After he gently kissed each one, he explored the length of her other leg until his lips nestled between her thighs again.

A small broken sound escaped her. Her moan of pleasure brought a smile to his lips as he lifted his head to gaze at her. He pushed back as if he wanted to watch her. He studied her. She wondered what exactly he thought. His hands were splayed on her stomach, his long fingers moving until they were at the apex of her thighs. It was too much when they dipped lower spreading her folds, teasing her until she arched into his caress. He smiled again, a self-satisfied grin. A strange stillness settled around her.

"Kane?"

"What?" With tenderness she never knew before, he pushed strands of damp hair from her face. His mouth closed over hers again. She opened for him as his large hands were now between her legs. He stroked her. Touched her in ways she'd never dreamt of a man doing.

"I don't know?" her question was a slight cry that seemed to give him pleasure. She gulped air. "I don't know."

He stroked her again. "You're so hot and wet, soft and sweet in all the right places. A man could believe he'd died and gone to heaven."

He slipped a finger inside her, pushed it deep then deeper still. "So small and tight. So, hot and wet the thought boggles the mind."

Two fingers found their way inside her, moving slowly.

Her hips bucked desperate for him, for more. She bit her lips. He swept them with his tongue, easing the pain. All she wanted was for the culmination of this. No, she didn't want him to stop. When he stroked her so sweetly, her body assumed a life all its own. When his legs pushed hers even farther apart, she tried to reach him with her hips. He played with her intimately. Found a spot that sent more penetrating heat rushing through her. She pushed against him as if she could create more of those same sensations.

"Please..."

She was beside herself with need with uncontrolled wanting. Suddenly her body seemed to have a will of its own. Pulses of pleasure swept through her igniting her until she had no control. His fingers moved more quickly. "Kane!"

She was filled with shattering pleasure, with light then darkness. The sweetest of colors danced behind her closed eyes as the ecstasy seared her.

Unexpectedly, his member replaced his fingers. With great slowness, she felt him move inside her expanding her to take his great size.

"Hold still, Little Bit," he murmured as he eased himself into that place where his fingers drove her wild. "I don't want to hurt you more than necessary. Just a tiny bit of pain. Just a small stab then all will be pleasure."

"Necessary," she said as her mind seemed to blaze with other ideas. "You feel so good inside me, so hard and strong."

"In a few minutes you will feel even better."

His grin was wide and arrogant. It seemed he was filled with a man's confidence.

His heat completed her, made them one with each other. Slowly, he pulled out a bit before pushing farther inside. It was too much to stand. Once more her hips bucked sucking him deeper and deeper into the depth where she understood more ecstasy would erupt. She pulsed and coiled. Twisted then turned. Her hips rose and fell. This was heaven yet hell. Beneath his hard body, she moaned and heaved.

"I'm there." Gently he kissed her cheeks, the hollow of her throat seeming to savor the moment.

"Where?"

"At your thin membrane that proclaims you are a virgin. When I push through, you will feel the pain, only for a moment though. I don't want to hurt you. If there was any other way." Without further preamble, he thrust hard.

"Kane!" she cried out again, her nails bit into his skin.

This wasn't a cry of pleasure. Tears rimmed her eyes, spiked her lashes. He saw the miniscule droplets of moisture on the tips. Softly, he kissed the tears, stroking them with his tongue until they disappeared. She bucked again attempting to rid herself of the cause of the pain. It wasn't with pleasure. Again, she tried to free herself of the man, purge herself from the pain. When she looked into his eyes, she saw his agony written in the fine lines surrounding them.

"Hold still. It will pass soon. From then on you will feel only the sweetest pleasure."

He kissed the drops of tears that slipped from her eyes. Kissed her lips with gentleness. Touched his mouth upon her eyelids then the tip of her nose.

The sensation of his moving inside her brought her to the realization that in truth she felt no more pain. "Only pleasure," she moaned softly as he moved farther and deeper inside her.

His satin length stirred within her. She was moving with him, matching his pace. He was so deep, so very deep, and hard, steel hard. He was plunging harder and faster. Spasms of delight swept through her over and over again. Her climax came when he cried out his pleasure, leaving his seed inside her.

Lyssa closed her eyes so exhausted she didn't think she could lift a finger to do anything else. Beneath him she was limp. He rolled to the side tugging her with him. She was flush against him, her breasts pushing against his broad chest. Tenderly, his hands soothed her flesh, moving down her back to her bottom cupping and squeezing.

"You have an adorable little backside, soft and wonderfully curved for a man's delight." Smoothly, he pushed strands of her hair aside so he could nibble on her neck.

"I can't move, Kane," her voice whispered in the night air.

"You will soon."

He turned her again so her body lay atop him, her legs spread across his thighs.

With his simple coaxing actions, his member seemed to spring to life. "Again? You can do that?" she asked, amazed at the thought.

He was inside her once more. She felt herself tighten around his rod.

"Seems I've waited so long for you, Lys. I can't get enough of you."

Again, he squeezed her bottom, trailed his hands between her legs, touched her, caressed her intimately. Another storm possessed her, the tempest writhing in waves of molten fury.

A broken sound slipped from her lips, soft purrs following delight. He made love to her again. When they finished, she thought she'd never felt so replete and satisfied in her life, exhausted too. He strode to the washbasin. Found a soft cloth.

He sat down on the furs beside her. "I'm going to wash your virgin blood from you, Lys. No more pain. I promise."

Embarrassment flooded her when he spread her legs then methodically proceeded to wash her, to look at her. When she was in the throes of passion, she didn't think about what he did or what he saw. Desperate to conceal herself, she tried to push them together. He chuckled as he stopped her attempts. Somehow this seemed so different from before when he coaxed her to her pleasure. At that time, she opened for him almost without thought. She saw her virgin's blood stain the cloth as well as the water. Blood pooled in her cheeks.

"Are you sore?"

Lyssa looked away from his gaze, the heat of her embarrassment potently sizzling though her. She couldn't face him. In any case, she didn't know how to do so. If she could, she would dress again. Had the incessant urge to hide away from his gaze. Heat flooded her face as she recalled shirking her undergarments from her body.

"No. Well, a little."

"We should probably have some of that delicious food along with the wine my cook sent us. What do you think? Are you hungry now? Can you eat? No more fluttering stomach to keep you from enjoying the delectable wedding fare that waits for us. We will need sustenance in order to enjoy our wedding night the way the time should be enjoyed."

"Believe I could eat something."

Her stomach chose that moment to rumble. She thought she could eat everything on the platter. She didn't think she'd ever felt so hungry in her entire life.

It seemed Kane ignored the less than subtle sound. "I'm famished too." He grinned at her showing white teeth behind the bronze of his face, "Even though you tasted delightful. Even though I can't wait to taste all your soft charms again. Would you like that? When we are finished with the first course, we can try something different?"

The cloth he washed her with plopped into the basin. He poured two glasses of wine. After that he brought the platter of food. Beside her, he sipped the red wine. His head rested against the back of the lodge.

She looked away in an attempt not to stare at all his male beauty. When she tried to cover herself, he stopped her, his large hand resting lightly on top of hers.

"I touched and tasted most every part of you. There is nothing for you to be ashamed for me to see. Don't be shy, Little Bit. I want to look at you until I cock up my toes. Want to make love to you every night or day or both for the next fifty years, even more if that will be possible. You will have to get used to that notion. In time you will."

"That's very British of you," she said unable to hide her smile, not that she wanted to hide anything from him.

It was just that his words surprised her. In most every way, Kane was more Sioux than English.

"What is?"

One dark eyebrow rose heavenward as if he questioned her comment. He grinned though, giving her the impression he knew exactly what she meant.

Before she answered she popped a berry into her mouth then chewed thoughtfully. "Cock up your toes," she repeated his words for him no longer feeling shy. "No one would say something that absurd in the states. I doubt if any warrior would repeat the phrase. Maybe I've stuck my oar into the water too soon. What do you think?"

"Ah, you call that British? I suppose it is. Have another berry, my love."

He ran the succulent fruit across her lips until she opened for him. He teased her, tempted her to bite then brought the mouthwatering fruit away from her lips only to then repeat the performance until she wanted to cosh him over the head.

Lyssa felt certain he had something else in mind with the teasing. She supposed she would discover the truth soon enough. Finally, he pushed the fruit into her mouth. After she chewed and swallowed, she asked him feeling a bit silly, "Are you trying to keep me quiet?"

"When do you want to travel to Baltimore?"

He twirled his wine in his glass watching her intently. The dark red liquid, lovingly kissed the sides of the crystal.

She couldn't help herself. She stared at his mouth, knew how soft and moist his lips were. Remembered exactly how they felt against hers, next to other parts of her too. "Didn't know we were traveling anywhere? Why?" She thought possibly to hold a wedding with the minister from her church. Maybe just to celebrate with her parents. A party might be in order, a cake too. "If we go to see my parents, I would like the reverend Brown to wed us."

She didn't know how he would feel about another marriage ceremony.

"Have to take your father the fifty horses I owe him as your bride price." After he said those words, he studied her intently, seeming to expect a reaction. She was stunned.

Fifty horses? Bride price?

Lyssa didn't understand what he wanted from her. The air she sipped stuck in her throat as she tried to swallow. While she understood something about his tribe's traditions, she never thought he would offer her father a bride price. She wondered how her father would take the gesture. He might be angry, in the process not accept the gift. That fact would anger Kane. He was a proud man.

"Fifty horses...don't you think that is a bit much? From what you told me, they are among the finest racers in England and Ireland. They must have cost you a small fortune." She wanted to understand. Truly she did.

"If your father asks for one hundred, I'll get them for him. You are worth every one of them and more," he said stoically.

Tender fingers brushed hair from her face. His knuckles roamed along the line of her jaw then lower. When he looked down, she knew he was seeing her breasts, remembering.

Lyssa found herself shaking her head in disbelief. "If I could find some way to understand..." She caught her bottom lip beneath her teeth.

"You are worth more than fifty horses. That is a paltry sum for a woman as beautiful as you. In case you haven't guessed it yet, you are my life. You hold my heart in the palms of your tiny hands. You mean everything to me. There is no price too high to pay for you."

Tenderly, he ran his thumb along her bottom lip.

She felt the rough callouses formed from hard work. At the contact she sucked in a breath of air. Once again, her body hummed to life. Wanted to feel his body next to hers, know the exquisite sensations he generated in her so effortlessly.

"How?"

She felt the gentle coaxing as his gaze caressed her, settled once more on her breasts, which were barely hidden by the sheet. She swallowed hard on a lump of air stuck in her throat. "How will you transport that many horses? It won't be easy."

He shrugged his broad shoulders while his fingertip explored her naked shoulder then lower to travel the length of her arm. A shuddering response to his caress bubbled in ribbons from deep in her belly. Her sigh of pleasure was whisper thin.

"A ship, perhaps two. I would have to make their voyage comfortable. Don't you think? Two ships. Fifty horses would need two ships. Do you think three would be better? I'll bow to your wishes. Just tell me."

This was all too absurd for further comment. He couldn't mean to transport fifty horses across the Atlantic to Baltimore, a couple, maybe even ten, but fifty?

"You're certifiably crazy. You know that, don't you?"

She drank deep of the tasty wine. Felt the slight sensations wine always gave her. She knew if she drank much more, she wouldn't be able to think straight. Would have a bit of a dizzy head. Ah, but did she want to think? No, all she wanted at the moment was to feel.

"Perhaps I am." He topped off her wine. "What would you like to do now? Make love again? No, that might not be a good idea even if you're willing. Are you willing, Lys? Can I count on that soft, sweet body to respond to my tender loving care?"

She ignored the temptation to give in to his sweet-talking. "You can leave all your business ventures to sail to America? It doesn't seem wise. What will people think?"

"Would like to wait until the duke and duchess return from their search for Nickie, your cousin. That might not be possible though. From the last missive I received, they still had no idea where the couple have flown too. They are probably making love in every port they come across. Why they could be all the way to Spain by now. No, they would not wait until they reached a port. I'm sure your cousin will return married as well as with child."

"You do, don't you? Want to make love again? Do you know where they are?" she asked wondering when they would get back to the original question.

Spain? No, she didn't believe they would travel that far abroad.

"I might if you do. Are you tender?" He looked down. "Want you to be able to walk when morning rolls around. As to Collin's whereabouts, it's none of my business."

He took her glass from her then set the crystal on the ground beside him. He pulled her between his spread legs, the sheet falling to her waist. Lovingly, he stroked her breasts, touched the tips lightly with his tongue.

The sensitive pinnacles hardened with the sensual contact. She responded, her body once more coming to life under his affectionate tutelage. "You're not going to tell me."

She supposed he didn't trust her yet. In this case, she wanted him to confide.

"Who would you tell? The people who are most interested in her whereabouts are too far away."

She turned in his arms. Her breasts floated against his chest.

Tingling sensations rippled within as they brushed across him, felt the smoothness of his bronzed flesh. Air sipped into her lungs. She wanted him again.

"They are in my hunting lodge in the most northern part of Scotland one can find. I'm sure by now the duke and duchess will be sailing in that direction. They are not stupid. They will figure out the course the amorous pair sailed. The duchess as well as the duke understands we are dear friends, also that I've a hunting lodge there. It is only a matter of time before they set their sights in that direction."

"You didn't tell them." Lyssa was surprised at that.

It seemed where Aunt Ella was concerned Kane was her loyal subject.

He lifted his broad male shoulders again. "I promised my friend. Had I not done that I would have told them where Collin and Nickie were headed in the beginning. As the facts stand, I could not. Ella understands loyalty as well as promises."

"Nickie went with him willingly. I'm sure of that fact. She must love him to defy everything she's been taught."

Lyssa sounded sure of that fact. Had Kane asked her to go to his hunting lodge with him before they were married, she would have done the same. She would have gone anywhere he asked.

"We should take the horses to your father before you begin to increase. The passage will be too difficult if you are huge with child." He kissed her lips then the tip of her nose followed by the corner of each eye.

Before this moment she hadn't thought of that, a child. Her eyes seemed to cross as she counted back in time. She never did keep track of her monthly. Doing so never seemed necessary. She didn't know how she thought about a child, a pregnancy.

"If you think about it, you could now carry my child at this moment. I emptied my seed inside you twice now. Although the chance of that happening would be highly unlikely, it is possible."

All her blood seemed to drain from her face. She swayed into him. He caught her chin with his fingers, lifting it so she had to look at him. Lowering her lashes to avoid the heated contact, she tried to think. Wanted to avoid him. Couldn't.

When she opened her eyes, she saw into his. Knew if he didn't love her, he cared about her. "If that is possible..."

"Oh, it is."

"We should travel soon unless you want me to have the baby on English soil. If we stayed until I conceive, we might not go for over a year from now. A newborn should not be subjected to a trip across the Atlantic."

~ * ~

Jonathan White sat with his friends at the top of a hill, looking down on Black's lodge. It had taken several discussions with his friends to decide how to go about his scheme. If he were to gain a title, he needed to marry an heiress. Lyssa Andrews was the heiress he wanted. He was willing to do whatever was necessary to achieve his goal. While David and Harry didn't agree that murdering the earl would be in anyone's best interest, they all concluded his death was the only way he could achieve his goals. As the situation stood now the couple were legally wed. That fact put a big hitch in the plans he made. At first taking her away to Scotland where a quick wedding could be performed was the best solution. Now, before he could do that, he needed to purge the world of the Earl of Blackmore. His death was the only answer that would solve his problem.

Yes, the Earl of Blackmore had to meet his maker for Jonathan's plans to come to fruition. Lyssa had to become a widow before she conceived his heir. If she did so, his plans would be further complicated. That was all there was to this situation gone terribly awry. With the two of them holed up at the edge of his property, no one would be the wiser as to the perpetrator of the crime. There would be no witness, no one to point a finger his way. If things went off as planned, even Lyssa wouldn't know the truth. She might have suspicions but she wouldn't know.

The two lovebirds had been here for two weeks now. That fact galled him to no end. In all that time, Black's Indian friend did not leave. He stood guard. The man protected with a loyalty Jonathan didn't understand. In the interim, he had not been able to spend all his days and nights watching and waiting. He would have to become proactive. Would have to do something to lure Still Water Runs away from his duties.

"Perhaps we need a diversion. Get Still Water Runs away from the lodge so you can shoot the earl. That would work. Unless we get the one and only witness away..."

"You don't have to expound on that fact. There can be no eyewitnesses. No one must know who shot the earl," Jonathan said while he tapped his finger on his jaw.

He just didn't know what could cause a diversion on a large enough scale to force Still Water Runs from his duties. What to do about Lyssa? She would know.

"We can shoot them both," Harry said with a touch of sarcasm to his words. "Though I don't like the idea of shooting either of them. Seems you should find another debutante with a title. If that is what you're wanting, finding a suitable gel shouldn't be too hard. One you could bend to your will. You're a wealthy man, good looking. When you want, you ooze charm. Don't think you've ever had trouble finding a willing woman."

"The fact of the matter is I'd have to find one who will inherit the title upon wedding me because there is no son. That is not so easy. Lyssa comes ready made for that. She is the only woman I know who will work."

"It's all rumor. Who's to know if her brother won't up and decide he wants that title? Even her brother's son, when he has one, would be in line. If he does, all this will be for naught. No one can predict the future. You know that."

Jonathan didn't like this plan either. However, he'd invested too much time in this one venture to cease with his tactics. When he watched them make love outside the lodge one morning, he found he wanted her more than he'd ever wanted another woman, more than he ever thought possible. Her small white body tempted him more than he would ever admit. It would not be difficult to make love to her. No, he thought as he'd watched her respond passionately with wild abandon to the earl, she would be his. Soon, he would have her in his bed, a willing participant. He discounted the fact she might love her husband. Women were fickle creatures. They didn't understand love, only passion along with pleasure a man would dole out when he wished.

"If we're caught it'll be Newgate for all of us or Botany Bay. That's for certain," David spoke softly with a strange reserve Jonathan never heard from him before. "Don't want any part of the shooting. Not into murder. I'll claim ignorance if we're questioned. I won't jeopardize my future. Providing a diversion for Still Water Runs would be fine by me. That part I can do without guilt. Other than that small part, I don't want to know anything else."

"You're going to have to do the shooting, Jonathan," Harry agreed as he cast his attention his way. "I'm not going down for murder."

"What are the three of you doing here?"

Still Water Runs seemed to have come from nowhere. He approached so silently none of them heard. Negligently, he sat on his big bay stallion, his arm draped across his thigh. His hard-edged look riveted on Jonathan as if he'd heard the plans they were making.

Jonathan shuddered squirming at the expression the formidable man slanted him. For a moment, he had second thoughts about the sanity of this scheme of his. The man was huge; his thighs tree trunks, as were his arms. Physically, he was a formidable opponent. Jonathan might well squander his life over this conspiracy. The question remained. Was Lyssa Andrews worth his life? He would think on that fact. Strategies were not yet put into motion.

"Just out for a little ride," he replied nonchalantly wondering what kind of diversion would make this man leave his post.

The distraction would have to be serious, probably only if another life was at stake. He thought on all his acquaintances. Perhaps a whore if he paid her well enough would agree to this unique proposal. The lady wouldn't have to comprehend the particulars.

"On Blackmore land? Seems a bit out of the way for a little ride. I suggest the three of you leave immediately. If I see you again, I'll run you off." Still Water Runs didn't move, not even a tick on his jaw changed his stoic expression.

"I say, old man," Harry began as he wiped the beaded sweat from his forehead, "don't see that you have the right. We're not hurting anything. Just taking a little look around."

"You're trespassing on private property. I can do what I please. Have the authority granted by the earl. Carte blanche you might say. He won't mind if I rid his land of the likes of you three bounders. Or," he paused as if for emphasis, "I could rid the three of you of your scalps."

No, he most likely would not mind at all. Jonathan eyed the wicked knife hanging on Still Water Runs' belt. He wondered how many men Still Water Runs scalped.

Scalped. He tried to swallow the lump of fear lodged in his throat.

Chapter Eight

The day was exceptionally clear, the sky so blue he wanted to bask in the sight. He and Lys were going back to the estate today. They'd been luxuriating and enjoying the newness of their marriage for the past three weeks. There was too much to be accomplished, too many documents to go over. For this brief span of time, he managed to capture the freedom of his life so long ago. This was a short-lived respite in time, as duties called.

If he were a lucky man, Lys would be increasing. She would carry his heir. If not, they would have to keep trying. The trying was so very enjoyable so much pleasure. She enjoyed the efforts as much as he did.

Ah, they spent the fourth of July with a picnic of fried chicken and potato salad finished off with apple pie. She also insisted on lemonade. When he informed her as a warrior of the Sioux nation, he never celebrated that holiday, she sent him a disappointed scowl. Lyssa even managed to procure some fireworks that Still Water Runs set off for them.

He did relish the beautiful display in the sky.

Once he got all his affairs in order, they would sail to Baltimore then on to her father's ranch with the fifty horses in tow. It might take a week or two for all the preparations.

He would see.

Jeremy and Drew made the notion clear they wished to travel with them. Told him London was growing too boring. They needed excitement in their lives: a bit of adventure would cure the monotony of their everyday lives. America would be an escapade, an adventure in the making. Drew even had the audacity to say he wanted to see a real Sioux warrior.

After he got over his slight pique that his friend didn't consider either him or Still Water Runs a true and real Sioux warrior, he decided to give the man a tiny geography lesson. Kane explained to him that the Sioux lived in the plains nowhere near Baltimore, hundreds of miles away. He might see Cherokee or someone from another tribe. Odds were against that simply because most tribes stayed away from the populated areas. They were all finding themselves pushed west. He along with Still Water Runs were the closest humans to a Sioux warrior he would ever meet. He would have to make do even if he wasn't satisfied.

He left Lys bathing in the lodge with water he heated over the fire. While he wanted to watch, he understood what would transpire between them if he remained. A few minutes of privacy for her simply meant they would start for home that much sooner.

While he watched the water shimmer in the sunlight, the small pond they spent hours frolicking in was smooth as glass. He picked up a rounded flat stone and skipped it across the still water. Thought of his friend, Still Water Runs, he mused thoughtfully. This pond was very deep in the center. So was his friend. His thoughts were always deep and thoughtful though he rarely shared them. They grew up together on the plains. He'd been surprised when Still Water Runs decided to follow him to England. Never did give a reason. He was heartily glad of his decision.

A woman's shrieking caught his attention. He turned, concerned for Lys. The voice wasn't his wife's. What was some woman doing on his land, screaming like a banshee? There was something wrong. He heard horse hooves pounding the earth. Still Water Runs was seeing to this issue. The long breath he inhaled was one of gratitude for his friend. Long strides took him in the direction of his lodge, concern for Lys still prominent in his mind.

When he reached the edge of the woods, he saw more clearly. Sitting astride his stallion, Still Water Runs raced away from him toward the woman. He reached the lady who was running from side-to-side, frantically waving her arms. Her long dark hair spilled out in streaming waves behind her. Bellowing. Crying out that someone was after her. There was no one in sight.

This was passing strange. His gut churned. The woman veered then veered a second time escaping her rescuer. Still Water Runs closed in on her. She swerved again, eluding Still Water Runs attempts to help her.

Pain exploded in his chest. The pistol shot surprised him, caught him off guard. He'd been distracted, watching the woman flee the warrior. His hand rested atop the spot where the projectile had entered. When he looked at his hand, his fingers were covered with blood. His first thought was that someone shot him. His second was of Lys.

Slowly, he fell to the ground unable to reach her. Fear for her swamped him. Helpless, he reached out for her. He couldn't move.

Hearing Lys' screams, he tried to sit up, tried to go to her. She was beside him. Her hand rested on his forehead. "You've been shot," she murmured.

Yes, he knew that.

Her fingers fumbled with his shirt, tearing at the place where the bullet entered. He found the strength to hold her wrist, "Stop, Lys." His voice sounded like a hollow shell of itself.

"Kane, I have to help!"

"No, listen, run, run as fast as you can. Ride Ashes. Go home to Baltimore."

He licked his dry lips watching her. Somehow, he knew this was about her. He had to make certain she remained safe. He would find her. He would survive. What was important was that she live.

"Kane, you're—"

"Go home, I'll find you. Take Ashes." *If I'm still alive.*

Blackness engulfed him. Dreams assailed him. He was on the prairie, hunting buffalo. He was raiding settlers' homes. The houses burned. Charred remains were left. White folks died. The massacres were endless. Sweat beaded on his upper lip. He watched as the braves violated white women. Scalped the men. All of it was because whites raided their villages. Sioux women and children were slaughtered and raped.

He vomited.

The other warriors made fun of him. The breed couldn't act like a brave warrior. He became more and more determined. His age didn't matter. This was his first war party. He was all of twelve, large for his age. Not as large as Still Water Runs who rode beside him. Still Water Runs never abandoned him. He was always by his side, would always protect him.

Black Thunder drifted in and out of a conscious state. When he was semi-aware, Still Water Runs sat by his bed, singing, chanting the songs of the Sioux, healing songs. The base of his shoulder into his chest throbbed painfully. He closed his eyes, drifting back to sleep then the dreams came again. Lys was beneath him. He gave her pleasure. She cried out his name. He wanted her more than he'd ever wanted another woman. The thought struck him that he loved her. He loved her with all his heart.

When he saw her next, he would have to tell her. Where was she? He woke occasionally when the doctor examined his wound. He opened his eyes when Still Water Runs helped him drink the bitter tea.

The curtains in the master suite must be open wide. Sunlight slanted into the room making him squint. This time he knew he was awake, fully, and completely awake. Felt the throbbing pain in his chest, which told him he was still alive. Tried to remember what happened to him. For a moment, he let his eyes drift closed. Some gut feeling deep inside cried out to him, told him he had to open them. There was something wrong. The sixth sense he always had closed around his heart, coiled in his stomach. Deep poignant loss assailed him.

Lyssa was in trouble.

He lay on a bed nursing a wound while she needed him. She was strong. No matter what happened she would survive. He remembered he told her to go home. Prayed she obeyed him. Deep inside where all the pain was centered, he tried to smile. She never liked his commands.

He would find her.

Still Water Runs stared at him. "Ah, you're awake, this time for longer than a few seconds. Thought you would sleep another day away." His laughing smile turned serious. "How are you feeling?"

"Like those fifty horses I have for Lys' bride price just thundered over me. Where is Lyssa?"

Deep down he knew the explanation would not be something he wanted to hear. Understood his friend wanted to tell tall tales to minimize what happened to her but wouldn't.

"So, my friend, you want to know about your wife before I tell you what happened to you."

Kane didn't like the tone of Still Water Runs' voice or the shadows in his eyes. There was something terribly wrong. He didn't like to see the strain on his friend's face. "Yes, I want to know where my wife is. She should be here by my side."

"What you say is a truth that cannot come to fruition. Perhaps the tale would be better to share with you when you are stronger."

Anger seethed in him as he tried to sit up. "Tell me. Don't deny me and try to bribe me with this knowledge."

Still Water Runs looked out the window for a second. The sigh issuing from his lungs was long and deep. "Very well, you will get your wish. We don't know. Jeremy and Drew have been looking for her these past six days. They don't have the necessary tracking skills. Though they are doing their best. She disappeared the day you were shot. What do you remember about that day?"

"Bloody eyes, six days! I've been in this bed for six long days! You don't know where she is?" His heart broke into pieces. She could be dead. He calmed himself. "What happened?"

"You were shot. I left my post to chase after this crazy woman who was yelling and screeching, waving her arms wildly while I tried to help. It was only a moment. Heard the shot. Raced to find Lyssa. She was gone. Had to find you. When I did you were near death."

"You should have gone after Lyssa," he gritted out, his hands fisted, desperate for the strength to get out of the bed.

"I did as soon as the doctor told me you would live. All I know by the tracks that were left behind is that she was chased. She dodged the men on horseback until there was nowhere for her go. I had to come back to you. I'm certain once the two of us follow the tracks we will find her. She is smart. Not city bred. She will be a handful for the man. He might come to regret what he did."

"White or Ritter?"

He clenched his fists, pushing from the bed. He was still so weak he couldn't get the desired results. Lyssa was in trouble. Lying back, he felt bone deep fear coupled with exhaustion. Defenseless was not a feeling he was used to. Only once before had he experienced anything as devastating. This was far worse. This time, Lys, needed him.

"They headed north to Scotland. She rode pillion with one of her kidnapers. By the time we were able to track more thoroughly we lost the trail. There just wasn't the time to search thoroughly. I know now that you are safe, we can pick it up again."

In his heart he knew what was happening. White believed him to be dead. Now, he raced to Scotland. "An uncontested marriage. Gretna Green?"

Kane drank the beef broth. He had to regain his strength.

"Most likely."

He slept. The night was tormented by his fears for Lyssa.

When morning light careened into his room, he felt stronger. Still Water Runs nodded off in a chair next to where he slept. "I can't stay in this demandable bed," he gritted out, his teeth clenching with the raw fury and contempt he felt for Jonathan White. It had to be White. Ritter would be too frightened of him to try something like this.

His endeavors to push himself from the covers failed miserably. He fell back, drained and weak from his efforts. The worst of it all was that he knew Still Water Runs could have tracked Lys. He didn't because his first loyalty was to him.

Another week passed before he was strong enough to walk from the bedroom to the drawing room. Negotiating the stairs left him sweating profusely. He found he was so exhausted from his efforts all he could do was sink down into the chair by the fireplace and watch the flames lick at each other. When he closed his eyes, all he saw was his wife. She needed him. He couldn't come to her aid.

"Lyssa…" Her name whispered longingly from his lips.

Two more days passed, his improvement tangible. He rode Ashes with Still Water Runs beside him. He remembered he told her to take Ashes. She must not have had the time to reach the stallion before the men captured her. Lyssa would have fought. He prayed she used restraint then bided her time. Hoped she understood that tactic. He'd never had time to teach her even though deep in his heart he understood she might need to use that deception.

Together they examined the tracks left by White and two other men, the dodged footsteps left in the soil by his terrified wife, which left him furious as well as frustrated. She'd tried to get to the stallion. Ashes would have flown like the swiftest wind. She could ride like that same wind. The stallion would have saved her. Diligently, they followed the tracks north, taking great pains to study thoroughly every small detail.

Three days into the ride the tracks changed. "They stopped here for the night. Something happened. What do you suppose that was?"

"I believe so," Still Water Runs said. "It is at this place I thought maybe one person traveled north with all the horses." He touched the ground. "I think, somehow, your brave wife got away from her captors. She took the horses leaving White along with his cohorts to walk. Why would she go north to Scotland? Why not return home? Though by the looks of what we're seeing here, your wife showed her true mettle. She is no wilting English daisy. She is made of sterner stuff. She is the woman for you."

He told her to go to Baltimore. Expected her to find her way to the states. In the back of his mind, he recalled telling her he would find her there, that she had to save herself and worry about him later.

"She was closer to Glasgow than London?" Kane asked himself more than his friend. "Do you think she knew someone there? A person who could help her return home or protect her from the bounders who were after her? At this point she was indeed closer to Glasgow than London."

Still Water Runs lifted his broad shoulders as if questioning, "Anything is possible." His friend's voice was stoic. "She is alive. Your woman still walks this earth. I know this in my heart."

Lightness assailed him at his friend's words. Lyssa was strong and resilient, a warrior's woman. This was good, all good. Now all he had to do was figure out who she knew in Glasgow. He searched his head for possibilities. Her family lived in the states. Her aunt was the duchess, her husband Drake Montgomerie. The duke kept numerous contacts close to his heart as well as in his confidence. She might very well know someone.

"Where do we go from here?" Still Water asked, his gaze straight ahead as if he knew the answer. "London or Glasgow?"

Kane understood he would have to travel to Scotland. He had an idea who she might have gone to see. The notion stemmed from something Ella once told him. He would have to take a bit of time to mull that over in his head. The man was the only one who made sense. Well hell, he didn't have time to think about anything.

The Duke of Southcliff was a friend of Ella and Drake. He along with his wife lived in Glasgow. She would go to him. Seek him out if she needed assistance. If his memory served him right, Southcliff had been involved in espionage hence the connection. He had visited Montgomerie numerous times according to Lyssa. The question he had to wonder about was if Lyssa got herself buried into something so deep with intrigue, she might not ever escape the consequences.

The two men spent the following days racing to Glasgow. They didn't sleep. Kept three horses each so they could switch without stopping. Kane prayed Lyssa found refuge there. Prayed too that she was still in the city safely tucked away in Southcliff's household. He did remember telling her if anything happened to him, to head for home. If she did so, he would find her. He wanted to go to Baltimore as did Drew and Jeremy. They would bring the horses, fifty of them. The bride price. Now, all he needed to do was see this duke and find out if his guesses were correct.

A few polite inquiries brought them to the Duke of Southcliff's home. Kane stood on the doorstep, his heart in his throat, nerves stretched thin. Too many days had passed since the men kidnapped Lyssa. More time than he wanted to admit he spent in bed while his woman needed him. Up one side then down the other he berated himself, not that the condemning words would change the facts.

A little over a month passed. By now, she could be somewhere on the Atlantic. If not sheltered by Leslie Stewart, the duke, at least he prayed that was where she was.

This wasn't one of his finer moments. He should have paid closer attention that day. Should not have left her at the lodge by herself. He had been so sure of himself. Positive his threats would keep White from attempting to abscond with her. His scalp would bloody well leave his head if he ever saw the man again. It wasn't just that fear he needed to put to rest. Lyssa would have spent several days as well as nights alone during her travel. Thieves were abundant on the roads. She would have been at a man's mercy if caught by some despicable rogue. Kane tried to push his fears aside. His Lys wasn't like any other female he'd ever known. She was competent, had skills no women should have. For the first time since he understood her, he was glad about that fact.

Annoyed and exasperated beyond reason, he pounded on the door with the gold knocker in the shape of a lion's head, the Duke of Southcliff's door. After that, he waited, rocking on the balls of his feet, impatient, frustrated with not knowing. When the door finally opened, he wanted to howl with his irritation at the delay. He stuffed his annoyance to the back of his head for the further good.

"Yes?" The aged butler stood at the door, a bland expression on his face. Then, he continued, "We've been expecting you, much earlier of course. What took you so long? The duke hoped you'd arrive a couple of weeks ago. Must have been a dastardly bullet wound. The sweet girl told us all about you as well as what happened."

What the devil?

Bending at the waist and slightly sideways, he tried to see around the man. Didn't succeed. He held out his hand, "I'm the Earl of Blackmore. I'm looking for my wife. Need to speak with the duke. Is she here?"

"The duke is not home at the moment. Neither is your wife. Lyssa Andrews left just as she told us you instructed her. Seems you told her you would find her. However, the duke's wife is expecting him within the hour. Do come in, both of you." He moved aside so Kane could enter. "You can wait in the drawing room. I'll tell his wife that you have finally arrived. Would you like a brandy? Something to eat?"

His stomach clenched with fear. Yet there was something about the situation that gave him pause. The butler was smiling. Since he knew now that Lyssa came here for help, he was certain she received what she asked for. This fear of his was absurd, unfounded now that he realized she used her ingenuity to save herself. He'd like to find out exactly how this woman he fell in love with got away from the men who kidnapped her. More than that he wanted to drink in her loveliness while he made love to her. Thoughts of his wife, her lovely white breasts, the sweet curves of her hips, the softness of her belly, hardened him to steel. These thoughts were well out of order. Nor were they his best thoughts when there were other priorities. He needed to concentrate on the pertinent facts. In doing so discover her whereabouts.

The comfortable armchair looking at the fire appealed to him. He sat then accepted the glass of brandy offered by the butler. Still Water Runs sat in another chair. It was simply a polite gesture, a means to pass the time before the duke returned home. He wondered if he'd be left to wait over long with his muddled thoughts. The crystal the drink was served in was expensive. Everything about the duke's home reeked of expense, the finest money could buy. Sipping slowly, he watched the flames. They danced and played with each other within the grate casting a warm glow on the room.

"Lord Blackmore?"

The voice behind the chair startled him. He jumped. Usually, he was tuned into all sounds. Once there was a time his life depended on his hearing. Kane sucked in a deep breath of air before he turned, smiling at the apparition in front of him. The woman was exquisite. She was about the same age as Ella, perhaps a few years younger. Approaching him, her hand held out to him in greeting.

"Yes." Unable to help himself he smiled at her.

"I'm Lacie Stewart. You are looking for Lyssa Andrews. I'm glad to meet you and equally glad you figured out where she would go to seek help. This arrival took longer than we expected."

"Murphy, Lyssa Murphy is her name. She is my wife after all. You do understand," he said as he took exception to the fact this lady didn't recognize the marriage between them.

Perhaps, Lys never had a chance to explain all that transpired. After all they'd been married twice.

"My apologies. We were, are, quite fond of Lyssa. She stayed here for several days. We made sure she found a ship heading directly for Baltimore with no stops at other ports. A safe ship," she amended. "We did offer her refuge in our home until you could come for her of course. She denied the safe harbor telling us she needed to be where you would expect to find her when you recovered. If you didn't figure things out, you would assume to see her with her family. She was worried about your health but tried to keep a positive attitude."

It would have been nice to find her here safe and sound. Instead, he would have to find passage on a ship to America. First, he would have to return to London where the horses were stabled so he could see to their transport. "I see," he murmured thinking of all the time wasted in bed then looking for her. Even though he knew he couldn't leave the island until he was sure she obeyed his wishes, it was still time he could have put to better use. When perhaps it would have been wiser for her to pursue other avenues, she chose to obey. He would never understand her.

"I will be going now." He stood to leave thinking of all the things that needed his attention before he could set out to bring her home. "Thank you for your hospitality as well as the information."

"You must stay for dinner. I'm sure there is a great deal for you to discuss with my husband. Also, we would like you and your friend to stay the night with us. You do understand your appearance was not a surprise. Your wife described you perfectly. She knew you would come here as soon as you could figure out her destination. Told us you would have followed her tracks. The fact it took you over a month is disconcerting. You were shot, she told us. Are you well now?"

"I'll accept your offer of dinner. I would like to speak with the duke. Want to know as much as possible about what happened to my wife. Yes, I was shot. It wasn't mortal. However, the recovery time was quite disconcerting. The bullet in my chest laid me up for some time, which is the reason I'm tardy arriving here. We did make the trip in few days however."

"Believe your wife's trials are a tale she will want to tell you herself when you finally catch up to her. She left over three weeks ago for Baltimore. By the time you return to London…you do plan on returning to London. Well, in any case, more time will pass before you will see her, another number of days."

Another week would pass before he could secure the ships to take him to the states. He groaned thinking of the last time, "I must return. There is no other choice in the matter. I can't delegate this task to another. The horses..."

"Ah," she said, sporting what appeared to be an all-knowing grin.

"From what I understand, you were bringing her father a bride price. What was it she told me?" Lacie put a slender finger to her chin. "Fifty horses? That will be quite the feat to transport."

"She is worth every one of them." He would pay one hundred if the man asked.

"Oh, I would never argue with that. She is a very beautiful woman, also intelligent and sincere. She is complicated though, so unlike the typical English debutante. I hope you've noticed. There is so much about her of interest. Lyssa is also very much in love with you. I hope you know that pertinent fact about her feelings." Lacie paused again as she directed her gaze unerringly toward Kane, "I see you didn't consider her feelings for you as important or mayhap worth your consideration."

He wasn't totally surprised by the last statement yet he was. She had never stuck her oar in the water about her feelings for him. The memory of her saying how very British he'd become swamped him. Back to the last thought, she never told him she loved him either. Yes, he agreed wholeheartedly with Lacie's statement concerning his wife's beauty along with her sincerity. There were depths hidden beneath a quiet façade left for him to uncover.

He would thoroughly enjoy uncovering each and every one of them. To do that, he would have to catch up with her.

Frustration built. If he hadn't been shot, incapacitated, he would have waylaid her here before she set sail. Further bothering him was the thought she would not have gone if he hadn't requested that very thing. The idea had been the best he could think of at the time. She needed protection. If he couldn't, who better to protect her besides her father? He'd wanted her to obey. This time he wished she had not.

Food was brought into the room. The conversation revolved around many things that he didn't care about. Time passed. Finally, the duke entered then poured himself a drink.

For the longest time, he watched without saying a word. "I see Lacie made you comfortable. You will want me to tell you about your wife. What has happened to her."

More than anything he did. Though the duke's statement was probably foolish. At this point he was certain Lacie told him everything.

"What do you think?"

His sarcasm hit home with the slight grimace he saw on the duke's face. He wasn't proud of that moment. These people helped a stranger. "I'm thankful for all you've done."

Leslie imbibed a long swallow of his expensive French brandy then nodded as if conceding the thank you put in front of him. "She came here, yes. Told us that Ella Montgomerie was her aunt. I'm quite fond of Drake as well as Ella. Booked her passage on the first ship sailing to Baltimore at her insistence. She wanted to make sure she arrived ahead of you. Didn't want you to worry over her safety." He stopped speaking to drink again. "If truth be told, I made sure that she found passage on one of my ships captained by my best man. She will arrive safe and sound in America in another month or so depending on the weather."

"It's a blessed long time. By the time I get there it will have been more than four months since I was shot."

"It is too much to grapple with, you know. You were shot. She thought you could be dead or she might have waited here. She was very afraid for your life. For several days, she vacillated between going and staying. She did, however, tell me she couldn't return to London in case you did succumb to the wound. I told her she needed to obey your last wish. Assured her you had her best interest in mind when you commanded she return to the states. I agreed with the sentiment. It is certainly nice to know you didn't pass into another world. Although, I never thought that was what happened to you. Figured it would be bloody difficult for a bounder such as the man Lyssa described to do you in."

"I feel the same, although I was unconscious for longer than I cared to admit. I will take your wife up on the offer to stay the night as well as dinner then I'll head home, back to London as quickly as I can. Want to set sail to retrieve my wife as soon as possible. It's a long journey. As I said before, it will be months before I see her again."

The next morning, he met with Drew and Jeremy along with Still Water Runs with the news. More days passed before they were back in London, even more before they set sail. By the time he saw her again, held her close, more than four months would have gone by.

He wondered if she conceived.

What would she look like if so? He needed to be with her.

~ * ~

When Lyssa knelt beside Kane and saw the blood fear for him pooled in her gut. She wanted to howl with the terror of it all. As to who could have done this to him, her mind turned blank. She supposed one of the suitors she turned away might have played a part. Understanding was impossible. He moaned then moved slightly. Tried to speak to her. She bent close to hear his words, weak as they were. For a fleeting moment, his hand brushed against her cheek.

Kane told her three things. One was to take his stallion, Ashes. Another was to go home, go home to Baltimore then on to her father's ranch. The last was to run, run as fast as she could away from here. Oh God, oh God...she didn't want to leave him. He needed her, needed his wound tended to. She heard Still Water Runs yelling at her to run. She couldn't see him though. He would be here for Kane. Everyone she trusted expected her to flee from the man she loved who was bleeding, possibly to death. She wanted to stay, stop the blood flow, reassure him with every breath and word. Pounding hooves seemed to close in on her. Bile rose to her throat when she turned her head to see Jonathan White along with his friends bearing down upon her.

She remembered that Kane told her Still Water Runs would find her if anything happened to her. He would take care of her, bring her back to him. First, she had to get away. Flee when she still had the chance. She had to take care of herself. Lyssa knew Kane lied. Understood Still Water Runs would stay and take care of him before anything else. That was good, all good. Kane would be angry though if Still Water Runs didn't go after her.

In time he would. She was smart. She would save herself. She possessed all the necessary skills. Once Kane felt hale and hearty again, Still Water Runs would do anything in his power to obey Kane while he helped her. He would probably even go to American to find her.

When she left the clearing, she raced for Ashes, hoping the stallion would out distance these men. Strange how a mind works during distress. All she could think of was the fact the horse's coat was the color of ashes unlike most thoroughbreds.

Men on horseback cut her off before she could reach Kane's horse. She tried to run around them to dodge them. Every time she tried, another man with his horse would block her way. They were laughing, jesting at her expense, yelling and whooping. There were too many of them. She was frantic now, unable to think as she fought for her life. Her heart pounded. Every breath of air that she gasped into her lungs hurt dreadfully. Fear escalated then consumed. She wanted to yell she was married. She saw the man. Knew it was the horrible person that tried to see her the day after the recital. Jonathan White couldn't have her. She would never give in to the man's wishes whatever they be. Would never allow him to touch her.

"Get her!" Jonathan cried out as he whirled his horse to the left to cut her off. "Stop her now! Don't let her get away. She's headed for the stallion. Stop her now!"

"Go to the right, keep her from reaching the horse! Hurry!" The horses chasing her kicked up dirt clods. Mud splattered all around her.

A large clump hit her square in the back. She slipped to her hands and knees, her hair falling from its pins pooling around her. She couldn't see. When she struggled to stand, she stumbled again. Finally, she found her footing. A hole between two of the mounted men opened. She raced for the tiny opening. Jonathan closed the distance, cutting her off.

"She's on foot, just a girl. Stop her, you fools!"

She whirled in tight circles, her lungs burning, her muscles cramping as the men rode nearer until they surrounded her. There was nowhere for her to flee. "No! Bastard! Oh god...oh god...No!"

What to do? Tears spiked her lashes. She didn't have time to cry.

This was it then. They would take her God knew where. Would force her against her will to wed this man. If she did, if Kane lived, she couldn't be forced...not now not ever. She would never say the words that would bind her to this man.

Never!

Keep your head, Little Bit. As if Kane was in her mind, she heard him speaking to her. *Stay calm. Fear does not win battles. Fight them when you get the chance. Don't exhaust yourself when you're cornered. You will find an opportunity to best these men. They are nothing but dust in the wind. Be patient and fight the good fight. Until then, you must remain quiet as well as calm. Fight with your mind not your body. Your strength is your intelligence.*

She gave up the ghost. Head held high Lyssa waited for what she didn't know would come her way, as she felt certain she would find out soon enough. The men leered at her. They laughed. She clenched her teeth together, her hands clamped tightly at her sides.

In seconds she was hauled on to Jonathan White's thighs. Forgetting her earlier thought to wait with her stomach curdling at his touch, she curled her fist then sent it flying into his face.

He yowled when her fist hit him. His head jerked back. Cursed profanely. She understood she was in trouble. He would punish her for her audacity. She didn't care. She would slam her fist into his nose again given the chance.

Blood spurted from his nose. He wiped the blood away with the back of his arm. "Bloody bitch!"

He tossed her onto her stomach, as if she was nothing. His hand came down hard on her, holding her still as she squirmed and wiggled hoping to fall. Ashes grazed within a few feet of them now. She thought she would rather fall onto the ground and be trampled than suffer what this man intended. She would never wed the man. Would never let him touch her as Kane did. She would fight until she could fight no more. Would make sure Jess claimed the title if there was no other recourse to her situation. He couldn't keep her prisoner forever. At some time, he would have to give her free reign to come and go. When that happened, she would run hard and fast. If something happened to Kane and he didn't survive, Drake would come to find her.

No, she assumed as her husband he could do whatever he wished. He could keep her locked in a room if that was what he wished.

When the horses picked up speed, she thought her stomach would rebel. Her head ached. She could barely sip in a breath of air. In time the men slowed to a walk.

"Let me up," her voice croaked as she tried to speak. She pleaded hoping to find some release. "I can't stay this way."

"Not on your life, sweetheart. Not until we stop to rest for the night. I'm not a stupid man. You almost broke my nose."

"I'm going to be sick all over your boot," she whispered.

She couldn't seem to put volume to her voice.

"You just go ahead and puke your innards up. Don't care after what you did to my nose." Jonathan settled his hand more firmly on her back pressing her down hard. "It's broken."

His pretty countenance won't be so pretty anymore. "Kane will come for me."

"The man's dead. He won't be coming for anyone. You'll be my wife. The title will be mine. There is naught you can do to change any of this."

"Jess will come to claim his title just to spite you. Still Water Runs will tell him what you did. Jess will come."

"He doesn't want the title. Everyone knows that."

"Kane's not dead. I felt his heartbeat. It was strong and sure. Still Water Runs will save him, doctor him until he is strong. He will come for me."

She felt the certainty of her words as if she understood what the winds were telling her. Maybe she just prayed for all this to come to fruition.

Jonathan's hand came down hard on her backside. She flinched in pain. "Shut up, just shut up, bitch! If you keep talking, I'll stop and gag you. Tie your hands and feet. Don't think for a second that I won't. Might not be a bad idea to do so in any case."

Lyssa inhaled long and deep. She kept quiet. She understood if she was bound and gagged, she would have no chance to escape. She did, however, still have the knife Kane insisted she keep strapped to her leg. After a while the men picked up their speed. The upside-down bouncing made her stomach as well as her head thunder horribly.

The pattern remained the same. They rode fast then slowed, over and over again. She thought she would die from the constant hammering in her head along with the rolling of her stomach.

Hours later the sun began a slow descent behind the hills. She prayed they would stop soon. Instead, they continued. When they finally came to a halt, the sky was dark. A few stars twinkled overhead between wisps of clouds. The moon, a tiny sliver in the night sky provided meager light.

One of the men pulled her roughly from the horse. Before she could get her legs under her, he pulled her hands in front of her then tied them with a leather thong. He guided her to a tree then bade her sit.

Jonathan dismounted in front of her. She saw that his nose was crooked, broken from the blow she hurled at him. She did break his nose. She was pleased with herself. Thought Kane would also be pleased. Just as he suggested, she would fight the good fight.

"Tie her feet too. Don't give her a chance to run," Jonathan said, eyeing her as if he thought her the devil in disguise.

Well, let him believe whatever he wished. She wasn't going to give him the satisfaction of getting her wherever he meant to take her; Gretna Green most likely. She would bide her time, stay calm just as Kane instructed her. All she needed was one of the horses. She could outrun them all on the big stallion Jonathan rode.

Amused, she watched them set up camp. The fire blazed. Flames shot upward that would attract people, any kind of person, good or bad. Perhaps they would attract Still Water Runs as well as the men he would send to track them. She smiled, relaxing with her thoughts. She needed to rest. If she couldn't get away tonight, she would have to make sure she lulled them into thinking she wouldn't try.

The food offered was sparse, some scraps of bread along with ham that was so salty she thought to spit the pieces in her mouth into the fire. She had to hold back. Despite the disgusting taste, she had to keep her strength. Starving herself would not help her cause.

"Best you get some rest. We've got a long day tomorrow. Want to make it to Gretna Green as soon as possible." Jonathan handed her a blanket. Leaning against a tree, she held the coarse covering in front of her. At least the summer evenings in July were still warm.

They took turns guarding her at night. No, perhaps they guarded the campsite. As one day turned to another, Harry and David consumed more whiskey. Harry was the worst. He usually slept most of his guard time, inebriated. His watch was the one she decided would be her best chance to escape. As for the timing, she wanted to be closer to Glasgow as she didn't like the idea of being alone on the road. If she had the coin, she would flag down a coach. As it stood now, she would have to keep to the side of the road. Perhaps even forge a trail of her making. She knew how to stay inconspicuous.

The same ritual went on for a few more days. By her calculations they would change course soon. She was only a day or two away from Glasgow. It was time she found a way to escape these men.

Her knife was still pressed to her thigh, in easy reach even while she was bound.

Obviously, Jonathan underestimated her. Life on her family's ranch prepared her for hardship, for forging a trail of her own. If she'd been brought up in the city, she probably would know less than nothing. She was a country girl. Her father made certain if she ever lost herself in the wilderness, she could find her way home.

Her golden opportunity came the sixth night away from London. All the men celebrated by drinking too much whiskey. It seemed they were pleased neither Kane or Still Water Runs came for her. They believed they were safe from retribution. They even slowed the rapid pace from the first two days to something more sedate. It seemed they were in no hurry.

She wasn't happy at all as she was afraid for Kane. The bullet wound might have taken his life. Though, he would have requested Still Water Runs to save her. The Sioux warrior would have traveled twice as fast. Would have covered the distance quickly by using more than one horse. She would know if Kane was gone from the earth. She would feel the loss in the wind.

No, there was something terribly wrong but he wasn't dead. She understood she would feel his death.

Rescuing herself was the only plausible answer to this situation. When it was time for Harry to take the last watch, he didn't show up for the duty. David slept soundly, his snores echoing through the quiet of the night. She looked to Jonathan who also seemed to be sleeping soundly, a bottle of whiskey tucked neatly under his arm.

Cautiously, ever watchful, she removed the knife from its sheathe. For a few seconds, she held her breath. Nervous sweat beaded on her forehead. She willed her breathing to slow. The blade fit her hand to perfection. Kane picked the weapon out especially for her use, for her small grip, sharpening the blade every day. Sawing at the ropes binding her wrists, she knew these men to be utter fools. Either that or they didn't expect a woman to use her wits and escape them. The sharp blade cut the soft leather easily.

In minutes she was free.

A few seconds later, she untied Jonathan's stallion as well as the other two horses. She took as much food as she could carry in the saddlebags. Leaving the saddles behind, she walked the horses south toward London along an animal trail dusting the prints as she made her way through the foliage.

In her mind, she saw the image of the men, waking up, realizing they had no mounts or food. They would be walking home or to the next village where they could purchase horses.

Where would they go? Would they follow her? Would they return to London thinking she headed in that direction?

An hour later, she mounted then found a different trail heading northeast. Now, she needed to put as much distance between her captors and herself as she could. Changing horses every hour or so, she kept her gaze on her back trail. When she stopped for the night, she ate sparingly of the bread and cheese she took from men's saddlebags. The meager fare would have to last her until she reached the city, which was two days away, maybe less if she could stay on her mounts for more than eight hours.

One day and a half later she rode through the back streets of Glasgow. Her stomach rumbled from lack of food. The sun had not set. A stiff breeze blew off the nearby river. She rubbed her arms in an attempt to warm herself. She hoped she could get directions to the Duke of Southcliff's home before the sky darkened to black velvet. She knew she was bedraggled and dirty. Understood no one would give her directions to a duke's home without some type of bribe.

She had no coin.

The people she stopped to ask continued on their way without replying to her. Minute after minute passed with no help forthcoming. Depression bit deep into her heart. If she couldn't find someone to help...she would, she told herself as she fisted her hands. She didn't know what to do until she spotted two women and a large man, handing out food to some of the homeless on the street. Her breath stalled in her lungs. She debated whether to approach them. Knew Kane would tell her to be cautious.

When she stopped in front of the trio, she dismounted, her heart in her throat, she walked toward them. "Excuse me," she began. Reminded herself she needed to be guarded. She swallowed the lump of fear in her throat, "Can anyone tell me where the Duke of Southcliff lives?"

A beautiful woman, well dressed with raven black hair turned to address her. "Who is asking?" she asked politely. Delicate crease lines formed on her brow. Nevertheless, she appeared friendly, just careful.

The woman didn't seem dangerous or a threat. "I, well…" She pressed her fingers against the bridge of her nose.

This could mean life or death. No, she shouldn't get overdramatic. Lyssa didn't want to mumble. She was having a devilish hard time not to do so. She was so exhausted, so terrified, "He, the duke, doesn't know me. However, we are both acquainted with the Duke and Duchess of Richmond. They are my aunt and uncle."

Lyssa liked the smile she saw on the woman's face. The ensuing grin was warm and in a way comforting. Perhaps luck was with her tonight.

"Well, anyone can say as much," said the lady who spoke first. She didn't sound mean or belligerent. "What is your name?"

She wiped her sweaty hands down her soiled dress. "I'm Lyssa Murphy, the Earl of Blackmore's wife. He was shot, you see. I was kidnapped by people who want the title I will bring to my son if I have one." She was breathing hard, trying to think of everything that needed to be said. "So, they tried to kill him. Before I married the earl, I was Lyssa Andrews. My mother and aunt Ella are sisters. They are Hepburns."

She looked to the other three who nodded seeming to tell her they also believed her to be telling the truth. "We won't hurt you. Come let's go to the bakery down the street. You can tell us the rest of the story over a hot cup of tea and a pastry. You appear half starved. My sister, Daryl, is sure to be still at work on the books. She always makes a mess of them. After she tries to make all her markings balance, I feel duty bound to correct all her errors."

"Let's hope she doesn't make too big a mess of them in your absence," the woman who so far remained quiet said with a small chuckle.

"I would have to spend hours fixing her miscalculations," the first lady snorted softly. "She is my sister and I love her dearly. However, she has no sense for numbers."

Pastry and tea. With the thought of food, her stomach rumbled in pleasure. "Thank you. I'd appreciate that."

"How long have you gone without food?" the woman asked. She sounded concerned. "We'll have to make sure you get plenty to eat. Is that alright with you?"

"Almost two days."

"Well then, we'll have to do something about your condition. I'll send a message to the duke that we will be home shortly. That is, after you tell me your story from the beginning to the end. Come along. We have to get you fed."

"Who are you?"

The lady turned a brilliant smile her way. "Why, I'm Lacie Stewart, the Duchess of Southcliff. You've found the right person to show you to the duke's home."

Her delicate laughter caused Lyssa's heart to bounce beneath her ribs.

"Thank you," she murmured again.

"No need for a thank you yet. We will see what transpires after I hear your entire story. As the tale stands now, to me you've told only bits and pieces. After the duke evaluates what we choose to tell him. I'm sure this will be interesting."

"Life is never boring around here. By the way, I'm Justine. I work for Daryl," the second woman said.

When they walked through the door, a little bell sounded their arrival. Inside the bakery, the aroma of freshly baked bread sent her stomach into another tailspin. She ate two blueberry muffins then a ham sandwich made especially for her. The sip of tea was hot and delicious. When she finished every crumb, she sat back contented for the moment. She felt sure this woman would help her find a way to America. If not, perhaps, she would help her back to London.

The little bell above the door rang a soft inviting sound again. A tall, very handsome confident man strode inside. With raven dark hair, a few white strands around his temple and well-chiseled features, he presented a striking picture. He grinned lovingly at his wife and opened his arms for her. Lacie jumped up then ran to greet him with a hug along with a kiss that went on forever.

So, that must be the duke.

Lacie sent for him and he came just like that. A snap of her fingers and the man was there.

Lyssa didn't see her send a messenger.

Lacie smiled at her before she patted her hand. "Yes, you're right. You didn't see me send a message. My husband always comes to the bakery to pick me up on the nights I help deliver the leftovers. I think he follows me too."

"I feel I'm at a disadvantage here," Leslie said while he gazed at his wife then to her.

The way his eyes shimmered when he looked at Lacie, reminded her of the way Kane stared at her.

"She has had a few bites to eat. I assume after her story is relayed to you, she will be coming home with us. She can stay with us at our home until we can figure out how to best help her with her problems. She does retain some interesting troubles."

Leslie Stewart, the Duke of Southcliff, sat back in the chair, his long-muscled legs stretched out in front of him as he listened. His long fingers formed a steeple beneath his chin. Lyssa didn't leave one word out of the telling. She was afraid for her husband's life. He might have died during these seven and a half days of her travel. The men who captured her might not give up. They might, even now, be looking for her here in Glasgow.

He nodded. When he smiled, he appeared devilishly handsome, "Well, Lady Blackmore, we will have to fix this situation the way your husband wished it to happen. For now, we will take you to our townhouse here in the city. We will figure out what is to be done as well as how to best accomplish the feat."

Relief flooded through her. She wiped her sweaty hands down the folds of her well-worn dress. The torn and mud-spattered gown certainly had seen better days. Once inside the carriage, Leslie asked her questions to clarify what she told him. She left so much out including the reason Jonathan White wanted her even after she married Kane. The duke assured her the horses would be taken care of. If the owners showed up to claim them, they would have to be returned. However, he wasn't positive they could be prosecuted for kidnapping her. It would be her word against theirs. He even praised her on taking all the mounts telling her she was quite inventive. He would have second thoughts about going up against her.

At the townhouse, Lacie showed her to a room then ordered a bath. Lyssa sunk into the steaming hot water, relishing the heat. Days of grime needed to be soaked off. Blood from her husband still clung to parts of her gown, which had been taken away, to be laundered the maid said. Lyssa had the distinct feeling it would be tossed in a fire. That is what she would do if it were left up to her. Nonetheless, without the old thing she had nothing to wear.

She was wrapped in a bath towel when Lacie knocked on the door asking if she was out of the bath.

"Come in," Lyssa said wondering if Lacie had a gown for her.

The dress would not be one of Lacie's as she was magnificently endowed. Although Kane told her that her breasts were marvelously large. Perhaps… Lacie did lay a gown on the bed as well as a negligée and a robe.

Lacie laughed then, a soft sweet sound. "The dress is mine. Seems you are…well…almost as well endowed. I believe a few tucks will do you just fine. You will fit into my dress nicely. We are close to the same size. When you are dressed, please come meet us in the drawing room. We will talk some more, make plans for your future then eat dinner. I expect you are still hungry."

Lyssa was nodding as she watched Lacie leave. It seemed the effects of her meal at the bakery vanished more than an hour ago. She was still hungry. How odd? Quickly, she dressed and fixed her hair. She was in the drawing room in less than thirty minutes.

"Would you like a sherry?" Lacie didn't wait for an answer but poured her a small glass.

"Thank you," she murmured thoughtfully as she watched Leslie shuffle through a few papers he held on his lap.

Leslie looked up, his smile broad. "Tomorrow, I believe I'll speak to Captain Carstairs. He is a fine captain. My ship, the Pegasus, should be in port to take on cargo headed for the states. I'll have him sail to Baltimore as soon as I can make sure the hold is filled. He will return with tobacco. We'll make a fine profit on this endeavor."

"Thank you. This all seems so fast. I can barely catch my breath."

She sipped the sherry. The drink was delicious. She looked at the plate of pre-dinner delicacies sitting on a small table, her mouth watering.

"Would you like to wait to see if Kane will come here looking for you?" Leslie asked seeming to watch her with close scrutiny. "He will come here. You understand that, right?"

Lacie interrupted before she could answer. "Before any of this can take place, we will have to go to the dressmaker. She needs clothing, dear, everything from the tips of her toes to the top of her head," Lacie interrupted before Lyssa could answer, holding her hand in the air to forestall her words. "We can't send her off to Baltimore with nothing to wear. Besides, she needs time to process what you just asked her. I know that I would need time if in a similar situation. Could you send a messenger to London to see if he lives? Or...would that take too long?"

"You would think of clothing." Leslie turned to her a wicked shimmer in his eyes, "Lyssa, I do hope you have better taste in what is suitable for you to wear than my wife. If not, I'll have to go along with the two of you just to make sure you don't pick out something so unflattering that your husband will run the opposite direction when he sees you again."

Leslie was laughing and staring at his wife who looked as if she wanted to cosh him over the head with the bottle of sherry she was holding. Instead, she set the bottle down, folded her hands then placed them in her lap before sending her husband a demure smile.

"I have adequate taste, sir. You will not need to go out of your way to see me clothed properly. I will keep a tab. Whether or not my husband still breathes; I will see you paid back. I do have funds of my own that I have access to. My father sent me to London with adequate amounts of coin to see me clothed for the season. I've spent very little of that."

"That is all well and good, Lyssa," the duke said eyeing her thoughtfully. "Tomorrow then Lacie will take you to the modiste. I'll make sure the carriage is sufficiently guarded." He paused tapping his finger to his chin. "Just in case the men who kidnapped you are in town. Do you think they would guess you came here?"

"No...well, maybe. Mr. White wouldn't know that my mother and the duchess are sisters. At least I don't believe he would. He also wouldn't know of the tiny connection there is between you and my uncle."

Waving her hand in the air once more, Lacie began, "None of that matters at this time. As for clothing, hopefully we can find readymade gowns for you. I doubt if we have enough time to commission even one frock." Lacie turned to her husband. "When do you expect the ship to leave?"

"Within the week. You are absolutely right, my dear, there is no time for that. Unfortunately, she doesn't have normal proportions. We might have to have some of your gowns refurbished a bit."

He grinned at Lacie while he stared at her bosom.

Lyssa watched the blush slowly climb from the top of Lacie's corsage to her cheeks.

~ * ~

"Bloody eyes! She's gone. Who was supposed to be guarding the damn chit?" Jonathan turned his fury on his friends.

Harry held up his hands in submission. "If you recall neither of us wanted to be involved in any part of your scheme. If the breed dies, we'll hang for sure. I for one don't want to return to London until I know the outcome."

"Yes, and I for one hope he doesn't survive. At least with the Andrews girl gone from our keeping, the earl, if he lives, might not kill us," David said looking at the spot where Lyssa was supposed to be resting. "I've heard too many rumors. They must be founded in truth. Kind of like my head of hair to stay where it is."

"She bloody well took all the horses! She stole the horses..."

What to do now? Jonathan paced around the circle that was their fire pit, jabbing his hands through his hair until it stood on end. He turned on Harry, "You were the last watch. Was she still there when you woke David?"

He pointed to the spot where Lyssa had been tied, the thongs binding her lying on the ground.

Red stained Harry's face. He slipped his hands into his pockets. "Don't recall ever taking over for David. Seems we both slept through the watch. She was bound hand and foot. She wasn't going anywhere."

"So, she did go somewhere. Either of you idiots have a clue about that? How did she get lose? This leather was obviously cut." Jonathan tugged in a deep breath of air while he tried to calm every shattering nerve he possessed. "Neither one of you spent any time last night guarding the chit." He kicked at the cold ashes in the pit, his fury escalating.

"If it means anything—" David began.

"It doesn't." Jonathan was quick to slash his hand in front of them cutting off the excuses he was certain he would hear.

"She was tied up tight. There was no way she could've unbound those leather thongs," Harry said. "What the devil happened? Someone must have come to her rescue."

Jonathan picked up the remains of her bindings. Studied them for several seconds. "Slick as a whistle, as I said before they've been cut through. She had a knife."

"Do you think Kane found her?" David asked.

"Kane's dead or incapacitated. He wouldn't have had the strength to ride this far if he did live. The other one, what was his name?"

"Still Water Runs," Harry offered.

"If the man found her here, he would have scalped us then taken off with the girl," Jonathan said quietly. "Kane would have done the same. No, Lyssa Andrews got herself away from us all by herself. She must have had a knife strapped to her leg."

Jonathan cursed himself for not thinking of something so simple. Kane knew Jonathan wanted her. Most likely guessed he wouldn't give up easily. The girl was different too. The usual debutante would never carry a knife.

"It's all the breed's fault," David said with disgust heating his voice. "Don't understand what you want with the chit after the warrior had her. She's tainted now. Soiled. Dirty."

"He's right. You do know that," Harry agreed with his friend. "You've got time to find the right female. There will be other seasons. Other debutantes who have access to a title."

Jonathan clenched his fists tight, his nerves strung taunt. Never in his life had he felt the humiliation so bone deep. Now it was a matter of pride. He meant to find her then have his way with her. "She won't get away with this. The girl has made a fool out of me. If I have to follow her to the ends of the earth, I'm going to make sure she regrets refusing my polite advances."

"You can count me out," David said. "All I care about now in hightailing it back to London. Perhaps living to see another day with my hair intact."

"Me too," Harry said quietly. "Don't want to go chasing after the gel. You might not like what comes next."

"The two of you will stay with me until I have Lyssa Andrews in hand once more. If not, I'll tell the authorities exactly what you did to Kane and his wife."

Jonathan saw Harry's eye twitch. Noticed the ticking of David's jaw. His words were not a bluff. His power would bring the authorities knocking at their door. They both understood the influence Jonathan wielded despite the fact he didn't hold his coveted title. The right money placed in powerful hands served Jonathan well.

"You wouldn't?" David whistled through his teeth. "We told you we didn't want a part of this before you shot the man."

"Whose to believe your sad tale of woe over my word. As you both understand, I've the money to continue this until I have what I want. I've judges in my pocket. Hold vowels from many prestigious noblemen. In case the two of you haven't noticed, money buys power."

He felt smug. His intelligence far outweighed his two friends who seemed to rely on him for their entertainment. Well, their amusement with him was finished if they didn't toe the line. He would no longer be their source of diversions.

"What do you wish?" Harry asked clearly displeased, obviously unable to figure a way out of this. His sigh was long and deliberate to make him feel guilty.

He felt no guilt.

"We follow the tracks she left. Got to be prints. A girl would not know to cover her back trail," David said with a matter-of-fact tone to his voice. He looked up with an expression of confusion in his eyes. "Would she?"

"Once again, I do believe we underestimated this particular girl," Jonathan said wishing he were wrong.

Before he confronted his friends, he quickly perused the area. All signs of tracks were gone. She had indeed covered her trail. They needed to figure where she would go before they set out after her.

"The breed taught her how to cover up her tracks?" Harry asked clearly bemused by the thought.

"They didn't have time for him to teach her anything except for bedding her. They've only been together as husband and wife for three weeks. Most of that time they were holed up in the teepee," David argued.

Jonathan stood, his hands behind his back, staring at the road. His stomach curdled as he thought of the repercussions from this debacle. "No, this time I do believe you're right, Harry. Kane didn't teach her. The two of you do recall she is not from around here. Her folks live in the western territory of Maryland. We can assume Damian Andrews taught her much more than Black ever did. She most likely wore a knife before she met the earl. It is what she cut the leather with. Never thought to check her for weapons other than the obvious which she didn't possess."

"How are we going to find her?" David walked up to him. "We

don't have any clues. Don't know if she went on to Glasgow or back to London. Could have headed for Edinburgh for all we know."

"No, doesn't appear we do. So, as to your question, David, if you were Lyssa where would you go?"

"Back to the man she thinks can keep her safe," Harry said obviously not too sure of his answer. "Maybe she knows someone in Glasgow. It's only a couple of days ride from here. She doesn't know if Kane is alive. The duke and duchess are gone on what seems to be a lengthy trip. As far as we know she doesn't have anyone in London to protect her. Except that breed."

"Glasgow, that's my thought. From here the journey is only two days ride to the city," Jonathan said softly still staring down the trail they followed. "However, in case you haven't noticed, we are on foot."

"Sad but true. Sure there is a village where we can catch a stage to the city or buy horses. That's what we should do," David said thoughtfully. "She went to Glasgow. Now who would she know in the town?"

"Maybe we should follow her, but then what?" Jonathan asked clearly miffed now that he understood how stupid he had been. "What happens when we arrive in Glasgow? We could search for days upon days and never find her."

"No, we'll return to London. She's bound to show up sometime. We'll keep an eye out for Kane if he is still alive as well as Still Water Runs. They are bound to show their hand sooner or later. They will want revenge."

Chapter Nine

Too many days passed before Kane and Still Water Runs arrived in London. They spent most of the time in the saddle. He was tired and hungry. His chest where he took the bullet meant to kill him ached. He knew the healing was slowed by all his activity. There was nothing to be done about that.

Kane pinched the bridge of his nose willing the pain in his head to vanish. Lyssa, where was she? Somewhere between here and Baltimore. He prayed to all the gods he could think of that she was safe on board a sturdy vessel with a good captain. He had Leslie's assurance that he walked her on board his ship with the most competent captain that money could buy commanding the boat.

At this moment, he stood at the docks peering out at the river Thames. Ships, ships everywhere, nevertheless there were none at the present who were headed to Baltimore. Oh, he could go to different ports. The trip would take three to four months instead of just a little over two. He could wait it out until a ship, no, he needed two ships, would make port here. The devil, one of his ships left port two days before they arrived in London.

It wasn't to be believed.

Bad luck seemed to haunt him.

He needed the duke's help. Where the devil were the duke and duchess? Off hunting for Nickie Gray who ran off with her lover. Obviously, the two intended to stay on Collin's trail until they resolved the issue. He needed to call in a few favors from those who owed him. Just didn't know who to call on now that he needed help.

His mind seemed to be filled with quicksand. He was slowly suffocating in the mire.

Even the Andrews shipping line had no available ships. One was due in to arrive in port soon, he was told. How soon was soon? There were two that should arrive within the week weather permitting. He didn't want to wait one second let alone a week to set sail.

No one should have to rely on weather. He strolled down the docks, searching through the various ships, seeking someone he might know. He would pay whatever the owner wanted. The seconds ticking by haunted his thoughts.

Frustration as well as annoyance at this untenable situation ate at his heart and soul. He wanted to howl at the moon, except there was no moon. With Still Water Runs beside him, he entered a dockside pub. A dark corner in the back of the room beckoned to him. The pair ordered ale and bread, some cheeses to go along with the food.

He wasn't hungry. Hadn't been since he recovered to learn Lyssa was missing. Learned Jonathan took her right out from under his nose. Bloody eyes, he'd been to Glasgow and back. Two weeks passed. He hadn't seen her in five.

Wracking his brain for ideas was doing him no good. There just wasn't anything to do except wait for the two ships from the Andrews line to find their way to London. Patience wasn't his strong suit. The ale left a hollow pit in his stomach. He did need food.

"Can you think of any of her uncles or aunts who might have ties to the shipyard? We could search someone out. Seems your wife has more relatives than the two of us put together," still Water Runs asked between bites of the fare they were eating.

"Don't you think I've wracked my brain since we returned here? I just don't know enough about her family. About all I know is that Ella is her aunt. There were four sisters. Ella was the second oldest, Lyssa's mother the oldest. That leaves two sisters to account for." He drummed his fingers on the table wishing his head wasn't so muddled with fear.

"Why don't we start with what you do know?" Still Water Runs kept the fear they were both feeling from showing.

It irritated Kane to no end that Still Water Runs was so calm. Why wouldn't he be? His wife wasn't missing. "Not a bloody lot," he said as he drank deep of the ale. His gaze roamed the room as if the smoke-filled chaos might give him some ideas. Nothing in the room facilitated his imagination or brought any new facts to light.

Too composed, Still Water Runs began to speak. "We know Ella is her mother's sister. Has she spoken of any other sisters that you remember?"

The tone infuriated him yet at the same time got him thinking. Kane knew his friend tried to soothe his rattled nerves. "Twins. Ella told me once her younger sisters were twins. Ella was afraid she would have twins and was thankful her children came to her one at a time."

Still Water Runs chuckled continuing to pull information from him. "Suppose any mother would be happy not to give birth to two at one time. Where are these twins living and what do their husbands do? Would they have anything to do with shipping?"

"Well, believe their names both start with a T. That won't help us much. Don't have any idea what their surnames are."

Kane felt as if he sweated bullets. Perspiration dripped down the back of his neck. He needed to magically pull names that he'd never heard out of his head. They had not been wed long enough to know much about her except the fact he wanted her desperately. He did know every beautiful part of her intimately. It seemed at this second he was too frazzled to think.

"Yes, I recall very easily that a man named Jamie Lundin arrived in town about the same time Collin disappeared with Nickie. Seems to me he was a relation of sorts. Ella and Drake confiscated his ship."

"Keep thinking. We're getting somewhere now."

"That's it!" Kane's fist slammed down hard on the table relief inundating him. Ale sloshed from the topped off glasses while the bread bounced on the platter.

"What is it?" Still Water Runs prodded him.

"Jamie Lundin went with the entourage to find Collin and Nickie. He might have returned. He has a shipping business in Baltimore. Let's go. "I know the man builds Baltimore clippers, lives in the American city near the docks."

Still Water Runs reached out a hand to stop him. "We need to finish our food. I'm sure the office will still be there in fifteen minutes. The tide is wrong for sailing so, nothing will be leaving the docks anytime soon, not for at least four hours. Don't think we can get the horses loaded in that amount of time."

Kane stifled the urge to disagree. He knew his friend was right. Impatience, he was just too damn impatient. "Very well," he murmured as he sipped his drink and ate the food in front of him.

The fare tasted like sawdust. Still Water Runs was right. They wouldn't be able to retrieve the horses and load them in four hours.

When they finished their meal, Kane was relieved beyond measure. Striding down the docks they stopped at several offices asking for the whereabouts of the Lundin shipyard office. With the directions in hand Kane set off.

They found the headquarters open. Kane let out a long sigh of relief as the man asked him what he needed.

"Transport to Baltimore...as soon as possible," Kane said, leaning against the counter. "Is Jamie Lundin around? Need to talk to him first about his niece. In retrospect, I need two ships."

"Well, there are two in port right now. Mr. Lundin docked last night. He'd been gone on a long trip. Said the mission was successful. Didn't ask him for specifics though. He most likely would like to leave for home as soon as possible too. Said he missed his wife."

"Yes, believe we understand each other. I miss mine also. He went searching for another of his nieces."

Kane turned to Still Water Runs. "With these two ships along with the Andrews ship which is due in port soon, we might be able to leave within the week. What do you think?"

"If that's so, we should see Mr. Lundin as soon as possible," Still Water Runs said with a laugh. Don't want to see him depart London without us. If he plans to quit London before the Andrews ship docks, you can go with Lundin. I can take the other twenty-five horses with me on the second vessel."

"Where can we find Mr. Lundin?"

"Sorry, sir, can't give out private information."

Well hell!

"Someone looking for me?"

When Kane turned around, he saw a tall man with striking dark hair beginning to gray around his temple. He had the look of a sea captain, tanned and broad of shoulder. His eyes twinkled as if he knew something amusing he wasn't about to share.

The man held out his hand. "Jamie Lundin, who are you? Why are you looking for me?"

Relief washed through Kane. His prayers were answered. Perhaps his luck was improving. They shook hands. "I'm the Earl of Blackmore. Call me Kane or Black. This is my friend, Still Water Runs. We need passage to Baltimore as soon as possible."

"You sound as if the trip is a matter of life or death. Tell me..."

Kane looked down the street to the pub where they ate. "Let me buy you a drink. I can explain everything in detail. The tale is long. Possibly boring."

The men talked as they walked to the pub. The ale tasted better to Kane than it had before the food they ordered earlier. The smoke-filled room seemed less stuffy, the air less thick, the serving wenches more attractive. Kane sat back his arms extended, more stress-free than an hour past. His nerves no longer felt stretched to the snapping point.

"So," Jamie said with a soft chuckle his eyes alight with humor, "You plan on offering Damian fifty horses as a bride price for his daughter, Lyssa. That should be interesting. I'd like to see his reaction."

Kane nodded. Saw the humor on the older man's face. Knew he was contemplating what Mr. Andrews would think when he rode onto his ranch herding fifty of the best racehorses in the British Isles. It didn't matter. This was something he felt driven to do, part of his heritage he couldn't overlook when it involved someone as important to him as his Lyssa.

"You're a brave man, Lord Blackmore. Not many would venture to pay for his bride. It's not done."

Kane lifted his shoulders in a controlled shrug, one meant to tell Jamie Lundin how little he thought of the white man's ways. He would proceed along the lines he planned, by doing so show his respect for Lyssa as well as her family. "It's the tradition of my mother's people. I would honor Lyssa as well as her mother and father by paying as much as he asked. She has assured me her father will accept the horses, might even ask for more. According to Lyssa, her father is a formidable man. If that is the case, I would have to ride west to find the wild ones that travel the plains. When and if he requests more, I would do so. To me, she is worth more than fifty horses."

"As I said, you are a brave man. I have two ships here in London. The one I just disembarked from along with one that arrived from Baltimore two days ago. We can set sail as soon as I..." he paused, "Suppose there won't be room for additional cargo, not with the horses."

"I will make up the difference, pay for passage. You shouldn't be imposed upon," Kane was quick to say.

"No, I shouldn't. However, Lyssa is family. We've come to know her quite well over the years. I would accompany you to the ranch as well. As I said earlier, would love to see the look on Damian's face when you ride in herding fifty horses."

"I insist on paying for the passage. Still Water Runs will sail with the rest of the horses on the second ship. I've two men, friends, who will accompany us. If you wish to go to the ranch when I deliver the horses, I would never say no. When can we set sail?"

"You are eager to see your wife?" One of Jamie's eyebrows shot skyward. "Suppose I'm just as eager to see Tira. She offered to come with me, bring the children for a visit. As it turned out, my wife would have been disappointed not to see her sister. The trip would have been wasted."

Two days later Kane stood at the bow of Jamie's ship. Thinking of his wife a surge of longing swamped him, flooded his senses. Four months would have passed since he held her in his arms. In all his imaginings, he would have never foreseen something so senseless as this.

From what he heard about Jonathan, the man returned to London along with his cohorts. They continued to attend the balls and festivities the season offered. There would be no consequences to his shooting, at least not in the courts of England. Jonathan did hold a great deal of power. He had enough money to buy judges. Kane heard there were at least two in his pocket. No, nothing would happen to the man, at least not through the courts.

He talked the situation over with Still Water Runs. They decided on a different course of action. Rather than going to the constables, they would hit White's pocketbook, in doing so ruin him. After visiting his solicitor along with his financial consultant, they set the wheels in motion. The first realization there was something terribly wrong would most likely come in a couple months, about the time his ship sailed into Baltimore harbor.

There would be no suspicion cast his way. Mr. White would feel the sting of the loss. He would try to counter the actions taken by his solicitor. Nothing would work. By the time they returned to London, Jonathan White might very well be in debtor's prison or quite possibly on his way to a work colony Down Under. His two friends would also find themselves in a similar loss of funds. The knowledge left him with a good feeling in the pit of his soul. It was justice.

The scent of salt air filled his nostrils as they drew closer to the North Sea. Gulls followed the ship. After that they would head west through the English Channel before reaching the Atlantic. Kane hoped the weather would be calm. He had ways to keep the horses in place if a storm brewed. Nonetheless, he also hoped the tools would not be necessary. Before he turned to go to his cabin, he said a prayer to the People's gods, Christian gods as well.

Just shy of two months and under sunny skies they sailed into the harbor in Baltimore. The trees abounded with autumn colors. Tira heard the news of the ship's arrival. She stood on the dock to meet her husband waving her hands in greeting. When Jamie stepped off the gangplank, she ran into his open arms. Jamie whirled her around in tight little circles. She laughed, tossing her head back. He kissed her hard. Kane knew what he would do when he saw his bride. Lust filled him at the thought, spiraled to his groin. Settling for a kiss upon their reunion was not enough. He had big plans for the two of them. Plans that would shock her to the tips of her delectable little toes.

Time without her had been too damn long.

The horses were herded to a large coral. Guards were posted for the night. Over dinner, they spoke of their ideas to head inland to the Andrews' ranch. It would take another day to purchase the supplies for the overland trip. To Tira's disappointment, Jamie wouldn't allow her and the children to travel with them. With the horses in tow, the journey would be too dangerous.

A storm stopped them from leaving on the second day. Rain muddied the roads creating quagmires. They decided to wait for the afternoon to begin the expedition so the roads would dry.

Kane paced and swore, his body tense with annoyance. If something could go wrong it seemed that it did. He needed to see his wife, to hold her in the shelter of his arms. She needed to find out he still lived along with what would happen to her kidnappers. The morning of waiting passed slowly.

When they finally set off, the sun shone brightly lifting his spirits. If all went well, he would see Lyssa in two and a half days, possibly less. His heart pounded in anticipation. The weather held.

He thought this out, his entrance. He hoped she would be outside watching for their arrival. Damian should understand the heritage as well as the tradition of his people. Near the Andrews ranch he stripped to his loincloth and moccasins. As a proud Sioux warrior, he would present the father of his bride with the horses, the bride price. After that he would see to his woman.

"You intend to go through with this?" Still Water Runs laughed watching him as he mounted his favorite of all the steeds. "You have no idea how her father will react. If I were you, I might not be so eager."

"Damian will believe his daughter wed a crazy man," Jamie chuckled as he eyed him closely. After that and with a wealth of doubt in his voice, he asked, parroting Still Water Runs' earlier question, "You sure you want to go through with this? If you do, her father might not let you near her. Might refuse to acknowledge the marriage."

He grinned, his eyes softening as he was sure he saw his wife standing near the stable, her hand shielding her eyes as she searched for him. The long strands of her raven dark hair were picked up by a brisk wind. His friends didn't know half of what he planned. The entrance was just the beginning of his ideas.

"Lyssa is waiting for me."

The thought filled him with pride. The frustration of the long absence slowly vanished, as he watched her begin to run toward him. She was running, her skirts hitched up to her lovely knees. Ah, but he intended to see more than her beautiful knees very soon.

"Set the horses to a faster clip." He urged his mount to a run. "Ai-ye, Ai, ye ye ye..." His war cry carried through the sunbaked air.

He yelled again and again as he pushed his mount faster, the rest of the horses following. His hand he held high his fist clenched tight in an expression of victory. His heart pounded beneath his chest as excitement also churned.

Behind him he heard the pounding of fifty horses racing the very wind. The rhythmic pounding was music to his ears bringing back his past clearly in his mind. More people streamed from the stable as well as the house to watch the exhibition. Beneath the hooves of all the horses, the ground thundered, the air swelled. When he looked over his shoulder, the display was magnificent. Dust churned from the hooves billowing around the herd. They raced with precision, with magnificent beauty.

Still Water Runs rode on one side of the pack, Jamie on the other side, keeping the horses in line. Drew along with Jeremy brought up the rear. The corral for them was opened, ready and waiting for the new occupants.

He reached Lyssa. Stopped. Her arms were lifted to him. He swept her onto his thighs. Quickly, he bent to kiss her warm moist lips. She greeted him with the play of her tongue against his as she eagerly opened for him. He didn't intend to waste another moment.

"I've missed you," she said as his lips framed hers. "Thought you would be here sooner. Knew you couldn't have died and left me to mourn."

She leaned into him, pressed herself close, the tips of her cloth covered breasts pressed against his chest. He meant to get rid of the barrier between them.

That was all she could say. He would show her how he missed her. Lust along with love coursed inside his hard all male body as they raced away from the ranch house. He couldn't wait. He didn't give a damn what anyone would think. He felt savage and wild, pure Sioux warrior. She was his wife. He wanted her, needed her now.

Her hands touched his naked chest, ran across him, stopped for a moment over the scar from the bullet. He heard her soft intake of breath.

Felt her lips against the puckered ridge.

"You are fine now?"

She looked at him while her eyes shimmered with moisture.

"Don't cry, Little Bit." The time for tears was over many months' past. "No, I'll be fine in a few minutes," he told her as he closed his mouth over hers again, savoring all that she was, seizing the moment along with all the passion she returned.

He didn't need to spirit her to a hunting lodge as her uncle Drake did to his wife Ella to know her raw passion.

One hand was beneath her skirt. The heat he felt seared his hands. "Lift your hips, Little Bit."

"What?"

"Just do it," he growled impatiently.

She did. He pulled her drawers from her body. The white frilly undergarment fluttered to the ground. Together they raced past the man he believed was her father. His hand was shielded over his eyes, watching them. They passed her mother along with the brother.

"What are you doing?" The question held a wealth of outrage even while her body quivered against him begging him for his attention.

"Straddle me, Lyssa. I want you yesterday, months ago. Don't want to wait one more second."

"You can't mean..."

Without answering, he lifted her so her legs clung to his flanks. His nimble fingers found the buttons on her shirt, then the ribbon-laces of her chemise. Her breasts pushed against the hard, smooth planes of his chest. He needed to taste her, touch her, every sweet inch of her. She was so adorable. He inhaled the scent of jasmine and woman.

"Hang on to me. Don't let go." He maneuvered his horse with his knees while he uncovered himself. "Are you ready for me? Are you hot and wet waiting for my body to become one with yours?"

"Kane! You can't..."

He wasn't' going to allow her to protest. Bending close to her, he touched her hard pink nipple with his tongue, sipped and laved until moans of delight echoed from her throat. A small broken sound followed. She writhed sending surges of lust deep to his groin.

His hands slipped beneath her chemise. Cool delicately satin-soft skin caressed his palms. Her back was almost as enticing as her front, her legs, behind her knees, other parts as well. A low rumbling groan rose from deep in his belly. He couldn't touch her everywhere but he wanted to do so. Rampant desire surged hot and fast in his loins. Raw passion for his wife flooded his body.

"Are you holding tight? Don't let go." He chuckled softly as her fingers bored into his shoulders before wrapping around him. She clung to him. He felt her muscles tighten as she did his bidding.

"Why?" her voice wobbled.

"Isn't it obvious," he queried as his hands continued to sightsee over sensitive flesh.

He didn't need to coax or sweet-talk, no seduction necessary. She was hot and wet, ready and wild for him. Of that fact he was certain. He slipped his fingers through slick wet feminine folds.

A shiver spiraled from her into him then he thought back to her as she coiled and arched against him. She was shaking her head. "Nothing you do is ever obvious, Kane..." her voice was a thin wail.

Once again, he touched her intimately. Found the tiny pearl hidden between the soft damp folds guarding her core. He caressed her there. Watched as her eyes darkened with the raw deep passion he created solely for her.

"This should be understandable," he murmured while he continued his campaign to generate the ecstasy he knew she craved. He touched the sensitive spot behind her ear with the tip of his tongue. Delighted in the clenching of her muscles. The way her body drenched his fingers with the sweetest nectar. Once more his lips found hers as her body spiraled and burned for him, only him.

Their tongues played and toyed with each other, dancing to the rhythm he set. She tasted of mint. When he inhaled deeply, jasmine and woman filled his senses. Again, he settled his mouth on a taut pink bud. His tongue curled around the tip while he caressed the other breast, playing with the tip, rolling the velvet hardness between his fingers.

"You don't mean to do this on the horse? Do you?" A broken sound left her then her hips lifted as if she asked for more exquisite attention.

He didn't want her to climax until he was deep inside her dark velvet sheathe. She would be hot and sultry, wet with her passion raining down upon him. Her tight core would kiss and caress his length. He moaned at the thoughts flooding his mind centering deep in his male parts.

She was ready for him. Her honey ran sweet and hot.

There was no reason to wait.

"Is there someplace private we can head?" While he spoke, his lips caressed her neck following across her jaw.

She nodded; her head tilted back giving him greater access. Her breasts heaved as if she tried to absorb as much air as she could. "Yes..."

His laughter joined with the wind, enjoying the picture of her bouncing breasts along with the long white column of her neck. Soon, she would find him deep inside her secret depths, touching her womb.

"Where?"

Without answering she tilted her head in the direction he should go.

He felt her climax building. She purred softly as his mouth framed hers. For a moment he withdrew his hand from between her legs. "Lyssa? Tell me. I can't read your mind."

"Oh! What did you ask?" The sound emitted was a shrill cry. Her need grew with each second.

"Where can we go that is private?" He slipped a finger inside her then followed with a second one.

She swallowed hard before closing her eyes. "I can't think. You have to, you..."

"Yes, you can. Tell me or I might stop right here and I'll be deep inside you with all to see." He wasn't going to do anything of the sort. She wouldn't know that. They were leaving the crowd of onlookers behind them. They were fading into nothing. With the advent of seconds, they were far enough away to do as he pleased.

Her tongue swept across her bottom lip leaving a dewy trail of moisture. "Northeast, there's a small lake with an island. We can go there. It will be private."

His back was to his watching audience. They would see nothing. In one fluid motion, he swept her high then settled her on his steel-hard member.

"Kane!"

In that second, he spurred his mount to race. Her body moved with the tempest of the horse. He drove into her harder and faster. He'd never experienced anything so damn sensual. She climaxed almost immediately. He felt the deep dark spams of her release coupled with her cries of pleasure. He joined her, his seed filling her. By his command the horse slowed to a gentle cantor.

The process began anew.

She panted. She heaved. She moaned. Her breaths were raw and deep while he enjoyed the movement of the tips of her rounded globes against his naked flesh. To him they were beautiful round jewels meant for him alone. They were more valuable than any diamonds or sapphires. His intimate attentions once more sent her into a heated spiral of need. Again, he set the horse to race with the; wind. Again, within seconds she climaxed.

"Kane..." Her head rested in the hollow of his shoulder. "I cannot breathe, my heart races. What are you doing to me?"

"Neither can I." Bloody eyes, he emptied himself three times inside her. Still, he wasn't sated. He wanted her more than ever. One more time as now he saw the island. He could wait.

Slowly, the horse drew to a halt. He looked upon the lake. A rowboat sat on the edge. Ah, good there was only one. He dismounted with Lyssa in his arms. They would spend the afternoon on the island making love, talking.

They had much to talk about.

~ * ~

When Lyssa watched Kane riding in front of the racing horses, the delight she felt couldn't be contained. He was tall and proud, a Sioux warrior. Her warrior. Her heart lurched wildly beneath her ribs. He was here. He was alive. She would hold him close. She'd never seen anyone ride so fearlessly. He put all the men she knew including her brother and father to shame. The muscles of his naked chest rippled while he rode, his arms strong and bulging with innate masculine strength.

After he picked her up to sit in front of her, she understood this ride would be like no other. Giving him whatever he wanted was at the forefront of her mind. Before he bade her lift her hips, she was running her hands along the expanse of his body, across his shoulders then lower wishing she dared find him beneath the skimpy cloth he wore. When he pulled her drawers off then left them on the ground, heat flooded every part of her. She wanted to think it was love. Knew the sensations were created from sexual hunger, lust, the fierce passion they felt for each other. Wondered if it was a bad thing to lust after one's husband.

She felt blindsided when he told her to straddle him. Her legs parted. He turned her to sit astride him. His member hard and deliciously throbbing pressed against her sensitive flesh. She gasped at the contact. Understood he meant to make love to her while riding. The thought sent another wave of raw passion storming through her so intense she groaned with the frenzy the sensations created.

He didn't stop. It seemed the spasms continued one after the other, never-ending. She didn't have time to breathe or to think. When he finally pulled to a stop in front of the lake, he helped her from the mount. She couldn't walk. Her body lay flush against his, learning the strength of her husband for a second time. If he wanted her to move, he would have to carry her for certainly her legs would not accommodate her commands to move.

He laughed softly while he brushed errant strands of hair from her face. "You are beautiful. Do you need time to recover before we start again? I intend to make love to you all afternoon. No one will stop us here. Am I right? There is only one way to the island."

She looked up. His smile was broad, so very arrogant the sight stole all the air from her lungs. He looked pleased with himself, confident in himself. Between sharp pants of air, she managed speech, "We should take the rowboat to the island before mother and father catch up to us. Doubt if either one is delighted at what they just witnessed."

"They couldn't see anything," he was quick to say in his defense.

"All they know for sure was that you sat on me, straddled me with your long white legs, held my flanks tight."

Weakly, she punched his chest not regretting what they did. The raw sensations were heavenly but she wouldn't tell him that. "Neither one is stupid. All watching from the field must have known what you did. You did toss my pantalets onto the ground."

"What we did," he corrected while he scooped her into his arms to stride to the boat. "I will row and you will tell me about the baby you are growing inside your womb."

She sipped air, felt startled at his blatant comment. "How did you know?"

"To begin with," he paused grinning besotted at her, "your breasts as well as your belly tell the entire tale. You can never hide anything from me, Lys. I remember how you were. Know how you are now."

"How?" She puzzled over his comment. She didn't show yet, well, was just beginning to guess. He couldn't possibly know she was pregnant. His was a lucky guess.

"They are not the same as I remember. Your breasts are more sensitive as well as larger and there is a tiny bump where your belly used to be flat. How far along are you?"

"Are you pleased?"

"Immensely, now, how far along are you. Eventually, we will need to take some precautions with our lovemaking. Not today though."

"I'm guessing about three and a half months possibly four." Truly, she didn't know the exact time.

"Do your parents know you carry my child?" he asked as he watched her, seemed to study her in depth.

She shook her head. "I…" Nervously she moistened her lips, sent her tongue across the bottom one then back again. "Wanted to tell you first. Knew you would find me here, since you orchestrated this scenario."

"I took that away from you. I'm not sorry though."

"No, I don't suppose you are."

It didn't take long to reach the island. She'd never been here with a beau. She never knew anyone before Kane she would want to take here. After he set her in the boat, he retrieved a few items from his saddlebags.

She saw a canteen along with a bag.

"Yes, I suppose I was as much a part of the lovemaking as you were. I never told you to stop. Imagine I was too shocked to say the word no. After that I was too..." she didn't have the words to describe what she was feeling.

"Shocked?" He nuzzled her ear, sipping behind then giving his attention to more tender, sensitive spots. "Too?"

"Yes, everything you do shocks me in some way. I don't know what to say." She didn't. "You always manage to leave me breathless as well as without words."

The little structure hidden away was exactly as she remembered. When she opened the door, the sight stole her breath. Her mother must have updated the tiny space during her absence. Bright orange and yellow pillows adorned the small platform bed in the center. On each side of the bed there was a table just high enough to set a glass of wine or food."

"Do your parents still go here or is this Jess' doing?"

His grin spread across his face as he seemed to envision her parents lying on the quilts and pillows naked, stroking and caressing each other.

Heat flooded all of her. The images were too much for her to contemplate. "I don't know," her words wobbled from her lips. "Don't want to think about my parents or Jess doing the things we do."

Kane pulled her into his arms. Her back pressed against his chest. His large bronzed hands cradled her belly. He pressed and kneaded the contours spreading his fingers so they reached to both hipbones.

His fingers moved through her hair while his lips warmed the empty spots on the back of her neck. "I want you naked. Need to look at all of you, explore as well as seduce all of you." She moved against him, feeling the instant rise of passion his words always spawned.

"Not before you are naked," she teased, her voice rough, filled with need.

"Are you positive no one can get to the island? Don't want to be interrupted." He looked to the spot where the rowboat was moored.

"It's been an unspoken rule. As children we always understood mother and father were here if the boat wasn't on the bank. We understood that unless the situation was a matter of life or death, they would not be pleased to find themselves disturbed. I guess the rule was the same with Jess."

"You?" He turned her, lifting a perfectly arched eyebrow upward. "Does this unspoken rule apply to you also? First hand, I know you've never been here with a man."

"Me? You knew I was a virgin." She felt anger as well as indignation rise at the thought he questioned her. "Would then assume I never used the island."

"You never brought a boy here just to kiss? Perhaps explore a tiny bit?"

"No." He wasn't going to receive any more of an answer than that. She was riled beyond belief.

"Did you kiss anyone before me?"

She wanted to yell at him that her past wasn't his business. The chance evaded her when his lips framed her mouth, savored, claiming all of her. Heat swamped her. All her innate sensuality aroused; she returned his intimate kisses. His fingers closed over her buttocks while her breasts pushed against his chest. He pulled her so close she felt the steel hardness of his arousal against her belly, experienced the heat, felt the power along with the strength of him.

"No? Is that your answer? I understand you were innocent. Never thought for a moment some handsome, arrogant boy didn't try to steal a kiss or two from your soft pink lips."

"I was homely." She could think of nothing else to say that wouldn't bolster his ego.

"Little liar, you were never unattractive." He pushed the fabric of her gown to her waist along with her chemise. "Your nipples are pink. Do you know you taste pink?"

"That is the stupidest thing I've ever heard." She stretched her hands across his chest. "Don't know if I can do this again. It seemed you stole every breath as well as all my energy from me. You've rendered me exhausted."

"You can." He paused then, seeming to think. "Are you sore?"

She was but she wasn't about to tell him simply because she

wanted him deep inside her again. She needed to feel as one with him. When they returned to the house, she was positive her parents would do all in their power to keep them apart.

"No," she whispered softly.

"For some reason, I don't believe you're speaking true. Nonetheless, I will make love to you once more. I will be gentle. After that we will talk. I've brought wine in the canteen along with a bag of foods that are meant to delight all your senses."

Slowly, reverently, he finished undressing her. For himself, there was little for Kane to remove. The cushions were soft, the lovemaking this time was slow, not fast and hard as it had been when they rode. When they finished and he pulled her into his arms, her head rested in the hollow of his shoulder. Her hand settled on his back, smoothed along the scars left by the whip so many years ago. She hated the woman who caused this yet thanked her. He didn't like to speak of the disfigurements on his back or of that time. Neither did she even though she could not help but think of his pain.

She was breathing deeply, lost in thought as his fingers gently moved along her arm.

"A penny for your thoughts?" he asked when he pulled back to look at her.

Lyssa knew she enjoyed these moments after the passion as much as she did the fantastic explosion of sensations she always experienced. He was always so gentle. His tenderness belied his hard body. "So many things," she murmured.

"Just one." He sat up then handed her the canteen to drink from. While he waited for her to speak, he set the food items he brought with him on a cloth. She drank. The wine was delicious, soothed her parched throat.

"My parents don't believe we are truly married. Not in the eyes of our Christian God. I made the mistake of telling him the man who wed us was your chief cook as well as dishwasher. They won't let us stay together tonight. I'm as sure of that fact as I'm certain they will insist on separate bedrooms. I'm so glad to see you again. There was a time...there was a time I was afraid you were gone from me forever."

"You did? He doesn't wash dishes. He simply gets them dirty. Did you also tell them he is an ordained minister?" Gently, he moved damp strands of hair to behind her ear. "Hmm..."

"I told them everything. Nevertheless, they want to see us wed in the Methodist church tomorrow. Reverend Brown will agree to do the honors. You could refuse. However, I would appreciate it if you give into this one bit of parental decisions. My entire life...well...I always believed he would say the vows at my marriage."

His brows drew together eyes shimmering in a way she didn't understand. "They don't trust your word?"

She was so afraid he was angry. "It isn't a matter of trust. At least I don't believe that." A breath of air escaped when he traced a path to the hardened tip of her breast.

"What do you believe then?" He teased her lips with an apple slice.

"If you want to talk, you've got to stop seducing and charming my socks off."

"You aren't wearing socks."

She pushed off his chest to look at him. His grin was wicked. She continued speaking while trying desperately to ignore him. The scrumptiously wild light in his eyes was making ignoring impossible. "The simple fact is that I'm their only daughter. I believe they thought when they sent me to Aunt Ella's that they would have time to sail to England for the wedding. That wasn't the case. From their viewpoint, they missed an important event in their daughter's life. They won't let that go easily. They will insist."

"So, if I'm understanding the situation correctly, they would like to watch their female child wed."

Lightly, he kissed her on the nose before doing the same to the corners of her mouth. With a look of sensual longing in his eyes he gazed at the tips of her breasts.

"Are you terribly set against another wedding?"

His eyes sparkled with humor. It seemed he did not intend to reply in the negative.

"No, the more weddings the better. No one will question the

legitimacy of my heir. We will have wedding certificates coming out our ears. If a third wedding makes you happy, I won't stand in your way. I did expect this to happen when we returned."

"They will put up a stink about our sleeping together tonight. You understand that, don't you?" she went on to tell him. "It seems to be a long-standing tradition in our family that the men don't get to go to bed with their women until the wedding night."

The grimace on his face brought forth a giggle. He touched the tip of her nose. "I've been celibate for four months now going on what seems to be a year. Tonight, one way or the other we will sleep in the same bed even if I have to sneak into the room where you have bedded down. You are my wife, whether or not your parents choose to believe so."

"You will have to be strong in your convictions. Father will find some means to make you see the evening his way."

She didn't want to sleep alone. After all she'd also been celibate for the same amount of time. She missed his warm arms around her, the closeness, the protective touch missed much more than that.

Several seconds passed while she was absorbed in her thoughts. She wanted to know what happened to Jonathan White as well as why it took Kane so long to come for her. Gently, she touched his scar. Her heart wrenched while she thought about that day so long in the past. She didn't like feeling helpless and vulnerable.

Kane seemed to read her thoughts. His brows drew together forming a line above his eyes. "Three weeks, three damn long weeks passed before I could get out of bed. The last week nearly killed me by itself. All I wanted was to find you. I feared for you, for your life as I also knew you would fight the man. If you did, he would hurt you."

"You almost died. When I left your side, my hands along with the front of my dress was covered in your blood. I did try to run. Did attempt to reach Ashes before Mr. White caught up to me. They surrounded me."

"I felt so bloody powerless. The ability to defend and protect my wife ceased to exist that day. Nothing like that has ever happened to me before. I was a fool to not take that man more seriously." He drew in a long deep breath his eyes closed as if he remembered every horrific detail. "I don't see how they got the better of us. It was such a stupid mistake."

"Still Water Runs wasn't there. The men taunted me. They circled around me so I couldn't reach the horse. When I could no longer run, my breath heaving, Jonathan picked me up, set me in front of him. Even though you warned me against it, I fought him with all my strength. I was afraid..." She didn't want to voice her worst fears. "I did break his nose."

"The sorrow that swamps me at your pain cannot be described. Their plan was sound except for the fact they underestimated you. You are an amazing woman, Little Bit. When I was healed, we...I followed the tracks along with Still Water Runs the best we could. My men had already done so. They went to Glasgow to search as well as Edinburgh. Needless to say, they couldn't find you. Didn't know who you would turn to for help. I was unconscious. I couldn't tell them what I knew about you."

"With the knife you gave me, I was able to cut the leather they bound me with. They had no idea I possessed a means to defeat them. They never searched me. I took their horses. Riding hard while moving from one four legged beast to another I made it to Glasgow in record time." She finished the telling of her story including the random meeting of Lacie Stewart the Duchess of Southcliff.

He told her the rest of what happened to him those weeks he searched and waited to find a way to Baltimore. Recounting how he finally found Jamie, she giggled.

"It was Still Water Runs who helped me remember your aunt's name as well as her husband. I was so fraught with worry I couldn't think straight."

"Then we have a great deal to thank your friend for. You might still be searching for a ship. Are Mr. White along with his friends going to live their lives unpunished."

She prayed it wasn't so. Her father told her several times without a witness who saw him shoot the earl; he would not be brought to trial. The kidnapping was a different story. Nonetheless, it would end up her word against three others.

"Yes, for the crimes they committed concerning us. However, not the crimes they will be committing even as we speak. I understand men like them. They will not give up their fortunes without exploring every legal as well as illegal avenues to regain what I intend to see them misplace."

Kane proceeded to tell her all he'd done. "By the time we reach home, they will be out of our lives for good. If not, well then, I'll have to find some other way to punish them."

"You are a genius." Lyssa spoke sincerely from the heart as she nipped tiny kisses across his collarbone. "I never would have thought of something so underhanded yet efficient."

"Jonathan thrived with the power his money bought. He will be brought low. Is, I'm certain even now, paying the price for his greed. The man should have been happy with the money he earned from his successful endeavors. He wished for more. His title isn't to be. By threatening all I hold dear, he overstepped his bounds."

"The sun is sitting low on the horizon," she said softly. "Wish we could spend the night here. We have to return before my parents send out search parties or build another rowboat."

"The nights are too chilly for us to stay here even with my arms around you."

"We've lots of warm blankets. As long as it doesn't rain hard, we can stay," she sounded as if she didn't want to see her parents.

She didn't. Not after the display they created on their way to the lake gazebo.

He kissed her softly as if he didn't want to generate raw passion only wanted to confirm how much he cared for her. "You are not showing the courage I've come to admire in you."

"He is not your father."

"No, my father-in-law. In any case his respect is important to me. We must return before dark. At least for me a bath is in order, a hot one to be taken before we sit at the dinner table with your family for the first time. Would you prefer to bathe in the lake?" He chuckled beneath his breath as if he thought he could see any more of her than he already did.

It seemed their arrival back at the ranch was anticipated. A steaming hot bath awaited them at the guest cottage where she stayed since arriving at the ranch. Lyssa looked at it longingly. Kane grinned.

"Did they think we would share? That doesn't seem to me the thoughts of a man who wants to keep his daughter and her husband from sleeping together this night."

"Perhaps the ploy is to lull us into believing otherwise." She looked from him to the tub then back again. "We are too big to share. Go ahead take the first bath. Just don't use all the rinse water. I will be happy to wash in what is left over."

"A gentleman would never allow such a travesty. I'll give you the first one if you hurry."

She let a slow breath of air filter through her lungs. "You just want to watch."

"Yes." He grinned wickedly while lifting his dark eyebrows.

"Not that I care."

She undressed quickly. Spent as little time as possible in the hot water. She wished to dress in one of her new gowns, as she didn't want to spill out of the top of one of her old ones. It didn't surprise her he knew her breasts were larger, her belly not as flat. Over the months her body seemed to change. Every week or so, she would notice something different about herself.

An hour later they appeared at the front door of the house. When he brought his hand up to knock, she stepped in front of him holding onto the door's handle.

Her father must have seen them coming. The door swung open. At the expression on his face, Lyssa stifled a gasp of air. She felt mortified when Kane's grin seemed to tell her father what they had been doing for the last few hours.

"Are the horses taken care of? We will have to build you a new stable for the care of these fine creatures. We will do this before Lyssa and I return to London."

Those words brought a smile to her father's face. "You will help, I thought you would. You don't mean to leave tomorrow?"

"Yes, helping was my intention. My wife and I will not risk a journey across the Atlantic during hurricane season especially since she carries my heir tucked away quite nicely in her precious womb."

Well, that changed the smile on her father's face to a definitive frown. She tugged on Kane's arm as if to stop him from saying more condemning words. After that she sucked in a deep breath of air.

"Kane," she murmured softly while the heat on her cheeks grew.

The blasted man paid her no heed. "We will get started tomorrow after the wedding?"

"So…" Damian rocked back on his heels. "The two of you aren't married."

Her husband's grin was wolfish. "We've been wed twice. I see nothing wrong with a third or even a fourth time if it makes her father happy. As your son-in-law, I will respect most of your wishes."

His words didn't seem to sooth her father, not one tiny bit.

Damian looked as if he was at a loss for words. He bit in a shallow breath of air. "I think…"

"Dinner is ready." Amorica waltzed into the room then slanted a warning glance to her husband. "I've baked three batches of biscuits. You only get one, Damian. The second is for Kane if he wishes, after that the third is for the rest of us. Do not even dare to be greedy."

"What about me?" Jess asked as he strode into the room. "I can eat an entire batch too."

"You will behave yourself and share the third batch with Lyssa and me."

"Mother bakes the most mouth-watering biscuits," Lyssa said as she watched her father and brother scowl as if they'd been denied the tastiest treat of their lives. They got biscuits almost every night.

"You will learn?" Kane asked with a lopsided smile as if he anticipated that very thing.

Lyssa lifted her shoulders slightly. "Don't know how to do that. I will always be myself. Perhaps you will learn."

"Ah, we will be here for months. You can learn."

"Not likely."

~ * ~

"Do you see what they are doing?" Damian asked his wife as he watched Kane along with his daughter ride away.

She was straddling him, her legs wrapped around his flanks. When Damian watched her drawers float to the ground, he turned away. That wasn't something a father should see. His insides curdled while he tried desperately to accept the idea that his little girl was now a married woman.

"No, I've closed my eyes. Don't want to see. Don't want to know or hear anything about what they are doing. So, kindly keep your lips sealed," Amorica muttered softly as she made her way to the house. She turned back to say one more thing, her finger pointing at him, "Going to start dinner. You will behave yourself where the biscuits are concerned. After that I'll finish working on the new quilt."

Damian decided then and there he would make sure the new couple slept alone tonight simply because no matter how he tried he couldn't wrap his head around the pertinent facts. Kane would abide by his rules. This ranch where Kane stayed was after all his home. He followed his wife into the house then the kitchen. Venison stew would soon simmer on the stove. An apple pie cooled on a window ledge. The biscuits would give a wondrous aroma to the kitchen. Amorica's biscuits were the absolute best.

His stomach growled in anticipation of the meal to come. The biscuits, ah, her biscuits, he could make a meal of them himself.

"When do you think the children will return?" Amorica asked while she cut up strips of venison.

She was humming to herself, stirring the liquid in the pot. She added the precut vegetables.

Damian understood she hoped it would be sooner than later just as he hoped it would not be. He was realistic enough to know they would spend the afternoon on the island. "We have to remember she is a married lady," he said the words more to convince himself than to satisfy his wife.

"Yes, I know. We have fifty horses in the corral that says as much. A bride price." She puffed an errant strand of hair from her face appearing disgusted with the notion. "He must understand we don't sell our daughters. What he has done is outrageous."

When Damian stood behind her, she pressed against him. Her hair, piled on top of her head left her nape bare, susceptible to his lips. He nipped. He laved. The slim body he knew so well quivered in anticipation. After watching his new son-in-law with his daughter, he had parallel feelings.

"I do believe we should try it sometime. Might prove a delightful experience. What do you think?" His hands settled on her belly. One rose to cup her breast then flick hotly across the tip.

"Try what?" she murmured softly as she seemed to absorb his attentions.

Damian adored the way she always melted for him. He knew her eyes would hold a dreamy faraway look when she climaxed. The way they never failed to darken when he stroked her pleased him immensely. Slowly, very gently, his nimble fingers pulled on the hem of her dress. He wanted to caress the length of her leg, feel the satin finish of her skin.

"Making love while riding..." He bit tenderly the back of her neck then allowed his attentions to move higher to her ear. A soft purring sound rippled from her lips.

When his fingers closed over her woman's mound, she was damp and swollen. Her intimate heat seared his hand. A small broken sound broke from her lips while she parted her legs for him.

"We...no...Damian, we need to take this to the bedroom not to your horse. I won't do it."

"Want to go to the stable."

"No..."

It was too late for protest. He made up his mind. He meant to pleasure her in this new and unique way. His imagination understood how fast the ecstasy would come. Lust for his wife surged to his groin.

He swept her into his arms.

She struggled. Hit him on the shoulder. "Put me down! Beast! Arrogant rogue!"

After a moment of protest, Amorica set her head on his chest. Seemingly resigned, she played with the buttons on his shirt, slipping the buttons through the holes.

"Unfasten your gown," he told her when his shirt hung open baring his chest to her questing hands.

Amorica did. Her breath caught on a moan of pleasure as his fingers cupped and played with the globes. He wanted all the fabric to vanish. "You mean to do this? We could go to the loft. I wouldn't protest."

"Doesn't seem as if I've heard one word of descent from lips that will soon be kiss swollen and begging for more." He chuckled as her blouse opened. "Now your chemise. I want to feel you pressed against me."

It was so close to the dinner hour, thankfully all his men had gone home. Quickly, he left her standing while he put the blanket on his horse then the surcingle tying it down. He lifted her so she sat the horse backward then he quickly mounted behind her. Before she had time to say anything, she straddled him. He felt the intimate heat radiate from her parted legs.

They headed in the opposite direction from the children. Once they were away from the main house and outbuildings, he unfastened his trousers.

He was inside her then. Potent flames engulfed him. Felt her sultry core caress him, kiss the length of him with the hot intense tremors that were even now building sensuously.

They galloped.

The event was everything he hoped for then more. Together they climaxed then again and again as he changed the tempo of the horse.

Chapter Ten

With dinner finished they all retired to the main living room of the ranch. Lyssa told him this was when her father would make sure he understood a few relevant facts about this evening. Her father could lecture or talk until his face was blue. Kane wasn't going to give in to the man's wishes. He needed to relearn every adorable spot his wife possessed, especially the new places caused because of the baby she carried.

"You and my daughter will not sleep together before the wedding."

After Lyssa's warnings, Damian's words came as no surprise to Kane. Still, he hoped they would not be spoken. He didn't wish to argue with his new father-in-law. If given no feasible choice, he would.

Unable to stop himself, he nervously tapped his fingers on the arm of the chair where he sat in an attempt at a winning strategy in this new endeavor. Ah hell, the man didn't pull any punches. He couldn't either. Lyssa sent him a quelling look over her glass of wine. It was an I told you so look coupled with the question of how he was going to change her father's mind. Obviously, she didn't have much confidence in his verbal strategy.

Kane cleared his throat while he reached out for Lyssa's hand. He squeezed. Her fingers were cold. His smile didn't reach his eyes. He began, "I mean you no disrespect, sir."

"You and my daughter are not married in my eyes," Damian began as if he meant to continue in the same autocratic vein. "Under my roof the two of you will remain chaste. One night is all I'm asking."

Kane held his hands up in an attempt to silence Lyssa's father. "We have been wed twice. This third time is simply to humor her parents. We will sleep together as man and wife tonight."

"Humor?" Amorica asked a look of disdain caressing her features. "Humor her parents?" Her anger was apparent.

The last thing he wanted was to hurt Lyssa's mother. Obviously, his use of words was wrong.

"Not married to my satisfaction," Damian persisted, his voice rising, seeming not to notice Amorica's comment.

"Once in the way of the Christian God."

Kane had a lot to say. It didn't seem Damian meant to give him the chance.

"He was your damn chef, your cook," Damian grit out behind clenched teeth. "What kind of minister is that?"

This seemed to be going from bad to worse for them. Lyssa held her breath apparently waiting for his reply.

"An ordained minister who grew distraught at his congregation who came to church on Sunday pious then as soon as they left went back to ways that were not so Christian one might call them evil. The man quit preaching. Found he could do quite a lot of things, cooking as well as baking. He did not quit the church. We were also married in the way of the People. You accepted the bride price thereby accepting the marriage as valid. That gesture cannot be taken back. There is nothing more for you to do about this situation you are single handedly creating. We are wed. Tomorrow is just so Amorica can watch her child marry the man she loves." He certainly hoped Lyssa loved him. He looked at her for affirmative confirmation. Her face was a blank slate.

She had yet to say the words.

Perhaps he should plunge first into that treacherous territory. He didn't like the idea of putting himself out there when he didn't know how she felt. Vulnerability didn't become him.

She married you, you fool. Of course, she loves you.

That doesn't necessarily mean she loves me.

No, all she wanted was to erase the permanent scowl on my face.

That too.

"Those facts won't change my mind," Damian said as he looked from Lyssa to Kane. "The two of you will wait until tomorrow night to join together in one bed."

"Damian, give in for once. They are wed. It is but one night," Amorica said as she set her hand upon his.

"No!"

Well, that one word held a wealth of meaning, none of which he appreciated. Kane sucked in a long draught of air while he searched for the words necessary to convince Damian he wasn't going to sleep alone tonight. Believed the mention of the bride price would have done the trick. Apparently not. "I've been without my wife for four months now. I'm not spending another night without her in my arms."

"Seems the two you made up for lost time this afternoon." Damian's voice was bland as he stared from one to the other.

Well hell, what did he expect? Kane wished he knew what was behind the man's eyes, the hidden meaning. He promised Lyssa her parents couldn't see what was going on when she straddled him and he was deep inside the sultry heat of her body.

"That, sir, is overstepping a father's right to know about what goes on between his daughter and her husband."

Kane's anger began to overpower his good judgment, his fury escalating with every breath he inhaled.

"Father, you did accept the horses, did you not?" Lyssa said softly, her eyes wide with hope. "You acknowledged the marriage in the way of his people. We are also wed by a Christian minister."

"I didn't understand the rules," Damian bit out furious now. "One can't hold another man accountable in that case."

"Does all this truly make a difference in anything?" Amorica asked. It seemed she wanted the argument to cease. Deftly, she'd become the peacemaker. "If they wish to be together, I see no reason why we should refuse them."

"It does make a difference to me. Thank you, Amorica, we both appreciate your support," Kane spoke calmly. "If you don't want us here, we can leave. Don't have to remain under your roof if that is the way you see us. Don't have to partake of the wedding tomorrow. I'm quite capable of providing for my wife whether it is beneath the stars or in the home of her parents. I believe the choice is now up to you."

"The way I see you?" Damian asked clearly frustrated with Kane.

"All I expected from the two of you was one night sleeping alone."

"Lyssa is pregnant. Nearly four months now. There is no reason to pretend we have not made love numerous times. Including this afternoon," Kane spoke blatantly, understanding Damian would not change his mind easily. Probably would not change his mind at all.

Amorica set her hand on her husband's shoulder. "We will not insist that you stay in separate buildings hence separate beds," she spoke for her husband, her eyes shining with love when she looked at him. "We understand your need to be together. If that need weren't so potent and strong, I would worry about your marriage. As it is, I see no reason to deny either of you."

Nonetheless, it seemed Damian persisted in his arguments. "Doesn't make a difference in my mind if she is increasing. What the fact does mean is that she needs to be married as soon as possible."

"Father, we are wed. Don't persevere. It's not one of your finer moments. I don't want to see a rift between my husband and my father, one that could not be mended. Kane will insist to the point of leaving here with me tonight. If that is the case, we most likely will not be wed tomorrow. Is that what you want?"

"You need to compromise with the children," Amorica said sweetly her lashes lowering for a moment, "meet them half way. They are willing to hold a third wedding for us so we can celebrate their union with them. Let's not ruin tomorrow by an argument that cannot be won by either of you tonight. I, for one, don't wish them to leave."

To Kane it seemed Damian might give in to Amorica's gentle plea. He positively hoped so. As Lyssa pointed out, they would leave here if forced to sleep in separate rooms.

He heard Lyssa tug in a bit of air, "I will follow my husband's commands, not my father's. He is, after all, my husband. My loyalty as well as my obedience lies with him."

Once again, she spoke softly yet what he heard in her voice was firm commitment to him. He was well pleased. He wanted to pull her into his arms while kissing her senseless. After that he wanted to finish with the lovemaking.

"More wine?"

Amorica topped off everyone's glass. She seemed pleased with the change of atmosphere. Neither man was still bristling.

"Seems to me," Jess spoke up, "this conversation is the most ridiculous one I've ever heard. If it were me, I'd feel the same as Kane. Would want to sleep with my wife."

"It's not up to you," Damian was quick to say flashing his son a look that should tell him to keep his opinions behind his teeth. "A son is different."

Kane stared hard at Lyssa after he heard the sharp gasp of air. Her eyes darkened with anger he didn't understand. If he didn't miss his guess, Lyssa was now furious with her father.

"You've never treated us...said anything that implied I didn't have the same rights as Jess. What do you mean a son is different? I'll have you know that I'm the same...well...except for that."

"Perhaps you should also explain that statement to me as well," Amorica said.

She seemed to withdraw from her husband who now had his sight on the couch. Kane wondered if he got sent to the couch very often.

"Wish I could," Damian said as he ran a finger around his collar clearly distressed by the words of both women. "Where a woman is concerned, my daughter, sex is different. Jess can't get pregnant."

"That's a damn poor excuse. You best figure out something better," Amorica told him, her hands now fisted one around the stem of her wine glass. "I seem to remember times...well I'm not about to elaborate now. You best remember them. It seems to me that if a man gets a woman with child, he is not absolved of responsibility because of his gender."

Kane thought for a moment that he wouldn't be surprised if she tossed the remainder of her wine at her husband. Wickedly he grinned.

"It's easy," Jess began, his words spoken with the arrogance of a young pup who knew he owned his part of the world. "A man wants to know he has fathered the child his wife is to bear him."

He turned to stare at his sister. "In the Earl of Blackmore's case, there is more at stake. He will want to know for certain that Lyssa carries his heir, that he is the sire because of the title."

"You are evil, brother," Lyssa shouted, her rage obvious. "I'm so tired of talk about titles I'll certainly explode! You have the audacity to toss out that impertinent observation as if you have the right to do so. You've no right whatsoever! How many girls have you bedded?"

She was adorable in her rage. Kane felt the urge to laugh. If he wanted to sleep with his wife tonight, he didn't dare do something so foolish as join his opinion in this conversation. She was an indelible picture of anger all that fury directed toward her father and brother. The passion she exhibited was always delightful. When she turned that statement his way, he would have to have a ready answer.

"Your brother is merely making an observation," Kane said blandly not believing that fact for an instant. "While it should never be different it seems to be so…in polite society." He felt proud at that statement. "Women have few means to keep from conceiving an unwanted child. Men don't have to worry about that." He lifted his shoulders in a masculine shrug. "If they did, well, I'm sure there would be more equality between the sexes. Don't you think?"

"Would anyone like pie?" Amorica seemed to wish this conversation ended as much as he did. "I've warmed it. So, it is ready. I've cheese slices to put on the top if you wish."

The question put a silence to the stilted conversation. Kane was eager to finish the dessert then head to the small guesthouse where he could have a simple conversation with Lyssa then make love to her and hold her in his arms. Tomorrow would inevitably be a long day, fatiguing. In her present condition, he didn't know how much stamina she possessed. Testing her limits would not be a good idea. He needed to take care of his wife. After all, her health along with the baby's came first. If she showed any signs of strain, he meant to put an end to this third installment of a wedding ceremony, one that wasn't at all needed.

After all, today he asked for a lot from his lovely wife. He had made love to her again then again. She never told him she didn't wish for him to bury himself deep inside. Never asked him to cease. No, it seemed she yearned for him as much as he lusted for her. He needed to take care. Having a pregnant wife was new ground for him to travel.

She could be exhausted.

If she were correct in her counting, she was beginning her fourth month. Well then, she would no longer feel sickness. Would she? After desert was served there was no more talk of their staying in separate rooms. When he walked Lyssa back to the guesthouse, he wrapped his arm around her pulling her close. Her body was flush against his. He gulped air to calm his raging desire.

She was warm as well as eager blindingly eager. He understood she would be willing. This was what he dreamt of during the long nights aboard the ship, during all the nights they were separated.

Once inside, he put another log on the fire. "Do you want to go to bed now?" He lifted one eyebrow while he waited for her answer. "Or talk?"

"I'm not tired yet or sleepy? Don't want to go to bed. Do you?"

She eyed the chair as if she wished for nothing more than to spend the rest of the evening doing absolutely nothing. "Suppose I'd like to talk. There are things you need to tell me since this afternoon was spent in other delightful pursuits."

She sat down by the fire before she looked to him. She tucked her knees close to her as she sprawled lazily in the chair. "You've had a long few days. How do you feel? You've dark shadows beneath your eyes. You, too, must be exhausted."

It was true. Over the days on the trail, he pushed the horses as well as the men. Still, he reminded himself he wasn't in her condition. Never would be so he didn't understand. "I want to make love to my wife. However, I can wait until later."

He watched firelight play against her dark hair. There were a myriad of colors shimmering in the glow. He wished he could yank all the pins out then run his fingers through the length. Understood if he did so, his actions would lead to other things. They wouldn't talk. Ah, but they would end up in bed together.

He found the brandy then poured them both a drink.

"You still want...?" She sipped staring at him over the brim. "To make love?"

He wished he could see into her mind. He would know the answer then. Wouldn't have to question. "Don't you?" He laughed softly while he watched her seem to ponder the inquiry.

There were things he wanted to tell her he would do if she agreed to come to bed. Talk could always be put off until later. They could, after all, make love in front of the fireplace on the fur rug. That would be a different scenario than in front of the fire pit inside the teepee. They'd done that a number of times. The loving had been delightfully delicious, sensual in every conceivable way...magic. They'd made love in the stream a few times also.

"What I want is to look at you naked, hold you in my arms then I want to..." she moistened her lips with her tiny pink tongue seeming to anticipate her next words. "I would like to touch you, run my tongue along..."

He groaned before he spoke softly to her. The devil, he seduced himself with the play of her words along with his encouragement. "What else, Lyssa? What are you thinking but not saying? I'd like to understand what is inside that lovely mind of yours."

Her lashes lowered, fanned darkly against her white flesh. He saw her swallow. "I...I believe I should not have spoken my thoughts. While I want you to hold me then...we do need to talk. You won the first round with my father. Don't believe anyone else has ever done that."

He did and he wasn't intending to gloat. "Your thoughts aren't clear and precise. Nevertheless, I believe I can fill in the empty spots. You want to take my rod into your mouth. Perhaps you even want to suck my..."

"Stop! All that yes, yes, that and more." She squirmed in her chair as she adjusted her skirts. "Too many days have passed since we made love...not counting this afternoon."

"You understand I wouldn't tell you no. This afternoon you could have used your mouth to bring me to my climax. What else do you want to use your lovely mouth for? I can tell you how I want to play with you. How I want my fingers to dance on your slender white body. My lips to touch you intimately."

She sighed softly, her eyes dark pools of blue, her hair falling down her back to her waist as she removed the pins from her hair. She fluffed the length with her hands. The gesture wasn't meant to entice. He understood at this moment their sexual conversation would end. She would pursue something that was bothering her. As much as he wanted her right now, he would have to wait.

"Do you actually believe a father would feel differently about his son and marriage than his daughter," she blurted the words before looking away for a moment. "I'm sorry. Have to know how you feel."

He pinched the bridge of his nose wishing she would let this change of conversation go to the devil. "Can we curtail this topic to another time? It is a moot point until or if we have a daughter and she wishes to wed. We've years before we need to pursue this topic."

"No, I want to understand how you think."

Nervously, she brought the crystal glass with the brandy to her lips. She downed the contents before she stared pointedly at him.

He heaved in a powerful breath of air, one meant to give courage to speak of a distasteful topic. Well, hell, he tried to put the conversation off. She would just have to come to understand men and women weren't seen as equals in this world. "Personally, I don't agree with Jess. However..."

"There is always a however isn't there?"

Her sarcasm didn't go unnoticed.

"Not always; in this case, yes." How could he ever explain how a father would think about his daughter differently than his son? "A man expects certain things from his daughter and the man courting her than he would a son. At all cost a father must protect his daughter from pain as well as humiliation. After she is wed then it is her husband's job to care for her and protect. A son doesn't need protection."

"I gather he doesn't expect his son to remain a virgin so the bride will understand he hasn't slept with anyone else," she spoke blandly, her eyes shimmering with anger she had not yet unleashed on him.

He very nearly let the brandy in his mouth spew outward. He composed himself. "That is correct. Men are better lovers if they are not virgins on the wedding night. It is not practical to think of a man abstaining."

She played with the empty brandy glass. "It's all wrong. You know that for a fact." It appeared Lyssa meant to challenge him, his words as well as his ideals, ideals he held for a lifetime. "I believe if a woman wants to sleep with a man or men before she marries, she should. Wouldn't that make her a better lover too? Wouldn't she know just how and where to caress and stroke her husband to give him the most ecstasy?" She paused to gaze lovingly at his crotch. "Both males as well as females can play at that game. The more experience the better they are at giving pleasure. Don't you think?"

"No."

"Ah, well, I'm sure it would."

"A man wants to teach his wife about sexual pleasure. Doesn't wish for her to come to his bed an experienced whore."

His words seemed to cause her to bristle in indignation.

"Why would she be a whore and not the man also? If they've both had multiple partners in the bedroom? Perhaps a woman, if wealthy enough, should be able to keep a man on the side. Pay for all his needs. Couldn't call him a mistress. What would you suggest?"

Kane waved his hand in the air, frustration and annoyance eating at him. He felt sure Lyssa baited him. "It's time to stop this nonsense. You want to get a rise out of me. It's working."

He downed the contents of his brandy letting the liquid burn the path down his throat. He stood then held out his hand. She kept her hands in her lap. "Come to bed, wife. Don't want you to be too tired tomorrow to say the words your parents want to hear."

"You don't want to hear me say I do?"

"My dear, you are obnoxious. Is it because the little one you carry inside you is treating you with kicks and jabs? A veritable fighter he must be. It seems to me I've heard you say it twice in two different ways. For me personally, don't need to hear those two words a third time."

"I haven't felt her as of this moment. She has not kicked or jabbed. Nor has she any part in my mood. Our little girl will be strong as well as liberated. I will bring her up to be an independent thinker just as I am. She will not have to be coddled and protected by her father or her husband. Perhaps she will do the protecting."

"Will you tell me when you do feel the movement?"

He extended his hand to her again while he was doing his best to put her wayward thinking to the back of his mind. He did want his daughter if he had one to take care of herself. Well, hell, he also wanted to feel needed. It was a conundrum he had no answer for. Lyssa brought up too many valuable points he wanted time to think about.

She nodded as she let him lead her to the bedroom. The devil he didn't wish to spend this evening in a conversation that would lead nowhere. Curse her father for opening his mouth about the differences between sons and daughters. Curse him for not immediately agreeing with her. He thought he could give her a different insight.

She'd done him in.

Once inside the bedroom, he slowly undressed his wife, soon to be married a third time. He understood tomorrow would arrive sooner than expected. They both needed sleep. After they made love, he cradled her in his arms savoring everything about his wife, her hot temper, her calculated questions, especially the soft warm and very loving woman she was. It seemed she forgot the argument.

When he woke, sunshine filled the bedroom. Lyssa wasn't in his bed. He wondered where she'd gotten herself. He slipped into his dressing gown. As he padded into the main living area, he sipped in a slight breath of air. Jess along with Damian were there as well as another man he didn't know. Jamie leaned against the mantel of the fireplace, his arms crossed. Still Water Runs lounged in a nearby chair. Drew and Jeremy were also there.

Another damn fine specimen of an older man, perhaps this was Aric Lakeland, their neighbor. The wife was another cousin. He searched his head for her name. Came up with nothing. Supposed he would find out soon enough.

He stood then introduced himself. Kane was right on his assumption.

"Where is Lyssa?"

He smelled food as he looked to the kitchen. His stomach rumbled hungrily. Saw water steaming, for his bath he presumed. After all, this was another wedding day. He suddenly felt weighted down while he hoped this would be the last wedding. He found he was tired of proving himself to others even though it had only been last night he had to do so.

He wished to get on with his life.

"With the wives and the daughters," Damian said smugly. "Aric's son is not here to attend the wedding nor is Jamie's oldest. It is sad. We could wait a week or so for them to show up. They are off together and are sure to be back home by then. Won't they?"

Damian looked to Aric then Jamie appearing to be in a better mood than the night before. "Or...we could always have a fourth wedding."

"I'm certain of the fact. Not a bad idea to wait," Aric agreed, his grin wide as he seemed to examine him from head to toe.

"We are not waiting. If you want a fourth wedding when your son arrives, so be it. However, I'm not waiting for anything."

He cringed at his words. The devil, these people might take him up on the absurd notion of another ceremony. Bloody, bloody hell! His fists tightened. He felt a powerful need to punch something, anything. Damian's smug face would be a great place to start.

Kane tugged on his ear in an attempt to keep his mouth shut then sent his hands into the pockets of his dressing gown. Bloody hell, he thought today would be something simple just between Lyssa's parents and him. He suddenly realized the wedding would not be modest. Simplicity didn't seem to fit in this family's vocabulary.

"That's most likely for the best. Mrs. Brown, the good reverend's wife, would have to bake another cake for the next occasion. This one won't keep a week or two." Damian was shaking his head clearly amused. "It would be too much to ask of the fine woman. The congregation would have to be informed a second time, the after the wedding feast cooked anew. Probably other things I'm not recalling would have to be done again. No, waiting just won't do."

"The what?"

Kane was beside himself with questions. His gut churned. Why didn't Lyssa tell him? How could all this be put together in just one day? It was absurd. He realized suddenly Lyssa most likely didn't comprehend any more than he did. They had both been blindsided by her parents. The smug win of last evening paled in comparison to the plans that had been set in motion.

"The cake, the congregation, the feast..."

Damian was now grinning widely as he counted off on his fingers. He appeared as a man who finally found the upper hand with his son-in-law and meant to enjoy the victory. He was a cocky arrogant man at the moment.

"You are liking this aren't you?" Kane asked frustrated that no one gave him warning as to what was going to happen today.

"How many people were at your first wedding?" Damian taunted him.

He probably knew there were few witnesses. After a moment of thought coupled with the fact he had no intention of answering, the man continued, "Lyssa doesn't know about all the people either although she will be as surprised as you when Amorica tells her about the plans that were set in motion just yesterday."

Aric poured coffee for all then laced each one with brandy. "Suppose we will be needing this extra fortitude. We need to get you bathed and dressed. Don't want you late for the ceremony."

"Enough," Kane waved his hand in the air.

"This one will be better. The village is small. News travels fast. There is not a single man, woman or child who won't want to see Lyssa wed. Even the good Catholics will be there." Damian laughed seemingly pleased with himself. What Damian didn't realize was that he was also pleased because this would please Lyssa.

~ * ~

When her mother woke Lyssa that morning, a finger to her lips to make certain she didn't wake her husband, she wasn't certain what exactly to think. She blinked a few times trying to make the sleepiness disappear. With a few deep breaths of air inside her lungs, she felt better. She was tired though. All she wanted was to return to sleep. As she looked at her husband the sheet at his waist, she wanted to run her hands along the broad expanse of his chest.

"Hush, darling, your father will be over in about five minutes to help Kane prepare for the wedding. Your aunts and I will get you ready in the main house." Amorica stood back for a moment, "Now, I do comprehend part of what you see in this man. Doing what your eyes are saying you wish will have to wait until this evening." Amorica spoke to her again after she was dressed and they left the bedroom. It was more than embarrassing to find her mother looking at her when she was naked and in bed with her equally naked husband. "You will be surprised, hopefully in a good way. I promise you I tried. Nonetheless, I could not deter your father. When he has his mind set..."

It seemed her mother let the sentence fade into nothing. Lyssa wasn't concerned until then, "Deter my father? Has his mind set?" A sick feeling swept through her while she thought about last night's conversations. "What has he done now?"

"We will have to make do with his plans. As I said there were no words I could utter that would change his mind. All has been set in motion. There is no turning back. He so wanted a huge celebration. You will have some family as well as a few friends as witness to this very important change in your life."

She swallowed hard as she watched crease lines mar her mother's forehead. Lyssa wished she could understand her parents. They were such an enigma. "You don't approve?" Before Amorica could answer, she realized what exactly was mentioned. "A huge wedding?"

"Your father is a proud papa of a very beautiful daughter. We didn't have a large wedding. Well, we barley had a wedding at all." She closed her eyes as if remembering that day. "It was in a small parish church. I didn't want to marry him. He gave me no plausible choice. The only person to witness our marriage was the minister's wife. I believe he doesn't want that for his only daughter. If given a choice, he didn't want that for us either. I think he's always regretted the way he mishandled our fledgling relationship."

Huge, she mulled the single word over in her head. What was huge for one person might be small for another. In this case, she guessed her opinion was not wanted. Nevertheless, she needed to ask, "How big is huge?"

Amorica opened the back door to the house. "Pretty much the entire village as well as the outlying farms. There will be a wedding feast.

Mrs. Brown took over and organized everything. All the foods you like best will be set on the tables outside for after the ceremony. Mrs. Chalmers has made a wedding cake that will feed two hundred. Thank goodness the weather is nice. We might have had a hurricane brewing instead of this wonderful sunshine. It is hurricane season."

Her stomach curdled, spiraling topsy-turvy. Two hundred people at her third wedding while at her first wedding, she had less than a handful. No, she had two witnesses, Still Water Runs along with Abernathy. She supposed she should be happy. However, what she worried about was Kane's reaction when he discovered what her father planned. She wondered if he would refuse to marry her again. In this situation anything was possible.

Lyssa understood how a community such as this one could come together so quickly. They pitched in for everything. "Do they know I'm pregnant? She didn't want to feel any judgment. They didn't make love until after the first two weddings. In that regard, she wasn't a fallen woman. At this point in time, she wondered if anyone would understand. "How did he have time to make all the arrangements?"

"Well, while the two of you were playing on the island, Jess and Damian went to Mrs. Brown. Of course, the woman knows everyone. There seems to be a line of communication that spreads as if someone set fire to dry grassland. We both know how that can consume everything in its path in record time. Mrs. Brown seems to have that effect on the community. Seems everyone volunteered their services. You are a favorite child in this area."

"This just seems so unnatural."

Kane was bound to be furious. She didn't know how she felt having never truly thought about a big wedding. Her brother told her she wasn't a normal girl when she told him she didn't care about all the falderal.

If she admitted anything to herself, she had to say she was a bit disappointed the duke and duchess were not at her wedding outside London so many months ago. She was also disappointed Nickie, her cousin, hadn't been there.

Ah, where was Nickie?"

Her father must have found her by now. If they did, Nickie would be married to Colin McInnis. She didn't harbor a single doubt about that. At least she did things in the proper order. She didn't run off with Kane before they were wed.

Colin and Nickie...she wished she could attend their wedding.

"My sweet child, this is very natural. Your family and friends wish to celebrate your nuptials with you. You didn't have that in London. I can tell you both your father as well as myself were disappointed when we learned you wed without anyone who cared for you to witness the ceremony. It seemed to us you could have waited the two months it would have taken us to cross the Atlantic."

"Still Water Runs was there along with his butler, Abernathy..."

Yes, well he was a friend of her husband after the fact her friend. There was no one there for her. Everyone she knew in England was away searching for her cousin. She sipped in a breath of air. "Suppose we didn't want to put the bedding before the marriage as we believe Nickie did. I wanted him desperately, you know. He lusted for me. Don't think we could have put off making love for two months. We did the only thing we could to keep everything in the proper order."

"Yes, after the heated race of yesterday to the lake, it does seem he feels the same about you," her mother said a bland tone to her voice. "Suppose the two of you made an appropriate choice."

Lyssa felt heat rise to her cheeks. Her mother knew what she did. When she looked at her, there was a healthy pink glow to her mother's cheeks also. Lyssa couldn't help to wonder what put the rosy glow there.

She stepped into the parlor. Her breath caught in the back of her throat. She supposed seeing both Tira and Ravyn standing near the fireplace should not have come as too much of a shock. Beside Ravyn, her daughter, Chauncy, stood sporting a broad smile. Tira must have been only a half-day behind the men herding the horses. How would she have known about the wedding that wasn't planned yet? She must have also comprehended what her father would expect.

As if Tira read her mind, "I know your parents quite well, at least I know your mother, my sister. Took a gamble and despite Jamie's probable disapproval, I took some of his men and followed him here. He did seem pleased to see me last night. However, so I could travel quickly, I left our small children in town with their nanny."

Lyssa accepted the hug from Tira as well as Ravyn. She was thrilled to see both her aunts to have them witness her wedding. "I'm happy you are all here." She didn't lie. She truly felt happiness along with a weight seeming to be lifted off her shoulders. Later, much, much later she would thank her father.

"Then..." Amorica paused, tapping a finger to her chin, her smile broad. "We must get you ready. A bath waits in one of the guest rooms. Let us know when you're prepared to dress. We will descend upon you and help. I remember Ella's wedding. We were all there. The Duchess, Charlotte, lined us all up in order of age. Aidan was so angry with Blade, she almost refused to walk with him. They are married now."

When Lyssa entered the room, the water in the tub steamed. Quickly, she slipped from the clothing she donned a few moments ago then into the bath. Once she was bathed and dry, the aunts joined her to help her dress as well as do her hair.

The wine was poured. Her first sip was delicious. Small cakes baked the day before sat on a tray in the bedroom. Her aunts chatted and tasted the sweet red wine that most likely came from her uncle's vineyard in Bordeaux. The wedding gifts were given. Tears filled her eyes. She understood she would remember this day forever, as she would also recall the first two ceremonies, all with fondness. She blinked back tears. This was what dreams were made from. This was the wedding she always yearned for.

"Now, don't cry," her mother, murmured. "That is for the mother of the bride, not the happy bride."

"It's...well, I didn't know what I was missing. Thank you everyone. I'm so glad you are all here."

"You still believe Kane will be angry about the number of wedding guests?" Amorica asked while Ravyn fixed her hair.

When she looked in the mirror everything was lovely including the white gown meant for the wedding. It was simple, perfect for this occasion. Her hair was swept on top of her head, ringlets flowing softly to frame her face. There was a rosy glow on her cheeks. She recalled the first wedding dress, made lovingly by Kane's mother. They were both beautiful.

"No, not when he realizes how happy I am. He's a good kind man," she turned to her mother. "He will be pleased. I'm certain of it."

"I know he is. If he wasn't, my daughter would not have fallen in love with him."

"Sometimes I think I forced him into marriage. At first, he adamantly put me aside whenever it seemed we grew close. His scowl always deepened when he saw me. You know, mother, until we were wed, he was known as the stodgy earl. At one point, he spent hours and hours chopping wood. I would watch. I told him I wanted to wipe his scowl permanently from his face. When I think about what happened between us, I believe Aunt Ella thought this would happen when she brought me to him and asked if he would be my chaperone. In my case, she is very definitely a matchmaker."

"A man such as Kane doesn't do something he doesn't wish to do," Tira told her softly. "Though, I wouldn't put our sister past setting the two of you up. She is much like Aunt Charlotte. You're right. Ella does love to play matchmaker. There must have been something she saw in the two of you, some promise for the future. Why else would she have made him your chaperone then leave the two of you alone?"

"It does beg the question," Amorica said thoughtfully while she tapped her chin. "Next time we see her we will have to put her on the spot and ask. What she did could have gone horribly astray."

"No, I don't suppose he would. I love him."

Oh, how she wanted to hear those words from her husband. While she knew he wanted her body, lust was not love. Once she believed lust to be enough. Now, she understood passion wasn't sufficient If that was all he could give to her though, so be it. She could live with that as well as the notion love between them could grow."

When she saw him standing tall in front of the altar, her breath caught. She struggled for air. He appeared so handsome in his elegant clothing, so different from his breechclout from the day before. Shamelessly, she grinned at that recollection. Both types of clothing seemed perfect for him. He was so at ease with everything he did. She wondered why he brought the attire with him to this out-of-the-way place. Perhaps one of the uncles supplied the necessary finery. They were all close to the same size. He would wonder too how she obtained a wedding dress. She thought the gown might have been Tira's.

The ceremony passed in a blur. She heard the proud tones of her father when he said he would give her to Kane. Saw the shine of Amorica's eyes when she watched, her hands clasped tightly in front of her. Before she could blink, they were announced as husband and wife. Suddenly, Kane was kissing her his tongue playing across her lips demanding more than was acceptable at such an occasion. She didn't dare open for him. If she did, he would take wicked advantage. By the time he lifted his head with a smirking grin, she was breathing hard.

Gently, he touched a finger to her swollen lips. The breath from his softly whispered words caressed her ear. "Your lips are damp. Are you wet anywhere else? There will be more of this later. I promise you that."

Heat flooded her at his suggestive words. She didn't doubt his motives for a moment, hoped there would be more.

By the time all the friends and family greeted them giving them their best wishes, she was exhausted. Kane kept one hand on her elbow, seeming to sense the fatigue flowing through her. She needed to sit for a short time. The festivities were far from over. It would never do to create a wealth of gossip by leaving too soon. People would speculate. She wanted none of that. As it was the babe would arrive long before the allotted due date if people understood this to be their wedding day. They would not leave America until her child was born.

"Come, we've been asked to serve ourselves of this delightful fare. It seems Mrs. Brown has been a busy lady. Was told the bride and groom must eat first. Believe there is more food here than all our guest can possibly finish tonight." He wrapped his arm around her then settled his hand possessively on her waist. "Are you hungry, my countess?"

She jerked slightly surprised by his comment along with the voicing of the title. His hand tightened. He never called her his countess before. Indeed, she didn't know what an earl's wife should be called. "I'm your countess?"

She was also a lady by English standards. She never cared about a label or a title.

"Yes." He stole a quick kiss to her forehead before leading her to the table meant for the family. "Stay here," he told her while he pulled out a chair then helped her to sit. "I'll bring you a plate of food. Anything special you want?"

"I like everything."

True enough, when he returned, he held two plates piled high with food. Damian followed with two large glasses of ale for them. "You are a beautiful bride," her father said then kissed her cheek. "Eat, you look fatigued. You will have to rest so you can dance with your father. I do expect one dance."

With the food in her belly, she felt energized. The slight dizzy feeling the alcohol gave her made her giggle. Kane slanted her an all-knowing stare. For the next few hours, they danced and talked. More food was brought to the tables. She enjoyed the dance with her father. Kane danced with her mother.

In the distance, she noticed Still Water Runs speaking with Chauncy, her cousin. They seemed interested in each other. Chauncy set her hand on his chest. He took her hand in his before kissing her palm. A moment later they walked away to disappear behind the church.

So that was the way of it? Lyssa wondered if anything would come of this sudden infatuation with each other. Still Water Runs was a Sioux warrior while he wasn't labeled a half breed, there was white blood running in his veins. His eyes were green. Chauncy wasn't stupid. She would understand what she was getting herself into. Perhaps she didn't. If she fell in love, nothing else would matter.

When she was too tired to dance again, Kane held her in his arms so they could watch the others whirl and dip around the grassy dance floor. The evening breeze was cool. No one seemed to mind. It was true the entire village showed up for the wedding. Before the festivities ended there were fireworks. The sky lit up in a dazzling display of colors for almost fifteen minutes.

She looked up at her husband, "Did you see Still Water Runs with Chauncy Lakeland?"

"No," he chuckled softly. "What did you see?"

"They looked enamored of each other. After that first look, the two of them disappeared behind the church."

"Do you want me to search them out?" Again, he laughed. "I would not like to catch them at something inappropriate. I'm not at all certain what I would do."

She tapped him on the chest. "No, of course not. He will not compromise her."

Lost in thought, the newlyweds for the third time swayed to the beat of the music. His hands rested on the curve of her hips. He squeezed gently. She understood what he wanted. Slowly, he bent to kiss the nape of her neck. Ribbons of pleasure rushed through her in sensual swirls leaving her breathless.

"You will not seduce me here where everyone can see." Her words sounded weak to her. He knew he could seduce her just thinking about where his hands were creeping ever higher. The pressure beneath her breasts generated a purr she tried to keep behind her lips.

"Have you kissed any of these young pups?" he asked his voice quiet yet she sensed a threatening tone beneath the softness. "If you have, I would have to stake them out and let the fire ants eat them. If you have offered your bountiful lips for them to taste," he paused thoughtfully, "or allow the sun to bake them until they were burned to a crisp."

Using her elbow, she jabbed him in the ribs. "That's disgusting. You know the answer. I'm not going to give any more credit to your question by answering a second time."

"Just checking if your answers are consistent."

He kissed her ear, nipping it slightly.

"No, no one here as ever even tried to kiss me as you've been told. As a child I was quite the ugly duckling."

She felt a bit indignant she had to say the words again. They were true.

"Don't believe you." He stopped to look more pointedly at her. "About the ugly duckling part. However, the deterrent was most likely generated by the dark looks I'm certain your father directed their way."

She felt his breath float against sensitive skin. His teeth scraped gently down her neck. She tried to keep the shiver from reaching deep inside. Tried to quell the racing of her heart along with the short stabs of air she tried to inhale.

"I believe it's time for us to cut that monstrous cake then make our getaway." His hand cupped her breast. He rubbed his thumb across a rapidly hardening tip.

She heard the masculine groan rumble from his chest. "Believe you are right. Don't want you to lose control here with everyone watching us."

He laughed, one hand at the small of her back he guided her to the table with the cake. The sampling of the cake went off without a hitch. She savored the icing on his lips when he kissed her in front of the crowd of cheering people. After he finished, he swept her into his arms. While he didn't run, his long strides covered the ground quickly. It seemed he was impatient to get her to the wedding bed.

This was their second wedding night. She wondered if the evening would indeed be as sweet as the first. Her virginity wasn't an issue tonight. This evening there would be no pain. Once inside the bedroom, he set her down so her feet touched the floor. To no avail, his hands worked on the fasteners of her gown. He ran his hands down her sides until they rested on her hips. His chin settled on top of her head. Felt his heavy breathing behind her.

She understood his frustration along with the annoyance he must feel. She was aggravated too. "Don't rip anything. Believe this is Tira's. We need to return the gown in perfect condition. After all the gown survived the first wedding night. It must survive this one as well." She tilted her chin upward her eyes bright with the love she felt for this perfect man. "I never wanted to be royalty. I'm an American. We fought a war, two wars to show the English that democracy works. You understand I never cared about a title."

"Don't want to speak of things such as that. I never wanted the title either. Roaming the plains was my happiness. Now you are. You are enchanting, magic to my soul. I will be happy wherever you are."

He kissed her long and hard. The caress was urgent, demanding she meet him with her passion the raw hunger that composed him. He turned her. Slowly unfastened each button. He nipped and laved where he uncovered flesh. By the time he finished and parted her legs, tremors deep inside her grew. When he entered her, she cried out his name.

What seemed like hours later they sipped wine and ate the food that was on the tray waiting for them. It appeared they were both sated for the time being. He ran a finger along her arm while they sat against the backboard of the bed, pillows behind them shoulder to shoulder.

"You know, Lyssa," he began softly, "I dream about you all the time. Before we wed, I used to dream that you were naked in my arms. Imagined I was making love to you. I even dreamed of making love to you as we did yesterday afternoon while you straddled me."

"I had dreams too," she confessed her voice weak, soft with the memories. "They were only about your kisses though. I didn't know what else there was. I didn't understand the height you would bring me to."

"You didn't know anything else. What do you dream of now that I've taught you so well?" His question was too impertinent.

She didn't want to answer. Heat overwhelmed her. Gently, he squeezed her shoulder. She spoke softly, "Now I don't get a chance to dream. You keep me up all night."

He let his head fall back as he roared with laughter, "What about all those months we weren't together?" His roving hand stopped where her pulse thundered at the base of her neck. "What did you dream about then?"

"My dreams were of you. Of your beautiful man's body deep inside me bringing me pleasure. I missed you so much, Kane. Some of my dreams were of you smiling. Now you smile more. I accomplished that feat. You are no longer the stuffy earl." She giggled.

"Stodgy. I didn't smile when I spent so much time chasing after you." His thumb teased the tip of one of her breasts. "I was afraid to say the words, terrified of the vulnerability the words would bring, Lyssa. It's time though."

Her heart leapt to her throat. "What words? Time for what?" She hoped and prayed they were what she wanted to hear.

He ran his knuckles across her jaw then lower. His eyes shimmered a deep, dark blue. "I love you, Lyssa. Didn't know a man could love a woman so deeply and so possessively. I do love you that way, that much. You are mine."

He waited as he turned her so she gazed into his eyes.

She understood he needed the words returned. With a fingertip she touched his lips. "I've loved you since the first day I saw you sitting behind your desk in your study scowling at me. The day the duchess told you that you would be my guardian until they returned. I love you too, Kane."

"As a woman should love her husband?" His mouth framed hers while he deepened the kiss his tongue playing sensually with hers.

The wedding night seemed to take on a different life after they confessed their love. Lyssa didn't believe she'd ever felt so cherished. Kane was both tender as well as demanding. Love as well as lust poured from him into her then back.

This second wedding night was better than the first in too many ways to count.

Epilogue

1838

Sizzling hot was the only way Lyssa could describe this August day at the Blackmore country home outside London. More than a year had passed since she left Glasgow fleeing for her life. Kane insisted they remain on Damian's ranch until their baby boy was at least three months old. While she was happy and content at her parent's home, she wanted to begin her life with Kane here in England.

Before they left for London, he was christened Colton Jacy Murphy, the sixth Earl of Blackmore. Kane was thrilled she agreed to a Sioux name. Jacy means moon, he told her. The little boy possessed the same striking features as his father. His hair was dark black, his eyes the same clear gray rimmed in changing shades of blue. Lyssa understood many babies' eyes changed color. She didn't believe Colton's would do so. At the moment, he lay on a blanket in the shade of a great oak tree. His little arms and legs waved wildly. She felt sure he watched the light playing and shimmering on the leaves above him. He would feel the sweet breeze flow across his face. He would need to eat soon. Kane loved to watch her feed his son.

Nickie McInnis, her cousin, sat next to her watching the baby girl she gave birth to a month before Colton was born. Byrony Cora McInnis possessed very little hair, as she was to be as blond as her mother. Her eyes were green though, as green as the Scottish Highlands as green as her father's. Byrony would be brought up to be an independent thinker, a woman with values and ideas. Lyssa was sure she would lead her parents a merry chase.

"Your little girl will grow up very Scottish in her way of thinking. I suppose," Lyssa said while Colton grabbed on to her finger, holding it tight. She loved his grip, so strong. His gaze seemed to light on hers when she played with him. He smiled. She placed the boy on his tummy with a scattering of toys around him. He grew stronger daily. His head barely bobbed anymore when he was on his tummy. He arched pushing himself away from the blanket, his head held high so he could see what was going on around him.

"As your son will undoubtedly be English," Nickie said as she handed her little girl a toy ring. She clung to the object waving it wildly all the while cooing softly. "I wonder, will he scowl at everyone?"

The children were both adorable.

"Colton will be as much a Sioux warrior as his father can manage here in England. He will cling to the People's traditions as much as possible. I'm sure he will ride and shoot as if he grew up on the northern plains. He will ride as one with his horse. Perhaps in time we can visit the territory where Kane grew up. Now, it is far too dangerous."

"If Collin had his way, pour little Bryony will learn to toss a caber. He treats her as if she is a son. She is only six months old. In not too many more months, he will be tossing her in the air." Nickie cringed at the words she spoke. "She seems to love it when he holds her high above his head. If she could giggle, I know she would. All she does now is allow the drool to run from her mouth on to Collin's face while her besotted grin makes him even more intent. It's always fun to see him grimace when that happens. Needless to say, he doesn't learn that his actions are not smart if he wishes to stay dry. He doesn't seem to care. In his eyes, she can't do anything wrong."

"Too many times I need to close my eyes when Kane has his son. He does like to play rough with the boy. He takes him on Ashes when he rides, puts him in front of him, bracing his head against his chest. Says he'll probably ride before he can walk. The way he's going at the task, I won't be surprised."

Heat rose to Lyssa's cheeks when she remembered her husband's outrageous behavior the day before her third wedding. They'd make love with her straddling him while he rode his stallion. They'd done the same several times since they returned. She just knew sometime someone would see them. When she brought the possibility up, he would simply tell her she had nothing to fear. With her long skirts around her ankles no one would be the wiser.

Hah!

Kane and Collin appeared striding toward them, their long strides taking them quickly across the grass. Their horses were tied near the stream, which provided a cooling breeze. The two men chatted as they walked. Before they met their wives, they'd been close friends. Nickie and Collin stayed at Kane's hunting lodge in northern Scotland when they ran away together. It seemed to her that Nickie and Collin had their honeymoon before the wedding. The two told Nickie's parents they handfasted. That news did not go over well.

Both women ran to greet their husbands. Kane twirled her around before setting her feet on the ground for a quick kiss. Collin did the same with Nickie. Lyssa knew she would love him forever and ever. He meant the world to her. He possessed her heart as well as her soul.

"I see the two of you didn't wait for us to open the wine," Kane said, his arm draped over her shoulder as they strode toward the babies.

He bent to kiss a tender spot on her neck, grazed that same place with his teeth sending shivers of pleasure through her.

"No, the two of you said you would be here fifteen minutes ago. You are late. So, of course we didn't wait. What was so important that kept you from being here sooner?" Lyssa was grinning thinking about Colton's naptime. Ah, they had company. Today, there would be no afternoon private time in his lodge. He would not seduce her on his furs.

When he reached Colton, he picked the boy up, held him high over his head while he laughed. The little one grinned charmingly while drool slipped from his soft lips to land on his father's moccasin. It was always the same.

Collin did the same with the little girl, asking "Do you think it is too hot out here for the babies?"

"They are in the shade. Fresh air is good for them. In an hour they both will be ready for a nap," Lyssa said while she watched Kane hold Colton close. He was cuddled tenderly in the crook of his big arm. The child looked so tiny nestled against his father's chest. For his age the little tyke was a big boy. Undoubtedly, he would take after his father in size.

"Ella and Drake are behind us. They are bringing your cousin, Chauncy."

Ah, she recalled the day of her wedding when Chauncy and Still Water Runs disappeared behind the church. Later she learned that was Chauncy's first kiss. Still Water Runs was a Sioux warrior. While she didn't believe the Lakelands would care, there would obviously be problems if they wed. If they loved each other, Lyssa felt certain they would survive any issues that might arrive. Nonetheless, Chauncy followed Still Water Runs into Lakota territory. They left for London before the two returned. She wondered what their story was.

"I haven't seen her in so long," Nickie mused.

Collin sat down beside her with Byrony cradled in his lap. "I hope she's a better chaperone with Chauncy than she was with us." He winked at his wife.

"With us as well," Kane said laughing when he caught his wife's expression.

"You can say that?" Nickie punched Collin on the arm. "You would have left for Scotland without me. What would have happened then?"

He arched one eyebrow upward, "Would I?"

"You said you were going whether I decided to come or not," she told him indignantly.

He lifted his rugged shoulders a quirky half smile on his lips. "Doubt if I would have done so. I wanted you so badly. The first time I saw you in my third-floor bedroom, I knew I had to have you. The fact that you fell in line with my plans so easily told me you felt the same."

"Arrogant!" Nickie punched him in the arm.

"Aunt Ella made Kane my chaperone. It seemed she gave the fox permission to guard the hen house."

All in all, there was laughter as well as love in this gathering. Lyssa along with Nickie were both so in love with their husbands how the marriages came about no longer mattered. They would go on to be friends while their children grew up together.

Kane bent close to Lyssa, "Dream about me, Lyssa. You will always dream of me. I will always dream of you. I will dream of Lyssa."

Coming Soon
by the Author
at
Rogue Phoenix Press

Deke's MagicKiss

Boston Female Medical College
1846

Lights blazed in the large ballroom where the first recipients of a diploma from Boston Female Medical College danced and celebrated with loved ones. The waltz the band played was slow, making those who weren't dancing sway in time. They played a series of tunes. The golden glow of the gas lights touched on the vibrant face of Annie Lundin as she danced in the arms of a man she seemed to know. She smiled flirtatiously as the young man whirled her around the room. He held her too close. She pushed away, a flush to her once pale cheeks bloomed as if a flower was opening to the sun. She looked nice painted in the rose color. Deke wondered what the man said to her to cause the rise of embarrassment.

By the look on her face, she chastised the man, her lips set in a grim line. Her dance partner didn't seem to care. He tugged her closer his hand on the small of her back. This time she was able to dislodge herself from him. Her lips set tight, she strode from him, her back rigid. The man did not mean her well. Thinking he should intervene, Deke pushed himself from the wall where he'd been leaning, a soft curse on his breath. He thought better of his plan when another young man joined her. She laughed at something he said then turned from him moving away. What could be described as vicious, the man grabbed her arm, turning her to face him again. Her rescue came from an older man, possibly one of her professors. The tune began. The music livelier. The couple ended up at the punch bowl. As if hot or winded from the exertion, she waved her hand in front of her face, her smile infectious.

Deke Sullivan relaxed against the wall again. His arms crossed in front of him one knee bent, his foot braced on the wall. For the time being she was safe. For how much longer he couldn't be certain. He watched. He thought of his mission, something he refused several times, refused adamantly. Jamie Lundin, her father, paid him to escort Annie Lundin to Pine Flats, Colorado. She was going to be the new doc in town. What she might not understand was the fact that there wasn't a single man in the area surrounding Pine Flats that would come to her. She would have a few female patients if their men folk would allow them to see a female. She didn't belong in the west. She was silk and lace, a smile to grace ballrooms not barn dances. Her features so very delicate and fragile surely, she would suffocate or die in Colorado. Her soft hands would end up with callouses. That life couldn't possibly suit her.

Annie Lundin did not belong to the fierce west. She belonged in Boston or Baltimore, any Eastern city.

Geez, he thought of a woman such as this one examining him. He choked back his thoughts, his body hardening in response to the notion. With a quick readjustment to his dress pants, he tamped down the thought of her doctoring him. God, she was a fire brand. Her long blond hair expertly coiffed on top of her head showed the length of her white neck. The tendrils she artfully arranged to curl beguilingly around her face would tempt a saint. He wanted to get close enough to her to see the color of her eyes. Would they be blue, a crystal-clear shimmering blue?

Annie Lundin was dangerous to a man such as he. She could provoke and enchant create fire within that couldn't be extinguished with one taste. Her small slippered feet seemed to float magically along the floor to the tunes despite her inept partners. Hell, he had two left feet when it came to dancing. Nevertheless, he was tempted to ask for a dance. He wanted her in his arms. His hard gaze focused on her.

The night would end. He would have to follow her through the streets of Boston to her apartment. Protect her from the threat her father described in his letter. Jamie Lundin couldn't stay for the celebrations. He'd attended yesterday's graduation ceremony where she spoke. Business called him home. He and his wife Tira worried about her.

Objected furiously, when she told them she was going to Pine Flats. She was so spontaneous, impulsive too. Apparently, she didn't take the threats against her seriously. Either that or her father was a worrier. Deke knew Jamie Lundin well. He wasn't a man to exaggerate or drum up problems that didn't exist. The threats had to be real.

Pulling out his pocket watch, Deke stared at the hour. He was bone weary. He'd hoped Annie would grow tired of the dancing hours ago. Their train west would leave early tomorrow morning, dawn. The time to rise would come all too soon. He rubbed his chin, thinking about the miles that lay ahead of them. While he understood she would have a special car to sleep and live in for the short distance they could take the train, he would have to take special care not to soil her reputation. Jamie told him his car was in front of hers. There was a living area and two bedrooms. Her father trusted him with his little girl who wasn't quite so little any longer.

He was snapped out of his thoughts by the sight of Annie, striding to the cloak room. It was about time she put a period on this celebration. He waited a moment before following discreetly. Seemingly unwilling to admit she was female all the way down to her toes, she was headed out into the darkness alone. The streets near the campus were not well lit. Three well-dressed men trailed behind her. One might call them dapper. They were drunk, swaggering yet strangely quiet. At one time each had been a dance partner.

Beneath his breath Deke cursed into the bleakness of the night. She couldn't have made this easy for him.

This was what her father cautioned him about, the threatening men she'd been warned against. The same ones she dismissed as harmless. Didn't she understand a harmless man didn't exist? He slipped the badge he wore into the pocket of his jacket. If it came to a fight, he didn't want these men to know he was a sheriff. His jurisdiction didn't carry sway in Boston. He would do what was necessary to protect the woman who seemed to be able to flirt and carry on leaving her male victims panting with their tongues hanging out and in need of what she so eloquently offered. If she said no, the word should be heeded even if she seduced and charmed, even if she was a little flirt.

Tonight, she made several conquests. Apparently, these men

meant to taste what she suggested with her winsome smile coupled with the sensual shimmer in her vibrant blue eyes. Jamie didn't understand what his daughter with her innate allure was capable of provoking in the weak male species. She shouldn't be out alone in the night, in the dark without protection. He assumed he was her protection tonight as well as a host of nights to come. Street lights cast a subtle glow, elongating shadows. Anyone who wished to steal away in the gloomy night could do so without detection.

The men following her didn't seem to be hiding. She must know they followed. Her pace increased even while he mused once more about the inherent dangers for a female alone in the blackness. A prudent woman would have hailed a carriage. According to her doting father, Annie defied logic. She was an independent woman. He supposed any female who wished to be a doctor in an out-of-way small town in Colorado would have to defy more than rational thought. She would have to possess a good sense of autonomy. The west was dangerous territory. Women were few. Men obsessed over beautiful women. They either wanted them as a wife or a mistress. In either case men wanted a woman in his bed to ease his needs.

When she turned off the well-lit street, he knew the men would act. He picked up his pace, his heart pounding with energy, fighting energy. His strides lengthened. His body toned and hardened in anticipation of the looming fight. The shrill scream didn't surprise him. The silence afterward did.

What he saw ripped through him, blinding rage followed. She was pushed against the cold brick of the building. One man's hand covered her mouth his other ripped the cloth of her bodice and chemise. Even in the darkness he saw the white of her flesh, the pink tips that could push any man to lust. Her flailing body was caught by the faint light from the lantern on the far corner. She pounded on the man's back, screaming.

"No!"

"Ay-ee…ay-ee, ay…ay…yii…" The war cry honed from his time living with the Cheyenne never failed to send chills of fear into the opponent. He wasn't Cheyenne. Nevertheless, he lived with them, he learned their ways. The woman he called mother was fullblood Cheyenne. He was full blood Irish.

The first man he encountered, he leapt high, kicking him in the chin, toppling him backward. The second he tackled sending him to the ground with the force of the blow. The third man ran. The fourth, his hand thrust forward to ward him off never saw the blow that sent his head backward, blood flowing from his nose.

Deke straddled the man. His fist tucked into the cloth of his shirt. He lifted him inches off the ground. "You sorry son of a bitch." With force, he sent the man back to the ground. His head cracked when it hit solid stone. "She said no!"

He stood, dusting his hands. She'd left. All he could see now was her back, her skirt lifted as she ran. "Well, hell." He supposed given the same situation if he was female, he would have done the same. In a few seconds, he caught up with her. He walked beside her adjusting the length of his strides to hers. His hand rested on her elbow, which she tried to jerk away.

"What do you want?" She didn't look at him nor did she break stride, her rough breathing all that gave indication of the stress. One hand held her skirt high so as not to trip, the other gripped her torn bodice tight.

"Not what you think." He couldn't help grinning. Flushed to such a high color, she was adorable.

"Go away." Dropping her tight fist from her skirt to pick up her reticule, fumbling with one hand, she pulled out a key. With the door unlocked she tried to slip through the opening without him.

"'Fraid I can't let you do that." His hand stopped the door from shutting in his face. His foot straddled the door jam.

"Or wont?" Striding up the steps, she ignored him. Her back rigid as a boulder, she reached the door to her apartment. Once again, he couldn't allow her to enter without him. Sometime he would have to explain his purpose. She would object. Jamie warned him convincing her she needed him wouldn't be easy. He would have to stick to her, not let her use her cunning to get away from him. He did have his honor. Duty first. She was his duty, a repayment of debt he owed Jamie.

She inhaled a deep breath, turning on him. Her slim fingers still clutching the fabric. "What do you want?"

He massaged his chin for a moment, a slow grin forming on his lips, "A glass of whisky would be nice." He grinned at the slow mercuric spread of fire he watched growing along her neck to reach her cheeks. Her eyes shimmered spitting liquid heat. Obviously, she didn't know how to handle this situation. He pushed his hat upward, lifting an eyebrow, studying her. "Too much to ask?"

"Go to hell!"

Ignored now, she set about arranging papers that cluttered her desk still attempting to keep her grip on her bodice tight. Every now and then he caught a glimpse of rounded white flesh. A valise and a trunk were packed sitting next to the door. She was ready for the morning train. Even while she tried to put up a brave front, her shoulders shook. Beneath sooty, long lashes she eyed him, sized him up from the tips of his riding boots to the top of his hat.

"You should have hailed a cab." He told her his voice taking on a soft edge. "If I hadn't been there… A safe ride home would have been prudent. He looked at his bruised knuckles. "If you'd done so, I could have avoided the skirmish. Don't like to fight though I'm damn good at it." He'd been wishing for more than a skirmish since he first set eyes upon her a week ago. Until now, she didn't know he existed.

"I didn't ask for help." The prickly little female was bristling with outrage. She waltzed into the bedroom. A few seconds later she emerged with a shawl draped around her shoulders and tied in the front. He'd wondered when she would take care of that small inconvenience that kept her one handed.

"You needed it or…they weren't forcing you?"

Shaking her head, pointing a long slender finger at him. "Who are you?" She now stood in the farthest away corner of the small living room.

"You should have asked that a long time ago, Annie Lundin."

Her gasp of surprise didn't mean anything. He knew her father never told her about the protection he hired to take her to Pine Flats. Understood she was far out of her realm of expertise when it came to living in a small western town filled with miners and gamblers dotted with a couple of whores. The men were rough, the women easy. She didn't fit the bill. He understood protecting this woman would be a formidable task. She was a brilliant, beautiful menace.

"I'm asking now."

Deke found the whiskey bottle he knew she purchased for Jamie.

The bottle wasn't packed. He poured two fingers before downing half. "Sherriff Deke Sullivan." He finished the whiskey keeping his gaze on her.

"You could have said so in the beginning. Will you leave now?"

"Nope to the leaving. Those men could return. Do they know where you live?"

"I'm not your concern. I've got a train to catch in the morning."

He stepped toward her, "So?"

"I've got to sleep."

"As, do I." He placed his hat on the table by the door, took inventory of the apartment. The bed was too small for both of them. He chuckled thoughtfully. She didn't seem in the mood to share the mattress though he would never form the words to object if she changed her mind. "Suppose the sofa will have to do."

"Never!" Her hands fisted on her hips. She stood her ground.

"Sweetheart, I'm staying here to make certain you and I reach the train in one piece in the morning. I don't intend to sleep on the floor outside your door."

With her mouth clenched tight, she raced to him, pushed on his chest. Taken by surprise, he fell backward, bringing her with him. They landed together on the rug with a solid *oof*. He grunted with the impact. When she tried to push from him, her eyes blazed female fury.

"Let me go!" With those tight little fists, she pounded on him; his chest, his shoulders. Her hair fell around her shoulders, the soft strands sliding against his face and along his hands.

He grabbed the pummeling hands then rolled. He lay atop her, her hands held above her head. "You should stop when you're in over your head." The shawl fell away. Her partially covered breasts pushed against his chest. The small puffs of air she inhaled to fill her lungs had to hurt. "Will you promise to keep your hands to yourself?" This was not something he anticipated. What he hadn't anticipated was the fabric of her torn bodice opening, her breasts delightfully pushing against his chest.

Annie clenched her teeth then nodded. So many more silken strands of her coif came undone to taunt him further, sliding with silken heat across him, catching in the stubble on his face.

"You're hurting me."

"Sweetheart, you hurt me."

"*Oaf!*" Her breasts pushed against his chest.

"As soon as you promise, we can begin again. I'll tell you everything you need to know about me as well as my purpose here. I will also tell you why." The press of her body next to his sent an inferno seething inside flying straight to his groin, his response so swift and hard the sensation caught him by surprise. He should remove himself from her person.

She nodded, her dark lashes briefly closing over her eyes fanning across her cheekbones.

"I need the words. Who the heck could guess what you are nodding at? Say the words, my darling."

"I promise," she spit the words out too quickly.

His lips quirked in a half-smile. He didn't trust the promise. Hell, he wasn't born yesterday. He wasn't a half-wit who would fall for her female charms. Who did she think he was? An untried boy? He stood, holding out a hand to help her to her feet.

She ignored the offer. "What are you doing here?"

"Protecting you," he said his voice bland.

Annie stomped to the whiskey. Poured herself a stiff drink. After she downed a goodly portion, she closed her eyes, grimacing, straining as the heat slipped down her throat. Her shoulders unyielding, she pointed an accusing finger in his direction, "I don't need protecting. Go find another woman to guard."

His laughter barked from his throat. "Someone important to you believes you do. At least he believes enough to have hired me. You'll get used to me. I'm easy to get along with."

"Liar!"

He tugged her into his arms intending to make his position to her crystal clear, clear as the devil inside him. Her hands on his chest, she stared at him with the bluest damn eyes he'd ever seen. Unable to stop himself, he slowly lowered his mouth to meet hers. Softly, he brushed his lips across hers, teasing, touching, caressing the fulness he encountered. Heat, enchantment, liquid fire erupted. He expected a slap to his face. Instead, her fingers rose to his shoulders then his neck her nails biting. He pushed her lips apart as he explored inside the dark sultry heat of her mouth. His hands cupped her buttocks, pulling her closer, so close she was certain to feel the heat of his heavy arousal.

Realizing he was about to take this farther than he should, he let his tongue slip from the warmth of her mouth. When he was inches away, could smell the scent of aroused woman, he grinned then winked. "I make my point."

This time the slap startled him. Dazed by the sensations she elicited, his mind was in a fog. He touched his hand to his throbbing cheek.

"Bastard!"

"You didn't say no."

He ignored his blinding need to show her how foolish her action was. He was angry with his stupidity. "We will leave at dawn. Best you get sleep." Through clenched teeth he grated out his comments.

Annie finished her drink her body quivering with pent up emotions. He sat down to take his boots off then followed with his shirt leaving his clothing on the floor. His pants unfastened he rose, watching, studying her. She liked the kiss.

"What are you doing?" She stood in front of him so close he could reach out, pull her once more into his arms. If he did so, they would end up in the bed together. "Get out!"

"Going to sleep as per your suggestion." He winked at her knowing that would infuriate her further.

"Not in my home you're not." She picked up his clothing and boots tossing them toward him. One boot hit him square in his chest.

He grunted. "I am staying in your home. Over the next several weeks, we are going to be close, very close. Now, my suggestion is that you retreat to the bedroom. If you don't, I'll trade sleeping arrangements with you or we could share."

Head in her hands, she sat on an old ragged chair near the fireplace. He thought he saw her shoulders shaking. Finally, she looked at him. Her eyes shimmered with the tears she refused to shed earlier. Despite her efforts, when she looked at him again, she questioned. "Who hired you?"

Damn, he hated women's tears. Time for teasing her ended minutes ago. He should have never caried this so far. In his defense, she was so damn adorable when she was angry, he had a devil of a time thinking straight. "Your father."

When she flew at him again, he was ready for her. "How dare he!"

The answer to him was obvious. She was a menace to all males everywhere with those soft white breasts, the beguiling curves of her wasp thin waist and that delectable little butt not to mention her beguiling blue eyes he was drowning in every time he looked at her. He wanted to taste and squeeze every deliciously delectable part of her. "You're in need of protection from every male here to Colorado," he said unemotionally.

Her hands held once more in his, "You promised you'd keep these," he placed tender kisses on her knuckles, "to yourself."

"Oh!"

"You did." He drew in a long deep breath needing the raw restraint the air might give him. He needed to hold his temper in check. "Sweetheart, don't like this job. You're trouble from the start. Whenever possible, I stay away from trouble. Told your father no, until I couldn't."

"Are you trying to tell me it's my fault those men attacked me?" From the get go she sounded indignant. She had every right to be. She looked as mad as a hornet gettin' ready to sting.

"Well, honey, you flirt outrageously. Every male at the celebration panted after you. They looked at your breasts popin' out of that dress of yours..." He lifted his shoulders in a careless shrug." What did you expect?" He did regret the words. The attack was not her fault. He should tell her that. For some reason he didn't understand, he couldn't keep the taunting words behind his lips.

Her fists were on her hips again her eyes flashing with heated color, ice blue fire. She pulled in a breath of air, her breasts rising as if to put a period on the point he was making. "How dare you blame something so ludicrous on a woman when a man thinks with his cock and not his head." She stared pointedly at his groin which was rising to the occasion as she spoke.

He regarded her tiny weapons with care as well as her words. She was spittin' mad. Her audacity intrigued him. For her size she was a whirlwind of hot air. Her attacks always came out of the blue. About this she was right on all counts. He grinned at her. "Think with my cock, do I? Why, sweetheart, where did you hear such things? Thought you were a lady."

"From every male on this earth," she retorted while her eyes blazed ferociously.

She looked as if she meant to fly at him again, fists blazing.

"Don't even think to hit me. I won't tolerate more than one time. You've already passed once. That slap packed a wallop."

"You're not worth the effort," she gritted the words out through clenched teeth as she stomped to the bedroom again. She came out with a derringer pointed at his chest. "For the last time, get out!"

"Do you have an extra pillow or blanket for me?" After he sat down, he kicked his feet onto the sofa. "Wasn't looking forward to the hard pallet on the wood floor. This here sofa's mighty comfortable for a sofa."

Her hand shook, the gun still pointed his direction. "You aren't listening. I told you I want you out of my home."

He let out the air he'd been holding since he saw the gun. She wasn't going to use the weapon. He'd stake his life on the fact. "Use the damn thing or put it away. We both need sleep. Dawn will be here early. I for one am tired of arguing. Would rather bed you than exchange more words."

"Bastard! Devil! I should…"

"Shooting me won't solve your problems. You still have to get to Pine Flats in one piece. Without my expertise you won't make it more 'un five miles out of Denver." The girl was going to be the death of him, not death by derringer, death by headache or…death by arousal. This journey would take forever if he had to listen to her rant and rave all day as well as all night. Kissing her mouth closed was one solution that he'd take more interest in than her war with words.

"Don't come in my bedroom." She didn't walk to the bedroom but to the whiskey. Not reaching for a glass, she tipped the bottle to her lips. She drank long. Coughed. Wiped her mouth with the back of her hand her eyes firing hotter and bluer.

He lifted his shoulders, staring at her eyes. "Bedding a viper is never pleasant. Might be able to tame the viper to my way of thinkin'."

"You've bedded a viper?" she asked sweetly her eyes brimming with laughter now.

The about face surprised him. Caught him off guard. Her smile jammed him in the gut before his stomach twisted. "No." He wanted too though. During their conversation and struggles, her torn bodice gaped farther open. When he kissed her, it was all he could do not to test the softness of her those beautiful white globes of hers.

"How old are you?" The question popped out. Even he understood never to ask a woman her age.

Annie Lundin stared at him as if he lost his mind. She swiped her hands along her dress pulling the fabric lower. As if she suddenly understood what he stared at, she pulled the fabric to cover her, found the shawl that dropped to the floor earlier. He'd seen more than she intended. She was perfection. A man, this man could get lost in those curves of hers, die and go to heaven in her perfection if invited.

"You're going to stay here?" She pointed a shaking finger at the sofa. "Don't you have a place of your own?"

"Damn straight. Right on that sofa unless a certain viper gives an invitation I can't refuse."

"Why?"

"Believe we've hashed over that...the numerous reasons."

She disappeared again. He caught the pillow and blanket in the face. He grinned.

~ * ~

Sheets and blankets were wrapped around her sprawled legs. Sunlight poured through lace curtains leaving patterns on the floor. Her eyes burned from lack of sleep. Her head pounded in aggravation at the infuriating man in her living room. She drank too much whiskey.

A viper, am I?

I will show him viper!

Throughout the night she pounded her pillow, pushed off covers before reaching for them again when the cool morning air chilled her arms. She urged straggling damp hair from her sweaty face. The glass of water she always kept by her bed was empty. The audacity of that man. Her protector? Never. How dare her father hire a man to guard her. She was an adult. She didn't need any man to shadow her.

He did come in handy last night.

"Good you're up. I wasn't relishing having to shake you awake."

His darkly raspy voice caught her attention sending a sensual thrill down her spine. She turned to look at him. All she saw was his back. He left as quickly as he showed himself.

All through the night she hoped he was a figment of her imagination. "Go away." Her words lacked conviction. It seemed he wouldn't go anywhere until he was good and ready until they reached Pine Flats. While she understood he didn't want her in his town, he meant to fulfill the contract he signed with her father. Quickly, she scrambled from the bed, hoping to put some clothes on before he barged into the room again. She slept wearing an old thin chemise that was very close to wearing nothing at all.

Dressed, feeling the protection of fabric against her body, she brushed her hair into a severe bun. She was going to disavow him from the notion she was a flirt. She wasn't. Having a good time, laughing, talking to men, was not flirting. He was from the west, a backwoodsman. What did he know about balls? He shot at men to keep the peace. He was a gunslinger. How dare he assume to tell her how she acted?

When she stepped from the bedroom, he handed her a cup of coffee. "Drink up. Time's a wastin'."

Her trunk along with her valise no longer sat by the door. Her medical bag was gone. The room looked so empty. She had spent two years here, studying. At one time she thought herself in love. Two weeks ago, the man she thought would be hers announced his engagement to a wealthy Bostonian lady. The man vowed undying love the night before. Her heart ripped apart. He'd been at the celebration, danced with her. Told her he still wanted her. He'd been one of the men who accosted her. Peter Bentley was his name. Along with his friends, he attacked her once before.

Flirt she would if she wanted. However, she'd never fall again for a man's vows of love. She was never going to fall in love, period. When she looked at Deke, she saw pure male power, fascination, strength, intrigue. Control was evident in the way he stood, by the look in his dark eyes. His broad chest, his height, the way his lips curved sensuously all spoke of male dominance. She would never allow a man to dominate her. She would never take orders from this man.

"You have time to sit, drink your coffee, have a doughnut. You do need to eat something. Gotta keep up your strength." He sounded as if he spoke to a little girl. She wasn't. Couldn't he see that?

Giving in to the realization that all because of her father he controlled her now, her life, she knew couldn't get rid of him by wishing him away. She touched her lips remembering the sweetness of his kiss, the sensuously sweet way his tongue explored her, the way she melted into him became liquid heat in his arms. In hind sight, she should have slapped him hard then. Instead, she clung to his broad shoulders, ran her fingers through his dark hair.

"Thank you." The coffee was delicious, the doughnut sweet and sticky. Butterflies twitted around in her stomach sending strange tendrils of heat to parts of her she'd never actually thought of before. He leaned against the doorframe watching her. His broad arms were crossed negligently in front of him while his eyes studied her drifting along the length of her form. She squirmed against his boldness.

Half-eaten she set the delicacy back into the sack. "I'll finish this later." She sipped the last of her coffee.

One dark eyebrow arched toward the ceiling. He pushed away from the wall. "Not hungry?"

"Can't eat a bite while you stare at me." She sounded petulant. She didn't want to give him a reason for amusement. Apparently, she did.

Grinning, he offered an arm. She ignored him again, smiling softly when she heard the swear word follow her out the door. He picked up the sack. The sound of his boots tramped on the hard wood. At the bottom of the stairs, he caught up to her then opened the door for her. A hack waited for them. When she tried to ignore his assistance, her foot caught in her skirt. For a moment, she thought she would end up nose first on the floor. So much for her defiance, too bad she never learned from her mistakes. He picked her up before she fell, setting her on her feet.

He led the way to the train cars they would share during the trip west. She rode in these cars with her family when they traveled. This was her first trip alone.

She wasn't alone.

"My bedroom is the first car. Yours the last." His husky voice behind her snapped her out of her reverie. She turned, her skirts whirling around her ankles. "We will share this living space. Did you know your father made these arrangements for you? You would have ridden in the main cars if not for his consideration."

"My father always uses these cars. This luxury is nothing new." Now she sounded peevish. She didn't want him to realize the startling affect his presence had on her, on her nerves.

"That's what I thought. You're not going to like Pine Flats. The town is rough around the edges. There is no luxury anywhere in Pine Flats," He paused watching her closely. "Hell, the western town is rough everywhere. You should change your mind. Find a place to be a doctor here in Boston."

"I'm a doctor, Mr. Sullivan. I go where I'm needed."

"Deke."

"I'm a doctor. I'll set up practice in your rough western town. All will be fine. You'll see." Stunned by his rudeness, she scrambled for more words. He didn't have the right to assume she couldn't make it on her own. "You don't know me."

"That's true. However, in the last few hours you've shown me quite a bit about who you are."

"What did you learn?" She couldn't help her curiosity even though she understood she shouldn't ask. Would most likely regret the question. Everything he would say would come out negative.

"I'm going to do my damndest to convince you to turn your delectable little backside around and go home. You're not a woman who is cut out for hard living. The men won't want to call you doctor. They won't drop their drawers for you to examine them. You will have no clients."

She bristled, outraged at his words. "You can't drive me away. What about you? Would you come to me if...?"

"Well, now, oughta tell you no, however," he paused raking her slowly with his heated gaze, "Depends on your bedside manner. I could get used to your sweet hands examining me."

"Ass..." she breathed softly. Knew he heard the word.

"I'm the sheriff of Pine Flats." He pushed his hat back a trifle, his dark blue eyes focused on her face now. "The way I see this situation once you're in town, I'll be defending you day in and day out. Men want one thing from a pretty little woman such as yourself. It's not the kinda doctorin' you've gone to school to learn."

"Go to Hell!" With just a few words and outrageous comments he managed to make her bristle with fury. He tapped into something she didn't understand. His dark blue eyes turned to black when he spoke of her, of her future in Pine Flats. He had nerve, damn him. She was terribly afraid he was speaking the truth.

"Right along with you." He sat down in a chair by the window. The train was on the move. "Nice place. I'm going to enjoy this trip much more than the one I took to Boston. Though the train doesn't go far enough. Rode in the regular car with all the regular folks. Before that the stage. You're goin' to like that stage real well."

His legs were stretched, long and lean in front of him. The jeans he wore molded around the solid muscle of his thighs. His shirt was unfastened at the top. She caught sight of crisp dark red hair poking from the opening. He was a unyielding wall of muscle and sinew.

"Like what you see?" His lazy drawl startled her out of her musings.

Flushed, she turned away from him. Back stiff, she marched through the cars to the last one, her sleeping chamber. A few moments of peace and quiet would be nice. He rattled all of her, every nerve stretched thin, every thought convoluted. When she entered, she saw her trunk as well as the valise. Her medical bag sat on top of the trunk. While she slept, he cared for her belongings.

His hands rested on her shoulders.

"Oh!" she gasped out startled by his presences quickly moving away from the heat of his body, from the frightening energy that possessed him. Her hand atop her chest, "You could let a person know you were there."

"I called your name twice." His voice deep and husky seemed to fill the tiny space. "You must not have heard me."

"What are you doing in here? This is my room." She didn't want to be so close to this man who stripped her to nothingness then sent flames of fire heating her. Something about the confidence he exuded transfixed her. She'd never know a man such as this one. Even the man she thought she loved never touched her senses as Deke did. She did need protection. Guarding her heart against this man would take all she possessed.

"Checking on you."

"Stay out of this room!" She wanted to be alone with her thoughts free of his overwhelming presence.

He tipped his hat, "As you wish." He grinned.

The man didn't move. She caught her lip beneath her teeth. "Go!" She pushed on his chest. The mistake was obvious the moment her hands touched him. She felt the sensual heat, the pull she couldn't resist.

His large hands surrounded her waist. "When I'm ready." He paused as he seemed to think, "…or when you tell me no."

She leaned back, staring into his fathomless dark eyes. He was a man to do things his way not hers. Tell him no? "Mr. Sullivan…"

"I've kissed you, sweetheart. Call me Deke. A man can only take so much formality with a woman he's going to become intimate with."

His face was inches away from hers. She swallowed hard, wishing for another kiss, not wanting him to touch her again. He tapped a finger on her nose. After that she watched his broad back as he sauntered through the door. She heard his chuckle from the other room.

Deep inside she seethed, her body becoming an inferno of molten liquid fire. He was the most audacious man she ever met. She collapsed into a chair, trying to control her breathing as she stared at the empty space where he stood a few minutes ago. He didn't want her in Pine Flats. He hated her. She tried to tell herself she despised him. She didn't. He intrigued and fascinated every sinew and bone in her body. His dark looks, the way he didn't let his emotions show sent chills of fire down her spine. She wrapped her arms around her as if that small gesture would smother the flames ignited by his presence. The single kiss touched a part of her she never knew existed. Her finger flew to her lips. Damn the arrogant man. She wasn't going to allow him to treat her so callously.

Quickly, she decided that she would tell him his duties. He needed to understand a few rules about this journey. She wasn't going to let him walk all over her. She fixed her hair, smoothed her skirts until she felt confidence grow. When she entered the living area, he wasn't there. He had left.

Damn the man.

She found the sack that held her doughnut. She ate. The food churned inside her stomach somersaulting rolling around as if it was doing his bidding. She walked from one end of the small room to the other. Back again. They were moving faster. When she looked out the window, she watched the city speed in front of her eyes as the hours dragged. Before, when she travelled with her family, they spent time in the other cars talking and laughing with the travelers. Right now, she didn't want to see anyone.

Especially not Deke.

Especially Deke. There were rules he had to learn. She opened the door. Shut the door. She was a mass of confusion, a maelstrom of frustration.

The sun was high in the sky before he reappeared. He stepped through the door without speaking. She spent all the morning as well as most of the afternoon wondering just where he was, gambling or drinking. He might have found a woman to wile away the time with. The pillow she held in front of her became a launched missile. She wanted to hurt him. To show him he couldn't treat her like so much unwanted baggage. She wasn't going to let him walk out on her.

Deke caught the projectile before it hit him. Once more, he quirked an elegantly shaped dark brow upward, "What did I do?" he asked sounding perplexed as well as a bit angry. "I left you alone as you requested. Did you want me to stay? I would have obliged you if I understood what you wanted."

"You ass!" she bit out clearly showing him her feelings. She was jealous and she hated the thought. The idea of a woman in his arms...

He shrugged from his jacket, tossed his hat onto the coat stand. "If I'm accused of something untoward, I'd like to know what it is."

"You've been gone." When the accusatory words left her mouth, she thought to bite her tongue. If he discovered she missed his company, he'd become insufferable. She'd wanted to be alone. He obliged her.

"True." He loosened the buttons on his shirt. "Did you miss me?"

"You're not going to undress again." She closed her eyes. He was insufferable.

He lifted his broad masculine shoulders all the while staring at her. "Thought I would get more comfortable. You have an objection to comfort? It's a long trip. We are going to be in close quarters for a while. After we leave this train, we'll ride a stagecoach. Then...well...then we will be alone together on the trail from Denver to Pine Flats. You're going to have to get used to me."

God in heaven what would he have to take off to get more comfortable? She didn't want to guess. Unable to help herself, she peeked at him from beneath lowered lashes. He stretched out on a chair, his shirt open to his narrow waist muscles rippling on his flat belly. Crips hair descended lower. She gulped air. She remembered all the rules in her head. Now because of his insolence she added another.

"You are not to remove your clothing in front of me," she blurted, her voice shaking with pent up emotion. Heat rushed to her face. The implication of what she said startled her.

His eyes darkened to fathomless pits. He barked a hoot of laughter as he leaned toward her his forearms resting against his thighs. "Anything else?"

She ran her tongue along her bottom lip. Oh God, she couldn't do this. His eyes narrowed as if she was quite insane. "Yes. I have a list of rules."

"Why am I not surprised?" His husky sigh of displeasure or fatigue didn't go unnoticed. "Go on..." He crossed his legs at the ankles while his back now rested on the chair. His hands were folded on top of his hard stomach.

"Coming into my private room is expressly forbidden." She started to ramble more rules.

He halted her with an upraised hand. His lips quirked in seeming amusement, "I see. Nonetheless, I'm being paid to protect you. If there is danger, I will go wherever I need to be. If it's in your private space, so be it."

Apparently, he didn't see how his clothing or lack thereof was the problem. He didn't understand how he created unease within her. He didn't understand how his simple touch could set forth a maelstrom of emotions inside she'd never encountered. If he chose, he would do whatever he pleased. She couldn't stop the sudden outburst. Her fists clenched while her temper soared, she yelled at him, "You don't! You don't see anything."

"Of course, I understand. You want me so much that in order for you to keep your innocence intact, you have to demand certain things of me. You don't want me to invade your sacred space nor do you want to see me with little to no clothing. You haven't mentioned anything about sharing a bed."

"I don't want you!" she yelled out.

His grin sent a wave of newfound butterflies rippling in her stomach then lower to between her thighs. She caught her breath in the back of her throat. Her protest fell on deaf ears.

"Should we test that theory?" he queried softly looking as if he was going to devour her whole. "I think...if I kissed you again..."

"N-no..." She was too quick to object, her hands outstretched as if that simple gesture could hold him off. "My feelings are not an experiment or a theory to test. I don't ever want you to kiss me."

"I think testing your rules would make the trip more interesting. You see, I'm bored. Would love to make the days and nights fly by with lightning speed. With you in my bed, we could do just that. We would only have to stop to eat. You know, come up out of the sheets for air."

"Why would I want to be in your bed?" She found herself backing away. She wanted to turn, to run. There was nowhere to run.

"You tell me, sweetheart. You've men drooling and panting over you since we first met. You can be damn certain I won't drool. I saw them at the dance. Watched one man push you against a wall, his hand exploring your..."

"I screamed."

"You did. I distinctly remember the weak yell that brought me to your defense. Was the sound made from fright or sexual excitement? Did you want the man's hand on your breast touching and weighing? Did you want to be rescued?"

Her eyes crossed. She frowned at him, unable to put a coherent sentence together. "I don't want any man's hand there...on my..." She clenched her teeth, reasoning with this man impossible. She wasn't going to talk about her breasts with a man she didn't know.

"Should that be another rule I intend to break? Should I see if you want my hand caressing you intimately, exploring parts of you that will make you hungry with desire? Perhaps between your lily white thighs?" he taunted her. "There are so many places I could caress you that would make you scream with pleasure."

Another pillow flew his way. She tried to leave. He caught her in her bedroom. He held her shoulders. His dark eyes blazing. With a wobbling voice she continued. "You're not going to break my rules. You're not going to test theories. You're not going to explore any part of me."

"Hmm...we'll see." His lips touched upon hers. "Shall we experiment with what you want as well as what you might not want?"

His mouth was warm and soft. She held herself stiff, unwilling to allow him the sweetest of intimacies he talked about. Giving into this wicked ploy of his was not a choice. His hands drifted downward. His lips swept across her neck then found more dark secret places to explore, along her collarbone, higher to a sensitive spot behind her ear. A soft sigh rippled from her lips. She closed her eyes wishing he didn't have such a potent effect on her.

She didn't want him.

She didn't want to want him.

His kisses stopped. Her lashes flew open. Her lips parted, moist from the fervent play of his mouth upon hers. She looked into the depth of his dark penetrating eyes. "I could have you right now, sweetheart. If I wanted you, I could have you in my bed anytime. You melt for me."

He caught her arm as she attempted to slap his face. She was furious with him. He goaded her. She fell into the game. "You cannot, not now not anytime. I will always tell you no!" She hated him. She wanted him.

"Another theory to experiment with. Time will tell the true tale. I'm not going to rush you. You are a novice in the ways of love. While you can flirt with the best you cannot tell a man no when he wishes to make love to you. Something you need learn."

"If you're trying to dissuade me from my plans your ploy is not working." She pushed against his chest. She wanted him to kiss her again, needed to feel the warmth of his mouth on hers.

He tightened his hold upon her. Once again, his lips descended to meet hers, the taste evocative. When he pushed inside, she met him, dueled and explored. She leaned into him. Heat exploded within her. A cool breeze touched upon her shoulders. He'd removed her clothing, moved the fabric down her arms. His lips explored everywhere across her shoulders, lower until she thought her knees would collapse beneath her. Still he held her, his hands tightening around her buttocks. He squeezed. Stroked. Explored. She moaned. Purred. The sensation was delicious. Her breath caught in her throat when his mouth closed over a nipple. She gasped at the sweetly painful pleasure. He laved then nipped softly, raked his teeth along tender flesh. She pushed against him. Her body constricted with need. She didn't understand what was happening to her.

"D-Deke..."

"What?" he asked without stopping as he turned the same heated attention to her other nipple.

Her fingers wound into his hair. She arched closer to him, giving him more access. Oh, dear God she knew this was wrong. Understood she should tell him no. If she didn't, he would be more arrogant than before. She didn't want him to stop. He was right. She couldn't tell him no. Didn't want to in any case. Wanted to learn what came after the kiss.

Suddenly she felt the backs of his fingers brush against her. He closed her gown then set her aside. "End of experiment." His voice was raspy, harsh. "I was right. You were wrong. Pretty damn simple."

She was shaking violently, her entire body trembling with anger along with the embarrassment and the knowledge that he so easily bested her. Now he tossed her aside as if she meant nothing to him. She would have to be stronger. Finally, gaining more courage. "I've more rules."

"Thought so." He stepped away from her. Sat on her bed, stretching his legs in front of him. He patted the spot beside him. "Come relax while you spout the list I intend to ignore. Don't abide by rules set down by a woman. They're usually foolish."

His grin infuriated her. Under the current circumstances, she would have to be an absolute idiot to sit next to him. Damn his never-ending gall. "No."

"Then...there will be no more rules, Annie. From now on you'll abide my terms. Your rules, when you tell me, we can discuss the pros and cons. My terms are nonnegotiable."

Her hands clasped in front of her. "No." She needed to make certain he understood who his employer was.

"Come sit. We can iron out all our differences in a matter of seconds."

"I'm firing you."

His grin broadened. His fine white teeth flashed in the dwindling light of the waning afternoon. "Your father told me you'd eventually say that. Won't work. You don't pay my fee. Your father does."

She wasn't going to stand in front of him and let him abuse her. Whirling, she swept out the door heading to a new destination. On the train she wouldn't go far. In this instance, she didn't get past his bedroom before she found herself plucked off the floor. She sifted in a mouthful of air then on a startled gasp the miniscule amount of oxygen she held there rushed out. He tossed her onto his bed. He followed. Her hands now above her head, he straddled her. His hard muscled thighs pressed against hers. He stared down at her. She was breathing hard. She knew what he looked at.

"Listening?" His gleaming white teeth were inches from her face. "It's well past time you listened to me."

Fire raged inside her while she willed herself to calm. She didn't understand how he could raise her temperature so quickly. "We don't know each other."

"I'm willing. How about you?"

"You can't tell me what to do or not to do. Well, you can say anything you want. It doesn't matter."

"Believe me, Miss Lundin, you will comply with my wishes."

"No."

"You've an infuriating way of not listening to me. You can't say no to something that hasn't been spoken."

"You're hurting me."

Immediately, he let go. She struck his chest with her tiny fists. He grunted. The blow was hard, harder than he probably expected. "Why, Miss Lundin, you can't seem to keep your little hands to yourself. I can think of other things your hands could be doing."

"If you weren't sitting on top of me waylaying me, I would never touch you." Her indignation caused his smile to widen.

"Oh, but I do think you will touch me. Explore my body with fingers as well as lips, teeth, tongue." Tenderly he ran his knuckles along her cheek. "You've the softest skin I've ever had the pleasure of feeling. Are you this soft everywhere?"

Heat flamed to her cheeks. His chuckle at her discomfort didn't suit. "No."

"I take that as a challenge. Shall I discover exactly where you are not soft?"

~ * ~

With a turbulence of thoughts raging in his aching head, Deke sat in one of the lavish compartments of the train. He sipped the glass of whiskey the sweet little doxy serving this area set down on the table. Raking in his coins, over a thousand dollars, he sat back to watch the other gamblers. At the moment he was done. He didn't want to go back to Annie. She touched him in ways he didn't want to consider. Making love to the woman wouldn't be wise or prudent. God how she tempted him though. Everything about her enticed him.

Hell, that was one little lady who didn't belong in the west. The little lady who bedeviled him the first moment he saw her belonged in fancy drawing rooms on the arm of a gentleman. He was no gentleman. He couldn't help thinking about her. In less than twenty-four hours she became ingrained in his blood. What would happen over the next weeks? They would travel from Denver to Pine Flats alone. She would be dependent on him for every need.

He wasn't going to spare her feelings. No way in hell would the menfolk of Pine Flats allow her to treat them as their physician. The ones who were wed wouldn't allow a woman to tend to their wives unless it was in childbirth. He didn't know how to convince her she didn't belong in a remote western town. She was so damned determined the fact boggled his mind.

Damn, on the other hand, he didn't want to let her out of his site. If he bedded her, she would be exorcised from his head. She couldn't possibly be a virgin. She was twenty-six years old. Her father told him her age before he finally agreed to the job. He never thought she would become a fire in his soul. Never thought she would be irresistible. No, she was another woman, nothing more, nothing less. He could bed her and not be touched by the fire she possessed, the response that heated like quicksilver.

He sipped his drink, cashed in his chips then headed for his sleeping car. The days from Boston passed much the same. He argued with her. He left. He won and lost cash. The journey by stage wasn't much better. He found games at the posting houses where they stopped. She sat next to him on the vehicle, sleeping, sometimes her head on his chest. She bedeviled him. Now, one day from Denver he was ahead of the game. He would leave it like that.

He followed her rules. She'd yet to be informed of his terms. They weren't necessary yet. Once they started on the trail from Denver to Pine Flats, she would learn soon enough she would have to do exactly as he told her.

What the devil were his terms?

He supposed the most important one was to keep her safe. She couldn't wander outside the town. She was not to leave her office unless he accompanied her. Blast it all, even in the tiny town she wouldn't be completely safe walking along the boardwalk. When passing by the saloon, she should move to the other side of the road. If there was a shootout, she would have to duck for cover. The list went on from there. On the trail her behavior would be even more important. If he gave her an order, she couldn't argue.

This was hell. He kept his hands off her. He'd done so by staying away from her at least until they got on the stage. The miles on the trail would be murder to his unruly body. All that was needed for him to lust after her was to look into her sultry blue eyes. She was fire in his blood. He needed to find a means to send her back to the east coast before he did something they would both regret through eternity.

Mentally, he ticked off what needed to be purchased in Denver before they left. She would need warmer clothing. The coat she brought with her wasn't heavy enough for the winter snows that would come their way if she managed to stay in Pine Flats until October. If she remained until October, she would be there until spring.

He should have spent the hours regaling her about the dangers she would encounter instead of gambling and drinking. He'd thought to find a woman to ease himself with. Whenever he looked at another lady, his mind traveled to the little viper residing in the plush cars at the end of the train.

Tomorrow.

The next few days would be trying for both of them. Barely two words had been shared between them the last few weeks. He ushered her on the stage in the morning then rode shotgun whenever possible sitting by the driver. When he did see her, she looked away. After looking at his pocket watch, he decided it was late enough to retire for the night.

The animosity between them would help him keep his hands to himself. The last night on the train, he strode through the cars. Slipping inside the main room, he was shocked to see Annie standing by the window looking out at the blackness of the night. A lump formed in his throat. He understood the only way to keep the distance between them was to bait her. He was just too damn tired to do so.

She turned when he cleared his throat, her clear blue eyes shimmering with emotion. She looked as if she wished to speak.

"Shouldn't you be in bed?" He sure as hell didn't want to see her, let alone talk to her right now while he was thinking of the trip to his town, while he thought of her alone with him in the vast forests of Colorado.

"I'm not tired. Where have you been?" Her voice sounded accusatory. Her bottom lip trembled. "I haven't seen you."

"Didn't think you wanted me around. I can be obliging when necessary. We could test some of those theories of yours." As soon as they came together sparks flew. He saw the fire rush to her eyes, the flames igniting with the few words spoken between them.

"I never said that."

"Well, honey, I'm not one to cotton to rules set down by a woman. Told you that on the first mention. Had to stay away from you or risk your temper flaring." What he wanted was to wrap his arms around her, pull her against him. If he did so, she would end up tumbled on his bed. "Best you go to bed."

~ * ~

"What's going to happen tomorrow? We are going to reach Denver by afternoon?" She was tired of spending days and nights alone in the uncomfortable stage even if it meant haggling with Deke Sullivan to have someone to speak with. She was now looking forward to conversation. The first week of the trip, she relished the solitude. This last week she was bored to tears. She was in the mood for a good fight.

"Early morning," he corrected her while he tugged on his boots.

"What will you do?" Pulling teeth might be easier than getting questions answered. Was he going to leave her alone in a hotel while he gambled and drank? Good lord he'd done enough of that during the trip out here.

"Need to buy supplies for the trip into the wilderness." His reply was curt as he didn't appear to offer more information.

She bristled. He stepped forward. His hand rested on her shoulder. She felt his heat, the inferno he always generated when he stood near when he touched. She choked back the reply hovering on the tip of her tongue.

"Supplies?" All she needed was a few simple answers.

"Food, blankets, my horse is stabled in town. Do you ride?" He looked at her as if he knew the answer.

Her terror of horses was well known. Her father elaborated understanding at some point she would have to conquer her fears. She was shaking her head, "No." She could learn quickly. She didn't want to learn.

"Didn't think so, Boston. You need a caretaker out here. A woman who can't ride, don't fit. You oughta go home. As soon as we pull into Denver, I'll set you up on the first stage headed east. We can be finished with the foolishness that brought you here."

"Don't call me Boston!" He could be such an ass. His language always changed when he wanted to make her leave. She pushed his hand off her shoulder.

Before she could blink or step back, he was holding her. His hand touched her neck. He pulled her close too near for her comfort. "That's who you are to me. You're Boston, all city girl, all fancy parlors and pretty dresses. A fancy little teacup held with your pinky sticking out. You don't belong in the wilderness where life can go from bad to worse in a blink."

She tried to turn. He held her tight. His lips found hers, touched, caressed, generated the magic she remembered. Heat whipped through her as if lightning struck. With his large callused hands, he framed her face. She opened for him. He groaned the sound husky. Just as always, she began to liquify. His tongue delved inside, explored touched deeply into secret places. A tiny sigh broke from her.

When he pulled away, he stared at her, his thumbs danced

seductively along her neck. "You're dangerous, a flirt. You leave a man with no wits. Go to bed, Boston." He gave her a tiny nudge in the direction of her room. Tomorrow will come soon enough. Once we're on the trail you'll be beggin' me for more time to sleep."

Dazed she stared at him wishing he would hold her again, wishing he would leave. She wanted to curse him. She should run as fast as she could. She wanted him to touch her, caress her as he'd done that first day. If he would hold her, the fear she felt might melt away. She didn't want him to know she was afraid. She wouldn't beg him for anything.

"Annie," his voice softened. Tenderly, he ran his knuckles along her cheek. "Go to bed. Tomorrow is going to be long as well as difficult for you. You need rest not a night of playing in my bed with me."

Heat raced to her face. She needed to refute his words. "You're crude, Mr. Sullivan. I would never play in your bed." She wanted to find out what he meant. Wanted to know what he could teach her about love. Love, no, she was never going to love a man. Though she did want to know what he meant by play in his bed.

Other Books by Christine Young
Available at Rogue Phoenix Press

Nick's Tender Rogue
Naughty book One

Once a McClellan lass

Beautiful, naughty and audaciously daring, young Nickie Gray is a McClellan princess through and through—as wild and reckless as the most incorrigible of her male cousins. Now that she has reached a marriageable age, Nickie has set her amorous sights on a most unsuitable male—the notorious rake and womanizer known to all mamas on the debutante scene in London as dangerous. When her chaperone tells her all rakes are off limits, she finds the challenge one she sets her mind to.

Always a McInnis rake

Not expecting to find a ravishing woman throwing herself at him yet blatantly willing to accept whatever overtures she makes, handsome Collin McInnis is thrilled by the brazen escapades of this naïve creature and is willing to experience her high-spirited advances with no expectations of commitment. On the high seas, he is bested by a vivacious beauty whose love of freedom and adventure rivals his own...and by an inescapable tidal wave of passion that threatens to engulf them both.

Connal's Eternal Love
Sweet McKenna Book One

A few days shy of All Hallows' Eve Connal McKenna, Laird of

Clan Chattan stands on the parapets of his castle. Bonfires line the hillsides while his clan prepares for the upcoming festivities. Drawn by the whispering of the wind, Connal McKenna feels a strange restlessness in his soul. Setting out to discover the wickedness that is calling to him, he discovers his mate. With gentle words and sensuous kisses, the auburn-eyed highlander conquers his mate, the beautiful, defiant Wynnie Adair who he comes upon during an evening ride. She must ultimately put her trust in the only man who can save her from the ruthless plans of her father and succumb to his gentle coaxing.

In Brady's Arms
Sweet McKenna Book Two

Forced to run from the only home she knows, beautiful, headstrong Lillian Townsends seeks shelter in the wild highlands where the McKenna clan live. Trying to avoid a betrothal contract signed by her stepfather to an aging lord, she is desperate to find a means to sidestep the inevitable, including a marriage to the oldest son of the laird. Lilly is enamored of the young lord who pursues her with unrelenting determination flashing his devilishly handsome charms. She is hard pressed to resist.

Besotted from the first moment Brady McKenna sees Lilly, he is determined to find a means to coax her into his arms and bed. With only the promise of carnal pleasure as his mistress, Brady relentlessly pursues the woman who has unwittingly forged a place in his heart. She is like no other woman, proud, defiant and enchanting. Despite his father's advice to stay away from her, he cannot. He boldly seeks her out and makes her his own.

Nobody but Walker
Sweet McKenna Book Three

The Highland Lass...

She was brought up, adored and loved by a doting mother and father ardently protected by her brothers. She was everything sweet and innocent until she was faced with betrayal and an unexpected and out of wedlock pregnancy. When she gave her love to a man who couldn't return her passion and commitment, she was left devastated and furious. Faced with the loss of her child if she didn't comply to his demands, Crissie McKenna followed him to Belfast then on to his country home to discover he was already married.

...The Irishman

Stunned to find out his one and only encounter with the woman he wanted to love forever created a child, Walker Endicott, Earl of Briarwood, claimed his child as his only heir. Walker threatened all her previously held values even while he thrilled her senses. From the moment he first saw her to the second she ran after him begging him to make love to her, his captivating masculinity held her fascinated. In his arms she would know tempestuous passion, bitter despair, and a soaring joy that would humble them both before the power of love.

Roby's Moonlit Night
Sweet McKenna Book Four

Once she'd been a pampered child with high expectations for her future blessed with love. Then she became an innocent pawn in a terrible game of greed and power. Now, with a noose around her neck, Pippa was to hang before she had the chance to unveil the men who drove her from her home, before she had the chance to live.

Roby McKenna was a man blessed with endless charm and wit. While he searched for his eternal love across the Atlantic in a new land, he would have to come home to find her. His silver blue eyes could sparkle with amusement or harden to steel gray with displeasure. He had all the women a man could want or need. As he grew older, mistresses were not enough. A quirk of fate brought him to the gallows, a spark of destiny made him claim the condemned Pippa as his bride.

Made for Houston
Sweet McKenna Book Five

Leah Kennedy is as wary of people as she is strikingly beautiful. However, the shocking death of her father that forever changed her girlhood has left her terrified of the very love she desperately longs for. Only in the untamed splendor of the Scottish crags does she feel safe from the feelings she stirs in men and the cruel mockery of Selkirk's villagers.

Debonair, well-educated doctor Houston Stuart has turned his back on social privilege along with professional honors to set up a medical practice in the lowlands of Scotland. There, serving those who need him the most, he hopes to forget the bitter memories and disillusionment that disturb his days.

Coincidence brings the cultured doctor and this fey mountain girl together. Something as bizarre as destiny disrupts the obstacle of birth and breeding, stubborn pride and fear which has kept them apart...as each seeks to heal the other's wounds with a raw passion neither can deny and all the odds against them cannot defeat.

Say You Love Kit
Sweet McKenna Book Six

Fascinated…

When the woman stepped through the door of the pub, the sun setting her fiery red hair glowing around her delicate features, Kit Stuart finds himself captivated by the sight. The moment he sees her he knows she will be his. Convincing the fire-haired lady of that fact isn't easy. After she calls out another man's name when he kisses her that night, he is instantly enraged as well as jealous. The road they travel is fraught with secrets that neither can tell. Trust is an elusive quality that neither can give.

Intrigued…

Forced to run for her life, desperate and afraid, Aila MacDuff willingly enters into the Kinnel Stones, a mysterious place where people disappear then appear magically in different times. At the first sight of Kit, she finds herself inexplicably drawn to him. She's been told to search for her mate and that she will know when she finds him. Aila doesn't know what this man's name is or what he looks like. Nonetheless, she is certain he will be similar to her mate from one hundred years earlier. Despite the fact she is falling in love with Kit, he can't be her mate. Her mate is a shifter. Kit is not.

My Sweet Broc
Bad Boys Book One

He's a bad bad boy...

Broc Wallace is a fun-loving rake who never thought any beautiful woman could melt his heart. He lives life in the present enjoying the camaraderie of his friends and the pleasures of his mistress. When Bliss races into his life, he is ill prepared to deal with her secrets or give up the tenor of his life. When the truth is revealed, he finds himself unable to forgive and forget the betrayal.

...but she's sweet for him

Bliss MacTavish knows she's playing with fire when she refuses to tell this bad boy her name. He tempts her with sweet whispers of seduction knowing her innocent nature will be unable to refuse all he yearns to give her. Deciding to follow her heart, she finds the repercussions more than she bargains for when she gives herself to this bad boy.

Crazy for Cam
Bad Boys Book Two

He's a bad bad boy...

Lord Cam MacEwen, Viscount of Rosehill, tries his best to be proper and court the lady of his dreams in the acceptable way. The feat proves impossible when the lady in question uses every means at her disposal to tempt him. He fights his jealousy for another man as well as the need to make her his own, finally giving in to her irresistible passion.

...but she's crazy for him.

Chelsea MacTavish wants the bad boy she fell in love with and kissed just before her eighteenth birthday. With feminine wiles and irresistible allure, the sensuous lady plans to best Cam at his game of hearts and make him forget his need to court her properly.

Falling for Flynt
Bad Boys Book Three

He's a bad, bad boy...

Fascinated by Hope's loss of memory yet haunted by her sultry beauty, Flynt is irresistibly drawn to the stoic miss—and into her troubles with the sultan who wants her for himself. When he discovers she is the sister of his best friend, his pride keeps him from pursuing her and making her his.

...but she's falling for him.

Raised in a harem but now penniless, alone and without her memory, Hope must discover a way to remember all that she has lost. She finds a way to continue with her life as a servant in Flynt's home. The first sight of Flynt steals Hope's breath as well as her heart. Can she overcome her fears and give herself to the man she fell in love with.

Dancing With Donal
Bad Boys Book Four

He's a bad bad boy...

Once a bad boy always a bad boy, Donal Chamberlin's carefree ways come crashing down around him when he meets the ravishingly beautiful Daryl MacTavish, the innocent little sister of one of his best friends. He is determined to win her heart as he sets his sights on marriage and an heir. His past gets in the way of his quest when a woman he once loved threatens Daryl's life.

...but she's dancing with him.

Daryl has seen the control her sister's husbands hold over them.

She yearns for a life where she makes decisions for herself. No man will have power over her. But no man kisses her the way Donal does. No man can make her forget all her goals leaving her helpless to give up her dreams. Yet Donal is determined to dance through all the barriers she thrust in front of him, pursuing her until she says yes.

Loving Leslie
Bad Boys Book Five

He's a bad bad boy...

Leslie Stewart, Duke of Southcliff is stoic, set in his ways, a spy who is used to having his life well ordered. He expects life to continue on in this perfectly conventional fashion. He assumes his bad boy status while keeping mamas and debutantes at arm's length. An heir is needed but Leslie has every intention of finding a woman who doesn't covet his wealth and tittle. He is irresistibly drawn to the headstrong young lady who becomes more beautiful as she develops into a woman.

...but she is loving him.

When Leslie kisses Lacie MacTavish, she knows even at the tender age of fifteen this is the man of her dreams. Forced to wait until she comes of age, Lacie withdraws into herself. Now she is eighteen and Leslie has returned from a mission for the British Government ready to claim her as his bride. She refuses him and he must find a way to seduce her and in the process create a burning passion within her, which she cannot deny.

Pleasing Arie
Bad Boys Book Six

He's a bad bad boy...

Arie Demir has never been denied anything in his life. He takes what he wants. What he undeniably yearns for is the beautiful redheaded spitfire he sees in a restaurant in Glasgow. At every turn, she confuses him by disputing his power over her. Alison refuses to accept the fact he owns her. While Arie tries desperately with patience and tenderness to drive her wild with new sensations, his scorching kisses ignite the fires of her very soul to make her understand he is all she will ever want.

...but is she pleasing him?

Alison Fletcher never expected to find herself kidnapped and sold to a whorehouse then bought by a Turkish sultan to become his slave. She vows to never surrender to the arrogant man who believes he owns her. She is stunned by the magnificently handsome man who awaits her compliance. Unexpectedly, she finds Arie the lesser of all the evils. The hidden depths of his mesmerizing dark brown eyes hold her into their power; his muscular embrace makes her weak with desire. She is his to do with as he wishes.

Graham's Wicked Kiss
Bad Boys Book Seven

He's a bad bad boy...

Graham Chamberlin is stunned to find three young boys dangling from the trees lining the drive to Runningmead Manner. On further inspection, he is astonished at their obsession to protect a young woman who has been brutalized by her pimp. The woman he discovers hiding in a third-floor attic room is gravely injured. He takes the silver haired stowaway under his wing. Clearly, Graham's new guest is a lady with many secrets. He is determined to unlock all the mysteries surrounding her.

...But she can't resist his wicked kiss.

The years since Ria left the convent where she was raised have been a nightmare. Her secrets are dangerous—as is the powerful man determined to find her. Handsome Graham Chamberlin is clearly a gentleman with secrets of his own, but staying with him could mean the difference between life and death for Ria. With each passing day, her handsome host turns Ria's convalescence into an increasingly sensual escape. Now her greatest challenge may be imagining anything less than a future in his arms.

Feeling Etienne's Love
Bad Boys Book Eight

He's a bad bad boy...

Etienne Dubois is the son of a wealthy vineyard owner who craves the excitement of putting his life on the line. Working with the French government and as a confidant of King Charles X give him reasons for living. An encounter with a beautiful young woman in a plush bordello in Paris has him rethinking his roguish ways. Etienne never expects to become a father especially from one encounter with an innocent prostitute who whispers his name and has him rethinking his well-ordered life.

...But she can't help feeling his love.

Elisa Moreau, the only daughter of Angelique Moreau, the owner of an exclusive bordello in Bordeaux, France, has loved Etienne Dubois since she was six. Unfortunately, until an unexpected encounter at a brothel in Paris puts the two of them in the same room, Etienne doesn't even know she exists. Confused but wanting Etienne and this chance meeting to never end, Elisa gives herself to the man who has held her heart in hands for what seems like her entire life

All I Want Is Link
Bad Boys Book Nine

He's a bad bad boy...

Merry Stewart is wildly unpredictable. Left alone to run wild over the Bordeaux and Scottish countryside she becomes impetuous and daringly bold. Over the years, she's found she can bedevil her softhearted brothers into allowing her exploits to go unnoticed. As a young woman she has learned she can do as she pleases when she pleases. Now, Merry has set her amorous sights on the Duke of Weston—a man she has never met but has every intention of marrying. No other suitor will satisfy her—especially not the exceptionally striking, horse breeder, Devlin Mathews.

...she's the woman of his desires.

Posing as commoner Devlin Mathews to escape a potentially fatal confrontation, Devlin is enthralled and infuriated by the audacious, duke-hunting dark haired vixen. Bedeviled at every opportunity, he finds dealing with the tiny she-devil exasperating as well as intriguing. Without revealing his true identify, the infamous rogue pledges to thwart Merry's plans to wed the man of her dream-never imagining the bewitching strategist would turn out to be the only woman he would ever dream of marrying.

Devlin's Angel
Bad Boys Book Ten

He's a bad bad boy...

Merry Stewart is wildly unpredictable. Left alone to run wild over the Bordeaux and Scottish countryside she becomes impetuous and daringly bold. Over the years, she's found she can bedevil her softhearted brothers into allowing her exploits to go unnoticed. As a young woman she has learned she can do as she pleases when she pleases. Now, Merry has set her amorous sights on the Duke of Weston—a man she has never met but has every intention of marrying. No other suitor will satisfy her—especially not the exceptionally striking, horse breeder, Devlin Mathews.

...she's the woman of his desires.

Posing as commoner Devlin Mathews to escape a potentially fatal confrontation, Devlin is enthralled and infuriated by the audacious, duke-hunting dark haired vixen. Bedeviled at every opportunity, he finds dealing with the tiny she-devil exasperating as well as intriguing. Without revealing his true identify, the infamous rogue pledges to thwart Merry's plans to wed the man of her dream-never imagining the bewitching strategist would turn out to be the only woman he would ever dream of marrying.

Needing Gill
Bad Boys Book Eleven

He's a bad bad boy...a man with no heart.

Gil Allemand wants to be left alone, especially by the beautiful outcast who's invaded the vineyard where he meant to wallow in his grief. She has a ton of impudence and brazenness, a talent for trouble, and a child who brings back memories better left in the dark recesses of his mind. Yet Jenna's feisty spirit might just be heaven-sent to save a hard, inflexible man

...she's a desperate young mother

Jenna Bonnet's bad luck has taken a turn she never imagined. With twenty-five silver francs, a mare that can't walk up the hill to the chateau that is her five-year-old son's birthright, a son she is desperate to keep alive, she's come home to a village that despises her. However, this single-minded young widow with a shocking past has learned how to fight. She'll do anything to keep her child alive—even take on a man with no heart.

Just For Michael
Bad Boys Book Twelve

He is a bad, bad boy…

Michael Flannigan has burgeoning ideas the moment he meets the woman who has inherited Mayfair. Clare will fit into his big plans quite nicely. Mayfair Plantation is his heritage. Even before the Revolutionary war Flannigans owned this land. No woman is going take what is his. Realizing the only way he can possess the land that is his birthright is to marry the impulsive woman who waltzes into his life, he sets his sights on making her his, slowly seducing her until she unwittingly falls into his scheme.

…but she is determined

When Clare Carter-Brown returns to Mayfair Hall in Virginia after several years absence, she intends to claim her inheritance. Bypassing Leslie Hall, she moves into Mayfair without a chaperone intending to take over from the manager. Michael objects to her tactics. At every turn, he adeptly points out her failings. As the fires rage around them they find a love that burns more fiercely than either could ever imagine.

Foolish for Piper

The pickpocket…

Piper has spent her life surviving the streets of St. Giles Parish in London, a den of iniquity and crime. Masquerading as a boy she escapes the whorehouses the young girls are sent to as they come of age. The day she encounters Brett MacLachlan begins the same as every other one. When she picks his pocket, she has no idea her life is going to change irreversibly.

…and the mark

Handsome aristocrat Brett MacLachlan has come to London for his amusement only to find his world turned upside down by a thief and her dog. From the moment he spots her, Brett knows there is something intrinsically wrong. In his arms, Piper discovers passion and joy. Yet secrets of her past haunt her, and a scar will tell the true tale as well as her identity.

Taylor's Destiny

She traveled to another time and place to change destiny...

Enjoying a day of sailing, Taylor Maxwell never expected after a suffering a concussion she would wake up in another century. A resilient independent woman in the twenty-first century, the blond beauty is ill prepared for life in the 1800s. Her first sight of the naval captain who rescues her makes her heart stop, giving her hope for her future.

His life is transformed by a woman who appears from nowhere...

Born to a life of ease, Reid Stewart defies the dictates of those born to aristocracy and chooses a life of adventure in the navy and as a spy for the crown. When he discovers a nearly naked woman on the bow of small sailing ship, his heart warms. His love for Taylor and his need to protect her from a man who pursues her might cost him his life as well as hers.

Caitlin's Duke

She played a fiddle in an Irish pub...

Caitlin O'Shea Is the most beautiful woman Roc Leighton has ever seen. With her blue violet eyes and long black hair she captivates him. In turn he mesmerizes Caitlin. Caught in the power of his gaze as he watches her, she is wise enough to know he desires her but will never give his heart to her. Caitlin has vowed to never be any man's mistress.

And fell in love with an English Lord...

Roc knows the first time he watches her play the fiddle and dance around the pub, she will be his next mistress. Despite her protest, he will find a way to convince her that her place is with him. While Caitlin's determination to keep her vows, fate takes a cruel turn and she is forced to seek refuge with Roc.

Catching Meara
Book One in the McKenna Clan Series

Meara Thorton was a feisty, world-class computer hacker—cornered by the FBI and shockingly given the chance to be their newly acquired technical analyst. Brilliant and intuitive, yet aching with the loss of everyone she has cared about, her restless heart led her to discover a love she fought and a world she didn't know could possibly exist.

Sweet Sexy Sadie
Book Two in the McKenna Clan Series

From the first time Sadie's eyes met those of Brody McKenna in the hot Sierra Madre Mountains, theirs was a potent attraction—not gentle, slow, and easy, but hot, hard, and all-consuming. The daughter of a dysfunctional family, Sadie had dreams no man could wrench from her with hot sex and an all-consuming passion. She'd challenge this alpha male with all the strength she possessed. But her red hair, fiery temperament, and indomitable spirit obsessed Brody...and he knew he had to find a way to show her he was more than he appeared and convince her to make a life with him.

Sweet Misbehavin'
Book Three in the McKenna Clan Series

Cast adrift after fleeing the home of Jokul, the ice demon, Atantsi, a firestarter, grew to womanhood as she moved through time to keep the demon from finding her. Though stubborn and courageous, she was ill prepared to use powers she had not been taught. Her first sight of the intoxicating Carr McKenna left her breathless, and her second encounter gave her hope for a future she never thought she had.

A playboy, a second son and a shifter, a man who thought his life would be carefree, Carr McKenna was shocked to discover the woman he'd paid as an escort is a firestarter who is running for her life. He is the leader of all the McKennas around the world and that he has multiple powers. His passion for Margo and the need to defend her might cost him his life as well as hers.

Sweet Talkin' Sugar
Book Four in the McKenna Clan Series

Lyonesse McKenna, was dreaming, or was she? From the instant Lyn saw Deacon McClain across a black jack table in a crowed Las Vegas casino the unmistakable attraction sent Lyn's senses flying into overdrive. Her family of shapeshifters believed in soul mates. She'd always been skeptical yet she couldn't help but question the way her heart sped when he looked at her.

When Deacon appeared in Las Vegas he knew his first job was to save Lyn from a Sea Demon, but the next order of business was to convince her he would someday mean more to her than she'd ever expected. But her stubborn nature and unbendable spirit consumed Deacon...and he had to chase away all the demons real and imagined in order to win her heart.

Sweet Surrender
Book Five in the McKenna Clan Series

Ripped from her family at the top of Infinity Cliff, Kimi McKenna finds herself thrust somewhere into the future. Dark elements threaten to destroy the earth unless Kimi can work together with the white witch to stop the destruction. Confused by her mate's role in the conspiracy, she refuses to acknowledge the connection. But amidst raging fire and attacks on the people she is coming to hold dear, she allows Maska O'keefe into her heart.

Maska O'keefe has loved the beautiful shapeshifter for years. Unable to save her life years ago, he vows to watch over her as he is given a second chance to convince her that even though he is a witch and not a shifter, they are indeed soul mates. Kimi's divided loyalties between her family and the cause she is now a part of will determine their relationship. Only the part she plays as the messiah can bring this to a conclusion in the final battle.

Sweet Dreams
Book Six in the McKenna Clan Series

For Cas Doyle finding the shifter of her dreams was a matter of life or death. She walked into the Red Neck Bar and Grill in Cactus Junction with a hope and a prayer he would be there and she would recognize him. What she needed was for him to take her home and take her virginity. Cas never thought to be a one-night stand. She had no choice.

Guy McKenna knew eventually he'd find his soul mate. He didn't expect the reality to happen this night. When he saw her he knew. She was dressed provocatively, enticing him to an extreme he never felt before. What he didn't know was if he could convince his protective family that Casidhe Doyle was indeed his soul mate.

Dakota's Bride
The first book in the Lakota/Pinkerton Series

When Emma St. John received her brother's letter imploring her to escape her stepfather's vengeful scheme and to trust Dakota Barringer with her life, she was willing to chance it. But the handsome, brooding riverboat owner Emma found in Natchez a danger of another kind. For Emma soon found herself surrendering to an unrelenting desire.

Raised by the Sioux when his parents were killed, Dakota had been betrayed once before by a white woman. He wasn't about to trust another, especially one claiming that her stepfather, a powerful U.S. senator, had framed her as a murderess. But he couldn't let Emma's intoxicating effect on him. Now Dakota would risk his very life to protect the innocent beauty who had seduced him with her tender love.

My Angel
The second book in the Lakota/Pinkerton Series

A BEAUTY IN BUCKSKINS

When her father decided to send her to a finishing school back East, Angela Chamberlain refused to be confined to stuffy drawing rooms. Instead, the daring spitfire who could shoot like a man and ride like the wind longed for a life of adventure and romance—and she knew exactly who could give it to her. Devil Blackmoor was a hired gun with a dangerous reputation. But Angela was willing to go to the ends of the earth to capture the handsome devil's heart.

A DEVIL IN DISGUISE

He'd come to America looking for excitement, but Devil Blackmoor got more than he bargained for when he encountered a beautiful rebel who answered his kisses with a wild innocence that touched his very soul. Yet standing between them were more obstacles than either ever dreamed. For Devil had strapped on a gun for the wrong man. And that made Angela his enemy. Now he'll have to choose between his duty and the woman he loves more than life.

The Locket
The third book in the Lakota/Pinkerton Series

The year is 1894. Seeking revenge for crimes against his family, Misha Petrovich follows a path that leads straight to Ariel Cameron's boarding house in Mist Harbor, Oregon. A family heirloom in Ariel's possession leads Misha to believe she is guilty. The locket has been handed down to the oldest girl in the Petrovich family for generations. Ariel is innocent of wrong doing, but her father is not. Misha is torn by his feelings for Ariel and his need for restitution against her father. Knowing that the relationship between them is fragile, Misha does everything in his power to protect Ariel's father. His efforts are to no avail when her father is shot. Ariel comes to realize Misha's steadfast courage and determination to protect her and her father despite what has happened to his family. Ariel's love and devotion heals Misha's heart.

The Talisman
The fourth book in the Lakota/Pinkerton Series

Running from a marriage that lasted one night, Dr. Moriah McKeown discovers the land she has settled on is coveted by determined and lawless men. Yet the proud young woman who once vowed never to abandon her home has second thoughts when her adopted children are threatened. Her only recourse is to enlist the aid of a dark, dangerous gun for hire.

Haunted by the past and a betrayal he will never forgive, Ian Civanovich uses his fast gun and his reckless courage to forget the faithlessness of a woman in his past. He will trust no female—nor will he rest until the threat hovering over Moriah McKeown is put to rest.

Forever His
The fifth book in the Lakota/Pinkerton Series

Struggling to come to terms with the part she played in Jacob St. John's death, Etta Barringer resigns from Pinkerton Agency and seeks peace and solace in a Rocky Mountain Cabin.

Jacob has vowed to discover the reason Etta has betrayed him, sold him out to his enemy and left him for dead.

Isolated in their cabin, they discover their love for each other and learn to trust. But the trust is shattered when Jacob learns she is married to his sworn enemy; the man who left him in the desert to die.

Allura's Secret
Twelve Dancing Princesses Book One

Allura McClellan is horrified by her father's decision to take out an ad in the Times awarding her to the man strong enough and smart enough to win her hand and uncover her secrets. She's an intelligent young woman who takes great delight in the freedom allotted to her by her father. She's well aware that marriage would effectively curtail the adventures she's shared with her sisters and cousins.

Hunter Gray is nothing like the other men who've arrived to vie for Allura's hand in marriage and everything that goes along with it. However, he is the first to refuse to concede defeat and pursue her despite her attempts to disguise her true appearance. It's her temperament that is of more concern to him than her looks. Hunter has worked all his life with the hope of someday owning his own land. Now that it looks like there's a very real possibility that everything he's ever wanted is within reach nothing is going to deter him – including Miss Allura's disagreeable disposition.

Amorica's Wager
Twelve Dancing Princesses Book Two

Amorica Hepburn was sent to London to find a husband. Finding a man was the last item on her agenda. With her two cousins, Amorica wagers she can dissuade her suitor before the others. Despite her efforts she discovers a chemistry that cannot be denied. Suddenly she is the arrogant man's wife, pledged to a marriage neither desire. But swept off to his ancestral home above the Dover cliffs and into his strong embrace, Amorica is soon possessed by a raging passion for the husband she had vowed to despise...

Damian Andrews couldn't afford to trust the emerald-eyed spitfire who happened upon his secret. Amorica's hatred of all men of his kind only inflames the war that rages between them. Still, he can not control the intense desire his stubborn bride inspires, or make her surrender to his will until he has conquered the headstrong beauty on the battlefield of love...

Ravyn's Marriage of Inconvenience
Twelve Dancing Princesses Book Three

A REGAL BEAUTY

When the duchess decides to wed her to a wastrel and a fop, Ravyn Grahm takes matters into her own hands and declares her engagement to another man. Instead of fessing up and telling her great aunt what she has done, she goes through with the pretense. Ariec Lakeland is the bastard son of an earl and has a dangerous reputation. But Ravyn is willing to do most anything to keep the duchess from discovering the lie.

A DEVIL-MAY-CARE SMUGGLER

He'd bought land in America, looking to put down roots and end his life of adventure, but Ariec Lakeland got more than he bargained for when he encountered a beautiful heiress who made a promise she didn't want to keep. But the promise could not be undone and standing between them were more obstacles than either ever dreamed. Ariec had made plans to spend the rest of his life in America and that was at odds with Ravyn's plan of living in England and running her father's estate. Now, he'll have to choose between his dreams and the woman he loves more than life.

Christel's Sunrise
Twelve Dancing Princesses Book Four

He Made Her An Offer...

Life has thrown Christel McClellan some experiences that could have devastated a less determined woman. Beautiful, self-assured and fiercely independent, she is trying to forget the loss of her stillborn child. But is the child alive?

She Couldn't Deny...

Life is carefree for Ryder MacLaren who loves to see what is on the other side of the sunrise. Laird of Clan MacLaren, he is wealthy, handsome and happily unencumbered...until stunning Christel McClellan enters his life. When he hears her story, he believes the child she thought dead has been sold to a wealthy buyer.

Storm's Passion
Twelve Dancing Princesses Book Five

SHE MADE A PROPOSAL...

Life strikes Storm Graham a shattering blow when she learns her father has bartered her to a man she detests. Storm is beautiful, self–assured and fiercely independent, and refuses to be a pawn in her father's schemes, yet she can find no way out of this bargain made in hell. Going on the offensive she asks the wealthiest man on the eastern coast of England to marry her, never believing she might fall in love.

HE TRIED TO REFUSE...

For Hadden Johnston life has provided everything he ever wanted, including a sanctuary for homeless children. He is wealthy, handsome and happily unencumbered...until stunning Storm Graham marches into his life and proposes a marriage of convenience. Yet this type of marriage to a woman who inflames his senses is far from acceptable. If he's going to be tied down, he will move heaven and earth to have this woman warming his bed.

Gotta Have Fayth
Twelve Dancing Princesses Book Six

A regal beauty with raven hair and piercing blue eyes, Fayth Graham is unwilling to parade herself in front of the wealthy Lords of England during the season. Seeking a means to dissuade any man wishing to wed her, she seeks a way to ruin herself for marriage. When she unexpectedly meets a man with sparkling gray eyes and an infectious grin, she decides this is the man who will keep her from agreeing to obey.

He returned from six months at sea, looking for a few nights of pleasure with a willing lass, but Jarret Kinsley got more than he bargained for when he met a beautiful debutant who responded to his kisses with a wild innocence that touched his heart. Yet the obstacles looming between them might rip them apart. Both had vowed never to marry, so when consequences of their dalliances got in the way, Jarret would have to choose between the life he's always desired and the woman he loves more than life.

Ella's Pleasure
Twelve Dancing Princesses Book Seven

A WHISPER OF PLEASURE

Ella Hepburn was an auburn haired debutant from the harsh Scottish coastline—a wild innocent to be seduced and tamed. A spirited beauty, she captivated Drake Montgomerie's jaded heart—while succumbing to the smoldering desire she felt for her unyielding suitor.

A WHISPER OF DANGER

In Drake Montgomerie's glittering world of money and privilege, young Ella discovered passion and desire could overcome everything she'd been taught to resist—entangling Drake, the heir apparent, in a lethal coil of aristocratic family intrigue. But grave peril would only nurse the sparks of a love that knew no limits and a magnificent ecstasy that would not be denied.

Eveleen's Seduction
Twelve Dancing Princesses Book Eight

A WHISPER OF SEDUCTION

A brutal attack on Eveleen Hepburn's cherished island off the Scottish coastline leaves her shattered and bewildered. Learning a man she once trusted can kill as easily as he can breathe even though the deed saves her life, creates questions that need answers. An innocent beauty, she enchants Logan Maxwell's cynical heart—giving in to the raging passion she feels for her mysterious suitor.

A WHISPER OF INTRIGUE

In Logan's Maxwell's world of espionage and privilege, young Eveleen discovers truths about herself she never expected, and a need for passion and love can overcome all her fears if she learns to accept certain truths. She finds herself entangled in a lethal battle for land that was once owned by French nobility, taken from them during the revolution and sold to Maxwell. But grave peril would unleash the flames of love that simmers, creating a magical union that cannot be refuted.

Tavia's Deception
Twelve Dancing Princesses Book Nine

WHISPERS OF DECEPTION

When her father decides to send her to London for her season, Tavia Hepburn resolves to see the world instead. The raven haired beauty decides to disguise herself as a lad and find employment on a ship bound for Barcelona as a cabin boy. But she never bargains on finding passion and love to a red haired sea captain who rescues her from certain death.

WHISPERS OF MURDER

For James Macmurra, the world is black and white until he meets a young debutante, who turns his world upside down. He's unable to deny Tavia's intoxicating effect on him. In a match tense with obstacles, unwillingness to divulge secrets, and unforeseen peril, irresistible desire and passion grows into undeniable love. James would risk his life to shelter and protect the innocent debutante who seduces him with her sweet love.

Larena's Fascination
Twelve Dancing Princesses Book Ten

WHISPERS OF FASCINATION

Fiery, free spirited Larena Graham never wanted to marry a duke.

She is thrilled to be in love with the fourth son of an aristocrat, Gavin Broon. But when it seems Gavin ignores her, she set her sights on politics and bettering human life. Unsuspecting intrigue and a plot against her, she continues her dangerous plans despite Gavin's wishes.

WHISPERS OF TRUST

Gavin has every intention of properly courting the beautiful Larena until he must leave the city in order to put his affairs in order. Returning to London, he finds the woman he means to make his own is embroiled in political protests that could lead to a prison ship. Larena must learn to trust the handsome Scotsman whose most pressing mission is to protect her and keep her from harm.

Tira's Education
Twelve Dancing Princesses Book Eleven

WHISPERS OF EDUCATION

Learning how to build ships is Tira Hepburn's only dream until she meets Jamie Lundin and her world is turned upside down. With her raven black hair and vivid green eyes, she tempts Jamie and pushes him to defy his vows. She never bargains on finding an irrevocable love and a passion to a man who cannot fulfill her dreams despite his burning desire for her.

WHISPERS OF A BARGAIN

Arrogant and self-assured Jamie is brought up short when Tira captures his heart. All his carefully made plans are put to the test when he decides to teach her the art of ship building if she will spend a week with him alone on his ship. He is unable to deny Tira's intoxicating effect on him. When Tira leaves him behind unwilling to live with him without the benefit of marriage, he races after her. Jamie will risk everything to shelter and protect the innocent debutante who seduces him with her sweet love.

Aidan's Love
Twelve Dancing Princesses Book Twelve

Whispers of Love

Aidan McLellan has loved since she first set eyes on him as a young girl. Spontaneous, wild and eager to grow up, Aidan haunts his waking thoughts day and night, insinuating herself into his life. With her fiery red hair and sparkling sapphire eyes, she seizes Blade's heart even while he tries to resist the innocent child until she becomes a woman.

Whispers of Courage

Blade has waited what seems a lifetime to claim the woman who captures his heart as a little girl. Claiming his inheritance before his younger brother takes what is rightfully his, Blade must convince Aidan of his sincerity after years of avoidance and wed her before his father dies so he can return home, securing his rightful place. Everything is put to the test when his life as well as Aidan's is threatened by the man who once called him brother.

Don't Hustle Letty
Good Girls Book One

She's a good girl...

As tempted as Scarlett was, she had too many secrets to let someone enter her world—secrets that would send any reasonable man to the farthest ends of the earth. Bobby was far from reasonable and despite her desperate attempts to hold him at bay, he would not let her past destroy their future. With her escort service, Scarlett used men and their insatiable lust for women to capitalize on the means to survive and prosper. She vowed to never wed, to never put herself in the control of a man.

...nonetheless he has other ideas.

Lord Robert Munroe, with his newly acquired title of marquis goes to Scarlett's for training on how to comport himself. The marquis, better known as Bobby, knows how to pick a pocket as well as get into a bloke's home to steal them blind. What he doesn't know is how to be a gentleman. When he sets his sights on the prim Miss Scarlet, Letty, to his way of thinking, he decides she is the woman he wants to call his wife. He tempts all that she is with sweet words and tender coaxing until she is unable to refuse all he hopes to give her.

Only Caro's Baby
Good Girls Book Two

The Scheme

Genius botanist with theories of inherited traits, Caroline Kenworth desperately wants a baby. Finding a suitable father won't be easy. Caroline's super-intelligence makes her feel pushed aside, unwanted as a woman. As a bluestocking she is determined to spare her child the suffering that plagues her life. Which means she must find someone very special to father her child. A person very...well...ignorant.

The Target.

Duncan Murray, the Earl of Downsberry, well known for his lack of intelligence as well as his rakish ways with women, seems as if he is the flawless man to fulfill the role. His amazing good looks and Scottish brogue are misleading. Caro learns too late that this debonair earl is a lot smarter than she first thought—in addition he's not about to be used then abandoned by any woman who has schemed to steal his sperm.

The Detonation

A dazzling solitary woman whose desires to learn what it would be like to become a mother... A man who is in control of all he does never allowing anyone to usurp his role will settle for nothing less than surrender... Can lust coupled with physical attraction drive two strong-minded yet vulnerable people to a completely unforeseen love?

Only Caro's Baby
Good Girls Book Three

She's a good girl...

Born a bastard, Honey McRae is taunted and bullied by her half-brother most of her life. Branded with a tattoo of the Saber and the Rose by the men's association, she is desperate to be free and escapes the country estate where she was held prisoner. Resigned to a passionless life devoid of men, she fights the nightmares that haunt her. Despite her past fears, she accepts the fact she will never be able to give herself wholly to the man she loves. Until that man, bold and breathtaking, decides he will find a means to woo her into his arms.

Nonetheless...

Stolen at birth and sent to live in the bowels of London, Billy–once a pickpocket and thief–discovers he is actually the Duke of St. Aubries. He is determined to win the woman he fell in love with the first time he saw her, the lady with a tattoo on her breast, a woman who has been cruelly used. He disputes her notion that men are only capable of inflicting pain...instead he binds her to his heart with his gentle and patient loving.

Twelve Days to Love

When Archer Steele shows up at Calanthe Durand's failing plantation with an alligator over his shoulder, Cali thinks she's never seen a more handsome man. During the war she had to defend herself and her servants from both union and confederate soldiers. Independent and self-sufficient, she vows to never marry.

But Archer Steele has different ideas. The first time Archer sees Cali in town, he feels an instant attraction. He decides he will do everything and anything to convince the beautiful Miss Durand he is worthy of her love. During the weeks leading up to Christmas, he gives her twelve gifts in hopes she will fall in love with him. Yet they are faced with challenges they must overcome before Cali can commit to a marriage.

Door to Heaven

Jessica Lawrence is the stepdaughter of a woman born in the twentieth century transported back in time to the year 1868. An acclaimed suffragette, she raises Jessica to believe in the equality of women. Jess Law believes everything she was taught, and when the time is right she becomes a private investigator. Courageous and impetuous, Jess finds danger in her quest to save all women from white slavery. Her passionate mission results in a wedding to Roc Newman, a man she knows can steal her heart...

Roc can't trust the sapphire-eyed spitfire who invades his home in search of secret papers and knocks him flat with her karate moves. Jessica's refusal to obey his wishes serves to inflame the war between them. Still, he cannot control the intense desire his reluctant bride inspires, or make her surrender her independence, until he has conquered the headstrong beauty on the battlefield of love...

Rebel Heart

HER REBEL SPIRIT DEFIED HIS OUTSIDERS SOUL...She was velvet and silk, eyes the color of a summer storm and amber hair. Victoria DeMontville, because of a promise and a codicil to her father's will, was forced to marry one man to protect her from another. She hated Cameron Savage with a fierce passion. But to hold on to her genetic research and find a cure for the deadly Signe virus, she must pretend to love the enemy at her door, come with weapons of fire to melt her icy heart...

HIS OUTSIDERS TOUCH IGNITED RAGING PASSIONS...
He wore a mask, disguised as the Phantom, a true legend come to life.
Even as war and debate over new genetic research engulfed them all, he
would find his greatest adversary in the beauty who'd branded him an
outsider and barbarian, the woman he was born to possess, his soul mate.

Safari Moon

Solo St. John, a wildlife photographer, is preparing for a trip to
Alaska. Suddenly, Solo finds women of all sorts invading his privacy, his
home and his office, all cooing nonsense words and blatantly throwing
themselves at him. Solo doesn't know why, and he has no idea how to rid
himself of the persistent women. He finally decides to beg a favor of his
best buddy Nyssa Harrington.

In love with Solo for the past ten years and knowing he doesn't
return her feelings Nyssa doesn't want to talk to Solo. She knows if she
accepts his phone call, she will not be able to resist the temptation to hope
again.

Straight to Heaven

Running from demons, Alexandra McMurdie stumbles into
Forbidden Ground where up is down and elements of nature are
contested. Though a strong independent woman in the twenty-first
century' she is unprepared for life in the 1800s. Her first site of the
formidable James Lawrence makes her heart skip a beat, giving her cause
to reconsider her desperate need to find a way home.

Born with a silver spoon, James' life was torn apart during the
War Between the States. Moving west he vows to put the life he once
knew in the past. When he discovers a half-frozen woman near Gold Hill,
his heart begins to thaw. His love for Alexandra and his need to keep her
from a man who has pursued her through time might cost him his life as

well as hers.

A Valentine's Anthology

The Lending Library-a fantasy by Christie L. Kraemer
Faeries try to fit into the human world when the forest where they make their home is destroyed by a mysterious enemy.

Chasing Rainbows-a contemporary romance by Genene Valleau
An eccentric aunt, an inventive uncle, a mother who wears poodle skirts, and a brother who wears pearls provide a hilarious backdrop for the courtship of a young woman who yearns for a "normal" family.

The Gift-an historical romance by Christine Young
A man and a woman on opposite sides of the Civil War get a second chance at love after one final battle returns soldiers to their war-torn homes to rebuild their lives.

A St. Patrick's Day Tale
Christine Young, C. L. Kraemer, Genene Valleau

Tumble through time...
...to Ireland in 1817, when tensions are high between Protestants and Catholics and fae people guide the fate of villagers. A lovely Catholic lass stumbles upon the weakly ritual fisticuffing between Irish lads. She falls into the lap of a handsome young Protestant. Family ties, grudges, and two conniving faeries threaten their budding love. But the faeries outsmart themselves when they hijack a time machine that has mysteriously appeared in their forest and are whisked to...
...Eugene, Oregon in the 20th century, amid a property feud between the local faeries and night elves. The conniving faeries from Olde Ireland try to stir up more mischief. However, a warrior gnome convinces the magic folk to control their own destiny, and forces the intruding faeries to take refuge in the time machine again, spinning their

way toward...

...A modern day castle in western Oregon. An eccentric inventor is determined to reclaim his wayward time machine and save his beloved wife from her latest misadventure. If only they can travel safely past the black hole...

a May Day Anthology
Christine Young, C. L. Kraemer, Rosemary Indra, Genene Valleau

Highland Miracle — Christine Young
HURTLED THROUGH TIME, Sean Michael Sterling, landed in the midst of a May Day celebration he didn't understand, assuming the role of Laird Sterling.
ILLIGITAMATE CHILD OF NOBILITY, Reagan Douglas searches for a way out of her half brother's house.

Defying the Odds — C.L. Kraemer
The night elves on the hill aren't happy without their magic. They concoct a plan to punish those who were involved in the act that rendered them almost human. Meanwhile, Uther, the rogue night elf, has returned to woo the Librarian to be his eternal mate.

Love in Bloom — Rosemary Indra
When childhood friends reunite it takes two fairies and a matchmaking daughter to help them admit their true love for each other.

No More Poodle Skirts — Genie Gabriel
After drifting for years in the innocent age of the 1950s, a woman struggles to join today's world by finding a career and a new love, with some help from her zany family.

Once Upon a Christmas Moon
Christine Young, C. L. Kraemer, Genene Valleau

TWELVE DAYS TO LOVE

When Archer Steele shows up at Calanthe Durand's failing plantation with an alligator over his shoulder, Cali thinks she's never seen a more handsome man. During the war she had to defend herself and her servants from both union and confederate soldiers. Independent and self-sufficient, she vows to never marry. But Archer Steele has different ideas. The first time Archer sees Cali in town, he feels an instant attraction. He decides he will do everything and anything to convince the beautiful Miss Durand he is worthy of her love. During the weeks leading up to Christmas, he gives her twelve gifts in hopes she will fall in love with him.

BOOTS AND BLADES

An ancient evil from the old country has arrived in the high desert of Oregon. Gnome children are vanishing then re-appearing, showing various stages of traumatization. Tiamoon, warrior gnome, will put her skills to use alongside Killian, a handsome warrior, also in need of a cause.

CHRISTMAS PAWSIBILITIES

With their world destroyed and their space ship malfunctioning, the dogizens of Planet Canid have little choice but to crash land on Earth. They face tortuous experiments at the hands of the Geeks in Green...or they can trust an eccentric inventor and his zany family to deliver the Canine Queen's puppies and help them celebrate new lives.

www.ingramcontent.com/pod-product-compliance
Lightning Source LLC
Chambersburg PA
CBHW070637180626
46817CB00006B/2148